Hawaii.

Specifically Maui. A total dream, a seduction of the senses. After their plane landed and they stepped out of the pressurized, recycled air in the first-class cabin and into the tropical, flower-scented warmth, Kate totally understood the lure of just abandoning everything and escaping to a tropical island somewhere in the Pacific. She'd never been to the tropics before, and the whole island seemed like a dream. From the moment she'd looked out the plane window and seen the purple and turquoise waters ringing soft sand beaches, the jagged volcanic cliffs and the lush, vivid green of tropic vegetation, she'd known she was far away from anything she'd ever known before. . . .

The Fling

Elda Minger ❀

JOVE BOOKS, NEW YORK

This is a work of fiction. Names, characters, places, and incidents either are the product of the author's imagination or are used fictitiously, and any resemblance to actual persons, living or dead, business establishments, events, or locales is entirely coincidental.

THE FLING

A Jove Book / published by arrangement with
the author

PRINTING HISTORY
Jove edition / September 2002

Copyright © 2002 by Elda Minger
Cover art by Tsukushi
Cover design by George Long
Book design by Julie Rogers

Visit our website at
www.penguinputnam.com

ISBN: 0-515-13372-8

A JOVE BOOK®
Jove Books are published by The Berkley Publishing Group,
a division of Penguin Putnam Inc.,
375 Hudson Street, New York, New York 10014.
JOVE and the "J" design
are trademarks belonging to Penguin Putnam Inc.

PRINTED IN THE UNITED STATES OF AMERICA

10 9 8 7 6 5 4 3 2 1

To Gail Fortune, who always believed. This one's for you.

*And to Frank Sinatra, whose style, originality, and music
kept me company while I wrote,
and reminded me to keep it romantic, always.*

Acknowledgments

A writer rarely works alone.

To Nancy Cochran, Terri Farrell, and Beth Wellington, treasured friends and fellow writers, for giving this manuscript a thorough reading and finding the inevitable mistakes.

Any that remain are certainly my own.

Fling

n.

A short period of unrestrained pursuit of one's wishes or desires. A brief period of indulgence in pleasure.

Chapter One

❀ Kate Prescott would have never considered herself capable of cold-blooded, premeditated murder. That is, until Roger Geisler didn't bother to show up for his wedding to her cousin, Patti. On *Valentine's* Day.

Now she was seriously considering it.

Roger the rat wasn't going to show. And Kate, standing on the front steps of the church and looking out over the snow-covered grounds, had no idea how she was going to break the news to her cousin. Even worse, Roger had sent one of his buddies to deliver the bad news. The minute she'd seen the sheepish look on Bob Dixon's face as he'd loped toward her, note in hand, she'd *known*.

Kate knew Patti's heart was about to be totally broken. She knew the entire wedding would have to be called off. Though she disliked opening and reading her cousin's note, this was an emergency.

Why, she thought as she unfolded the single piece of

white paper she'd managed to confiscate from Bob, did men do such stupid things and make it so easy to hate them?

Glancing quickly around to make sure no one was watching, she scanned the hurriedly scribbled note. Roger, though he was thirty-five, had the handwriting of a six-year-old child—and not a terribly talented one.

> *Patti,*
> *I know you'll understand. I couldn't go through with it. I just need some time to find myself—*

She didn't read any further. Kate folded the note closed, then tapped it against the long, pale lavender skirts of her iridescent chiffon maid of honor dress, then wrapped her platinum-colored satin wrap more snugly around her shoulders.

She'd really liked her dress and the wrap that went with it, and that was so unlike her usual pre-wedding bridesmaid's experience that it should have been her first tip-off things weren't going to go smoothly.

How was she going to break the news to her cousin?

Kate didn't hesitate long. Patti was with her mother, both of them getting more nervous by the minute as they rearranged her veil and the train of her dress. That absolutely exquisite wedding dress of hand-embroidered English tulle over crepe with a fishtail train, a dress that had set Patti's father back almost two grand. Patti, who'd had her heart set on getting married since they were old enough to play dress-up.

Patti, whose heart was quietly breaking because she had to know something wasn't right.

As Kate stepped back inside the church and out of

the cold, she knew she wasn't doing her cousin any favors by delaying the inevitable.

There were just over five hundred guests sitting in the church, waiting for Patti to come floating down the aisle decked out in all her bridal finery and looking gorgeous. Waiting for Roger, the rat—no, make that *worm*—to approach the altar so they could get this whole show on the road.

The money and time that had gone into planning this wedding was immense. But neither would be anywhere near the pain her cousin would suffer from Roger's cruel and fearful last-minute abandonment.

Her uncle had a ton of food back at his restaurant, and the entire place had been cleaned and decorated to within an inch of its life. White twinkling Christmas lights had been strung from the ceiling, the dance floor had been waxed and buffed, hundreds of dollars worth of Patti's favorite salmon-pink Tuscany roses in full bloom had been placed everywhere, and the great band her uncle had hired was gearing up to play everyone's favorite songs.

Only there wasn't going to be anything to celebrate.

Kate sighed. She'd baked the most magnificent wedding cake, light vanilla layers with a raspberry filling and classic butter cream frosting, which right now rested in one of the huge refrigerators in the restaurant's kitchen. Patti had picked out the two adorable little china doves for the top layer.

None of it would be used for what it had originally been planned for.

Kate's vision blurred, but she quickly blinked the useless tears away. What had to be done had to be done. This wasn't going to be easy. Patti couldn't go on pretending Roger had gotten stuck in traffic or had gotten sick, or whatever excuse she was running through her mind to keep panic at bay.

"Kate?"

She turned at the sound of her uncle Albert's voice. Alberto Cannelli looked exactly like Belle's father in the Disney animated cartoon *Beauty and the Beast*. All round curves and of short stature, he came bustling up to her, looking like a plump penguin in his good suit. He wheezed slightly as he caught her hand, then glanced around the front of the church to make sure none of the relatives were within hearing distance.

"She's starting to cry. Even Connie's getting upset."

This was a bad sign. Her aunt Connie was usually a rock.

"What's going on?" Uncle Albert continued. "Why isn't he here yet? I don't understand!"

She handed him the note without a word.

Uncle Albert studied it for a moment, not opening it, with the reluctance and fear one would have for a live grenade. He was out of his depth in feminine, emotional waters, and he knew it.

"He's not coming, is he?"

Trust Uncle Albert. He was a fantastic judge of character, hadn't liked Roger from the moment he'd met him, and didn't need to read the note to know what was about to happen to his beloved daughter. But Patti had loved the jerk, and her father had been willing to set aside his dislike for his only daughter's happiness. He had welcomed Roger into the Cannelli family with open arms, which only made this betrayal, especially the way it had been done, more horrible.

"Nope."

"Oh my God."

"Yep."

They stared at each other for a moment, then Kate

said, "I'm going to go and tell her. What should we do about all the guests?"

Uncle Albert straightened his shoulders, though his dark eyes glistened suspiciously. "Tell them that dinner is still being served at the restaurant. That everyone should leave the church immediately and get over there. I'll go right now. We'll open a few more bottles of wine, I'll send the band home—"

"Let 'em stay. You've already paid for them, and dancing might help. Just ask them to change the song list and take out all the wedding references."

"You're right," Uncle Albert said, absently scratching his head.

"Have Aunt Connie take Patti home," Kate said, thinking quickly. "And I'll come help you at the restaurant."

"Yes."

She could tell her uncle was grasping at lifelines, trying to stay calm.

"You're a good girl, Katie."

Kate's throat tightened. His heart was breaking along with his daughter's.

Along with hers.

"No, I have to go home with them," he said, changing his mind. "I'll meet you at the restaurant as soon as I can."

"Take whatever time you need, Uncle Albert. I'll make sure they all start eating."

He grasped her hand, clasped it hard. "Thank you for being strong, Kate. This is going to be hard for Patti."

Kate hugged her uncle fiercely, then kissed his cheek. "I know," Kate whispered. "Because she loves the jerk."

*   *   *

Kate worked swiftly and efficiently in the restaurant's kitchen, taking the layers of the elaborate wedding cake apart and creating a simple sheet cake out of the bottom layer. Dinner had been served, and as with most dinners with the large Cannelli extended family, it had been mostly predictable.

Amid the filet mignons, lobster tails, and homemade lasagna, Auntie Mannie had drunk way too much red wine and was arguing with Uncle Sonny, something about a sizable loan that had never been repaid. Auntie Carmella had criticized all the food, claiming some of it was too salty, while the rest of it was too bland, but none of it measured up to what their mother used to make in Italy when they were children. And Uncle Tony kept telling everyone how much money he'd been making at the racetrack.

Typical.

She was just finishing up the last touch with some decorative frosting, swirling on roses and leaves over the small hole where the layer had been joined to the one above it, when her uncle came back into the large restaurant kitchen.

"Just coffee and cake, and then they can all go home."

She set down the pastry bag of frosting and gave his chubby arm a comforting pat. "The family. What would we do without them?"

Her uncle laughed, and she was glad she could help him see the smallest bit of humor on this black day.

"So Auntie Carmella liked Grandma's lasagna better, hmm?" she said, picking up her cup of *café latte*. She took a sip. *Heaven*. No one made better coffee than her uncle.

"It's the same recipe as our mother's, and always has

been. The specialty of the house, the same to the ounce. But she'll never admit it."

Kate laughed. "It's always something with her."

"I know." Uncle Albert's face creased into a concerned frown. "I got a call from Connie at the house. Patti's not doing so good."

"I can imagine." She glanced up at the large clock on the kitchen wall. "When do you think we can leave?"

"Another hour, maybe an hour and a half. I'll get them all out."

She put her arm around her uncle and squeezed his shoulders. "I'll come out and help you serve the cake."

They drove home in different cars, and as Kate navigated her blue Toyota Corolla through the quiet streets of the Chicago suburb of Oak Park to her uncle's house, she thought about Patti.

Their relationship was really more like sisters than cousins. Her parents had been killed in a car accident when she was only five, and she could still remember Uncle Albert and Aunt Connie coming to the house late that night. Kate had been with a sitter, who'd fallen asleep on the sofa with the television on. Kate had been upstairs in her bed.

Her parents had gone out to dinner to celebrate their eighth wedding anniversary. Her father, ever the romantic, had made reservations at a French restaurant in Chicago. On the way home, just a few blocks from their house, a drunk driver had run a stoplight, and that had been the end of two lives. And the end of her life with them.

Kate could still remember how her uncle had come into her bedroom. The sirens had awakened her, and she'd seen him in the doorway, looking down at her, tears streaming down his round face.

She'd known something terrible had happened.

He'd come and sat in the chair by the side of her canopied bed. She'd reached for her bear, and the stuffed bunny that was never far from her side.

"Where's Mommy?" she'd asked him. He'd always been her favorite uncle, and she trusted him implicitly.

"Your mommy's with the angels," he'd said quietly. "And your auntie and I would like you to come and stay with us."

She'd studied him for a long moment.

"Okay." She'd hesitated. "But can I go see Mommy later?"

"Sure, honey," he'd said, his voice breaking. He'd picked her up and carried her, her stuffed bear and her bunny, down the stairs. Wrapped in a blanket, she'd made the short journey to his home, and had never left.

Patti, her cousin, had been born a mere month after Kate, so the two of them had grown up together. They'd been inseparable. Years later, Kate had learned that her aunt Connie had desperately wanted more children, but none had been given to her. So Kate had been like Patti's sister.

Kate turned down the tree-lined block toward the familiar and comfortable home she'd grown up in. At thirty-two, she didn't live there anymore. She had an apartment closer to the city, but her uncle had asked her to come and spend the night in case Patti needed her. And of course, she'd said yes.

It had been a major relief to send all the relatives home. She and her uncle had piled them into their cars with various designated drivers, and they'd hired taxis for a few. Sad, how a day that was supposed to bring such joy and happiness to the family had resulted in such heartache.

There were a few gossips in the family, people who

over the years took total delight in other family members' misfortunes. But she and her uncle had been very discreet tonight, giving out as little information as possible. Protecting Patti. If the relatives wanted to talk, well, they wouldn't hear it from them. As far as they knew, it could have been Patti who called off the wedding at the last minute.

She pulled her car into the driveway alongside her uncle's white van with red lettering along the side that spelled out ALBERTO'S, then got out of her car, locked the doors, and started up the front walk.

It was going to be a long night.

She spent most of the rest of the night up in Patti's former bedroom, listening to her, hearing the story over and over. Biting her tongue when her cousin tried to make excuses for Roger's abominable behavior, tried to "understand" him and what he needed out of life. But Kate knew that was the way of grief, that you had to keep talking about it, you almost had to tell it to make it real.

It was so hard, looking at her cousin, feeling her pain. Patti, with her ethereal blonde looks, her golden hair and beautiful blue eyes, now swollen and red from all the crying she'd done. She'd lain in bed and cried and cried, choked out the words. Aunt Connie had taken the ill-fated wedding dress and hidden it in her room, along with any other little touches that might remind Patti that she should have been married by now.

Kate and her aunt switched off, never leaving Patti alone. Uncle Albert had hovered by the door, but Kate could tell he felt totally out of his element.

When Aunt Connie went downstairs to get a cup of coffee and spend some time with Uncle Albert, Kate was left alone with Patti.

She wasn't afraid to be alone with her cousin and those powerful emotions. Kate knew she had to be strong for Patti, because she couldn't imagine what it would be like to be betrayed by someone you'd loved enough to want to spend the rest of your life with. And what had possessed Roger? Why hadn't he told her the evening before, or even a *week* before? Why had he waited until everyone had been gathered at the church, and the organist had begun to play?

"*Why,* Kate?" Patti whispered. "Why do you think he did it?"

Kate didn't want to make up any more excuses for Roger. She didn't want to give Patti any sense of false hope. Kate was so sick of Roger, so angry with him. If she heard one more reference to the fact that this man needed a little more time and understanding to get his head on straight, she was going to scream.

"I don't know, Patti." She came over and sat down on one side of the double bed, taking the place her aunt had recently occupied. Patti was sprawled out on the other side, on her stomach. Her face had recently been buried in her pillow as she'd cried, but at least she'd raised her head up and was looking Kate right in the eye.

It was progress, of a sort.

"I do know this," Kate continued slowly. "Life's kind of a funny business, and every time I think I have it figured out, something else gets in my way. But Patti, I think that whatever's really meant for you, you can't lose it. Nobody can take it away from you. Just like if something isn't meant for you, or meant to be, no matter how hard you fight for it, it'll never be yours."

"Yeah." Patti sniffed and reached for another tissue from the bedside table.

"Remember that fortune cookie I got in that restaurant when we were sixteen?"

Patti smiled. "That was strange."

They'd both liked the fortune, and pasted it up on their bathroom mirror. Both of them had looked at it for years, until the paper had yellowed and curled, the tape had disintegrated, and it had fallen to the floor.

You cannot lose what is your own.

"You cannot lose what is your own," Patti whispered. "Kate, I know you're right, but—" Kate watched as her cousin's sad blue eyes filled. "It just *hurts* so much," Patti whispered, then she buried her face in the pillow as her slender shoulders started to shake.

Kate simply reached over and rubbed her back, as she blinked furiously against her own frustrated tears.

Her aunt had just come in to relieve her, and Kate was making her way down the stairs to the kitchen for another cup of coffee when her uncle's voice stopped her.

"Kate," he said. "I have a favor to ask you."

"Anything." She hesitated, halfway down the stairs. She would do anything for her uncle, who had really been more of a father to her. Uncle Albert indicated that she should join him in the kitchen.

He made her a cup of coffee exactly the way she liked it, then poured himself a cup and sat with her in the breakfast nook that overlooked the snow-covered yard in back.

"I want you to get Patti out of town."

Kate took a sip of her coffee, waiting. Her uncle was not a man who did things rashly. If she knew him, he'd been thinking about this since he'd seen that damn note from Roger.

"How? What did you have in mind?"

"Take her on her honeymoon."

For just a moment, Kate was shocked. What honeymoon? The last she'd heard, Roger the Rat, a tightwad as well as emotionally retarded, had planned on spending a couple of days in Wisconsin with his new bride. She couldn't see taking Patti up north on a bogus honeymoon.

What was Uncle Albert up to?

This was something she hadn't expected. But in fairness to her uncle, she decided to hear him out.

"I bought Patti and that . . . I bought Patti and Roger tickets to Maui for their honeymoon. Ten days. I wanted to surprise them at the reception. The travel agent is a regular customer of mine. I know he could fix the tickets so that you can travel with Patti instead of Roger. It's to one of those luxury resorts, right on the beach."

Kate took another sip of coffee, listening.

Her uncle thought for a moment, then said, "The Kalani Resort and Spa, that was the name of the place. Kate, everything is prepaid, and if you could get her out of town until this whole thing dies down and the family stops talking—"

Kate nodded her head. She could see the logic in this.

"You don't think she'd be too depressed, going on the honeymoon she was supposed to go on with Roger?"

"No. Remember, I was going to surprise them with this trip at the reception."

"Oh." Kate considered this. "So she didn't know about this."

"That's right."

"So instead of a honeymoon, we could say we were both going to Maui for a little rest and relaxation."

"Exactly."

"And keep the family from talking. Snooping around and upsetting her."

"Yes."

She took another sip of her coffee.

"What do you think, Kate?"

She set her coffee down and took her uncle's hand, wishing she could wipe the worried look off his face. The only man in a family of women, her uncle loved all three of them fiercely but was always confused by how women's lives and minds worked.

He'd have no idea how to deal with his daughter's emotions. Kate was sure they terrified him.

"I think it's a good idea. We have to protect Patti and do what's best for her. And beaches are always good places to heal. The ocean's therapeutic."

He frowned. "She might not want to go."

"I can talk her into it," she said, thinking, studying the pattern of the tablecloth in front of her. Fruits. Her aunt Connie loved fruits and vines; her kitchen was full of them, in pictures and stencils, on fabric, even a framed needlepoint on the far wall. The effect was stunning.

He laughed softly. "That's true. Ever since you were little girls, you could talk her into anything. Snow White and Cinderella."

Kate laughed, remembering the first trip they'd taken to Disneyland when she and Patti had been eight. Uncle Albert had nicknamed them Snow White and Cinderella because of their coloring—Kate had her mother's dark brown hair and vivid green eyes, while Patti was so very fair.

"You understand Patti in a way that her mother and I can't," he said.

"Only one of my special talents," she said, teasing him. *And speaking of talents* . . . She raised her eyes to his. "But who would do all the desserts?"

Kate had known she wanted to be a professional chef from the time she was a teenager. She'd won a scholarship to a prestigious Chicago cooking school directly out of high school, and had completed the entire program, specializing in desserts and pastries. After working at a few different restaurants, she'd come back to her uncle's business, and was now in charge of the spectacular desserts they served at Alberto's.

"Kate, if you do this for me, I'll make the desserts for the ten days you're gone."

"Hmm." She tapped her finger on the table. "I already have a bunch of cheesecakes frozen in the back refrigerator, that should take you through the rest of February. The tiramisu is easy enough, but the chocolate mousse—"

"Annette can handle that."

Kate smiled at her uncle. "Just as long as you don't give her my job."

He laughed, then said, "Never!"

"Well then," Kate said, "you've got yourself a deal."

Jack McKenna was feeling good.

Make that *great.*

He'd flown to San Francisco from the family's Boston property just yesterday and to Maui early this morning. Gaining time as he flew west, he was determined to see his father as soon as possible. He loved the man; the two of them were the only family each other had. Jack had missed his father while living and working on the East Coast. But there was another reason, as well.

His father was finally going to give him his dream.

After years of hard work and effort, Jack was finally going to be put in charge of the crown jewel of the entire luxury hotel and resort chain his father owned—the Maui property.

The Kalani Resort Hotel and Spa was perhaps one of the most luxurious vacation destinations in all of the

Hawaiian Islands. Located in Wailea, on the western side of the island, it was a little piece of paradise on this island that had long been described as being as close to paradise as possible. Though this side of Maui was often referred to as the desert side, there was no desert dryness here. The trade winds were kind to the skin, caressing both body and spirit.

The perfect place for the ultimate vacation.

Kalani meant "the heavens" in Hawaiian, and James McKenna, Jack's father, had worked extremely hard for many years to make sure that every single guest who visited the resort thought that the name reflected their experience. Guests were pampered and given first-class treatment, for an ultimate experience they'd remember forever.

And now James was preparing to retire and give his tropical kingdom over to his only son.

Jack had worked hard for many years to be deserving of such a kingdom, knowing how much this resort meant to his father. James McKenna had very exacting standards. Jack had known what was expected and had done the job. Long hours of discipline and sacrifice, years of effort had all culminated in this moment.

Straight A's in high school, undergraduate work at an Ivy League school, then an MBA from Harvard Business School. And it wasn't just his father's name or his money that had gotten him there; he'd put in the work, made the grades.

More importantly, he'd put in the necessary years working at various hotels and resorts. He'd made his way up the ranks through hard work and real experience. He'd done the job. And now he felt good this morning because he knew the end was in sight. And Jack knew that he'd truly earned it.

It felt damn good. *He* felt damn good.

"Hello, Meredith," he said to his father's secretary as he reached her desk, just outside his father's imposing office door. She never seemed to age, though she had to be somewhere in her sixties. Meredith Wilkins always appeared cool, crisp and efficient, with her shining cap of silvery gray hair and her simple shirtwaist dresses. Tall and slender, six feet tall without her heels—which she adored—she'd been his father's right hand for as long as Jack could remember. Her husband, Hank, a marine biologist, was now retired and gave lots of his time to local schools, teaching children about the ocean, the incredible world they had at their fingertips, and the responsibilities that came with that knowledge.

She came around the desk and enveloped him in a fierce hug, which he returned with just as much enthusiasm. Meredith was like a member of their family.

"How's Hank?" Jack said.

"Fine. He's doing a program for our granddaughter's class this week, on great white sharks."

"The kids should love that."

"Oh, he's got sound effects and everything," Meredith said. "He enters the classroom to the *Jaws* soundtrack."

Jack laughed. "I can just see Hank doing that. Does he still use those hand puppets?"

Meredith grinned, clearly delighted. "I can't believe you remember!"

"You don't forget a program like Hank's. How's the old man?" Jack said, referring to his father.

"He's waiting to see you, Jack."

"I can imagine."

"We're all very happy that you've finally come home."

Home. His father, James McKenna, had lived in one of the penthouses at the Maui resort for the last twenty-five years, since his mother had passed away. Jack had spent all his summers with his father at this resort, as a kid, then a teenager, and then his summers out of college. He knew this resort, knew the island, loved the place and the people.

There was no other resort in the McKenna holdings that he wanted to run as badly as this one.

His time had come.

"I'm glad to be home." He indicated the closed door with a nod of his head. "If he's ready to see me, then let's get this show on the road!"

James McKenna stood at the floor-to-ceiling windows behind his wooden desk, staring out at a view that was almost too beautiful.

His son, Jack, wasn't going to like what he was going to tell him. Yet James knew it was the only way.

He had to be sure.

He also had to get through to his son.

Oh, the boy was brilliant. That wasn't even in question. Jack had shown ability since he first started to walk. Smart as a whip and able to get into trouble faster than any child he'd ever known. He'd excelled in school, and later in college. He was a hard worker and had a good heart.

But it was that heart that James McKenna was worried about.

Though James had once been listed as one of the twenty wealthiest men on the planet, he would have given up all his money if he could only be sure that his son would have a happy emotional life once he was gone. He didn't have any plans of dying anytime soon, but in the natural order of things he would certainly leave this planet before his only son did. And that son worried him.

Because while Jack had an incredibly sharp mind and a work ethic that often put his own to shame, James was uncertain whether his son would ever really love, or chose to risk giving his heart to a woman.

At thirty-six, Jack was a brilliant businessman, a hard worker, a charmer, but he'd dated a succession of women and had never seemed to be able to find the right one. Though James had never pushed him for grandchildren, he was far more concerned that Jack seemed to be navigating through life solo.

And James knew how lonely that could be.

The love of his life, his wife, Caroline, had died when Jack was eleven. Cancer had claimed her, and James had taken the last two years of her life off from work to stay home with her. They'd tried everything they could find, medically, but finally surrendered to the inevitable. In Caroline's final months, they had simply been content to be with each other. To store up memories against the years he would be alone.

He felt her with him, at times. Never more than when he looked at his son, for Jack was the best of both of them. But he and his wife had both been concerned about what would happen to their son.

He seemed to skate along the top of an emotional life in the most superficial of ways. He dated, and he'd even brought home several of these women for various holidays. But James could tell, with the eye of a concerned father, that none of these women had ever engaged his heart.

It worried him. It worried him a lot.

The intercom buzzed, and he heard Meredith's crisp voice.

"Your son is here, Mr. McKenna. Should I send him in?"

James took a deep breath, preparing to face Jack.

"Yes."

He took one last look out the window, at palm trees blowing gently in the trade winds and the bright sunshine glittering on the ocean's surface. Then, he turned as he heard his office door open.

Jack wasn't going to like what he was about to tell him. No, he wasn't going to like it at all.

James grinned as his son entered his office. How he loved a challenge, and his son was exactly like him in that respect. Jack had never been one to turn down a dare, or back down from a challenge.

And so the next ten days at the Kalani Resort Hotel and Spa promised to be very interesting, indeed.

Chapter Two

The morning Kate and Patti boarded their plane, it was snowing heavily, the fat flakes coming down in a flurry of white. The day after Valentine's Day, February fifteenth, was still right in the middle of the dead of winter in the Midwest, so a snowstorm wasn't that unusual. It had been a hideous winter up until now, and most of the people boarding their flight would be ecstatic at the chance to trade in their bulky winter clothing and snow shovels for a bathing suit, a lei, and a Mai Tai.

Kate could take no real pleasure in this trip. In fact, she'd decided to do what she usually did when she was operating in crisis mode—just take things one day at a time. Today, she'd decided that all she had to do was get Patti to this resort. That was all.

Their flight from O'Hare in Chicago would take them directly to LAX, Los Angeles International Airport. From there, they would catch a direct flight to Kahului Airport on Maui, and once on the island, they had a rental car reserved and would drive to the resort. Uncle Albert had cancelled the limousine he'd originally hired, as both he and Aunt Connie had thought that would be too much of a reminder to Patti that this trip had originally been intended as a honeymoon.

And once there, Patti could lock herself in their villa and cry her eyes out. With no prying eyes or gossiping tongues to make things worse. She had ten whole days to get over the worst that had been done to her, the biggest disaster in her life so far. Ten days to begin to heal.

A lot could happen in that time.

As for herself—Kate glanced at her cousin, slumped over in the molded plastic seat near the boarding gate for their flight to Los Angeles, their two carry-on bags at her feet. Patti looked pretty bad. She had large, round sunglasses on to hide her red, puffy eyes. Her mother had packed for her last night, throwing things into a suitcase and telling Kate that if she forgot anything to just buy it, charge it, and Uncle Albert would certainly reimburse her when she returned.

The only errand Kate had run was to the twenty-four hour drugstore for several bottles of sunscreen and tanning lotion, because she didn't want to pay exorbitant prices once they arrived on the island.

Basically, what this trip was about, what her assignment was, and what her uncle had entrusted her with was his precious daughter and her entire frame of mind. Her mental health. Kate knew that Uncle Albert had utter faith in her ability to be a glorified caregiver. And a caregiver on one of the most gorgeous islands that had ever risen up out of the ocean and graced the planet. Yet right now, Kate knew she would have braved a blizzard and stayed right here, freezing and at home, if it could have meant that her cousin was happy.

She glanced at Patti. "How're you doing?"

Patti didn't even raise her head. "Okay," she whispered. Her voice quavered, and Kate found herself quietly hating Roger all over again.

Far from okay. Not okay at all. Not even close . . .

Usually when Kate traveled she loved looking at other passengers and making up entire lives for them. This time, she didn't have the heart.

They'd be boarding in about fifteen minutes. All told, with the flight to Los Angeles, and then their second flight to Maui, she'd be in the air, on a plane, with her deeply depressed cousin for just over ten hours.

Thank God for alcohol.

"What's wrong with her?" whispered the flight attendant as she glanced at Patti, huddled up in the window seat, her jacket over her shoulders and part of her head, a sweater wadded up and used as a pillow. She'd fallen asleep soon after takeoff, and Kate had gently removed her dark glasses and put them in her purse.

Sleeping in and of itself wasn't at all strange on a plane flight. But Patti's face was still red and swollen, her eyes mere slits in her face. She'd cried until she couldn't cry anymore last night, then cried some more this morning before Uncle Albert had loaded the two of them and their luggage into his van and driven them to the airport. Aunt Connie had stayed at home, because every time she'd looked at her daughter she'd started to cry, and she didn't want to make Patti feel even worse.

So Patti didn't look too good.

"Depression," Kate whispered. "Her fiancé dumped her at the altar. Yesterday."

"Oh my God, how awful," the attendant said. "I took one look at her face, and I thought someone had died."

"You know, it would have been better for Roger if he had," Kate said.

"I know what you mean."

"And it was a good thing he didn't show his face yesterday, or I would have helped him along that path."

"I know *exactly* what you mean," the attendant said. "Would you like a coke or something?"

"Tomato juice. But can I ask you for a favor?"

"Sure."

"I'm going to let her sleep as long as possible. She was up all night crying, so she didn't get much sleep last night. But when she wakes up, I'm going to press that little button for you, and if you could bring me either a Cosmopolitan or a Bloody Mary, that would really save my life."

"For her, you mean."

"You got it."

"Sure. Good strategy, booze to dull the pain."

Briefly, Kate told her about what her uncle had done, and the trip they were taking to Maui to get away and help Patti heal.

"Oh, you'll love it there, it's so gorgeous."

Kate sat back in her chair after the flight attendant left and was about to pull out the paperback true crime book she'd stashed in her carry-on bag when a breathy voice across the aisle whispered, "Tough break."

She turned toward that voice, and if a crème puff crossed with a fluffy Persian cat with a little Marilyn Monroe and Ginger from *Gilligan's Island* thrown in for good measure could actually exist, then that woman was sitting across the aisle from her, in the flesh.

She was gorgeous, in a sweet and sexy way, with a wide-eyed little girl's innocence. Her strawberry blonde hair fell to her shoulders, and Kate knew, even after the briefest of glances, that it either had to be totally natural or have cost the earth. Highlights like that came out of the most expensive and exclusive salons.

Her makeup was flawless, but applied in a way that it looked just a little more than natural, emphasizing a quite striking face, big blue eyes, full lips, and white, even teeth.

There was just a touch of Farrah there, as well.

And her body—suffice it to say that this was the sort of body that drove men absolutely wild, with a small waist, large chest, and seductively curved hips. She was dressed in a short skirt, incredibly high heels, and a fluffy pink angora sweater with a deep V neckline.

And to top it all off, she had legs to die for.

"I couldn't help but overhear what you were saying to our flight attendant," the blonde whispered, keeping her voice down. She glanced around, but most of the other passengers were reading magazines and books, listening to music on their headphones, or talking to their fellow travelers. "That's a tough break, getting your heart broken like that. In public."

The first thing that came into Kate's head, while looking at this woman, was, *a problem I'll bet you've never experienced in your life.*

"I've been dumped a couple of times, I know how painful it can be," the blonde said.

"You?" Immediately Kate felt ashamed of herself, for the thought she'd just had.

"Sure, Sugar. Men can be real rats, you know?"

"Tell me about it," Kate said, leaning toward her. "I've sworn them off for the time being. I haven't even gone out on a date in eighteen months."

"I know what you mean, I've sworn them off, too." She studied Kate, her blue eyes kind. "I'll bet you have some painful experiences of your own. We all do." The blonde leaned forward. "It's like this big, secret sorority of women, with all these horrible stories to tell. Those disaster dates in *Cosmo* don't tell the half of it."

Kate had to grin. "I kind of enjoy reading those letters, though. About what women do to men when they discover they're cheating on them, you know? I wouldn't have had the nerve to do half of what they do, but if I'd had a chance to say something to Roger . . ."

"He's the one who left her at the altar?"

Kate nodded. "In front of over five hundred guests. The day of the wedding."

"Poor little thing. That's complete humiliation. But it still isn't as bad as knowing that the man you loved didn't want to marry you."

"He sent her a *note,* can you believe it? After a five-year relationship, he sends her a note. He didn't even have the balls to tell her himself. A friend of his dropped off this note that had some crap in it about 'I need some time to find myself.' I hate that expression. It's right up there with, 'I need some space.'"

The blonde nodded. "I think it's just male code for, 'Honey, you're not the one; there might still be someone better for me out there, and I'm getting out while the getting's good.'"

Kate stared at the fluffy blonde with new respect. She'd been prejudiced when she'd first seen her, thinking that a woman who looked like this one did couldn't be all that smart. How wrong she'd been.

"Kate Prescott," she said, holding out her hand across the plane's aisle.

"Cherry," the blonde said, taking the offered hand and shaking it firmly. "Cherry Jubilee."

"For real?"

"Yeah. Well, it was my stage name." She lowered her voice. "My real name was Dora. Dora Kendall. But I didn't want to go through life named Dora, you know?

There's absolutely no excitement in that name, and it just wasn't me. So as soon as I hit Vegas, I legally changed it."

Kate had a feeling that this woman's life story would be fascinating to listen to.

"You're a dancer?" she said.

"Among many other jobs," Cherry said. "But now I'm headed to Maui to find myself a millionaire."

"Run that by me again," Kate said. "I thought you'd sworn off men."

"I have. As far as ever falling in *love* with one of them. But I've decided that I'm going to play by their rules."

"Their rules?"

"You know how men are right up front about what they want?"

"You think so?"

"I *know* so. Haven't you ever seen an ugly old fart with the most gorgeous young woman? Or a seventy-five-year-old man who should know better running around with a woman young enough to be his granddaughter? Men are right up front about what they want, and they let us women know, loud and clear. And it's only gotten worse in the last ten years."

"Looks," said Kate. "They go for looks. Boobs. Supermodels. Totally superficial," she said, thinking of the fiancée her last boyfriend had kept on the side and had conveniently forgotten to tell her about.

"Yep. It's like that program that was on television a while ago with that English guy, *Lifestyles of the Rich and Famous*? It made everyone upset because they knew they'd never live in a house like that or have a life like that or even *see* the French Riviera. And not everyone can marry a supermodel, but there's that same sense of discontent. So what does the average guy do? He marries a woman in town, then makes her life miserable trying to make her live up to some unattainable standard that he never even has to meet."

Kate stared at this woman with even more appreciation. "I'd never thought about it that way. But you may be right."

"Well, think, Sugar! How many times have you seen a man with a big fat beer belly whose main joy in life is watching sports nonstop on television and eating pork rinds. And how many times have you seen that man bitch and moan to his wife because she doesn't look like some kind of movie star?"

"Lots of times."

"Of course you have," Cherry said, leaning forward in her seat. "Because men don't have to have looks. All they have to do is bring home the bacon. It's the way of the world. I even read a magazine article that said this was all in our genes—you know, how we're programmed for survival of the species. Men want young, beautiful women, because youth and beauty signify fertility. And women want protection and money, the necessary resources so they can have a family."

Kate considered this.

"So I figured out that as long as we're all being driven by these genes, and nobody really knows what they're doing in the battle of the sexes, I might as well manipulate these powerful instincts to my own advantage."

"My God," Kate said. "That's pretty amazing." A truly formidable brain was hidden beneath that gorgeous hair.

Cherry smiled, and if a smile could be wicked and sexy at the same time, this woman had the look down cold. "Hey, even though it took me a few years of careful observation to figure things out, I finally got smart."

"I hate to say this, but—I think you're right," Kate said.

"I *know* I am. So, if a man's standards are that his partner has to look like a cross between a movie star and a supermodel, then the equivalent for a woman is that a man should have the earning power of a Donald Trump."

"That makes sense," Kate said.

"It's all really out of control. See, all you have to do is take those basic biological truths and blow them up, exaggerate them, and you can see how crazy it's all become. I've known women who were anorexic and bulimic and who mutilated their faces and bodies with a surgeon's knife. They went into deep depression thinking that they just weren't good enough and for what? A guy with a beer belly and an average job?"

"Wow," said Kate.

"So if a woman has to live up to these unbelievable standards, if she has to almost starve herself to death or get a boob or nose job to be considered good-looking, or if she has to give the best blow job in the entire Western World, then I ask you, what's the equivalent for a man? If he doesn't have to look good or have surgery, then he has to bring home the whole little piggy, not just the bacon."

Cherry snapped her fingers, and Kate jumped.

"When I realized that, Kate, I decided to fly out to Maui and find myself a millionaire. I'm through with playing all these games. They're up front about what they want, so I'm going to play the mating game the same way. Just remember, the equivalent of a supermodel is a millionaire. If they think they deserve that level of beauty, then I want that level of money. Period."

"I never thought of it like that," Kate said. "But why Maui?"

"Because I went on the Internet to do some research, and the island of Maui has the highest percentage of millionaires, per capita, in the entire world."

"You're kidding!"

"Have you ever been there before?" Cherry said.

"No."

"When you see how beautiful it is, how nice and easygoing the lifestyle is, you'll understand why all the people with money decided to go and live there."

"You're not kidding," Kate said with wonder.

"Nope. So as I was logging off my computer, I thought, 'If the mountain won't come to Moham-med . . .'"

Kate considered everything Cherry had told her. "I have to admit, I'm impressed. I mean, look at Roger. He's a fine representation of his whole sex."

"Exactly!" Cherry said. "Look, what's the alternative? Staying with a man whose chief job seems to be to make you feel that no matter what you do, you're not good enough? Not for me."

Kate was about to reply when she heard her cousin's voice, thin and fragile and still full of sleep.

"Kate?"

Cherry patted her arm. "Take care of her. But tell her if she wants to hear some real tales of heartbreak, come on over and sit by me."

"Dad, this isn't funny," Jack said.

"It's not meant to be."

Jack slowly counted to ten, fighting to control his emotions. Of all the things he'd thought his father was going to say to him when he arrived at the family resort in Maui, this had not even been on his list.

"I don't get it," Jack said, feeling his frustration start to rise up again.

"You don't have to," his father said. "You just have to do as I ask, for ten days, and the resort is yours."

"This is insane," Jack said, rounding on his father. "You're basically saying that I'm not good enough to take over the running of this resort!"

"I'm not saying that at all," his father countered smoothly. "I know you're more than capable. Jack, I'm simply saying that there's one little thing I want you to do before I hand over the reins to you."

"One little thing! *One* little *thing!* Only it's not so little! What's so damn little about pretending to be a worker here, a glorified *cabana boy,* for Christ's sake, for ten days in order to finally take over running this place?" Jack hated losing his temper, but his father had always known how to push his buttons. And he was doing a fine job of it today. This was *not* what he'd expected to hear.

"I want you to have a clear understanding of the everyday workings of this place, from the ground up, before I give it all to you."

"And how is that going to make me better at my job?"

"Because you'll know firsthand what the people under your guidance are going through, and you'll be in a better position to both lead them and understand their lives. Because you'll have a chance to really interact with the people who come to this resort to get away from *their* everyday lives, and a deeper understanding of exactly why they come here. Because you'll develop a high level of respect, as I do, for every single person who does their best to keep this place running smoothly, and for every customer and guest who chooses this resort over many other fine places on this island and ultimately pays our bills."

Jack stared at his father, silent. The horrible thing

was, his old man had made a point. Several points. Cogent, very precise points. He was beginning to understand his father's point of view.

But he still didn't have to like it.

"Okay. Supposing, just *supposing* that I agree to do this. Tell me one more time, exactly what does it entail?"

James McKenna sat back down behind his desk and pointedly waited until his son sat down as well, in one of the two chairs facing his desk.

"For ten days, you're not Jack McKenna, my son. You're Jack Cameron, new employee. You'll use your mother's maiden name for the ten days you work undercover, and will tell no one that you're my son or that you're going to be taking over the running of this resort very shortly. And during those ten days, you'll do a variety of jobs, get to know the functioning of this place in a real, hands-on capacity. You'll meet people, you'll meet our guests, you'll interact with everyone in a way that you simply couldn't if you were isolated up in this office."

Jack took a deep breath. "Go on."

"Then at the end of ten days, if you've kept your identity secret, if you haven't used any of your money beyond what your salary at the resort pays you, and if you've worked well and hard, then I'll turn this entire place over to you and retire."

"Where will I live for the duration of this experiment?"

"There's some employee housing that I'll show you. I already have a small studio apartment set aside for you."

"Great. What will I use for money? Will I have any cash at all, or do I have to wait for my first paycheck?"

"I'll advance you two weeks' salary. Your apartment

is already paid for, along with the utilities. The hardship won't be financial, Jack. That's not the point. This will be a lesson in how the other half works and lives."

"Dad, I know that you and Mom made your money all by yourselves—"

"We came up the hard way, and had a wonderful time doing so, and so we appreciated it." James held up his hand as Jack opened his mouth to speak. "Hear me out, son. I'm not saying that you wouldn't appreciate this resort if I handed it over to you this instant. I'm only saying that I know you'll appreciate it *more* if you have a real idea of how things operate around here. You've been kind of isolated from us, out in Boston, and this is my way of making sure that you understand what the running of this resort entails."

Jack knew his father well enough to realize he wasn't going to budge in this matter. The stakes were high— the resort he'd wanted to run since he'd been old enough to imagine it. And the price his father was asking him to pay for the privilege wasn't all that bad. He'd endured worse. He could endure working at the resort for ten days if he just kept his eye on the ultimate prize.

"Unless, of course, you don't think you're up to it."

Jack's head came up, his eyes narrowed as he looked at his father, and—saw his twinkling blue eyes.

"You almost had me there, Dad."

"I know." There was suppressed laughter in the older man's voice. "Give this some thought, Jack. Maybe you want a night to sleep on the whole thing . . ."

"No, I don't need any more time to think about it. I'll do it."

"Good."

"What will I wear? I'll be a dead giveaway in the clothes I brought with me."

"You'll leave those clothes with me, in the penthouse

suite. I went ahead and charged a few things for you at Costco. That's where you would shop as an employee—"

"Hey, Dad, I'm no snob. I do some shopping there now."

His father smiled. "I know. And I'm glad you've come to see the wisdom of my offer. It's only ten days, Jack. A lot can happen in ten days."

"Sure." Jack stood up. "Well, there's no time like the present. Just point me in the direction of my studio apartment . . ."

"Jack." His father came around the side of his desk and enveloped him in a hug. After a slight hesitation, Jack's arms came up and he hugged his father back.

His father stepped away, then said, "I thought we might have lunch together out on the penthouse's balcony. Catch up on a few things. Hiro can drive you to your new apartment this evening."

"Okay. What's my first job?"

"Tomorrow, you'll be one of the bartenders out by the pool, serving drinks and mingling with our guests."

Actually, that didn't sound too bad. "Can I change out of this suit before you order up lunch?" Almost no one wore a suit on the islands except for the most formal of occasions, but Jack had thought that seeing his father today had rated wearing one of his best. Now he was itching to change into a pair of shorts and a Hawaiian shirt.

His father smiled. "Sure."

"He did that to you?" Patti said, incredulous.

"Cross my heart," Cherry said. "It was awful. I had no place to live, nowhere to go. I had to call one of my friends from the club, she was a dancer as well, and I slept on her couch for almost a month while I got my life back in order."

"What a mean thing to do," Patti said, "throwing you out that way."

"Yeah, it was, but I survived, and that's what's important."

Kate listened with half an ear as she ate her in-flight breakfast. Miss Cherry Jubilee was an absolute godsend. After Patti had come awake and staggered to the bathroom, then drank a glass of orange juice, combed her hair, and slicked on some lipstick, Kate had introduced the two women, and they'd just clicked.

The Bloody Mary had arrived along with breakfast, and Patti had started to pour her heart out to the blonde woman, who had listened carefully and asked such great questions for details, questions Kate hadn't even thought to ask.

Cherry was a killer listener, and during the course of her conversation with Patti, Kate had overheard many more details about Roger the Rat.

Now she was thanking God Patti had never married him. For even if her cousin couldn't see it right now, Kate had a strong feeling that the Universe, God, whatever you wanted to call those forces out there beyond our control, had been helping her cousin. She'd been prevented from making a terrible mistake, one she would have regretted for the rest of her life.

Roger was no prize. Patti hadn't been able to see that, but she was starting to, now, thanks to Cherry.

Kate could see how talking to Cherry was helping Patti. She was telling her the same story she'd told them all at home, only this time it was different. This time, Kate noticed, Patti wasn't crying. This time, between earnestly revealing every single detail to Cherry, she actually saw her cousin laughing. One time she'd laughed so hard that tears had come to her eyes, but the right kind of tears, not sad tears.

And now, Cherry was telling her about what she called "Number three in the three worst breakups in my entire life," and Patti was taking it all in. They were comrades in arms, both victims of the dating wars, and Kate ate her breakfast. It was really quite good for plane fare, but then again this was first class. She'd never flown first class before, and she was starting to really enjoy it.

Her Uncle Albert had gone all out buying these tickets, and Kate was suddenly glad it wasn't Roger sitting in the seat beside Patti, but that she was sitting on this plane and Patti was across the aisle, next to Cherry, and laughing her head off once again.

Things were definitely looking up.

"How are you going to go about finding this millionaire?" she heard her cousin say.

Kate leaned forward, half a blueberry muffin in hand, her coffee cup in the other. She'd wanted to ask Cherry the exact same thing, and was glad Patti had thought to. Because she was starting to think that this idea of hooking up with a millionaire wasn't so crazy, after all.

Chapter Three

✿ Meredith walked into James's office with the usual midmorning coffee tray, then approached his desk. She set the tray down on the glossy wooden surface, then took just a second to look at her boss. He was standing, his back toward her, and staring out the floor-to-ceiling windows that ran the entire length of one wall and faced the Pacific Ocean. His shoulders were slightly hunched and that proud bearing was nowhere in sight.

She wondered what James McKenna was thinking, and thought she even knew. But Meredith had too many years' experience with the man to ask.

Turning to leave, she wasn't startled when he said, "Meredith? Would you stay for a moment?"

James always spoke up sooner or later. He was a man who had deep feelings he usually kept to himself, but over the years he'd confided in her. She considered him one of her dearest friends as well as her employer, and knew that his meeting with Jack had affected him deeply.

"Certainly. Would you like some coffee?"

"That would be wonderful," he said, then sighed.

Quickly and efficiently she fixed him a cup exactly as he liked it, then one of her own. She positioned the plate of freshly baked chocolate chip macadamia nut cookies where he could grab a few if he wanted to. They were one of the specialties of the resort's extensive kitchen, and one of James's favorite desserts. Then she sat back in her chair with her cup.

He walked back to the desk, sat down, picked up his coffee and took a sip. He set it down, then reached for a cookie.

And Meredith knew better than to rush him. He was exactly like her husband, Hank. He'd get to what was bothering him when he was good and ready, and there was no point in pressing the matter.

"Do you think I did the right thing?" he finally said.

He was referring, of course, to the wager he'd made with his son.

"I do," she said, then took another sip of her coffee. "It can't possibly hurt him, you know. And ten days is really nothing in the scheme of things."

"I want so much for him," James admitted.

"I know," she said, and waited.

James set down his cup and leaned back in his chair. "Oh, it really has nothing to do with running the hotel, and everything to do with finding the right woman."

Meredith had to grin. "And you think that will solve all Jack's problems, as opposed to adding to them?"

"I think he's missing out on the best life has to offer."

"I agree with you there," she said, reaching for a cookie. "I don't know what I would have done without Hank in my life."

"I was blessed to have Caroline," he said quietly.

He still misses her. As Meredith studied her boss, she

thought of all the attention given by the media to the fact that today's man seemed incapable of commitment. She found that fact to be so false. There were men like James McKenna, who had loved deeply and finally lost. There were men like her husband, Hank, who had made her own life so much richer. And there were men like Jack, who underneath all that false bravado, loved just as deeply and passionately as his father.

"I know," she said quietly. "But you have to remember, James, that Jack lost her when he was eleven. And as much as Hank and I tried to include him in outings with our own children, and as much as you did for him, you don't get over the loss of your mother that easily. I know. I lost my own when I was eight, and it was only when I had my first child that I began to really heal."

"What could I have done?" he said, and she heard the quiet despair in his voice. James was such a good man. She'd considered it an honor to work for him and had always known she was a fortunate woman.

"Nothing. You did everything a father could, but that's a loss that each child has to get over on their own. It's the hardest lesson a parent learns, that their child has to go through pain on their own. That there's nothing we can do."

She saw the way his handsome face tightened with emotion.

"James, it's never easy, and you did everything you could for him. But that's why he holds back. That's why he hasn't married. I'd put money on it. He's afraid."

"Of loving," James said softly.

"Of loving deeply and being left. Of feeling that kind of pain again. Why do you think he's so immersed in his work? Why do you think he ran the Boston property so brilliantly? Because work is *safe*, James. Work isn't the same as a flesh and blood person, and it's far less complicated emotionally."

"How can I get through to him?"

"You can't." Meredith reached for a cookie and sat back in her chair. "But don't lose hope. The right woman will."

Kate ran after both Cherry and Patti as they headed toward their nonstop flight to Maui. They'd had to change planes at LAX, and even though their second flight was only a few gates away from the other and they had almost forty-five minutes, they didn't want to take any chances.

Patti was a changed woman, talking animatedly and nonstop with Cherry. They'd just clicked, and Kate had watched, dumbfounded, as her normally shy cousin had bloomed beneath Cherry's skilled listening and questioning. And Kate found herself not as worried about her cousin's state of mind.

Now, all she had to worry about was getting on that other plane.

Getting Patti to the resort seemed a lot less complicated than it had been when they'd boarded their first flight early this morning. And she had Miss Cherry Jubilee to thank for that.

"How's your fish?" James asked.

"Fine, Dad." Jack speared another piece of the grilled ahi pepper steak with his fork and popped it in his mouth. First-class food, as always. The meal was fabulous, the weather as glorious as ever, the sunshine warm out on the penthouse's balcony, the trade winds gentle.

But his father was up to something. He could always smell a hidden agenda, and all of his senses were on red alert.

"I'm happy to have you back here, Jack."

"And I'm happy to be here," he said, wondering all the while why his father couldn't just come out with what was really on his mind. Sometimes they had a hard time communicating.

"I have a lot of faith in you," his father said, after a short silence.

That one sentence touched him. Jack set down his fork. He didn't quite know what to say.

"Thanks, Dad," he said quietly. The words seemed totally inadequate, so he added, "That means a lot to me."

"I'm glad." His father hesitated.

Jack sensed there was something more. What? He glanced at his father, studied him for a long moment, then said, "Are you okay, Dad? Are you sure there's nothing more on your mind?"

His father seemed to struggle with something, some inner emotion, but then he reached over and awkwardly patted Jack's arm.

"No. No, nothing's wrong. I'm just so glad you're here."

Hawaii.

Specifically Maui. A total dream, a seduction of the senses. After their plane landed and they stepped out of the pressurized, recycled air in the first-class cabin and into tropical, flower-scented warmth, Kate totally understood the lure of just abandoning everything and escaping to a tropical island somewhere in the Pacific.

She'd never been to the tropics before, and the whole island seemed like a dream. From the moment she'd looked out the plane window and seen the purple and turquoise waters ringing soft sand beaches, viewed the lush, vivid green of tropic vegetation, she'd known she was far away from anything she'd ever known before.

The mild temperature was a shock, coming from the bitterly cold, snow-swirled skies of the Midwest. The feel of the air, the moisture, the heavy, flowery scent she couldn't quite identify—all Kate knew was that it combined into something quite magical, and she was more than content to fall beneath the island's seductive spell.

They'd decided to share a rental car, once she and Patti and Cherry had discovered that they were all headed for the same resort. After gathering up all their luggage and standing in line for the rental car for a short time, they found themselves on their way. Kate decided to drive the sixteen miles to the resort, while Cherry expounded on her plan to find Mr. Right, the millionaire.

"So anyway, Chuck told me that if I flew out to Maui on these dates, he'd meet me and introduce me to a few of his very wealthy friends. He has a suite set aside for me at the Kalani Resort, and tomorrow I think we're going to some sort of polo match." She turned in the front seat and faced Patti, sitting in back. "You and Kate are welcome to come along with me if you want to, I think it would be a lot more fun with both of you there!"

"That sounds great," Patti said, and Kate glanced at her cousin in the rearview mirror. She never would have believed it, but Patti seemed as if she was actually ready to have some fun. And as Kate had envisioned her cousin locking herself in one of the resort's bedrooms and languishing away, this new attitude of Patti's was a welcome addition to their vacation.

They kept driving through flatland. Bright green sugarcane rippled, dancing in the soft wind. Kate kept glancing at the land as she drove, land so lush and voluptuous, colored with such profound shades of green, the heavy scent of tropical flowers and moist, rich earth all around her. They passed a few roadside fruit stands, and she saw tropical produce, along with actual coconuts, in bountiful piles.

Paradise.

Soon they would be at Kalani, the Hawaiian word for heaven.

Jack made his way to his living quarters after lunch with his father. As he opened the door to the studio apartment that would be his home for the duration of the ten days he worked at the resort, he glanced around, curious.

Not bad.

Though it was rather small, it was clean and the carpet was new. A small couch and chair were positioned near the front door, and he recognized a Murphy bed in the far wall that could be pulled down at night. The one bathroom had only a shower stall, toilet, and sink, and a small breakfast bar separated the efficient little kitchen from the living room area.

Not bad at all. Definitely doable.

He threw his duffel bag down in the center of the living area. He'd made the exchange of clothing in his penthouse suite, leaving all of his clothing in one of the spacious closets and taking the clothing that his father had purchased for him. He'd also noticed that this clothing had been run through a washing machine several times, so it appeared slightly worn, as if he'd had it for a while.

His father didn't miss a trick. It was part of the reason that James McKenna had been so phenomenally successful.

Of course, there had been a few negotiations. He'd insisted on some form of transportation, and his father had relented and allowed him his old motorcycle, a Harley Davidson that had seen better days but ran beautifully. Jack had it parked beneath the studio apartment, in his assigned parking space.

Now, as he checked the refrigerator and found it empty, then checked his wallet and mentally budgeted his money for the next ten days, he decided to take his bike and make a grocery run.

Grabbing his keys off the coffee table, he headed out the door.

They entered the town of Wailea, on the western side of the island, and Kate drove carefully as Cherry read off the directions.

"You're going to turn left at the light and—oh, *my!*"

Kate glanced in the direction her friend was looking and saw a man on a Harley. Her first impression was fast and furious as he raced by on the motorcycle.

Classic bad boy. No helmet and driving fast. Dangerous. And just her type.

Just the type that had gotten her in emotional trouble before.

Just the type to stay away from.

He had on dark glasses, and was dressed in well-worn jeans, black boots, and a red and white Hawaiian shirt. His straight, dark brown hair was longish and brushed the back of his collar. And sunglasses couldn't conceal first-class bone structure. The arms holding those handlebars and controlling that powerful bike had been muscular, those shoulders powerful . . .

"If he has blue eyes, I'm a goner," Cherry said, teasing her.

"What?" said Kate. "I was just looking. Just for an instant."

"But he's not part of your plan," Patti chimed in.

"Of course not, Sugar," Cherry said. "But who said I couldn't look?"

*   *   *

Kate had never, in her entire life, seen luxury on a scale like this. When they'd named this place heaven, they hadn't been fooling around.

She and Patti had left Cherry at the front desk of the Kalani Resort. And what a front desk! The whole resort looked like a palace out of the *Arabian Nights,* all white marble, with dramatic lacquered vases filled with sprays of exotic orchids.

Gorgeous women dressed in tropical print dresses had met them as soon as they'd stepped out of the rental car and had offered them crystal glasses of tropical juices along with rolled washcloths.

Kate hadn't quite known what they were for.

"If you'd like to wipe your face and hands," one of the women explained. "It can get quite hot outside."

Patti had taken to this luxury like a little duck to water, and Kate watched as her cousin wiped her face and arms with the warm, damp washcloth.

"It feels great, Kate," she said.

So Kate did the same. This place was seductive, her senses were drowning in it, and the staff at the Kalani started you out on this feast for the senses from the moment you entered their gates.

Their every need seemed to be anticipated, and reservations were handled with a minimum of fuss.

"Call us when you get settled," Patti said to Cherry, giving her a hug. "And if you aren't meeting up with Chuck, maybe we could all have dinner together."

"That sounds like a plan," Cherry said, returning the hug. "You keep your chin up, you hear?"

"I will."

And then, after they'd parked their rental car, all of their luggage was loaded onto a white golf cart. And soon Kate found herself rocketing along curved cement pathways, lined with exotic and tropical plants she'd never seen before, as she and Patti and their driver made their way to their villa by the Pacific.

She didn't even want to think about what her uncle Albert had forked out for this little adventure, first class all the way. She'd overheard one of the desk clerks saying that Harrison Ford had checked out the other night, and Tom Hanks and his family had just spent a few weeks there as well.

Lifestyles of the Rich and Famous, Kate thought, remembering her conversation with Cherry on the plane. Well, though most people would never have a chance to see how the other half lived and to mingle with the fabulously rich, it looked like for the next ten days she was going to have a chance to do exactly that.

For the next ten days, he was going to see how the other half lived.

The poorer half.

Jack stood in line at the market, weighing his options. He was a man who budgeted his money carefully, no matter how much he made. So now he studied the contents of his cart, wondering if there was anything he didn't really need.

He'd been told that he could take meals in the resort's kitchen, so he knew he would be fed well. But this trip had been more for munchies, juice, a few little things so that he wouldn't be caught short late at night.

He glanced up as he heard squealing laughter, and had to smile at the sight of a small child being swooped up into his mother's arms. Both mother and child were caught up in each other, the child laughing, the mother smiling down at her child, and as Jack watched them he felt a painful tightening in his gut as he remembered.

Why does it still hurt, so many years later?

He thought of it as the defining moment of his life, the death of his mother. His father had been a rock, and had told him the truth from the beginning, when she'd first become ill. But Jack had concocted a fantasy in which his mother lived, so when she'd finally succumbed to the cancer, it had shocked him to his soul.

He'd made an attempt to come to terms with it; he'd gone through some therapy trying to get to the bottom of the basic distrust that he had in the goodness of life. He was aware of why he buried himself in work, why he still hadn't found a life partner, why he avoided that particular intimacy. Oh, he was aware, all right. He even knew his father was worried about him. And he'd been wondering, as he'd sped up the coast on his bike toward this market, if that was the entire reason behind this little ten-day wager—to get him to open up.

His mother had loved these islands, and he saw her in every part of them. He remembered the days she'd taken him to the beach and they'd snorkeled for hours. He remembered walks on the beach at night, and the way she'd pointed out the stars to him. His father had been working hard at that time, on his ascent in the resort business, so he and his mother had spent a lot of time together.

His most cherished memory was the first time she'd taken him up to the vast crater of Haleakala, the house of the sun, a dormant volcano. He'd been six years old. They'd driven up to see the sunrise, and as they'd huddled together in the cold and dark, she'd carefully explained the spiritual significance of the area, and how all the Hawaiians from the different islands had met here because it was a highly significant place.

If he closed his eyes, he could remember the moon riding high in the pale night sky, and the way the first rays of sunlight had slipped over the rim and illuminated everything. They'd stood silent in that ancient, powerful place, and he'd never felt as close to her as he had that morning.

Just before her death, his mother had asked his father to take her up there one last time. He had, wrapping her in a blanket and carrying her to see the sunrise she'd loved so much. Jack had followed beside them, holding his mother's hand, and the three of them had watched the sun start to rise over this sacred place. This time, when the sun had finally broken through the clouds, he'd cried, his emotions choked and painful, the tears running down his face, because he'd known it was the last time she'd ever see it.

She'd died less than a week later. Since her death, he'd never been up there.

Sometimes, Jack felt that when she'd died, she'd taken everything good with her. He'd acted out after her death, driven his father to complete distraction. There had even been a short stint in military school, which he'd hated except for the friends he'd made. He'd finally pulled himself together, but at best he'd known that he'd only spackled over a completely broken heart.

And he was at a complete loss as to how to heal it.

Nothing her uncle had said prepared Kate for their villa.

She'd been in something of a daze when she'd walked in, taking everything in. But she'd had the presence of mind to tip the two bellboys who had assisted them with their luggage. Now they'd left, and she and Patti had the entire place to themselves.

And what a place it was.

Her uncle had told her that this villa boasted what was called "a deluxe ocean view." As Kate walked outside the sliding glass doors leading out from the living room and onto the spacious lanai, she stared at the short expanse of green grass that fell away to the beach and the surging waves of the Pacific. Kate actually felt light-headed. Beauty such as this didn't come her way that often.

It seemed strange to think about Chicago at a time like this, and of her uncle's restaurant. And all of it freezing and covered with snow. Today, right about now, she would have finished making all her desserts and been ready to help her uncle with the dinner crowd, serving up portions of tiramisu and *panna cotta,* gelato and *biscotti.*

Yet here she was, on the world's oldest island chain in the middle of the Pacific, on Hawaii's second largest island, and one of the world's most beautiful places. And a guest at a five-star resort.

She turned and took in the private plunge pool, the barbecue grill, the breakfast table with four chairs. *Incredible.* Heading back inside, she glanced around the living room and full kitchen. The coffeemaker caught her eye, and she walked toward it. Within minutes, she'd started preparing some of the complimentary Kona coffee, and then it crossed her mind that she'd better go check on Patti.

She found her inside one of the bedrooms, lying across the queen-sized bed, sobbing.

"Oh, Patti," she said, walking over to the bed, sitting down next to her cousin and laying a gentle hand on her shoulder.

Patti mumbled something into the pillow.

"What?" Kate said gently. "I can't understand you."

"No one . . . no one is ever . . . going to . . . *want* me . . ." Patti hiccuped on another sob, then rolled over and buried her face in the soft pillow.

"Oh—" Kate stopped herself from saying, *Oh no, that isn't true,* because right now, for Patti, it was. Right now, after what Roger had done to her, she really believed that no one would ever want her again. The pain, the abandonment was too fresh, too raw, and too new. Cherry had been a distraction on the plane and had made her laugh, but now that she was in this exquisite villa and remembering that she should have been on her honeymoon, Kate could understand why her cousin was going off the deep end.

Well, as she and Uncle Albert had plotted, this was just the place for it.

She sat next to her cousin, gently rubbing her back, until she heard a bell ring. For a moment, she thought maybe it was some ultra-special device on the coffeemaker, then when the bell sounded again, Kate realized it was the villa's front door.

"Hang on, Patti, I'm just going to see who's there," she said, then got up and raced down the hall toward the front door. The two upstairs bedrooms and bathroom and huge walk-in closet were along a hallway that also opened out toward their main front door.

She flung open the door and saw Cherry, her blue eyes filled with tears, her bottom lip trembling, all her luggage piled up beside her.

"I have to go," she whispered. "But I wanted to say good-bye to you and Patti. You guys made the flight over here a lot of fun."

"What are you *talking* about?" Kate said, her hand coming up to push her hair away from her face. Everyone was going crazy!

"There *is* no Chuck," Cherry whispered, then hiccuped on a small sob. "His name is Marvin, and he has a wife and three kids. There's no suite reserved for me here, there are no millionaire friends, and he's a shoe— a shoe—a *shoe* salesman in Cincinnati!" Her bottom lip trembled and she bit it, then glanced down at her watch.

"I'm headed to Kahului Airport in about twenty minutes. It's back to Vegas for me."

"Wait a minute," Kate said. "Wait. Stop. Don't do that just yet. Come inside and have a cup of coffee, and we'll figure this whole thing out, okay?"

"No," Cherry said. "*No*. Game's *over,* and I was the total *fool* for ever believing what that Chuck—I mean, Marvin—ever promised me—"

"Cherry?" came a small voice from behind Kate. "What's wrong?"

When Cherry glanced over Kate's shoulder and saw Patti, her eyes filled again. "I guess we're both having a bad day, aren't we, Sugar?"

Kate stepped aside as Patti ran forward into Cherry's arms, and both women began to sob.

Jack lay back in the Murphy bed he'd pulled out, his arms stretched out behind his head. He could stand a nap; it had been a long flight yesterday from Boston at the crack of dawn to San Francisco, then from San Francisco to Maui today. And he had a long day ahead of him tomorrow.

According to his father's chart, tomorrow he would be stationed out by one of the three swimming pools, the lagoon pool with the swim-up bar. He'd be bartending, which wouldn't be that much of a stretch because he'd been a part-time bartender while he'd been in college.

His father had sent up a detailed drink list, complete with the resort's tropical drink specialties served at the swim-up bar. As Jack read the list of drink names, the ingredients began to come back to him. Wailea Sunset, Piyi, Green Flash, Pirate's Treasure, Rum Runner, and assorted smoothies. And, of course, the resort's signature drink, the Lava Flow.

Jack began to memorize the various ingredients, the tropical juices, crème of coconut, the particular rums, vodkas, and liqueurs. The Mango Passion liqueur, the Mac-Nut liqueur, the drinks that called for a float of 151 Rum . . .

But before he was halfway down the list, he fell asleep.

"So there is no Chuck?" Patti said.

"Nope," said Cherry. "Never has been, and never was."

Kate sat back in her chair and listened as the two women rehashed their woes. She'd insisted that Cherry drag all her luggage inside and at least spend the night before she raced off to the airport. And she was trying to think of a way to get her to stay with them, but now was not the time to bring that up.

Kate had herded both sobbing women out onto the lanai, poured each of them a large cup of Kona coffee, found some cream and sugar in the fully stocked kitchen cabinets and refrigerator. Then, she'd broken open the gift basket that Uncle Albert and Aunt Connie had sent them from the resort's gift shop. It contained over two pounds of chocolate covered macadamia nuts, along with three dozen chocolate chip cookies with nuts. Kate's first bite had revealed that those nuts were macadamias.

She wondered, as she chewed, if she dared try to get the recipe. Chefs could be notoriously overprotective of their creations, but these cookies were killer. She didn't know how she would justify them on an Italian menu, but she knew they would sell.

But her first concern had been to take care of Patti and Cherry.

She'd found a plate in the kitchen cupboard, piled on

some cookies, and carried them out to the breakfast table on the lanai. And now both Patti and Cherry seemed a little better, having had some sugar and caffeine.

"What are you going to do?" Patti said. As Kate watched her cousin, she silently blessed Cherry again. The woman's disaster had temporarily diverted her cousin from thinking about her own life.

"I don't know. I don't know." Cherry set down her coffee as tears welled up once again. "I'm just so tired of my life being a complete mess!"

"Me, too," Patti said as she patted her friend's arm. "But I know one thing you're going to do, and I'm not taking no for an answer."

Kate turned away, trying to hide her grin before she gave it all away. She knew what her cousin was about to suggest, because she'd been wondering how to make Cherry the same offer. But she was glad it was coming from Patti. It would make her cousin feel so much better to do this for a friend.

"What?" Cherry said.

"You're staying right here with us," Patti said. "With me and Kate. For the entire ten days that we're here." When Cherry started to protest, Patti held up her hand. "Cherry, you *really* helped me on that flight. I don't think I would have made it without both you and Kate right with me. And my dad would be horrified if I let you turn around and go home because of that Marvin creep and what he did to you. Now, you're not going anywhere, you're staying right here and you're going to get that millionaire. And I'm going to help you."

Kate took a sip of her coffee, and felt tight stomach muscles slowly unclench. She'd hated seeing both her cousin and her new friend in so much pain. But now things were looking up for all of them.

This trip hadn't been ordinary from the moment she and Patti had met Cherry on the plane. How often did you just click with someone the way they both had with Cherry and become so close so fast? Then this island resort, this luxurious paradise, was so much more than she'd thought it would be. And they had ten whole days to go.

Kate had a feeling that the three of them were in for a lot more than any of them had bargained for.

Chapter Four

❀ Jack woke up from his nap, took a hot shower, then quickly dressed in shorts, a Hawaiian shirt, and sandals. He flopped back down on his bed and took the drink list in hand. No use looking like an idiot if he didn't have to. As he studied the drinks and the proportion of ingredients, he became more confident that he could actually pull this off. Bartending was a lot like bike riding; once you'd done it and mastered the necessary skills, they always came back to you.

After reviewing the tropical drinks and making sure he knew how the Kalani Resort liked to serve up their libations, he decided to take a walk and go investigate the actual bar.

"We have to have dinner," Kate said. "We can't just hole up in this villa and live on coffee and cookies."

"But what coffee and cookies!" Patti said, rolling her eyes. "Let's just order in room service."

"I don't think that's a good idea, Sugar," Cherry said. "I think Kate's right. We should get out of the villa and scope this place out."

"Look," Kate said, examining a brochure on the living room coffee table. "There's a little café, and it says it's a gourmet Italian delicatessen with full table service. Freshly prepared pastas and pizzas, and indoor or outdoor dining. Daily baked breads and exquisite desserts. I say we try this place for tonight."

"Oh, you and your desserts!" Patti said, then she turned to Cherry. "Did Kate tell you she's a chef? Everywhere she goes, she has to try all the desserts and compare them to what we serve at my father's restaurant."

"Now that's what I call a great job," Cherry said. Then she addressed Kate. "That Italian place sounds good to me."

"I know when I'm outnumbered," Patti grumbled.

"You'll feel better once you have some food in your stomach," Kate said, reaching for her purse.

"Boy, you sound just like Mom," Patti said.

"Where do you think I learned it?"

They watched the sunset in silence from their lanai, then exited the villa and started down the winding path at dusk toward the pools and lights twinkling in the main building. Kate was walking with her head down, looking in her purse to make sure she'd remembered her key card, when she ran into a hard, male chest.

"Oh!" She almost bounced back and would have fallen on her butt if strong, sure hands hadn't reached out and grabbed her upper arms.

She looked up into the most incredible pair of blue eyes she'd ever seen.

Motorcycle man. Bad boy. Uh oh . . .

"Are you okay?" he said.

That voice . . . That voice would put George Clooney's voice to shame, and she liked Clooney's voice. A lot.

Now she couldn't seem to find her own.

"Are you okay?" he said again.

That touch . . . Something about the way he touched her made Kate realize how long it had been since a man had touched her. Actually, it made her realize how long it had been since anyone had touched her and made her feel like . . .

No. It had to be Maui. The whole island was just one big assault on the senses.

"Yes, I'm . . . sorry. I wasn't looking."

He smiled down at her, and her heart did a curious little flip-flop. This guy had it all. Tall, dark, and handsome didn't even begin to cover it. Dressed in shorts and a Hawaiian shirt, he had a body to die for, with broad, strong shoulders, muscular arms, great legs, and a presence so palpable she could almost feel it coming off him.

He must have just gone for a swim or taken a shower, because his thick dark hair was still slightly damp. He had great cheekbones and a strong jaw, but it was his eyes . . .

Kate caught herself staring and started to step back, then realized he still had a hold of her by her upper arms. And he was looking at her too, as if trying to place her.

For an instant, she was tempted to tell him they'd met before, she'd seen him on his motorcycle, but the moment passed, he dropped his hands, and she stepped back.

"You're looking just fine," he said, smiling. "And I can't say that I'm sorry. Not really."

A little thrill shot through her at his blatant male honesty.

He smiled at her one last time, then turned and walked off down the path in the opposite direction they were going.

"My God!" Cherry said, fanning herself with one hand. "Kate, you've barely walked out the door and already hooked a live one!"

"Yeah, right."

"Now, now," Cherry said as they continued on toward the Italian deli. "He may not be a millionaire, but that man is *primo* material for a vacation fling."

"Just what you need!" Patti exclaimed. She turned toward Cherry. "Kate hasn't been out on a date in—well, forever!"

"Eighteen months, two weeks, three days, and—oh—about six hours."

Cherry raised an expertly shaped eyebrow. "Wow. You have it timed down to the hour?"

"Just joking. But it has been about eighteen months."

"What happened?" Cherry said.

"I just got tired of the whole thing. I was dating, and none of the men I went out with were even close to what I wanted. The last straw was a really bad breakup with a guy I was starting to fall in love with and a couple of disastrous blind dates, so I just decided to take a time-out."

They'd reached the main building, and Patti said, "I think I see the little Italian place." She pointed to a small restaurant, decorated with twinkling white lights.

"That's it," Kate said, spying the name above the door.

Later, after they'd ordered dinner and were waiting for their food, Cherry leaned forward and said to Kate, "You know, those time-outs have a way of becoming months, then years, and then one day you wake up and—"

"And you've forgotten how to be a woman," Kate supplied for her.

Cherry leaned back. "That's a great way of putting it."

"I'm taking a time-out," Patti said, twirling a bread stick like a cranky four-year-old. "I'm taking a rest from the whole mess. I mean, look at my judgement. Look at what I got myself into." Her eyes welled up and she blinked furiously. "And I feel so damn guilty, after all the money my dad spent on the wedding, and now this—" She gestured around the restaurant, but Kate knew she meant the entire resort.

She grabbed her cousin's hand. "Listen to me, Patti. I was there when Uncle Albert found out about the note, and I know how upset he was. This is his way of trying to make things better for you, so I think we should try to enjoy ourselves and not feel all guilty."

"I agree with Kate," Cherry said.

"Let's make a pact," Kate said. "Like blood sisters, or something."

"Cool!" said Cherry.

"A pact that says we'll do our best to take these next ten days and really look at our lives and try to move ahead. I think we should each have a goal, a very specific goal, and try to accomplish it. Even if that goal is only to kick back and relax here in paradise."

"Good idea," Patti said. "I'll go first." She thought for a moment, then said, "I'm going to try and be grateful that I have such wonderful parents who would care about me so much that they would send me on a trip like this after all the trouble I caused them. And I'm going to take these ten days and get over Roger, because he's not worth it!"

"Hear, hear!" said Cherry, raising her glass of red wine. Kate and Patti did the same, and they clinked glasses in a toast.

"Okay, now me," Cherry said. She smiled, and a mischievous gleam filled her blue eyes. "I'm still on the prowl for my millionaire, but I'm not against having a little fun along the way, like with someone like that guy you bumped into." Cherry laughed. "If you don't want him, Kate, send him on over to me!"

The women laughed, then playfully clinked glasses again. Several of the other diners glanced over at their table, clearly curious at what was going on.

"Okay, Kate, now it's your turn," Patti said. "And it can't be something safe. It has to be something that really scares you, that pushes you completely out of your comfort zone. Something you have to really go all out to do!"

"Hmmm." Kate thought about this, then all three women focused their attention on their waiter as he came to their table with a large cheese pizza. They'd selected the restaurant's *quattro formaggi* pizza, and the blend of mozzarella, ricotta, Parmesan, and Gorgonzola cheeses smelled heavenly.

The waiter set their pizza down in front of them, then came directly back with plates and flatware.

"Good choice of restaurant, Kate," Cherry said. "That pizza smells divine."

"No distractions!" Patti said. "Kate, what are you going to do?"

For some reason, the motorcycle man's face came into view, that killer smile, the touch of his hands, that voice . . . Kate didn't know why life had to be this way, but there were men you had chemistry with and men who left you cold. And for some reason, it was always the men with that touch of wildness in their souls that did it for her.

He was one of them.

"She's thinking about that guy!" Patti whispered to Cherry.

"She has good taste," Cherry said.

"I want to wake back up, to feel—*something* again," Kate said, and to her horror, she felt tears filling her eyes. "I want . . ." She hesitated, then covered her eyes with one hand, suddenly self-conscious.

"Oh, Kate," Cherry said, taking her free hand. "I know how you feel. It's so damn scary, the whole relationship thing."

"I'm sorry, you guys. This is our first night here, we're supposed to be having fun—"

"No, Kate!" Patti said. "You're always so busy being strong for me, I kind of like knowing that you need me, you need us, to lean on."

"Well, I do," she said. She wiped at her eyes, then reached for a paper napkin and dried her tears. "You know, Patti, I think seeing you get dumped brought all my fears about men right back to the surface. Then, I was so busy getting us both out here, and we all get here and this whole island was made for romance, and there are honeymooning couples all over the place. And now that I've finally had a chance to slow down and relax, I can admit that I want a relationship but I've just been so bad at it, and met so many jerks." Kate took a deep breath. "And to top it all off, I'm scared to death."

"Aren't we all," murmured Cherry.

"Your goal," Patti reminded her.

Kate took a deep breath and wondered if she dared to voice what she was thinking. What she'd been thinking since she'd bumped into that handsome stranger on the path outside their villa. Then she decided to go for broke.

"I'm going to have a fling," Kate announced as she reached for a piece of pizza, then slid it onto the plate in front of her. "I'm going to have a glorious, no strings attached, no holds barred, totally about the physical fling with a capital *F* before I forget I even *have* a body."

"Wow," said Patti, sounding clearly impressed. "I wish I was ready for one."

"Really, Kate?" Cherry said.

Kate stared down at the slice of pizza in front of her. "Oh, who am I kidding? I've always been so careful. I've never really thrown caution to the winds, even though I can't tell you how many times I've wanted to. Or fantasized about it." She glanced back up at Patti and Cherry. "I'll be lucky if I even go out dancing while we're here, let alone on a date. Forget the fling." She leaned back in her chair. "Forget it, it's hopeless. *I'm* hopeless."

"No, Kate," said Patti. "It's not, and you're not. Remember how many times you told me that after Roger dumped me? Why don't you start small, with a small goal, something attainable? Make a promise to yourself. How about if you decide that for the next ten days you'll put yourself out into situations where you might actually meet a guy, and then if someone halfway decent asks you out on a date, you'll go and try and have a good time, okay?"

Kate considered this.

"Just a date," Patti said. "Not a fling, not a lifetime commitment. Just a date. You, a neat guy, and an activity you can both enjoy."

"Now *that's* getting my mind going," Cherry said.

"Not that kind of activity," Patti said. "Something

like snorkeling together, or dancing, or maybe a walk on the beach." She turned her attention back to Kate. "It's a start."

Kate found herself touched beyond words at how her cousin was trying to help her. She was so lucky to have the family and friends she had. She glanced at Patti, then Cherry.

"Okay, that's my goal. I'll try to go out on a genuine date while we're here. Even more important, I'm going to change my attitude and be open to it."

"That's the spirit!" Patti said, reaching for a slice of pizza.

"It's a great goal, Kate," Cherry said. "A life-changing one. But I still think having a fling is a great idea. Don't let that thought go. Sometimes a woman just has to cut loose and go a little wild. For herself, you know?"

"Yeah," Kate said. "I know what you mean." She picked up her pizza slice and took a bite, chewed, then swallowed. "That's really good pizza." She took a slow, deep breath, then let it out. "I feel a lot better. Really." She hesitated, then said, "So I'm just going to stick my toe back into the pool and test the water, right?"

"Who knows?" said Cherry. "By the end of a few days in paradise you might be ready to dive into the _deep_ end—" She stopped talking in midsentence, then whispered, "Oh my God, there he is! Kate's guy!"

How Kate refrained from dropping her slice of pizza, turning around in her chair and staring, she never knew.

"What's he doing?" she muttered.

"I think he's getting a coffee. To go," Cherry whispered. "He can't see us, we're behind the potted palm." She giggled. "I can't believe I actually said that! Anyway, move your chair just a little, and you can see him."

She did. And she could.

She watched him as he talked with the girl behind the

counter, and even though she was flirting up a storm
with him as she rang up the sale, the mystery man was
polite, nothing more. And that gave Kate a little thrill,
because he'd clearly been flirting with her earlier on the
path outside their villa.

"He's a total hunk," Cherry whispered. "Bona fide,
in the flesh—"

"I like the way he wasn't wearing a helmet when we
first saw him," said Patti.

That surprised Kate. She hadn't even thought her
cousin had noticed him.

He got his coffee and started out of the deli, and all
three women stared after him.

"Wow," said Patti. "He even *walks* sexy."

"Kate," said Cherry, "you could do a whole lot
worse." She hesitated. "For that date, I mean."

"That wasn't what you were thinking," Kate said.
"Admit it."

"You're right," Cherry said. "Forget the date. That
man was *born* to be some woman's fling!" She stared in
the direction he'd gone and said softly, "Hel-lo Mr.
Fling!"

Patti laughed. Kate just stared after him. How could
one man hold so much appeal for her? And probably an
equal amount of danger . . .

She turned back to her food. "So he's a little too
much for me," Kate said, but her thoughts were definitely more erotic than she'd ever admit. Her mystery
man was the sort of man a woman fantasized about,
dreamed about, and wished she had the courage to have
a relationship with . . .

No, not a relationship, a fling. Sex. Really hot sex.
Besides, men like that usually didn't stay around to
have relationships.

So, that was that. He was off limits, but perhaps she

could give herself permission to try again, to see if she still had what it took to simply go out on a date.

"We could go dancing in Lahaina tomorrow evening," Kate said. "There are supposed to be some great clubs there. If we all went together, maybe it wouldn't be so bad."

"Maybe you could meet a guy," Patti said.

"Go on a date," Cherry said.

"Yeah," Kate said, but as she bit into her slice of pizza, she knew her mind was still on the man who had walked out the door.

Too bad he was off limits to her.

Jack was restless.

It had nothing to do with the ten-day wait his father had insisted on before he took over the running of the family resort.

It had everything to do with the woman he'd run into along the path tonight.

He didn't really have a type. He'd dated all sorts of women in his life, from the time he'd entered high school up until he'd flown out to the islands today. So if someone had asked him what he looked for in a woman, he wouldn't have been able to say.

Until now.

Now he couldn't get a certain woman out of his mind.

She'd been taller than the average. He'd put her at about five eight. Straight, dark brown, shoulder-length hair, the most amazing green eyes, and he'd been close enough to see a few freckles across the bridge of her cute little nose. He liked that, it told him she enjoyed being out in the sun.

Full lips. Quite an amazing mouth, glossed with

some sort of peachy lipstick. He'd caught himself staring at those lips, and fantasizing . . .

She'd been slender, but surprisingly curved. Her upper arms had felt strong beneath his fingers, toned, slightly muscular. She was no couch potato, he was sure of that. She had some kind of job where she used her arms, or else she was a demon at working out.

She'd been wearing some sort of sundress contraption, with tiny little straps so he'd been able to see her shoulders. Great legs. First class. And even though the full skirt of her dress had obscured the lower half of her body, he'd bet money that the rest of that body was as nice as the parts he'd been able to see.

He'd liked that she'd been flustered, that she hadn't moved away from him right away. He'd liked the way she'd looked up at him, as if trying to remember who he was, and yet as if she'd known him for a long, long time.

He wondered who she was, if she was staying at the resort, and if he would see her again.

And he found himself hoping he would.

Kate had known, from the moment she'd seen the two magnificent Italian marble bathrooms in their villa, that she and one of those deep-soaking tubs had a date with destiny. They had a bathroom on each floor of the villa, and each one of them was larger than her bedroom at home.

When they'd come back from dinner, both Patti and Cherry had decided to take it easy and see what was on cable TV. The villa boasted a twenty-seven-inch color television with cable in the living room, so they'd made some microwave popcorn Cherry had bought at the gift shop, and now were settled on the plush couches in front of the tube, talking and laughing.

Kate had retreated to the bathroom. She'd filled the huge tub with hot water and a generous three capfuls of the plumeria-scented bath gel that had been in the bathroom, compliments of the resort. Now she languished back in the tub, totally content, and thought about the brochure she'd found by the phone.

Renew your spirit in blissful seclusion . . . stroll through tropical gardens to private beachfront accommodations . . . white sands of the beach just steps away . . .

This trip was nothing at all like what she'd thought it would be. She hadn't even known places like this existed. Oh, she'd *known* they probably did, but kind of knowing and actually taking a vacation and being spoiled like this had been beyond her wildest dreams. Until now. Kate felt as if she were actually living a dream.

She could hear Patti's laughter from the living room and wondered at the fates that had brought them together with Cherry on their flight.

The fates that had let her bump right into a man who affected her like no one else had in quite a while. Ever, if she was honest. And that had been a dream of hers, late at night, on evenings when she'd driven home from the restaurant and wondered if her life was always going to be about work.

I want to wake back up . . .

She lathered her arms with a bar of scented soap.

Where had she gotten the nerve to actually say those words? To admit that her present life was nothing like what she really wanted it to be?

It had to be this place, this wonderful island and this fabulous resort. Maui, a totally sensual island, and a place out of time. The softness of the air, the smell of the sea, the scent just outside their sliding glass door that their waiter had told them was plumeria, the gentle trade winds and the palm trees blowing in that breeze, the path of the full moon on the ocean.

All of it combined to put a woman in a completely receptive mood, at one with her senses, to the call of her emotions, to totally opening up and *feeling*.

To realizing how long it had been since she'd been in the company of a man and really felt like a woman.

Maybe that date idea wasn't so bad, after all.

Kate ducked beneath the hot water and rinsed off, then slid back up. She stretched out one leg, then the other, then wiggled her toes.

It felt good to have her body back, to want her body back. To stop living up in her head, all disconnected from her feelings.

And she realized, as she took her leisurely bath, that she usually ignored her body and lived up in her head. Just got up as soon as the alarm sounded, raced for the shower, had a quick cup of coffee for breakfast, got dressed, jumped into her car, raced to the restaurant, and then worked herself into exhaustion day after day after day—so she wouldn't have to feel.

Hmmm. *Now* there *was an observation.*

Well, enough of that. When would she ever be able to return and have another vacation like this one? When would she ever again have the opportunity these next ten days represented? Yes, she would look after Patti, but she was also going to look after herself and have some fun.

She was going to find those emotional parts of her that were missing. And if being receptive to the idea of dating again was what it took, then that's what she would do.

But her mind kept drifting back to the dark haired,

blue-eyed stranger she'd bumped into on the path outside the villa. And she felt her body tingle, come alive,
as she thought of him, his touch, the look in his eyes,
that voice.

Taking a deep breath, she submerged her body once
again.

He couldn't sleep.

Jack knew it was foolish not to get a good night's
sleep the night before he started work, but he found
himself restless and decided to take a quick run along
the beach. The moonlight glinted off the water, and he
remembered when his mother had told him it was an enchanted path, leading to a magical kingdom . . .

He shook his head. A kingdom. This was his kingdom right here, and he was familiar with every inch of
it. A new restaurant might spring up, a bar might be laid
out differently than he'd remembered, but he knew this
piece of property the way you could only know an area
from walking it and being with it for many, many years.

Restless. He was restless and he knew it was because
of her.

He hadn't been in an exclusive relationship for almost two years. The last one had broken up as soon as
he'd found out that the woman in question wanted to get
serious. As in married. To him. He'd always been
scrupulously honest with any woman he dated, and had
let her know from the start in no uncertain terms that he
wasn't sure if he would ever marry or have children.
That he was extremely invested in his work.

It hadn't deterred most of them. Looking back, he'd
realized that he'd unconsciously set himself up as a
challenge.

It was a funny thing about women—they really
thought they could change a man. He'd told them what

he was about, who he was, and they'd flagrantly ignored what he'd said and set themselves up for heartbreak.

He'd never meant to cause any. And he'd been gen
uinely sorry when he had. But he'd been honest, and
he'd never lied. And he'd never, never, used those three
words—*I love you*—to get a woman into bed. It was
against his private code.

He'd also had plenty of experience with women who
went after him solely for his bankbook and credit cards.
And he found that he detested that sort of person and
tried to steer a wide berth around them. He'd been
fooled once or twice, but the moment he'd found out
what the relationship had really been about, he'd cut
those women loose without a backward glance.

He couldn't understand it, looking at a man like a
meal ticket. That type of life partner he didn't need.
Ever.

He jogged along the beach, finally relaxing, letting
the wind and the waves calm him, letting the sound of
the surf wash over him, the scents of the island, the soft
moonlight. Jack let it all relax him, and he slowed, then
dropped down onto the sand, breathing in the night air.

He decided to take the long way back to the employee quarters, and walk past the villas. On the same
path where he'd first seen her.

Patti and Cherry had both fallen asleep on the comfortable living room couches, using the couch cushions like
pillows, so Kate took some extra blankets out of the first
floor closet and draped them over the two women. They
both had to be exhausted after their long flight, so she
saw no point in waking them up. Kate turned off the
television, then turned off all the downstairs lights. And
she was just about to go upstairs and get in bed herself

when she stilled and heard that siren call of the waves coming from outside.

Just for a moment . . .

The beach at night would be gorgeous.

She went upstairs and changed into a bright red bikini, and wrapped the blue and white pareo she'd bought at the gift shop that evening after dinner around her hips and tied it. Then Kate headed downstairs and toward the sliding glass door. She slid it open and stepped, barefoot, onto the lanai. She felt like a different person after her bath, soft and gently scented, her body relaxed from the hot bubbly water.

Now she felt wonderfully alive and sensual and free as she walked to the far edge of the lanai and leaned on the metal fence. There was a gate to the left of her that led down several shallow steps and to the strip of green grass that dropped away to the white sand beach.

Kate breathed in the ocean air, drawing it deeply into her lungs, then closing her eyes and letting her senses be totally filled by the sounds of the waves, the feel of the breeze, the velvet texture of the night air.

Acting on impulse, she moved toward the gate and opened it, then made her way down the steps and across the grass, the soft blades tickling her feet, as she headed toward the beach. Glancing up and down, she ascertained that no one was there and, dropping her pareo on the sand, Kate waded into the midnight water, splashing around like a child.

No matter what their reason for coming here, she could have flown home tomorrow and yet never forgotten this one night out of time. And to know this place even existed, to know there was a tiny spot on the map, a magical island where a person could become totally sensual and free—well, she would remember it once she got back to Chicago and resumed her old life.

*   *   *

He'd been about to get up off the sand and walk back to his studio apartment when he saw her. The woman he'd run into by the guest villas. And she totally enchanted him, the way she ran into the sparkling surf and splashed around like a child. He heard her laughter carry across the clear night sky, and he smiled.

He watched her as she played in the surf, frolicking through the waves like some sort of water sprite. And Jack found himself liking the fact that she enjoyed the beach at night. He felt slightly awkward, watching her without her knowledge or consent, but he certainly didn't want to announce his presence and ruin her private moment.

Then he frowned, getting to his feet at the same moment with a swift, fluid motion. She'd turned her back on the incoming surf, something that everyone at the hotel was constantly warned not to do, both verbally and with signs posted by the beach.

Never turn your back on the waves. Sometimes it didn't matter, sometimes you weren't caught. But the surf at the beach was usually strong during a full moon, and a larger wave could catch you off balance, knock you down.

He saw the large wave that was surging up toward the shore as the woman stood there, totally unaware, totally innocent of its potential for harm.

And he started to run.

Chapter Five

❀ The wave came up behind Kate as she was taking
in the Kalani Resort, the huge white building rising
up from the beachfront property. One minute she was
standing in the surf, the water up around her thighs, totally at one with nature and the quiet night. Then the
next minute a huge wall of water had knocked her off
her feet and she was on her hands and knees on gravelly
sand, struggling to stand up.

And she panicked. While she was a strong swimmer,
she'd only swum in public pools and several peaceful
lakes, when her uncle Albert had rented a summerhouse
in Antioch, a small Illinois town north of Chicago.
Nothing in her experience had ever prepared her for the
force of these waves, the power of this ocean.

She swallowed some seawater, the taste bitter in her
mouth. And to her horror, the sand beneath her seemed
to be sliding back out to sea with the waves, shifting
out from beneath her hands and feet, the water sucking

at her body, pulling her with it, sweeping her out to sea.

She felt a strong masculine hand grasp her arm and she clutched it as if it were a lifeline. That arm literally hauled her out of the water, as if her 128-pound body was composed of down feathers.

She choked on the water she swallowed, then felt strong arms around her as they set her on her feet on the packed sand along the shoreline. She staggered against a hard, warm, masculine body, then wound her arms around that waist. She didn't care who it was; she didn't want to go back beneath that dark water.

"Easy," said a low, masculine, sexy voice. "I've got you."

She recognized that voice instantly, but her legs didn't seem to want to work. They were still trembling, and she found she didn't have the energy to move away.

When she could finally talk, she whispered, "What happened?"

"A wave knocked you down," he said as he handed her the pareo she'd left on the sand. When she didn't answer, he said, "Didn't you see any of the signs that say never turn your back on the surf?"

She laughed then, but it came out a sad little hiccup. "I'll never forget now." Her voice trembled with emotion.

"Hey." He tilted her chin up with a gentle hand so she had to face him. "You're really scared." He swung her up into his arms and carried her up to the grass, then deposited her on the soft, velvety lawn. He let her go, moved slightly away from her, but stayed close.

"I didn't know," she whispered. "I didn't think."

"I did the same thing," he said, leaning back on the grass, supporting his upper body with his elbows. "But

I didn't have your excuse. My mother had told me all the time to be careful, and I just forgot."

"Were you scared?" The thought of him as a little boy was so appealing. He must have been adorable.

"Yep. I got hit by a monster wave, and slammed right down to the bottom. My mouth and my ears were full of sand." He hesitated, looking up at the stars. "I never told her, though. But I think she knew."

"Moms have a way of doing that," she said, realizing that her heartbeat had slowed down, her fear had abated. He'd known exactly what she needed, just a little time and normalcy to put her fears to rest.

She glanced at him. "I'm glad you were here. If you hadn't come along when you did—"

"You would have made it out just fine," he said quietly. "But I'm glad I could help you."

"Me, too," she whispered. "Thanks."

"My pleasure."

They sat in silence for almost a minute, and Kate found that she didn't want to go back to the villa. She wanted to stay outside in the darkness, under the stars with this man. And he didn't seem to be in any hurry to go anywhere.

She studied him surreptitiously. He was dressed in a pair of shorts, but no shirt. Water glistened off a chest that had just the right amount of dark hair and well-defined muscles. He had broad, powerful shoulders and arms, and she remembered the strength behind those arms as he'd pulled her out of the waves.

She glanced lower, quickly, swiftly. His abdomen was beautifully muscled, and the hair on his chest narrowed into a thin line that disappeared beneath his . . .

She glanced away from him.

Don't go there.

Unbidden, she remembered the conversation she'd

had with Cherry and Patti at the deli when he'd come in and ordered coffee.

Well, hello Mr. Fling!

She shivered with reaction, and he glanced over.

"Cold?"

"No, just . . ." She scratched her arm. "I've got sand all over me."

"You know where the showers are?"

"Out here?"

"Sure. For the guests. No one wants to track a bunch of sand back into their room."

She got to her knees, then stood. "Lead the way." She didn't want to go back to the villa looking like she'd been dragged along the bottom of the Pacific. Patti and Cherry would be concerned and make too big a deal out of it.

She walked along beside him as he headed up from the beach and toward an area that had what looked like several large, striped tents.

"What are those?" she said.

"Cabanas."

"Oh." She'd read something about them in the brochure by the phone at the villa. The tropical sun here in Maui was a lot more powerful than most people were used to, so cabanas, rather like makeshift tents, could be set up along the beach to give guests some much needed shade during the hottest parts of the day.

And then she saw the outdoor shower, the large, flat showerhead coming out of the wall, a cement floor beneath with a slight slant to it so that the water would drain off and not pool beneath your feet.

"Step underneath," he said as he turned on the water.

It felt incredibly good to wash off all the sand and sticky salt with cool, clear water. Kate stood directly beneath the powerful spray and felt as if she were standing beneath a waterfall. She raised her hands up into her hair, running her fingers through the strands and working out any sand and grit.

And had no idea that he was watching her.

She was absolutely gorgeous. And watching her take a shower, even in her bathing suit and with that pareo wrapped low on her hips, was one of the more achingly sexual experiences he'd ever had.

She was so unself-consciously sensual, the way she turned toward the water, opened her mouth and tilted her head back, luxuriated in it. And he couldn't help but wonder if she would be as incredibly sensual in a more sexual situation.

In the dark, the two of them all alone, he thought she looked like a little pagan, a goddess. A woman of nature, her body such a thing of beauty, her enthusiasm for all things natural simply pure delight to watch.

She stepped back from the fall of water, slicking her hair back, and he was captivated by the fact that she looked just as terrific drenched as most women did in full makeup.

"Now you," she said softly.

It took him a moment to understand what it was she meant, then he realized she assumed he wanted to rinse off, as well.

He stepped beneath the strong spray of water and closed his eyes.

She was simply gorgeous, and she couldn't stop staring at him.

She'd never liked heavily muscled men, and his body, though muscular, wasn't muscle-bound. Yet those muscular arms and legs, that flat stomach, that perfect butt, spoke of a man who did some sort of physical work. He didn't seem the type who sat behind a desk all day.

It was one of the most pleasurable experiences of her life, simply looking at him. His hair, slightly long, clung sleekly to his well-shaped head, and she watched as he ran his hands through it, then turned so his back got the full brunt of the spray. Water glistened and ran over his chest, down his thighs, then splashed to the cement.

As Kate watched him, she wondered what would happen when he finished. Would they both just go their separate ways? Would he ask for her name? Her villa number? Was he a guest here, who had been out on a late-night walk by the ocean, and had simply seen her plight and come to her rescue? Or was he one of the men who worked here at the resort, like a lifeguard or something?

And she couldn't help thinking that this was the sort of man who could help her come back to her body, back to her senses. Who could help her feel alive.

She came back to the present with a start as she caught him looking at her.

He'd caught her staring at him.

She could feel her face flush, and blurted out the first words that came to her mind. "All done?"

"Just about." He grinned, and she sensed he had that little bit of a devil in him, that he'd known exactly what she was thinking.

He turned off the shower and came toward her. "There's still some sand on your shoulder."

"Where?" She glanced back down and over, trying to see her back.

"Here." His fingers touched her back, and that touch, those fingers sliding over her bare, wet skin, almost made her jump. She was so aware of him she couldn't stand it.

She hesitated, then said, "Could you help me get it off?"

He studied her for a long moment, looking down at her, and then Kate's stomach clenched in excitement as he took her hand, led her back toward the shower and turned on the water.

"Turn around," he said, and that voice was foreplay in itself.

She did as he instructed, and felt his large hand come up, then his fingers slid over her shoulders, gently massaging. And she felt the slight roughness of sticky sand, and knew that he was actually helping her. That was all. But that voice, that touch.

She turned so they were facing each other beneath the water. And she looked up at him. Their gazes locked, and she refused to look away.

Her lashes were spiked with water, her hair slicked back off her face, her lips parted expectantly. All the signals were there, but Jack didn't want to misinterpret anything, especially with a woman who was a guest at his father's resort.

"All done," he said, using the same two words she had.

"Are we?" she whispered.

He continued to look at her, to take his fill of her visually in the darkness as the water continued to cascade down around both of them.

"Do you want to be?" he said.

"No," she said, the one word coming out on a soft breath of sound.

That one word made up his mind about the direction the rest of their evening together would take. He didn't care if she was a guest, he didn't care if he hadn't even started working for his father and was already breaking one of the cardinal and unspoken rules laid out for the staff. He only knew that he wanted her, badly, and nothing was going to get in his way.

Unless she changed her mind. Unless she told him no.

Moving slowly and deliberately, he reached for her waist.

For one moment, she thought he was a guy who liked things rough and was just going to reach for her bikini bottoms and pull them off. Then Kate realized that he was slowly, so slowly, unknotting her pareo.

The material had been knotted low around her waist, and now he worked that knot free, taking his time. Then he had the whole length of material in his hands, one end held in either hand, while her bottom was cradled in it, like a sling.

He smiled down at her, then slowly fisted the material in his hands as he began to pull her toward him.

She'd never been so excited in her life.

She came willingly, until she was standing mere inches from his body, so close she could feel the heat coming off him.

He pulled her closer.

She rose up on tiptoe and put her arms around his neck.

He angled his head slightly as he lowered it, then slanted his mouth down over hers. Their lips almost met, then he hesitated.

She stared up at him, totally lost in the moment.

He dropped the pareo, and the material fell to the cement floor, where the water quickly soaked it. His hands settled on her hips, then her buttocks, cupping them. Shaping them.

He lowered his head and kissed her.

It was everything she'd ever thought a kiss should be, and then some. She leaned right into it, so excited, so turned on her body was practically shaking with it. He didn't stop at a quick, chaste kiss, but eased her mouth open and slid his tongue inside.

That tongue, that first touch of his tongue, she felt all the way down to the tips of her toes, then back up again. Kate felt as if the roof of her head was about to come off, not to mention the distinctly pleasurable sensations that were pooling between her thighs. And she was so close to him, fitted so tightly against his body, that she had absolutely no doubt as to what it was he really wanted to do to her.

He broke the kiss, then reached over and turned off the shower. She leaned against his strong body as she heard the water flow slow, then stop.

He stepped back and reached out one hand toward her.

Without any words being exchanged between them, she knew exactly what he was asking her.

Without a second's hesitation, she put her hand in his.

She absolutely bewitched him.

And Jack found that he liked her forthrightness, the way she'd taken his hand and come with him into one of the deserted cabanas. They were luxurious as far as such things went, like large striped tents fitted out with chaise lounges and piles of pillows, towels and bottles of suntan lotion.

They'd just stepped inside, and she was standing close enough that he could touch her.

He did. Jack reached out and threaded his hand through her wet hair, and that hair felt exactly like he'd thought it would, like raw silk. It caught the light of the moon through the front opening of the cabana. He played with the silken strands, overwhelmed by his good fortune, and she sighed at his touch, the sound one of pure pleasure.

She really was a little pagan.

His hand slid lower as he cupped the side of her face, then her chin. He eased her head up slightly so she was looking directly at him, her eyes wide and clear.

"You're sure?" he whispered, knowing what he was asking. He had to make absolutely sure she knew where this was going. And consented to it.

"Yes," she whispered, and he took that as consent, though he knew that if she became frightened at any step along the way, he'd stop. He wasn't a man who took any pleasure in a power struggle. He wanted her badly, but he wouldn't use force. The thought turned his stomach.

Jack moved closer, slid both his hands around her waist, pulled her gently so she was even closer to him. She gave in to the pressure willingly as she eased up against him, and he lowered his head and brushed his mouth against hers with the lightest of touches.

Electric . . .

He pulled back slightly, then came back, moved his mouth against hers and then took her lips in a kiss that he'd meant to be quick but it deepened the moment their lips met, almost as if neither of them could help themselves.

Her hands reached for his shoulders, gripped them, held on as if she were afraid she might lose her balance, so he moved with her, swept her up against him and guided her toward a cushioned chaise. All the while his hands were around her waist, his mouth searching, finding, easing her lips open so he could slowly, teasingly slide his tongue inside.

She shuddered with reaction, her grip tightened on his shoulders, and he found himself impatient with the fact that they were still standing up. He swept her up into his arms and lowered her down onto the chaise lounge. The cabana created the sense of a little room, a private space.

Then he came to her, stretched out alongside her on the chaise, and, her head pillowed on his arm, he lowered his mouth to hers once again.

She couldn't stop him. No, she didn't *want* to stop him. Kate looked up into his face in the moonlight just before he lowered his mouth to hers and kissed her again. She'd never been kissed like this, kisses that were almost like a drug, kisses that affected every single part of her body. Kisses that made her whole body ache with a sense of wanting. Kate never wanted him to stop.

She'd known it would be this way. She'd sensed it from that first moment when he'd grabbed her arms in order to steady her. She'd known, and she'd wanted him to kiss her, she'd wanted to find out what it would be like.

Well, now she knew.

But she also knew that he wasn't the sort of man to stop with a few chaste kisses. His kisses weren't chaste; they were carnal in their intensity, the movements of his tongue mimicking a far more intimate and sexual rhythm. She'd never been kissed like this before.

Other men she'd kissed had been careful, or tentative, or awkward in their exploration of her mouth. She'd caught their tension and become stiff and uneasy, and it had never been that good. Or they'd been demanding and rough and crude, and she'd cringed away from them, all the while wondering what was wrong with her and why she couldn't seem to relax and just respond.

Now she knew. It hadn't been them, or her. They simply hadn't . . . *fit*. They hadn't been right for each other. Though she didn't have a tremendous amount of sexual experience, she knew enough to know when something was right.

This was right. This was so sexually right it was almost overwhelming.

She didn't cringe or stiffen up when she felt his fingers unfasten her bikini top, then slide the material off her body. Naked to the waist and exposed to his gaze, she lowered her lashes and watched his reaction, feeling the most incredible sense of feminine power when she sensed she pleased him. And she felt beautiful at that moment, in a way she hadn't for a long, long time.

He lowered his head and kissed the soft skin between her breasts, and she grabbed his hair with her hands, held his head as she arched up off the chaise, taking in a breath with a sharp little hiss of pleasure.

"Easy," he whispered. "Easy." His hands, those large, warm hands, stroked her bare skin with just the right amount of pressure, and she relaxed. Her body caught his warmth and she moved closer against him, loving the feel of his hard, muscular frame. His hands moved over her body as he continued to kiss her, and she felt one hand cup her breast, shape it, while the other slipped around her waist, supporting her, his fingers splayed against her bare back.

Unbelievable, how good he felt, how good everything he did to her felt.

This time, when his head dipped lower and he

moved his mouth over her breasts, she didn't arch up, she merely bit her lip and then gasped sharply, taking in a deep, steadying breath. She could feel his lips tugging on her nipple all the way to her womb, all the way down to the juncture of her thighs. She felt as if she were burning for him, and one hand left his shoulder and moved down his body, slid over the solid muscles in his chest, the sprinkling of rough hair, the flat male nipples.

She rubbed one, and he groaned, deep in his throat. She smiled at that, then her mouth opened in a silent *oh!* as he moved against her, sliding his body up over her and covering her, pressing her back down onto the chaise. She felt her breasts, so sensitive, pressing against his hot bare chest, felt her thighs open to cradle his body. And felt his strong arousal against her, so hard, so large—so exciting.

She wasn't afraid of him, and she didn't know why. It was something her mind couldn't figure out, something that was of the body and its wisdom. This man, this particular man and his powerful sexuality, was something she'd needed for a long time, and her body had responded to his without any hesitation. Her mind could have found a way to rationalize her right out of this situation, but the call of her body, its needs and wants, had been denied for too long. Those needs were just too strong, and she'd answered that call tonight.

She'd answered her body when she'd left the villa and gone out onto the lanai. When she'd walked across the grass with her bare feet and made her way down to the beach. When she'd waded in the sparkling surf and laughed with sheer joy. When she'd let him kiss her beneath the outdoor shower and responded to his touch.

When she'd followed him into this cabana.

Nothing existed for Kate but this moment in time. She didn't want to think about tomorrow, or even ten days from now when she would leave this island and go back home to her real life. What she wanted was in the now, with this man, this moment, these sensations. She wanted so much, she'd wanted so much for so long, and this man promised to give her everything.

She was like liquid fire in his arms, turning and shifting and changing, growing hotter and hotter by the moment. Jack couldn't remember a woman who had given him as much pleasure as this one had, and he wasn't even inside her yet. But he had a feeling she wasn't going to stop him, and they would get there very soon.

He shifted to the side, carefully, taking her with him, and his hand slid down the side of her almost naked body. He slipped his hand beneath her bikini bottom, cupped her, felt that warmth, that wonderful heat. She groaned deep in her throat and her head went back, exposing the delicate line of her neck. He kissed her bare shoulder, then moved his hand against her, parted her, and slid first one, then another finger deeply, intimately inside her.

She groaned again, a sound of intense pleasure. And he found her open to him, so very wet and ready.

Searching, he found what he was looking for, that small feminine nub, then caught it, held it. Stroked it gently, so gently. She caught her breath, and he smiled, increased the pressure ever so slightly, kept it steady, pressing and rubbing, feeling her entire body tighten and quicken, catch fire. Her breath caught again, her head went back, and . . .

He felt her climax, the quick, sharp contractions that signaled her release. And he held her all the way through it, and let her relax for a long moment afterwards, not wanting to rush her.

He was looking at her when her eyes finally opened. She gazed up at him and smiled, then touched the side of his face. The gesture moved him in a way he hadn't been moved in years, and he caught that hand and kissed it.

She grinned, then pulled her hand away from his and ran it through his hair, over his chest, exploring. He caught that hand again, then slid it farther down, beneath the waistband of his running shorts, until he placed it against the base of his erection and pressed hard. And all the while he watched her face, measuring her response.

He couldn't have wished for a better reaction. She was delighted.

Kate couldn't believe how bold she'd become. As she cupped his erection, she slowly curled her fingers around the long, strong length and began to stroke him. He'd given her such exquisite pleasure, and now she wanted to return that pleasure.

She eased him out of his shorts, slid them down his legs. He kicked them off easily, and they dropped over the side of the chaise, then he pulled off her bikini bottom, slid it quickly over and off her legs, leaving her completely naked. He came back to her, moved up and over her, pushing her legs apart.

"Now?" she whispered, wondering why he didn't want her to touch him anymore.

"Oh, yeah," he whispered in her ear, then she felt his erection parting her, then sliding in, and she felt that burning stretching, that pressure before he finally filled her completely. She moved slightly on the chaise, then her eyes widened as he slid even farther in, touching her deeply, giving her such exquisite pleasure.

"Oh," she breathed, and he kissed her mouth, softly nipping her bottom lip.

"Oh," he said back, his face so close to hers, their position so intimate that for a moment she couldn't look at him. Then she did, and what she saw in a shaft of moonlight thrilled her. His face looked so fierce, so masculine, so incredibly possessive, so . . . *sexual*.

Then he began to move inside her, and she forgot to think at all. His strokes were long and hard, and she reached her second climax easily, clutching at him, grabbing his buttocks and pulling him even deeper. And her movements must have set him off, because he drove into her with relentless masculine power until she felt the powerful contractions that signaled his release.

He was crushing her into the chaise but she didn't even mind. Her eyes slid shut, and she wasn't aware of anything until she felt him gently kissing her cheek, then her eyelids, then the side of her mouth. Playing with her. Gently.

"Go 'way," she whispered.

"You want me to?" he whispered back.

She considered this. "No," she said, slowly looping her arms around his neck. "No, you can stay for a while."

"Good," he said, and started to move inside her, slowly, and she realized he was still inside her. "So we can play."

"Yeah," she whispered, loving the feel of him inside her. She found she wanted to tease him. "Hey, no fair," she whispered, gently pulling a lock of his hair. "Where's my foreplay?"

He laughed, a deep masculine sound, and she delighted in the fact that she could make him laugh.

"You're really something," he whispered, then kissed her again. And then he broke their body contact, slid out of her, and she panicked.

"Wait! What I meant was—" Then she felt him move down her body until his head was by her belly and his hands were pushing her thighs apart, and she realized what he was about to do.

The words didn't leave her mouth in time before she felt his lips and tongue caressing her in the most incredibly intimate way. Her head went back against the pillows on the chaise, and she knew this man would stop at nothing to ensure her pleasure.

He kept at it until she was whimpering mindlessly, then he slid up her body and entered her once again, this time riding her fast and hard until she climaxed again. He thrust into her again and again even as she reached her release, then reached his own and shuddered to a final stop in her arms, gasping for breath as if he'd run a long, long way.

Kate couldn't even speak. She could feel his heart thundering against her chest, but she couldn't even remember how to form words, that was how intense her response had been. If someone had shaken her shoulder and asked her what her name was, she couldn't have told them.

Her eyes started to close. But just before she drifted off to sleep, she knew it was imperative that she make him understand, make him see what this all meant to her.

"Thank you," she whispered, her lips brushing against his ear, and the two simple words had never seemed so inadequate. "Thank you *so* much."

"My pleasure," he whispered back, and she heard a hint of masculine laughter in his deep, dark voice. The humor in the situation struck her then, and she started to laugh, and he did, too. And as Kate drifted off to sleep, she thought there was nothing quite as intimate as shared laughter.

She woke several hours later, as the sun was just rising and tinting the sky with a delicate wash of pastels. Stars still sparkled faintly in the sky. Birds called from the trees, the waves boomed against the shore, and she heard the sound of a golf cart careening down a path.

As Kate blinked her eyes and slowly regained consciousness, she realized that someone had draped several large beach towels over her so she wouldn't be cold or exposed.

Not someone. Him.

She glanced at the powerful male body, motionless in sleep on the chaise, right next to her, a muscled arm wound around her waist.

She didn't even know his name.

That fact didn't bother her, because intuition told her she'd see him again. Though she didn't have a ton of sexual experience, she knew what they'd shared last night had been incredibly special. And even if she never did see him again, she felt so absolutely wonderful this morning, so alert and alive, that she knew she would never forget the adventure she'd had last night.

He'd helped her find a crucial part of herself, and she was never going to lose it again.

Sitting up on the chaise after she gently disengaged his arm from around her waist, Kate quietly reached for both pieces of her bathing suit that had fallen to the side of the lounge chair and swiftly pulled them on. Then she stood up, stretched, ran her fingers through her damp hair, gave her mystery man one long last look, and started back toward the villa.

For a moment she'd been tempted to wake him, to

kiss him awake and snuggle close. But what had happened last night had been so incredible, so unlike anything she'd ever experienced, she wanted some time to digest what had happened to her.

Yet as she saw the plumeria tree to the side of the path, she reached up and quickly picked one of the fragrant, yellow blossoms. Darting back, she took one more look at him, and placed the flower by his head, where her head would have rested if she'd come awake in his arms.

Then she retrieved her pareo from the outdoor shower area and started toward the villa, amazed at the fact that she'd actually had a fling. She, Kate Prescott, a woman who hadn't had a real date in over eighteen months, had shed all her inhibitions and totally enjoyed a night of wild lovemaking with a man who exceeded any of her wildest fantasies.

A night of wild lovemaking that had let her know that though her previous sexual experience hadn't been all that extensive, it had been a huge and complete waste of time.

But now that the night was over, she was a little . . . nervous. Kate knew that part of the reason, a good part of the reason she hadn't actually said good-bye to him this morning was that in the light of day, she had absolutely no idea what she'd say to him.

Things looked mystical and magical by moonlight, but when the sun rose high in the sky, it was time for a dose of reality.

First order of business, a hot bath. She'd used muscles last night that she hadn't even known existed, and they were screaming in protest.

Second order of business, she'd go upstairs to one of the bedrooms and get some more sleep. She couldn't face the day on less than six hours, and since they'd been up half the night, she doubted they'd even gotten three.

And third, she wanted to keep this evening of hers private for a while. If her fantasy man ended up searching her out, she'd probably have to tell Cherry and Patti what happened, but until then, she wanted to keep her memories to herself.

She jogged swiftly back to the oceanfront villa, breathing in the sweetness of the air, relishing how alive she felt, how every inch of her body seemed to hum with a new sort of energy.

Before Kate let herself inside the sliding glass door that faced the ocean, she glanced out over the green grass, the stretch of beach, the gentle sway of coconut palms in the trade winds, the booming surf.

Paradise.

It certainly was. Last night, she'd felt like the only woman in the entire world, wrapped up in her own sensuality, totally focused on one incredibly sexual man. Last night, she'd finally felt like a woman again, after a long stretch of feeling . . . nothing.

She'd sleep for a while, then find her mystery man. She'd have the courage to walk right up to him. And maybe they could go out on an actual date!

Grinning, she stepped inside the sliding glass door.

Jack stood beneath the hot shower spray in the bathroom of his studio apartment. He couldn't stop smiling.

What a night. What a woman. The flower by his head when he'd come awake this morning had been the final, free-spirited touch.

He couldn't believe what he'd done. She was obviously a guest at the resort, and one who could afford one of their most expensive, oceanfront villas. And he'd had sex with her last night in one of the cabanas by the beach. *Great sex.*

But she'd made the final decision. She'd consented. She'd given him all the most erotic feminine signals when they'd stepped beneath that shower and had made no sign of protest when he'd taken her up on her sensuous offer.

Still, fraternizing with the guests was such a total violation, something that he could be penalized for. Something that might cost him the resort, should his father find out. Yet he hadn't even cared. Nothing would have stopped him last night, except a word or action from her.

If he were truthful with himself, he hadn't been thinking straight since he'd bumped into her last night. And especially since he'd seen her on the beach. Hell, he'd been thinking about getting her naked from the first moment he'd seen her, touched her. Chemistry was either present or not, and they had it in spades.

Now what he had to do was find out how long she was staying here at the resort. And hope to God that it was longer than ten days so that he could drop this façade his father insisted on and go after her in style.

He wanted her. It was as simple as that. He wanted more time with her, both in and out of bed. He wanted to figure her out. He wanted to get to know her and get to the bottom of this attraction they had for each other.

He stepped beneath the shower spray and closed his eyes, washing the shampoo out of his hair.

Ah hell, he just *wanted.* It had been years since he'd felt so alive, so invigorated, so . . . *happy.*

He smiled as he reached for the water faucets and turned off the spray. Stepping out of the shower, he reached for a towel and began to briskly rub his hair dry.

Nothing was going to stop him from getting to know . . . he frowned suddenly.

Strange. He didn't even know her name.

You weren't in that big a hurry last night to find out.

True enough. But he'd find out what her name was. He'd find out all about her, anything she was willing to tell him. Because what they'd shared last night came along only once in a lifetime, if that.

And he certainly wasn't going to be stupid and throw it all away.

Chapter Six

❀ Kate woke late the following morning when she heard someone sneaking into her room. Cranky from lack of sleep, she sat up in bed and blinked, and both Patti and Cherry came into fuzzy view. They stood at the foot of the queen-sized bed, plates and glasses in hand.

"Kate!" said Cherry. "We didn't mean to wake you up, but you wouldn't believe the breakfast buffet this place has!"

With a mumbled, "I'm sure it's very nice," she burrowed beneath the covers, pulling them up around her shoulders and over her head.

"Let me handle this," she heard Patti whisper. Then, "Ka-ate. Oh, Ka-ate! Wouldn't you like to try a nice warm plate of macadamia nut Belgian waffles with fresh berries? Or perhaps some plantation banana pancakes—"

The covers twitched as Kate fought for control, then . . .

"Patti, you fight really dirty." She sat up in bed and reached for both plates.

"We also have some guava juice, along with a concoction called Ginger Blast," Cherry continued, picking up where Patti left off. "And incredible cinnamon rolls and a plate of tropical fresh fruit."

"Oh my God," Kate said after swallowing a mouthful of the Belgian waffle. "Oh my *God!* I have to steal this recipe. I have to. I'm not leaving the island without it."

"That's the spirit!" Patti said. She'd brought a second fork and cut a piece off the generous stack of banana pancakes and popped it into her mouth.

"Kate, you look *great!*" Cherry said. "You've got this little glow about you. You make me think that I should've slept in; they say sleep is the best thing for your skin."

Kate refrained from telling her that she'd gotten very little sleep last night, but what she *had* been doing was also well known to give a woman a little glow. But she didn't want Cherry examining her too closely.

"What's with the flower?" Kate said to her cousin, effectively changing the subject.

"Oh, this?" Patti touched the white plumeria blossom she wore tucked behind her ear. "When in Rome, do as the Romans do. When a flower's tucked behind your right ear, it means you're a single woman. And as that's exactly what I am, I decided that it was time to announce that fact."

Kate grinned at her cousin. Patti looked absolutely darling in a fuschia and white pareo tied around her body sarong-style, the white tropical flower behind her ear. She didn't look that brokenhearted at all, and that was a good sign.

She ate almost all the waffle before Patti said, "How

come you're sleeping in so late on our first day in paradise?"

Memories of the night before washed over Kate, and she was sure her face was on fire.

"Kate? What's wrong?" Patti said. "You look flushed. Do you have a fever?"

"Nothing. I just—took a little walk along the beach last night, and—and I walked farther than I thought and ended up out there for quite a while. You should see the stars at night," she rushed on, "they're like nothing you'll ever see outside Chicago!"

Patti bought her story. She was more interested in another bite of those banana pancakes, anyway. But Cherry—Kate sensed that Cherry thought something was up.

"Well," Cherry said, "time's a-wasting. You'd better get moving, get your bathing suit and sunscreen on, and join us out by the pool. We'll be by the bar."

"Drinking?" Kate said. "So early, and after the breakfast the two of you had?"

"No, watching all the cute men," Cherry said. "I don't know if you've noticed this yet, but people around here have great bodies and don't tend to wear a whole lot of clothes."

Ah—yeah, I noticed it last night . . .

"It's that tropical influence," Patti said.

"What'd ya know," Kate said, between mouthfuls of waffle and a small sampling of the banana pancakes. At least it was good to see Patti eating; it sure beat her pining in one of the villa's bedrooms with the blinds closed and wasting away.

"So we'll see you outside in a little bit?" Patti said.

"Yeah. You two go on, I'm just going to finish my breakfast and find my suit." She knew exactly where one of her bathing suits was—the red bikini she'd rinsed out early this morning was hanging in the upstairs bathroom, dripping dry.

"I went by the resort's tanning center and bought us a few bottles of their sunscreen," Cherry said. "There's one in the bathroom for you. They say that the sun here is a lot stronger than at home and our sunscreen doesn't work as well. And you know how it can age you."

"And I think we should lie around the pool today and check out that guidebook I brought with me," Patti said. "Places to go, things to do, that sort of stuff."

"Sounds good," Kate said, setting her plate down on the bedside end table.

Kate thanked them for breakfast, and Cherry for the sunscreen. She watched the two women as they headed out of the bedroom, then listened as they walked down the hall and went out the front door.

After Patti and Cherry left, she lay back in bed, the rest of her breakfast completely forgotten. And she replayed her evening with—

She frowned.

Oh great, you still don't even know his name!

This was *so* unlike her. The whole fling thing— totally not her, never had been. But last night . . .

Remembering, her lips curved into a satisfied smile.

Last night had been a memory she'd treasure forever.

Last night she'd completely lost her mind but come back to her senses, and that was reason enough to celebrate. If nothing else happened on this vacation, that was enough. More than enough.

The feeling that swept her body was like fine champagne, bubbly, such a bubbly feeling of pure happiness. In a funny kind of way, she felt she'd come home—to herself, to her body, to a sense of pleasure so intense, to *life*. To a feeling that life was wonderful again, full of surprises, anticipation.

She wanted to see him again.

Kate slipped out of bed and headed toward the bathroom. On the way, she pulled the sleep shirt over her head and tossed it, then once inside the bathroom she reached for her red bikini. She'd already decided to wear the same one. After all, it would make it that much easier for Mr. Fling to recognize her.

She found herself humming as she spread sunscreen on her arms and legs, then her shoulders and stomach. Her hands were actually trembling.

She couldn't wait to see him.

Jack was getting the hang of this. It was actually a lot of fun, hanging out at the bar and fixing tropical concoctions for their guests. He couldn't believe how early people began to congregate around the pool.

But of course, it only felt that early because he'd been up so late himself.

He scanned the area around the bar, alert for any sign of her. He'd already decided that he wanted to see her again and not just to rush her into bed. He liked her—a lot. That spirit of adventure, that willingness to really let go and experience sensuality—and that indefinable thing people called chemistry. Jesus, chemistry didn't even cover what they had. He didn't even stop to wonder why they had so much of it, he just was thankful that they did.

He glanced up as two women slid onto seats at the bar. One, with short blonde hair, looked rather sweet. She had a white plumeria blossom tucked behind her right ear. The other was a strawberry blonde bombshell; there was no other word for it. They made a cute pair, though. Mary Anne and Ginger from *Gilligan's Island,* courtesy of Nick at Nite. The girl-next-door and the show-stopper.

"Can I get you two anything?" he asked them.

"Anything at all," the strawberry blonde said, giving him an appreciative glance.

He laughed. "Something from the bar."

"Sure," she said. "How about a Pineapple Smoothie?"

"You got it." He glanced at the blonde. Sweet kid. "How about you?"

"I'd like a Midnight Mango Iced Tea."

He moved away, started throwing the proper ingredients into the blender for the smoothie, then when he had the blender whirring, he poured a tall glass of iced tea. Coming back to the smoothie, he turned off the blender and poured it into a tall glass, then returned to where the two women were sitting.

"You think Kate's really going to make it down today?" he heard Mary Anne ask Ginger.

"Sure. Though I wonder what it was that had her so tired out," mused Ginger.

"Here you go, ladies," he said, handing them their drinks.

They both thanked him, and he returned to his work. As no one else needed his attention at the moment, Jack began to wash some of the glasses.

"Any more ideas about finding that millionaire?" he heard Mary Anne say to Ginger. And everything inside him stilled.

Too bad. They'd seemed like really nice women. It just showed you could never tell. Both of them looked like women who would be an absolute blast to be with, to date, to go out with and have a wild time on the island.

But all they were interested in was a man's money.

He'd seen it before, and after a few mistakes, he'd learned to give women like that a wide, wide berth.

Glancing up as an elderly man sat down at the bar, Jack wiped his hands on a towel and headed toward his new customer.

She was nervous.

Walking along the pathway toward the pool, in the strong tropical sunlight, Kate found herself suddenly nervous. So nervous with those butterflies doing double time in her stomach that she actually had to stop walking and catch her breath, her hand coming up to rest low on her belly.

What was she going to say to him when she saw him?

Oh, hi. You know, about last night, I just lost my head completely. I'm really not that kind of a girl, whatever type of girl that is. I mean, it must have been the ocean breezes, the tropical ambiance, your gorgeous bod, your strong arms, no sex for as long as I can remember—who knows, I just went wild for a moment there and...

Nothing she said made what she'd done last night seem reasonable. But then again, look where reasonable had gotten her so far in life. And maybe she was just tired of being reasonable. After all, as someone had once said, "Life is not a dress rehearsal."

And she felt so *alive*...

Well, all she could do was put herself out into the world today and hope she'd run into him. Maybe he'd try to explain to her what had come over him.

Yeah, right. Fat chance. Men never seem to have to worry about their behavior, or even justify it.

Not that she wanted him to. As far as she was concerned, he'd behaved just fine.

As she came around a corner of the path, the pool came into view, its turquoise water shimmering in the sunlight. She hesitated, swallowed against the tightness in her throat. Kate had her sunglasses on, so she didn't squint into the bright sunlight as she scanned the pool area. Right at the bar, bellied up to the bar, sat Patti and Cherry.

Breathing deeply, trying to still her racing heart and fluttering stomach, she headed toward them.

He had his back turned toward the two women when he heard her voice.

"Hey guys, haven't you even been in the water yet?"

He froze, then slowly, cautiously, turned his head. Chanced a quick look.

The woman he'd been with last night was sliding onto the seat next to Ginger the Bombshell; she was sitting next to the two of them, the two women who were after their millionaires.

Two women who were on the prowl for money.

No, make that three.

What a complete idiot he'd been. What a *fool*.

Well, no longer.

The feeling of deep regret almost overwhelmed him, like a swift punch to his stomach. Incredulity flooded him, caused his heartbeat to speed up with a sickening rhythm. He'd been so sure she was different. He'd thought she was special, wild and free, with an unconquerable spirit. When they'd first sat out beneath the stars and looked up at the sky last night, she'd awakened something in him that had lain dormant for a long time, emotions he'd simply chosen not to feel.

Last night had seemed magical, deep and mysterious. But now, in the bright tropical light of day, he realized she wasn't any different from countless other women he'd dated no more than two or three times. Just long enough to figure out their game.

Disappointment tasted bitter as ashes in his mouth.

He gripped the corner of the center island tightly, his back still turned toward her, willing himself to stop feeling, stop regretting the night he'd spent with her. He had to move on, that much was clear.

Well, he'd do what he had to do. What he'd done before, but what he'd never thought he'd do to her. He'd cut her off at the knees and let her know in no uncertain terms that she'd meant absolutely nothing to him. That their evening together had been a diversion, that was all. That what had happened between them last night was absolutely meaningless. Because if she was looking for a rich guy, then she'd be in for a shock when she discovered she'd been slumming with the help last night.

But he couldn't shun her completely. She was still a guest, and he had to treat her as such. It was part of his job, part of the deal he'd made with his father.

"Can I get you something?"

She turned toward the sound of his voice, and he saw the color leave those beautiful, high cheekbones. Those cheekbones he'd kissed last night, those freckles he'd thought were so cute, that face he'd held in his hands while he'd . . .

Stop. Stone cold, that's what a woman like her deserves.

She was staring at him, and he could understand her shock. She'd probably thought he was a wealthy guest at the resort. What a comedown—she'd made it with a lowly bartender. A minimum wage man.

The woman was still speechless as she stared at him.

"Kate?" said the strawberry blonde next to her. "Kate? Don't you want anything?"

Kate. Her name was Kate. In any other circumstances, he would've been happy to receive this bit of knowledge about her. Now it meant less than nothing.

"Anything at all," he said, his voice low, just for her ears. "A chocolate smoothie, a Longboard Lager on draft, a Lava Flow . . . or perhaps a nice millionaire?"

Her cheeks bloomed with hot color, and he knew he'd scored a direct hit.

"Nothing," she said, her voice so low he could barely hear it.

He waited just a second, then said, "Good," and turned away.

"Kate," he heard the blonde he'd thought was so sweet say softly. "Is something wrong?"

No answer.

He refused to look at her and busied himself making a Coconut Smoothie for a customer at the other end of the long poolside bar.

And wondered why he was so furious with her.

Kate couldn't believe how something so right could go so completely wrong so quickly. If she'd had any hopes of even having a conversation with him, those hopes had been completely dashed.

She couldn't look at him, she could only look at the smooth surface of the bar. And she was dangerously close to tears, but she'd be damned if she'd give him the satisfaction of seeing her cry.

It didn't take a rocket scientist to figure out what had happened. Cherry and Patti had probably been talking about their favorite subject—how Cherry was going to snare her millionaire. And when she'd sat next to them, and he'd realized they knew each other, well, Prince Charming here had tarred and feathered her with the same brush.

Her head came back up, and suddenly Kate was angry. Angry like she hadn't been in . . . *never.* How *dare* he? How *dare* he even assume he knew *anything* about her? How *dare* he treat her so coldly after what they'd shared? While it was bloody unlikely they'd ever even share a *dance* again, let alone the horizontal *macarena,* he could at least have the decency to treat her like a human being.

"Yoo hoo," she called across the bar, directly toward his rigid back.

He turned, glared at her, his dark blue eyes narrowed.

"Oh yes, you," she said sweetly. "I've figured out what I want."

He seemed to be counting silent numbers in his head, but he walked slowly over toward her, then paused, mere feet from her.

"I'd like a Rum Runner," she said, remembering the potent drink from the drinks list: Chambord liqueur, pineapple juice, coconut, light rum, dark rum, and a float of 151 Rum. The perfect way to start the day. Perfectly potent.

"One-fifty-one rum this early in the morning?" he said.

"What's it to you?" she shot back.

"Nothing at all," he said, then turned on his heel and went to fix her drink.

"What the hell is going on—" Cherry began.

"Don't . . . say . . . a . . . word," Kate said softly. "Don't. Just let me handle this."

"Oh, no," Patti said under her breath. "Oh, Kate—"

He came back with her drink and set it on the bar in front of her.

"Thanks," she said.

"Oh, my pleasure," he replied.

"I'm sure it will be." Then Kate promptly picked it up and flung it in his face.

All conversation at the bar ceased. Everyone stopped talking and stared at Kate. Her bartender did as well, as he wiped the alcoholic drink out of his eyes. And for just a moment, Kate could have sworn she saw his mouth twitch. Just the tiniest twitch.

"Anything else?" he said, his voice low. "We have a killer shrimp cocktail." But this time there was a deadly edge to that voice that said as clearly as day, *don't you push me.*

"Yeah," she said, sliding off her bar stool. "Got a pack of matches?"

The implication wasn't lost on anyone, rum being highly flammable.

"Kate—" Cherry began, but Kate was already walking around the bar and out toward the pool, headed for the path that would take her straight back to the villa. But before she could get there, her bartender slammed down his bar towel and vaulted over the bar, heading straight toward her.

"What the hell was that all about?" he said, blocking her path.

"What do *you* think?" she said, standing her ground. She was totally unafraid of him, and for some reason he really liked that about her, even as he still disliked her.

"I think you're going for the gold, as in *digger,* and it pissed you off that you got it on with a bartender."

He watched as her hand seemed to come up of its own volition, heading straight for the side of his face— and caught that hand in midflight.

"No," he said, his voice low. Now he was really angry and wanted to hurt her. "Save it for your millionaire."

He knew the exact moment her temper blew out the top of her head.

"You are *such* a jerk!" She pushed at his chest, and he caught her hands. She yanked them back and then punched him in the chest, then flattened her palms against his coral-colored polo shirt and gave him a sharp push.

Right into the pool.

But as he started to lose his balance, he grabbed her arm and pulled her, shrieking, right in with him.

"You think they know each other?" Patti said as she reached for a corn tortilla chip and dipped it in some guacamole.

"Oh yeah," said Cherry, never taking her eyes off the couple rising out of the water. *Walk along the beach, my foot.* Kate and her bartender had started splashing water at each other while they squabbled, and guests were giving them a wide, but amused, berth.

"Know like in the biblical sense?" Patti said. She bit into her chip.

"I'd bet money on it, Sugar," Cherry said. "And I'd win."

"Will you stop—" He bit out the words as he tried to keep her from punching him in the stomach.

"You are *such* a pig—"

"Yeah, well what did you expect?"

"I expected you to treat me like a human being and not assume the worst—"

Kate's breath left her lungs in a *whoosh* as this—*barbarian,* for lack of a better word—swung her up over his shoulders and carried her out of the pool. With his hand clamped firmly over her bikini-bottomed butt!

"My God!" said a tall, elegant older woman in a crisp blue shirtwaist dress and sensible sandals who stood to the side of the pool. "Jack, what seems to be going on here?"

Jack. His name was Jack. In any other circumstances, she would've been delighted to have this little tidbit of information. Now, she could care less.

He set her on her feet and turned away from her. "She was having some difficulty in the water, and I jumped in and saved her."

"Mama," said a four-year-old blond boy from the fringes of the small crowd, "how come it's okay for them to fight and not me?"

"Hmmm." The woman eyed Jack, then her gaze fell on Kate.

Kate knew she had to look like a wreck. She was breathing rapidly, as much from their water fight as from being this close to—Jack—in nothing but a little red bikini.

"Is this man bothering you?" the woman asked her.

And Kate knew, in that instant, the power she wielded over him. She was a guest, he was a bartender. She could get him fired. She could say the worst, just a few choice words, and he'd have to turn in his uniform, his drenched khaki shorts and dripping wet coral polo shirt with the resort's logo on the left breast pocket. And he'd have to leave like the dirty dog he was, with his tail between his legs.

She couldn't do it.

Kate couldn't finish what she'd started. And actually, what she'd started had been a lot meaner than what he'd done to her. For a moment—a very *brief* moment—Kate was ashamed of herself.

But not that long.

"I actually was having some trouble," she said, glaring at him. "And—*Jack* here, well, he jumped in and saved the day."

"Hmmm," said the woman, eyeing the two of them, and Kate felt for all the world as if her first grade teacher—the mean one—had just caught her fighting on the school playground.

"Well," the woman said. "Jack, why don't you get some dry clothes on and report back." As he left, she turned to Kate. "And—excuse me, what was your name?"

"Kate. Kate Prescott."

"Ah yes, villa number six." She held out her hand. "Meredith Wilkins."

Kate took the woman's hand, shook it. "Nice to meet you."

"Miss Prescott, I'm sorry about what happened in the pool just now. Please have whatever you want from the bar menu today. It's on us."

"Oh, but I don't need—"

"Please." The woman lowered her voice. "It must have been a disturbing experience, being in the water like that. Please accept a free lunch today, with our compliments."

Well, yeah, disturbing, but not because of the water.

She knew this woman wasn't going to give an inch. Better just to concede gracefully. And a free lunch didn't sound that bad.

"Okay. Thank you very much."

"It's our pleasure, Miss Prescott."

"They were fighting in the pool." Meredith's bright blue eyes twinkled with glee. She'd gone right back to her boss's office after making sure that Kate was settled with her lunch.

"Really?" James had the silliest grin on his face, and she loved seeing it.

"Like two little children. Oh, it was *glorious*! Neither of them looked like they knew what had hit them."

"So you think my plan's working?" he said.

"James," she said, "I think it's working far better than either of us could have imagined."

He was silent for a long moment, and she could practically see the wheels turning.

"Kate Prescott, is it?" he said.

"Yes."

"Point her out to me the next time you get a chance, would you?"

She couldn't seem to stop smiling. "Certainly, James."

Chapter Seven

❀ Kate had to admit she enjoyed her lunch.

The older woman, who had introduced herself as Meredith Wilkins, insisted that she start with an appetizer, so Kate chose the crab cakes with roasted aioli, then moved on to a grilled Hawaiian fish caesar salad, all of it washed down with two glasses of Midnight Mango Iced Tea.

And, of course, a chocolate chip cookie, no nuts, for dessert—and another recipe to acquire.

"I'm not sure whether I like them better with macadamia nuts or plain," she said to a still-slightly-stunned Patti.

"I haven't seen you in a water fight like that since band camp," her cousin remarked.

"Yeah, what was that all about?" Cherry said.

Kate paused, then said, "He rubbed me the wrong way." The entire time she'd been sitting at one of the round white tables by the bar, she hadn't bothered to glance in Jack's direction. In fact, she'd managed to sit so she was facing away from the bar.

But that didn't stop her from thinking about him. And knowing he was there. Her stomach was still doing flip-flops, and it was all she could do *not* to look over at him.

Patti and Cherry had ordered some lunch as well, and when it came time to pay their bill, they discovered that the entire meal had been comped, courtesy of the Kalani Resort Hotel and Spa.

"Wow, Kate, you really know the right people," Cherry teased.

Patti laughed, then said, "You know how Dad always says, 'There's no such thing as a free lunch'? I'm going to have to send him a postcard about this one!"

"Yeah." Kate had barely been able to swallow her leisurely lunch, and now it sat in her stomach like a couple of pounds of cement. The first thing on her agenda was getting away from Jack. She consciously put her emotions on automatic pilot.

"Let's stake out some lounge chairs on the far side of the pool and get some sun," she said, ignoring Cherry's curious look and Patti's concerned one. "We can skim Patti's guidebook and figure out something to do tonight. And we can always ask the concierge."

"Is she ever going to tell us what's *really* going on?" Cherry whispered to Patti as they walked slightly behind Kate toward three empty lounge chairs on the far side of the lagoon pool.

"Nope. Not until she's good and ready. That's just the way she is."

"Damn. I was afraid you were going to say that."

* * *

Jack noticed that she managed to place herself on the lounge chair that was the farthest away from him. And that was just fine with him.

Well, if he was honest with himself, not really.

He couldn't believe she'd managed to fool him. He'd thought he'd had infallible fortune-hunting radar when it came to women whose basic battle cry was "Show me the money!" He couldn't understand how Kate had flown in under the wire.

She'd seemed so different, the woman he'd seen playing in the surf by moonlight. And he sighed. He had to stop thinking so—there was no other word for it—*romantically.* He hated to admit it, but he was.just as much a romantic as his old man, and James McKenna was one of the great romantics of all time.

But look where it had gotten his father. A marriage that had been blissfully happy, a wife who had adored him as much as he had her. A family that had been idyllic until illness had claimed his mother and intense grief had consumed him for a long time. And Jack wondered if his father would have risked it all, lived life the exact same way, had he had any inkling of the final outcome and the intense emotional pain involved.

Jack knew the answer even before he'd finished asking himself the question.

Of course he would have, no question about it.

Then why was it so hard for him? The world was a different place, had transformed itself since his father had romanced his mother. Mores and values were so different. His father's world, his parents' courtship, seemed centuries away as opposed to decades.

But Jack had always believed, in his heart of hearts, that some things remained the same. And one of those things was that one night, one evening, you'd meet a woman and look in her eyes and suddenly you'd just *know* . . .

He'd thought that had happened with Kate. He'd come awake that morning feeling so . . . so *right*. It had felt so right to be with her. There hadn't been any of that awkwardness, any self-consciousness. He'd felt that a part of himself, an emotional part he'd repressed for the longest time, had flourished that night, had bloomed just as surely as the plumeria trees that surrounded the villas.

Then the moment Kate had slid onto that bar stool, and he'd realized she was with those other two fortune-hunters, he'd felt all of it come to ashes, tasted a bitter taste in his mouth. Thought of himself as a complete fool for ever having believed she was different.

He glanced up as a guest approached the bar. He smiled, approached the thirty-something woman with three little kids. Jack went through the motions as he asked them what they wanted, then made them their tropical smoothies. Work helped him keep his mind off Kate, and he knew that he'd get over this. He had to.

But it didn't make him feel any better.

Kate feigned sleep, closing her eyes against the hot, tropical sun. She felt like a shrimp on the barbie, as they said in that Australian ad. But the sun felt good, relaxing tight muscles and warming her skin. And as long as she had her eyes closed, she didn't have to look in the direction of the bar and see Jack.

It still hurt, even after all the energy and emotion she'd expended in their pool fight. It hurt to think that he would judge her, condemn her, without even asking her about her side of it. After they'd been so close.

Yeah, that was a real swift move. Get that intimate with a guy before figuring out if you can even talk to

*him in a civilized manner. And with Jack, that's clearly
impossible.*

"Kate? How does dancing in Lahaina sound for
tonight?"

At this point, the way her life was going, she
would've agreed to a guided tour of hell, with Satan as
a tour guide.

"Sure. Whatever."

The silence was just a tad too long. She opened her
eyes and glanced up to see Patti and Cherry giving each
other a look.

"What?"

"Kate," Cherry said, "are you ever going to tell us
what's really going on with that guy?"

"What's to tell? I lost my temper."

"But why?" Cherry pressed. "He was just an innocent bystander."

"Okay." Kate rolled over on her stomach and reached
for her glass of iced tea. "What if I told the two of you
that I met him on the beach last night and we talked?
What if I said that I'd never felt closer to a man in such
a short period of time?"

"This sounds great," Patti said, leaning in.

"And what if I told you that the same man behaved
like a total ass towards me today because he assumed
something that wasn't true."

"But what—oh." Cherry fell silent, then whispered,
"Oh, no. Oh, Kate."

"Oh, yeah."

"Oh, what?" said Patti, moving closer

"Kate, I'm *so* sorry—" Cherry began.

"Will someone please tell me what's going on?" Patti
said. "Spell it out for me, okay? I just had a piña colada,
the sun's really hot, and my brain's not functioning so
well."

"That bartender—he heard us talking about my millionaire," Cherry said quietly. Kate watched as those incredible, kittenlike blue eyes started to well up with quick tears. "Kate, I don't know how to—"

"Hey, he's the jerk, not you."

"But I can see how he could—"

"Nope, no excuses—"

"But he's just a bartender—"

"I don't care. He had no right to make that assumption. Not after the way we—talked last night."

Cherry raised an expressive, expertly shaped eyebrow, but remained silent.

Patti waved her arms, then made a *T* sign with two hands as if she was a ref calling for a time-out. "Wait. So you're saying that he thinks you're after money, and he doesn't have any, and he's upset? But Kate, that's a *good* sign."

"No, it's a bad sign, Patti, because he didn't even bother to ask me about it, he just assumed the worst."

"But that's because when people are in love, they behave like idiots!"

Both Cherry and Kate turned to stare at her.

Patti smiled. "I rest my case. You're staring at Exhibit A. Look at the mess I got myself in with Roger by falling in love with him. It makes you crazy. It makes you do stupid things. Why else would you stay up half the night talking to a total stranger, Kate? I mean, how do you really feel about him, and why did you get so mad?"

"I got mad at him because he assumed the worst—"

"No. If you really thought he was a complete jerk, you would've laughed and walked away."

"I agree with Patti," Cherry said. "Even after all that . . . talking."

Kate glanced sharply at her friend, then sighed. Cherry wasn't fooled. Damn.

She lowered her forehead onto her folded arms as tears stung her eyes. She wished she could have blamed it on sweaty, coconut-scented sunscreen running into her eyes, but she couldn't.

"I can't talk about this right now," she whispered. As alive as she'd felt this morning, now she felt as if her body had turned to ice, emotionally dead.

She felt Patti come sit beside her and put a hand on her shoulder. "Kate, it's going to be okay. I think he's going to come around and realize what a moron he was."

"Yeah," said Cherry dryly. "Men do that *all* the time."

"No, I think he will. I mean, he pulled you into the pool after him, didn't he?"

"What's that got to do with anything?" Kate said, her voice muffled by her arms.

"He didn't let go. He pulled you in with him. If he really disliked you that much, he wouldn't have had that water fight with you. The opposite of love isn't dislike, it's indifference, and neither of you is indifferent to each other. Do you get it?"

"I think so." Kate raised her head. "What do you think I should do?"

"I think," Patti said, "that you should do exactly what you told me to do last night at the restaurant. Enjoy the ten days we have here, do all sorts of fun stuff, and I think that in a couple of days this guy will come around."

"Mr. Fling," Cherry murmured.

"Let's not call him that," Kate said.

"Any other suggestions?" Cherry said.

A short pause ensued, and several very specific and

quite unflattering names came to Kate's mind, then she sighed and said, "His name's Jack. I had no idea he was a bartender here, but that wouldn't have made any difference to me. I mean, here I am, struggling with ice and snow every winter, and here he is, turning out tropical drinks and smoothies in paradise. So who's the smart one?"

"I agree," Cherry said. "This is really the way to live." She glanced at Kate. "I'm really sorry about this morning, Kate. I can't believe I caused you so much trouble with that guy."

"It's okay. I know you didn't mean to."

"It's not okay," Cherry said. "It's awful. But I want you to know that I didn't mean to hurt you."

"I know that."

"It's going to be okay," Patti said, picking up the sexy contemporary paperback romance novel she'd stuffed in her straw beach bag. "These things have a way of working themselves out." She opened the book and started to read, but her gaze kept straying to the bar.

After a few hours, Cherry and Kate went back to the villa, taking the long way around so they didn't have to walk past the bar. Patti told them she wanted to read a little more, but as soon as they were out of sight, she closed her paperback novel, stuffed it into her straw beach bag, and adjusted her sunglasses.

Now was as good a time as any.

She headed toward the bar, totally oblivious to the admiring looks she received from several men. And she saw that Jack the bartender was sitting at one of the tables in the far back, taking a break.

Perfect.

*   *   *

"Jack?"

He glanced up and saw Mary Anne, the angel blonde who had been sitting at the bar earlier. And as much as he wanted to just blow her off, he couldn't afford to be rude to another guest—not after that little fiasco in the pool.

"Yeah?" He did manage to make his tone as curt as possible, then felt bad when the blonde flinched slightly. Hurting her was no challenge, and he felt like an ass.

"Sorry. I didn't mean to be so rude." He took a sip of his mocha frappuccino. He didn't normally drink this much caffeine, but after the night he'd spent with Kate, he needed it. "Can I get you anything?"

"No. But I need you to hear what I'm going to say."

"Okay." This was interesting.

"Kate's not after your money."

He stared at her for a long, tense moment, not sure if he'd heard her correctly.

"She's not after your money. She's my cousin, and one of the best people I know. She came out here with me after my fiancé dumped me at the altar in front of five hundred family and friends. My dad had already bought these tickets, and this was supposed to be my honeymoon, but instead he asked Kate to come with me and help me get over Roger. And she did, she gave up everything she was doing to help me."

He stared at her, and for a moment he really wanted to believe her.

"I love her more than any other person in the world. We were raised like sisters together. And I just want you to know that whatever you think about Kate, it's wrong. It's so wrong. And she's here for only ten days, so if you want to make things right, you have a small window of time. Okay?"

He considered all this. "So why were you and—"

"Cherry. Her name is Cherry. And I'm Patti."

"Okay. So why were you and Cherry talking about nabbing a millionaire?"

"Because she grew up in foster homes."

"What?" He wasn't following this woman's logic at all.

"Cherry never really had a home. Her parents didn't want her, and they gave her away. She grew up in a series of foster homes, and some of the people didn't treat her real well. So she hit the road when she was sixteen and went to Vegas and became a dancer in this show. Like a showgirl."

He could believe that story, with the body that woman had.

"And now she thinks that if she gets some guy with money to protect her, the rest of her life will be okay." She seemed to study him. "But you and I both know that's not true."

He couldn't believe this conversation. A long moment of silence passed as he studied her.

"And why do we know that, Patti?"

"Because money can't protect you from the really bad things that can happen. Like if you're sick, money can't make you better."

He thought of his mother, and how desperately his father had searched for a cure, using every dollar he had at his disposal. Something twisted in his gut.

"You know that, Jack. I know you do, I can feel it."

What was it with this woman? What did she want from him?

"You and Kate took a walk last night—"

So that's what she'd told them . . .

"—and I know my cousin, and she really likes you.

And she doesn't like too many men. They find her too—difficult to handle."

"I wonder why?" he said, and when she saw the expression on his face, she started to laugh.

"I've never seen her go after any man the way she went after you," Patti said, after she composed herself.

"So throwing drinks in a guy's face isn't her standard operating procedure?"

"No. She must've been really upset. I think she felt really close to you after all your talking last night, and then you hurt her when you thought the worst of her without even speaking to her and finding out if it was true."

"Hmmm."

"Just think about what I said, okay Jack?"

"Okay."

He watched her as she walked away and thought, *Either she's the real deal, or those three women are unbelievable con artists.*

But he decided to give Kate the benefit of the doubt. He'd keep an eye on her, and go with his instincts. And if those instincts told him that she was the real deal, then he'd make the most of her time here on Maui.

Cherry knew better than to push Kate to go to Lahaina with them that evening.

"What are you going to do again?"

"I'm going to one of the nicest restaurants in Wailea at a resort down the road," Kate said, as she adjusted the strap on her sexy black dress. "They have a reputation for serving the best desserts on the island, and I want to try a couple of them for myself."

"Occupational hazard of being a chef," Patti chimed in. "She has to check out the competition."

"Dinner by yourself?" Cherry said. "That doesn't sound like too much fun."

"It's actually very relaxing, especially when I want to center my attention on the food."

"If you say so," Cherry said. "So we'll drop you off, and you don't mind getting a cab back?"

"I'll be fine. I can even call the hotel shuttle to come and pick me up."

The dining room in this particular restaurant looked like the inside of a Japanese Ceremonial Temple. Exquisite. Kate had a small table all to herself and was enjoying a glass of very good white wine when an older man stopped by her table.

"Miss Prescott? Is everything all right at the Kalani Resort?"

She glanced up and saw an extremely handsome older man looking down at her.

"Everything's fine," she said, wondering who he was and why he was asking her this question.

He laughed, then held out his hand. "James McKenna. I'm the owner of the Kalani, and I know you're a guest there for the next week. When I saw you here, I couldn't help wondering if there was something we were doing wrong."

"Not at all. I just hear this place has a reputation with their desserts, and I came over to try a few."

"Very interesting. You're a dessert fan?"

"I'm a chef, and I specialize in desserts. Just checking out the competition."

"Now that's intriguing. Where do you work?"

"I make all the desserts at Alberto's in Highland Park, just outside Chicago. It's my uncle's restaurant, and it's one of the best places for Italian food in the area."

He considered this, then said, "Would you care to join me for dinner?"

She grinned up at him. "I was just about to ask you why you weren't eating at your very own resort."

He smiled down at her. "Checking out the competition."

Jack took a long nap after he got off work, and once he woke and showered, the world seemed like a better place.

He was actually hoping this Patti was right about Kate.

Why would a woman go to such lengths to make up such a story? Especially when she didn't think he had any money. If she thought he really was a bartender, then her steering him toward her cousin didn't make sense if they really were only after big bucks.

He was feeling better and better about Kate. He'd leave her alone for tonight, let her get some sleep as well. But tomorrow—depending on where he had to work and for how long, he was going to find her, and they were going to talk.

They'd finished their dinner, and Kate was trying to decide between pineapple crepes, coconut flan, a macadamia nut soufflé, a white chocolate cake with coconut and pecans, a chocolate cake, and a guava cake with cream cheese frosting.

"And these are just tonight's specials," she said, studying the dessert menu. "Where did they find this guy?"

"He's from Oahu. A native. I guess he's been something of an intuitive cook since he could read a recipe."

"That's how it was for me," Kate said. "I used to

watch my uncle cook, and there was nothing I wanted to do more than be in the kitchen with him."

"What about your own parents?" James asked.

"They died when I was very young. In a car crash. They were coming home from their anniversary dinner, and a drunk driver hit their car."

His handsome face showed his concern. "How old were you?"

"Five."

"And you went to live with your aunt and uncle."

"Yes."

She'd found James McKenna a very easy man to talk to and had ended up telling him all about Patti's wedding that wasn't, and the reason for their trip out to the islands. She'd even had him laughing over her meeting Cherry on the plane, and her plot to marry money.

"Do you think she's serious?" he'd said.

"I think she thinks she is. But I believe that as time goes on, she'll find out it's not what she really wants."

"And what do you think she wants?"

"Love. I think she just wants to love and be loved."

He leaned back in his chair. "You're a wise woman for one so young, Kate."

"Thank you." She glanced back at the dessert menu. "But not so wise that I can make up my mind about what I want."

He plucked the menu out of her hands. "Order them all. My treat, of course."

She stared at him. "What?"

"Order them all. And then let me know how they are, in your professional opinion. And afterwards, if you can't finish them, we can have them boxed up and you can take them back to your cousin and your friend."

She started to laugh. "Then we have to order two forks. You *have* to help me eat them."

"I'll do what I can. But as the owner of a rival resort, I'm really interested in your opinion. I'd consider it a real favor to have the benefit of your expertise."

Kate found that she really liked James. There was something about the twinkle in his eye that reminded her of someone, but she couldn't quite place who it was. He'd been an absolutely charming dinner companion, they'd never run out of things to talk about, ranging from the serious to the silly.

And now she was in absolute heaven, at the prospect of so many grand desserts spread out in front of her. A veritable feast.

"I'll do what I can," she said.

"Actually," he said, "there is one thing you could do for me, and if you could succeed in this, I would be forever in your debt."

Intrigued, Kate leaned forward.

Chapter Eight

❀ Jack roamed the resort, restless. The island at night was magical, with the sound of the waves, the scents of night-blooming flowers, and the magical, glittering path that moonlight made on the ocean.

And all the time he walked, he thought of Kate.

He hadn't been able to sleep, so he'd pulled on shorts, a T-shirt, then laced up his running shoes and decided to take a walk on the resort's extensive grounds. That nap hadn't been a great idea. Now he wasn't tired, and all he could think about was Kate. The way he'd bumped into her on the pathway to the villa. Stepped back. Looked into an amazing pair of green eyes and that face . . . He'd known he was in trouble from the moment he'd seen her.

The strangest thing was, up until he'd actually seen her for the first time, he'd been convinced that his life was exactly what he wanted it to be, that he was where he wanted to be. Convinced being the operative word.

He'd been convincing himself all right, because the moment he'd gotten a good look at her, all of his rationalizing and justifications, all the amount of emotional time he'd spent telling himself that his life was perfect just the way it was had crashed and burned. Totally.

And now he'd found out that she wasn't after a millionaire after all. That she'd flown thousands of miles to help her cousin, who'd been royally shafted by her fiancé and left at the altar in front of five hundred people. A big wedding that had turned into a complete disaster. And Kate had been willing to drop her life and come with her cousin and help her.

He had the feeling that was just the kind of woman she was.

Jack jogged down to the moonlit beach and stopped at the shoreline, just above the waves. He took a deep breath of the fragrant ocean air, then slowly let it out. He watched the moonlight dancing on the water for a few moments, then his mind continued down that path that always led back to Kate.

He'd overreacted, that was for sure. He felt like a fool for condemning her so easily. He'd been as close to her as was humanly possible last night, he'd trusted her enough to get totally naked with her, both physically and emotionally. It hadn't been just a one-night stand for him; there had been a powerful pull that he'd felt toward her, and he'd felt it from the moment he'd seen her dancing in the surf on the deserted beach.

Hell, from the moment he'd bumped into her near the front door of her villa, it had felt so *right,* being with her. Like they belonged together. He'd been totally amazed at his impulsiveness that night, because normally he didn't do much that wasn't pretty well thought out, almost calculated.

And then had come the morning and his damn assumptions. The way he'd condemned her without even listening to her side of it. The whole millionaire thing had pressed one of his most sensitive emotional buttons, and he'd reacted without really thinking it through.

What if she really was only on vacation with Patti and Cherry and had no intention of imitating the other woman's goals and snagging herself a rich man?

He'd assumed she was after money, he'd accused her without even talking with her, and he could see how that would make her angry. Remembering their squabble in the pool, Jack had to grin as he looked out over the moonlit-sparked waves. That temper. That glorious temper. Kate was a fighter, no doubt about it, and she'd been spitting mad today at the bar.

They seemed to ignite each other, sexually and just in general. She wasn't boring, not at all. He couldn't even talk himself into believing he was indifferent to her.

What to do.

He glanced across the expanse of lawn next to the beach, in the direction of the opulent villas. Villa number six wasn't that far away, but it didn't feel like the right time to talk with Kate. He'd barely calmed down from their encounter at the bar today, so he was sure she was still riled. A good night's sleep might go a long way toward fixing things. And then he'd offer her an apology, because she deserved one.

He took another deep breath, let it out in a long sigh, then stared out over the ocean. Usually the sound of the waves and the gentle ocean breezes never failed to calm him down. But he knew that since he'd met Kate, the only thing that would calm him down was to see her, talk to her, try to get her to listen to him. He'd apologize and try to explain that the only reason he'd been so upset was that he'd thought they'd shared something magical, something special last night. Something that, if he were honest with himself, he'd been secretly looking for for a long, long time.

And if he was very lucky, she'd listen to him. And believe him.

For just a moment, he wished Kate were down here on the beach with him, that they could walk along the sand together and talk this whole thing out. And then when they were done talking . . .

He started to slowly jog down the beach, needing to release the intense energy that had taken over his body since meeting a certain green-eyed woman.

"A cookie war over coconut shortbread cookies?" Kate leaned back in her seat and picked up her cappuccino, unable to repress the smile she felt. The remains of various desserts lay all around her and James on the surface of their table, like the spoils of a culinary battle.

Each one had been excellent. When Kate had told their waiter, "my compliments to the chef," she'd really meant it.

"Maurice and I have been going round and round for years," James admitted sheepishly. "Our dessert wars on the island are legendary, but he really trumped me with his secret recipe for coconut macadamia nut shortbread. Its status on the island has reached epic proportions."

"I can understand why," Kate said, then she took another bite of the rich, buttery cookie and let the sandy shortbread texture melt in her mouth. *Heaven.*

"So," James said, "what do you think of my proposition?"

"You may be wasting the price of an elaborate gift basket," Kate said. "I can't guarantee that I can duplicate the recipe, or come up with one that's considerably better."

"I'm willing to take that chance," James said. "You can have the run of the resort's kitchen, anything you need, but I want that cookie—or something better."

"This is really funny," Kate said. "I didn't think I'd be doing any cooking on this vacation."

James frowned. "I hadn't thought of that. You might not want to spend your time cooped up in a kitchen instead of going to the beach."

"Are you kidding?" Kate leaned forward. "Cooking is my great passion in life, and there's nothing I love better than a challenge. I can't wait to see if I can do this!" She glanced over as she saw their waiter approach, an enormous white take-out box in his arms along with an elaborate gift basket filled to the brim with the aforementioned cookies.

"What's in that take-out box?"

James laughed. "I ordered a complete second round of every single dessert for your cousin, Patti, and your friend, Cherry."

"Oh my God!"

His deep blue eyes twinkled, and Kate could tell he was amused. "Are you telling me that they don't like to eat desserts? Are they both on diets?"

"No, I can guarantee they're going to love these." She spread her fingers out in front of her, smoothing them over the white linen tablecloth, feeling as if she were grounding herself. "It's just that . . . it's such a generous gesture."

"It's not every day that I meet such a charming chef."

She studied his face for a moment. Such a handsome man, and yet throughout the entire evening she hadn't felt as if he were hitting on her or trying to be anything but one of the most charming dinner companions she'd ever had. Besides, he had a wedding ring on, and if that wasn't a sign of a man's total devotion to another woman, what was?

"Thank you."

"Thank *you*," James said. "I can't remember when I've enjoyed a dinner more. Shall we head back to the Kalani?"

Kate nodded.

She's perfect for him, James thought as he helped Kate out of her chair. A real person, with no pretension, and enough fire so Jack would never be bored. And a beautiful woman, both inside and out. He couldn't have been more pleased if he'd picked her out for Jack himself.

He could totally understand why his son had pulled Kate Prescott into the pool with him. Now if only Jack wouldn't let his fears get the best of him. If his son would just surrender to that glorious undertow love brought to a man's life and give over to the magic of it, James knew he could hand over the resort to Jack and be totally confident that his son's life would be well-spent and gloriously happy.

He also knew he would adore having Kate as a daughter-in-law.

They were silent on the shuttle back to the resort until another thought occurred to him. *Grandchildren.*

"Kate, may I ask you a personal question?"

She smiled up at him. "I might even give you a personal answer."

"Do you want children?"

There wasn't even a moment's hesitation. "Yes." She hesitated. "Why do you ask?"

At least he could answer her honestly. "I just see you as the sort of woman who should have a family. I know I'm a rather old-fashioned man, but it makes me feel good to know you've made that decision."

"Do you have children?" she said.

"One. A son. He's the joy of my life."

"You and your wife must be very proud of him."

The shuttle reached the Kalani's massive circular drive. James helped Kate down the short steps, then grasped both the huge dessert box and the basket of shortbread cookies.

"Let me take some of that," Kate began.

"Absolutely not," he said, finding it very easy to talk to her. "My wife was extremely proud of our son. She passed away when he was quite young."

"I'm sorry," Kate said.

The quiet sincerity in her voice caused emotions to well up inside him, and she seemed to sense it. He felt her place her hand very gently on his forearm and found himself looking down into a very compassionate pair of green eyes.

"You must have loved her very much," Kate said.

He nodded his head.

Jack was walking through the front lobby when he glanced outside to the circular drive and saw his father and—*Kate?*

She had her hand on his father's arm and was looking up at him. He was looking down at her, and as Jack stared in horror, he realized they were sharing—how did one say it?—a rather intimate moment.

His father . . . and Kate . . . his father . . . and Kate . . . *Dad . . . Kate . . . Dad . . . Kate . . .*

No.

His brain didn't seem to want to function for just a moment, then a voice reverberated inside his head.

Any more ideas about finding that millionaire?

He could hear Patti's voice as plainly as if she were standing right next to him.

No. No, *absolutely not. This could* not *be happening.*

Jack forced his stunned legs to move, and he managed to conceal himself behind a massive potted palm, where he was well hidden but could still watch the interplay between his father and Kate. And he found himself in the extremely weird and uncomfortable position of being dead jealous of his own father.

As he watched, she said something that made his father smile. Really smile. Tension coiled in Jack's gut as he watched the two of them. And what the hell was his father doing, loaded down with a huge white box and an enormous basket of cookies?

It took his shock-addled brain another moment to process the fact that his own father had bought Kate something . . . something from a restaurant . . . something . . .

His life seemed to flash before his eyes, one of those hideous moments in which Jack felt he didn't have enough oxygen, he couldn't breathe, and everything was slowly fading to pinpricks of black.

He'd taken her out to dinner.

They headed into the lobby, and Jack watched with a kind of fascinated horror as the train wreck that was now his life walked right past him.

Kate. In that dress. A killer dress, some little black number with a short skirt and thin straps that showed a lot of tanned shoulder and exquisite collarbone, all witchcraft and seduction. And those *legs,* in those sexy black high heels. And his *father,* laughing down at her, looking younger than he had in—forever.

Oh my God . . .

This was far worse than anything he'd thought could happen. Jack slowly put a hand over his eyes, as if the simple gesture could wipe out what he'd just seen. Tentatively, hoping desperately that he'd been hallucinating, he uncovered his eyes.

And saw Kate's sweetly rounded bottom, looking spectacular in that little black number. And his own father was offering her his arm as they headed down the steps from the main lobby toward the path that led to the villas.

Jack closed his eyes. He couldn't even begin to think about where this night might lead.

Jack, there's something Kate and I would like to tell you . . .

Gee, Kate, should I call you Mom?

This was like a bad rerun of *Dynasty*. Maybe if he were truly cursed, he'd get a little brother or sister out of this whole disaster.

Hell. This whole scenario was so twisted he still couldn't get his brain around it. His father hadn't looked at another woman since the day his mother had died. Jack had assumed he never would. And now, Jack realized, James McKenna had gone out to dinner with the one woman on this entire island, no, make that this entire *planet,* who had the power to tie his gut up into knots.

Fate, destiny, whatever you wanted to call it, sure could be a bitch.

"If I eat one more thing, I'm going to explode. But before that happens, I'm going to kill you, Kate," Patti said from her prone position on the couch, one hand draped over her flat stomach. The remains of all the fabulous desserts were scattered around on the surface of the living room's glass-topped coffee table, along with a semi-decimated basket of shortbread cookies and three cups of coffee.

"Not if I get to her first," Cherry said, lying on the

Oriental carpet. "As soon as I can move." She moaned, but it was a sound closer to ecstasy than pain. "Pass the last of that coconut cake down this way." She waved a fork languidly in the air.

"You do realize," Patti said, "that we're going to be up all night after ingesting all this sugar. Not to mention the caffeine."

"Another shortbread cookie?" Kate offered, smiling at her cousin.

"But of course." Patti didn't even try to resist.

"I can't get over how the owner of this entire resort found you at a restaurant, insisted on having dinner with you, and then bought you all these desserts," Cherry said, licking the last of the coconut-flecked frosting off her fork. "No wonder you wanted to go to dinner alone. And what an absolutely charming man he was."

"Well, there was a condition."

"There always is," Patti and Cherry said in unison, then laughed.

Briefly, Kate explained about the cookies.

"This is too funny," Cherry said. "Two grown men engaged in a cookie war? Wait. What am I saying? Men and competition go together like . . ." She thought for a moment.

"Like guava cake and cream cheese frosting," Patti said.

"Thank you," said Cherry. "Did we finish the pineapple crepes?"

"I think it's gone beyond that," Kate said as she passed the crepes. "Now it's a matter of pride between two rival resort owners."

"Is there a little bit of that white chocolate cake left, the one with the pecans?" Patti said, forcing herself to sit upright.

"Right here," Cherry said, and passed it to Patti. "We

need to sign up for one of those yoga classes out by the pool after tonight's excesses."

"Fine with me," Patti said. "I'm also going to sign up for a swimming class. That's something that will push me out of my comfort zone." She turned toward Kate. "So Kate, you'll be in the kitchen tomorrow morning?"

"Yeah. I'll call Uncle Albert at the restaurant and have him fax me my shortbread recipe. Then I'll see what I can do."

Cherry nabbed one last cookie and lay back down on the floor as she started to laugh.

"What?" Kate said.

"Sugar, I think you're the closest of all of us to actually bagging that millionaire."

Jack slipped stealthily up to his father's penthouse suite, making sure no one saw him. Technically he wasn't supposed to contact his father for the duration of the ten-day period, but this was definitely an emergency.

As he reached the door to the penthouse, the hairs along the back of his neck prickled, then rose.

Oh, no. His father had broken out *Sinatra.* He could hear the first few violin strains of "All the Way," then that beautiful, unmistakable golden voice.

When somebody loves you, it's no good unless he loves you,
All the way . . .

Jack rested his forehead against the wooden door and let out a long breath. *Shit.*

This was much worse than he'd thought. He'd have to nip it in the bud. His father was clearly delusional, totally infatuated with Kate and had no idea what she was really up to. Maybe he was going through a very late midlife crisis.

He'd have to set his father straight. And it wasn't going to be pretty.

James McKenna always listened to Sinatra when he thought of Caroline. And having dinner with Kate tonight, thinking and hoping that she and his son were on the road to a deeply fulfilling love had brought back all sorts of personal memories of his own courtship of the woman he'd adored.

From the first moment he'd met Caroline, he'd known they had to be together.

And they'd both loved Sinatra, so it only seemed right to listen to him as he remembered. He'd even taken the original engagement ring he'd given his wife out of the penthouse's wall safe and was looking at it, remembering how nervous he'd been right before he'd given it to her.

The diamond, though exquisite, had been small, but his dreams for a life with Caroline had been enormous. James studied the delicate ring as he angled it so he could read what he'd had engraved on the inside of the slender, platinum gold band.

All the way.

He knew of no other way to love. He suspected Jack didn't, either. And Caroline had made him promise, right before she'd died, that he would give Jack this ring when he found the woman of his dreams.

Now with Jack pulling Kate Prescott into the pool with him and squabbling in public with her, he had no doubts that his son would soon be telling him that he'd fallen deeply in love. And he couldn't wait for that day.

"Dad."

He glanced up and saw his son in the penthouse

doorway. And noticed an expression of absolute and deep concern on Jack's face.

Taking control of his emotions, James McKenna slid his wife's engagement ring into the pocket of his dress slacks and turned to face his son.

Things were getting more disastrous by the minute. Just when Jack thought things couldn't get any worse, he'd caught sight of his mother's engagement ring in his father's hand.

Was he thinking of giving it to Kate? What was it about the woman? She'd been at the Kalani Resort for only two nights, bagged him on the first, and now she'd ensnared his dad? The phrase "like father, like son" was starting to take on a whole new meaning.

One he didn't even want to contemplate.

"Dad?"

"Son?" His father had a carefully neutral expression on his face. "Is something wrong?"

"In a way." Carefully, so carefully, feeling as if he were navigating a minefield, Jack crossed the massive living room and approached his father. "There's something I have to discuss with you."

The look of utter joy on his father's face stopped him for a moment.

"Anything, Jack. I hope you know you can talk about anything with me."

Jack cleared his throat nervously. "Well, this might be the one subject that's going to test that assumption."

"Try me." James moved toward the built-in bar. "Drink?"

Jack hesitated, then said, "Double Scotch on the rocks."

James gave him a long, measured look, then turned

and began to fix the drink. "Did you have a nice evening?" his father asked him.

"Sure. Yeah. You?"

"I had a tremendous evening," his father replied, then crossed the room and handed Jack his drink.

"Well." Jack raised his drink. "Cheers."

"Cheers," James said, and Jack could see that he was puzzled. Clearly his father was waiting for him to get to it.

Jack took a long sip of his drink, then set it down on the large coffee table between two comfortable couches.

"Could we sit, Dad?"

"Certainly."

Both men sat down across from each other, and Jack stared at his father until James said, "If there's something you have to say, go ahead. I'm sure nothing is going to shock me."

"Don't bet on it, Dad."

"What's wrong?"

"It's Kate."

The look of utter delight on his father's face almost defeated him before he went any further. In the background, Frank began to sing, "I've got the world on a string, sitting on a rainbow, got the string around my finger, what a world, what a life, I'm in love . . ."

James leaned forward. "Miss Prescott? She's an utter delight, isn't she?"

Jack thought back to the night before, then steeled his mind against the sensual memories.

"You could say that. You could also say that she came to this island with the intention of bagging herself a rich man, and—damn it, Dad, I don't want you to be that man!"

                    *   *   *

James McKenna hadn't been a successful businessman for close to forty years without some street smarts. So now he sized up the situation in a heartbeat.

He's still resisting. He's scared, so he's grasping at excuses not to deepen the relationship. Something—or someone—has to push him over the edge.

"What are you talking about?" He decided to stall for time, get some more information.

Briefly, Jack told him what had transpired at the bar that morning, how he'd overheard Cherry and Patti talking about their master plan, and how Kate had bellied up to that same bar and joined them.

"So I saw the two of you coming back from dinner somewhere, and I just—Dad, you've got to be able to see through her and realize what she's really up to."

James took a slow sip of his drink as he thought.

It bothers him, seeing her with me. Good. I can use this to my advantage, as long as he's being so stubborn. The lesson, Jack, is to surrender, and if you can't see it, I'll help you.

"So you think she's after my money."

"Well, yeah! I mean, they talk about nabbing a millionaire, and there you are! Put it together, Dad!"

"She didn't approach me, Jack."

"What?" In that instant, it seemed to James that he was watching his son deflate. All the air seemed to go out of Jack's argument.

"I approached her. I had been told about your little . . . incident by the pool, shall we say? As she's a guest at this resort, I asked how she was, and why she was choosing to dine outside the resort. It turns out she's a chef, and she wanted to try some of Maurice's incredible desserts."

"She did?"

James almost laughed at the expression on his son's face.

"Yes. If you must know, I asked her if I could join her for dinner. And she was absolutely charming company. I'm sure you're aware that she's quite a . . . captivating woman, wouldn't you say?"

The expression on his son's face was priceless.

"We enjoyed our meal together, and I bought her every dessert on the menu—twice. Once for the two of us, then boxed up for her cousin and friend back at villa number six. And a huge basket of Maurice's cookies." He decided to leave out the request he'd made of Kate to recreate those cookies and figure out the recipe.

"Dad, dinner is one thing, but what I'm afraid of is that—"

"I might become overly infatuated with this young woman and end up marrying her?"

"Well . . . yeah. I mean, can you blame me? At your age? And considering what I know about her?"

He decided to ignore the remark about his age. "Jack, do you really think she's a woman who's after money?"

He could tell his son was struggling with the question and that told James all he wanted to know. Jack didn't want to believe the worst of Kate.

But he was still afraid.

Time for another little push.

James took another sip of his drink, then set it down. "Well, I appreciate the warning. I know you care about me, Jack, and what happens to me. I'm touched that you don't want me to get my heart broken."

He watched as Jack sat back with a satisfied expression on his face and took a large swallow of Scotch.

"So you'll be relieved to know that I'm only contemplating a fling with our Miss Prescott, nothing remotely serious—"

As he'd expected, his son's drink spewed out of his mouth, followed by a furious fit of coughing.

"Jack! What's wrong? Are you all right?" With utter concern and solicitousness, James came around the couch and thumped his son on the back.

When Jack could finally speak, he forced the words out, his face red, his eyes watering. "Dad, you can't! You can't have an affair with her . . ."

"Jack, surely we can be adult about this . . ."

"No, you don't understand . . ."

But suddenly James did. And he hid the sudden smile that his thoughts inspired.

Could these two have possibly already gotten together? He remembered how hot and bright the attraction had flared between him and Caroline and knew that if Jack hadn't been with Kate yet, they were headed on a collision course toward intimacy.

Of course his son wouldn't want him anywhere *near* this woman!

"Dad, promise me you won't go anywhere—do anything stupid. For me."

James pretended to consider this seriously, then said, "I'm afraid I can't. I don't share your low regard for our Miss Prescott, and as I find her an absolutely charming woman, and she's a guest at my resort, I have to say that I'm going to make sure that the remaining days she spends here are as much fun as possible."

"You can't possibly mean . . ." Jack began, but James had already taken the glass of Scotch out of his son's hands and was ushering him toward the door.

"You know, Jack, you were right. This was the one subject that tested the assumption that we can talk about anything."

At this point, Jack was outside the penthouse door.

Before he ended their discussion, James decided to drive home one more point.

"And as for Miss Prescott, Jack, I expect you to treat her with the utmost respect and courtesy while she's staying here. And if you see the two of us together, I trust that you won't make any sort of scene."

"This can't be happening! Dad, I have to insist—"

"Good night, son. Sleep well." James started to shut the massive double door in his son's face, then said, "Tomorrow night I believe you're going to be waiting tables in the main restaurant. You'll need your sleep, those trays are heavy."

He shut the door in his son's protesting face, then leaned against the wooden surface, a wide grin on his face. James listened as Jack walked away, then whispered, "Caroline, I wish you were here to see this. And advise me."

He stepped away from the door and walked over to the floor-to-ceiling windows that overlooked the Pacific below.

"Though I don't think I did a half bad job."

He continued to watch and within minutes saw Jack leave the main building and storm off furiously toward employee housing.

James grinned.

"Oh Caroline, this is almost too easy!"

Chapter Nine

It was as if Kate had died and gone to kitchen heaven.

She'd cooked in some pretty fabulous kitchens in her day, but nothing compared with the main kitchen of the Kalani Resort in Maui. Gleaming expanses of counters, top-of-the-line kitchen gadgets, gorgeous tile floors, enormous walk-in refrigerators, oven after oven, miles of ranges, gleaming copper pots, the finest ingredients, many of them organic and grown right on the island.

She was a totally happy camper.

Uncle Albert had faxed her a favorite shortbread recipe earlier that morning, and now Kate studied the rows of cookies cooling on one of the massive kitchen counters. Shortbread didn't take that long to whip up. What had taken some work were the variations she'd dreamed up.

Literally. Kate dreamed food, and after that bacchanalian dessert party last night, once she'd hit her bed, she'd had visions of shortbread cookies dancing in her head. The fun part had been entering this dream kitchen and attempting to actually make those cookies a reality.

"They smell fantastic," said Eduardo, one of the chefs on the morning shift. While the cookies had baked, she'd watched him create various signature dishes with open admiration. Two foodies, they'd talked shop for hours, and now he'd called James's office and told him that the first round of cookie tasting was about to commence.

And though Kate wasn't sure that these would be the final winners in her experimentation with shortbread, she knew that all the cookie variations she'd created this morning were in the running.

Patti and Cherry were sprawled out on chaise lounges by the pool when a gorgeously built man in dark blue swimming trunks with long, sandy-blond hair pulled back in a low ponytail came up to them.

"Patti Cannelli? Villa number six?" he said, scanning a list on a clipboard.

"That's me," Patti said.

"You signed up for a swimming lesson at ten," he said. "I'm Matt, your instructor."

Patti gazed up at Matt. *Gorgeous.* He was easily a head and a half taller than she was and built like a construction worker, with rippling muscles and powerful shoulders. "Are we going to use this pool?"

"Nope. There's one on the other side that's roped off. It's a little more private. We'll start there. Just let me find my eleven-thirty, and then I'm all yours."

He walked away, and both Patti and Cherry watched him go.

"Wow," Cherry breathed. "If I'd known that the hotel

swim instructor looked like Brad Pitt in *Legends of the Fall,* I would've signed up for the advanced class."

"He's fling material if I've ever seen it," Patti whispered.

Cherry narrowed her cat-blue eyes. "Sugar, don't rush things. You just got your heart broken."

"Yeah, but maybe he can fix it."

Jack walked into the kitchen in time to see Kate feed his father a cookie. And darted back into the hallway, hovering just out of view.

"Fantastic!" he heard his father say. "This one tastes almost exactly like Maurice's cookies, but there's something different I can't quite place."

"Rum," Kate said, and Jack could tell she was clearly pleased with her handiwork. She and his father looked and sounded like a mutual admiration society, and for some strange reason, it grated on his nerves, big time.

He peered inside the kitchen again in time to see Kate hand his father another cookie.

Things were totally out of control. He'd gone back to his Spartan quarters last night and thought about how Kate affected him. And he'd realized that his emotions had less to do with Kate being a fortune hunter and more to do with the fact that he was just plain jealous. Jealous that his father got along with Kate so well, while he'd botched things with her so badly.

But her ten-day stay at the resort had barely started, so he had time to make up for their fight by the pool.

"Batches three, seven, and ten," he heard his father say. "Especially the ones with the rum."

"I was thinking of combining three and ten," Jack heard Kate say.

"Now that would be a distinctive cookie," his father replied. "You're thinking of doing that right now?"

"No time like the present. I just wanted your opinion first."

Jack practically ground his teeth. What was this, now she was baking cookies for his father, playing Betty Crocker? Did the woman have no shame?

"Great. I'll be up in my office, waiting for the results."

Out in the private pool, toward the end of her first swimming lesson, Patti practically passed out as Matt led her toward the deeper end, then supported her body with his strong hands and told her to start moving her arms in the simple swimming stroke he'd showed her.

She couldn't seem to concentrate when he was around her.

And she'd never felt this way when Roger had touched her. *Never.*

Kate was wiping down the gleaming counter when she heard a familiar masculine voice almost directly behind her.

"Hard at work, I see."

Her stomach did a crazy little flip-flop as she recognized Jack's voice and turned.

"Hi." She'd decided last night that if she saw Jack again while she was here at the resort, she was determined not to get involved in another fight with him. After all, she was an adult woman and wanted to start acting like one. And having dinner with James McKenna had salved her badly bruised ego, allowing her to feel good about herself again. Like an adult.

Jack looked absolutely wonderful, in khaki shorts and another coral-colored polo shirt. She guessed that he'd reported for work in the kitchen, probably as head dishwasher. She wondered at the fates that should have put her there, baking cookies, right in his path.

Kate was so nervous, she could barely meet his eyes.

"Want a cookie?" she blurted out, unsure of what to do next, but only knowing that she didn't want him to walk away.

"Sure."

She found it rather hard to breathe, the way he was looking at her. *As if he wants to eat me up and to hell with the cookie.*

She handed him one of the shortbread cookies with rum, then leaned back against the counter. He ate it slowly, and she watched him the entire time.

"So," she said, "what do you think?" She couldn't believe how much his opinion mattered to her.

"I think," he said, "that you're an excellent cook."

"Thanks." Her stomach relaxed . . . a little.

"But I also think you should know that James McKenna's practically bankrupt."

The smile left her face. "What are you talking about?"

"Bankrupt. As in money. As in, he has none."

Her temper started to simmer, and she took a step toward him. "Why do you keep harping on that whole millionaire thing?"

"I'm not. I'm just telling you, one friend to another, that he's washed up."

She narrowed her eyes at him. "So you think I'm going after James for his money?"

"Oh, we're already on a first-name basis, are we?"

She turned away from him, hurt beyond belief. What was with this man? Why did he always have to think the worst of her?

Incensed, she turned toward him. "Who the hell do you think you are?" She brought her hand down with a firm slap on the counter onto a huge pile of sifted flour on parchment paper.

Which promptly exploded and flew all over Jack and his clean coral-colored polo shirt. He blinked through the cloud of flour, and she saw, horrified, that it had dusted his dark hair and covered almost half of his face.

He blinked again. Narrowed those dark blue eyes and gave her that *look*.

And she laughed. She laughed so hard she had to hold her stomach, and as she did, she noticed that the sides of his mouth were twitching.

"Very funny, Kate."

"I think so." Her eyes were starting to tear up. "The way you look . . ."

"Funny? You think so?"

"Yeah, I do—no, wait, don't you *dare!*"

He'd picked up a bag of powdered sugar. Before she could dart out of the way, he upended part of the bag over her head, and she squealed, trying to avoid the deluge.

Kate grabbed the first thing her hand came into contact with, which was a huge lump of unsalted butter. Taking aim, she threw it at his face.

Jack ducked, the butter hit the wall, and he grabbed a handful of freshly grated coconut and deftly slipped it down the back of her pink cotton dress.

"*You!*" She grabbed a handful of chocolate chips, he grabbed a container of cream, and both of them fell, grappling, to the gleaming tile floor.

Meredith hung up the phone on her desk, then trotted into James's office with a huge grin on her face.

"Food fight in the kitchen. Everyone's giving them a wide berth. Eduardo called, he wants to know what he should do."

James couldn't stop smiling. "Let them play it out." He glanced at the clock on his desk. "It shouldn't go too long. If it does, you and I can go down and break things up. And afterwards, I'll send in some maintenance men to clean it all up before the lunch shift."

"Right."

"You are such a . . ." Kate swung, then slipped on a hunk of butter and went down for the count.

"You're cute when you're mad . . ." Jack began, then stopped laughing when she grabbed at his waistband and pulled him back down onto the slippery floor, where she threw some macadamia nuts down the front of his shirt.

"Hey!" He grabbed both her hands, and they rolled, coming to a stop beneath one of the kitchen tables, both breathing heavily. He found himself on top of her, the weight of his body pinning her down as she glared up at him, breathing heavily, her color high.

She looked gorgeous to him. And so damn desirable.

And as long as he was in total trouble with this woman, he might as well go all the way. Lowering his mouth to hers, he kissed her.

She thought the top of her head was going to come off.

Kate had thought about kissing Jack again since their first night together, but she'd never thought she'd get another chance because of the low opinion he had of her. Now, as his mouth coaxed hers open, she found she didn't care. She didn't care what he thought of her, she only knew that she wanted him to kiss her, didn't want him to stop, didn't care that they were both covered in flour and sugar and eggs and milk and coconut and God knew what else.

She had a moment of uncertainty when his hand

cupped her breast, then sensation overpowered her, and she didn't care where they were or what they were doing. The kitchen seemed strangely quiet, and she realized that most of the other help had left, wisely getting out of the way of flying food.

She moaned as she felt his fingers gently pinch her engorged nipple, then he whispered in her ear, "I can't take much more of this."

"You," she panted, "are a really horrible man. And I hate you."

He cupped her bottom, gave it a squeeze. "Baby, I love the way you hate."

"What seems to be going on here?"

"Meredith!" they both said in unison. Jack tried to stand up, bumped his head on the underside of the table as Kate laughed and slid out from beneath him, then stood.

"How's the baking coming along?" James McKenna said, his voice sounding loud, almost echoing in the large commercial kitchen.

Kate closed her eyes. She knew how this had to look. She and Jack were covered, literally covered, with foodstuff. She hadn't played this down and dirty since her sandbox days.

She just didn't know what came over her when this man was around.

"Really well," she said to James, trying for a small semblance of dignity. She pushed back her hair with her hands, and when she looked at her fingers, she had melted chocolate all over them. Chocolate chips and body heat, what a combination.

"Has Jack been bothering you?" Meredith asked.

"Jack?" Kate said. She looked at Jack as if she'd just noticed him. The only way through this—literal—mess was to bluff her way out. "Oh, *Jack!* Bothering me? No.

He was actually a great help, we were starting on the second round of cookies, and I slipped on a small piece of butter I'd dropped on the floor. Then as I fell, I grabbed the edge of the parchment paper and everything came down off the table, and then when Jack tried to help me stand back up, well—you know, butter on the floor and all that."

She stopped chattering, registering everyone's reaction. Meredith was slowly nodding her head, James was smiling down at her, and Jack was giving her the most incredulous look as if he didn't even recognize her.

"I see," Meredith said. "Well, Jack, why don't you go get cleaned up and report back for the dinner shift." She turned toward Kate. "Is there anything we can do to help you, Miss Prescott?"

Kate smiled at the older woman, totally relieved that she and James McKenna had bought her story—sort of. She had a feeling that both of them suspected something else was going on. And if they could enlighten her as far as what that was, she'd be grateful.

"Nope. I think I'm just going to head off to my villa and that glorious bathroom and take a long, hot shower."

"Good idea," James said, nodding his head.

The four of them stood there for a moment, until James cleared his throat, and he and Meredith picked their way carefully across the food-strewn battleground and headed toward the kitchen's main exit.

"Nice save," Jack muttered as soon as they were both out of earshot. "You really are one hell of a con artist."

"Blah de blah blah," Kate replied, picking some coconut out of her hair. "Whatever. I don't care."

"You cared for a moment there, under the table."

"Lust, buddy, pure and simple. And I'm not going down *that* road with you again."

"But you've got to admit, it was a great piece of road."

"I don't have to admit a damn thing."

"Fine."

She watched as he started out of the kitchen, somehow managing to stride out without falling down on the food-slicked floor.

Kate almost had her temper under control when Jack turned around, and walking backward, called out, "McKenna would've bought the whole story if it hadn't been for that chocolate handprint on your left breast."

She gasped, then looked down, pulled at the front of her pink cotton dress so she could have a good view of—the obvious. In living color. Vivid dark brown. Melted chocolate. Jack's handprint, immortalized on her breast.

He laughed, and she grabbed the first thing she could lay her hands on, a small cellophane bag of walnut pieces. Heaving it toward Jack's head, she was mightily frustrated by the way he caught it and tossed it on one of the counters.

"And check out the one on your butt," he said, just as he walked out the door. "It's even better."

She didn't feel better until after almost thirty minutes beneath the shower. Once every trace of her food fight with Jack had been eliminated, and her dress was soaking in one of the pedestal sinks, Kate felt almost human again. She wrapped her head in a towel, turban-style, then slipped on one of the resort's plush white terry cloth robes and sat down on the sofa in the living room, facing the sliding glass doors and the ocean.

She got herself a glass of pineapple juice and was leafing through a fashion magazine Cherry had bought when she heard her cousin and her friend come in the front door, laughing and talking.

After listening to Patti's account of her swimming lesson and Cherry's account of the instructor, she felt a lot better. No one could make her laugh like her cousin could, and Cherry ran a close second.

"So, what are we up to tonight?" Cherry asked.

"What do you think, Kate? What do you want to do?" said Patti.

"Nothing."

As if on cue, the phone rang. Patti picked it up. "Hello?" Then she glanced at Kate and mouthed, "It's for you."

"Who?" Kate asked.

Patti covered the mouthpiece with her hand and handed her the receiver. "It's James McKenna."

For just an instant, Kate felt sharp regret that it wasn't Jack. But why would he be calling her? He despised her, and all women like her.

"Hello?" she said softly.

"You sound a little depressed," came James's comforting voice over the phone.

She didn't quite know what to say to that. He seemed able to sense her moods, and she had a feeling he could be quite a good friend.

"Here's a thought," James said. "I know this is very short notice, but I'd like to meet your cousin and friend. Could the three of you meet me for dinner tonight?"

Kate rubbed her temples. She'd had such an upsetting day, fighting with Jack again and then facing his contempt. And now this sweet man, despite his desperate financial straits, was trying to help cheer her up.

"James, I couldn't let you pay for dinner, not with all your financial difficulties."

There was a very pregnant pause over the line.

"Financial difficulties? Who told you that?"

"I won't breathe a word to anyone."

"Was it Jack Cameron?"

She sighed. "As a matter of fact, it was."

He laughed. "Oh, he has me mixed up with another resort owner. I can assure you, I have no financial troubles at the moment. The various resorts I own have been having a banner year."

"Really," Kate said quietly. "Because I would feel just awful if you spent money on us that you couldn't afford."

"I'm touched that you would care. But about dinner tonight—I think another night out might do you some good. Think of it as my way of saying thank you for those incredible cookies."

"Oh, I'm far from done with coming up with recipes."

"I believe you. How about eight, and we'll meet in the lobby of the Kalani Restaurant?"

"Okay."

"That's my girl." And with that, he hung up.

"What's going on?" Cherry asked.

"James McKenna wants to take all three of us out to dinner at the Kalani Restaurant. His treat."

"Dinner with a handsome rich man at one of the most expensive restaurants on the entire island?" Cherry said. "Let me think if I want to do this. Yes."

"Wow, Kate," said Patti. "That one tumble in the pool really netted you some outrageous results."

"Yeah," Kate replied. *And a broken heart.*

The three of them met James at the Kalani Restaurant promptly at eight, and were whisked to one of the main tables, a round table seating four that looked out over the ocean on a glorious patio.

"This truly is beautiful," Cherry said, sipping her glass of white wine. "I'm amazed at the thought of one man creating this entire empire."

Kate watched Patti and Cherry interact with James and had to admit that the evening promised to be a great one. They all seemed to get along, and she watched with admiration as James drew out her cousin, who sometimes didn't join in conversations with groups of people. To her relief, Patti was soon chatting with James as if she'd known him all her life.

"Where's our waiter?" James said. "He should have taken our order by now." The man who had taken their drink orders had clearly been a wine expert, but now that it was time to order, their waiter was nowhere in sight.

James stopped one of the other waiters and asked that he check out the situation. The young man assured him he would and hurried off.

Jack couldn't believe the evening he was having.

He'd done his share of waiting tables, but tonight the place was packed—and then he'd seen his father walk in with not just Kate, but Patti and Cherry as well.

What was he trying to do? Flaunt Jack's warning in his face? Even if Kate wasn't some sort of fortune hunter, Cherry clearly was. The woman had almost caused a few coronaries with the dress she'd worn tonight, an emerald green sheathlike thing that clung to her voluptuous curves like a second skin.

And now he had to go take their orders.

He wondered if Kate thought she was helping his father along the road to his supposed financial ruin by having this dinner with him.

Jack sighed, then squared his shoulders. As he headed toward the outside table where his father was chatting with the three women, he prepared himself for the worst.

Kate couldn't even look at Jack as she ordered—the cheapest entrée on the menu. Some kind of sweet and sour chicken dish with pineapple.

"Oh, no," James said. "It's a nice enough dish, but not one of our best. Why don't you try the lobster? The way we prepare it is out of this world."

"Works for me," Cherry said, closing her menu and setting it down in front of her.

"Me, too," Patti chimed in.

"And don't give a thought to those rumors concerning my financial situation," James said blithely. "Probably just some upstart who wants to try and make me look bad."

Kate saw Jack flush to the roots of his hair as he busily took down their order. But she still refused to look at him.

By the time they were ready to order dessert, Kate was quietly in agony.

It was a peculiar type of personal hell, being this close to Jack and not being close at all. She watched him out of the corner of her eye as he quickly and efficiently removed salad plates, replacing them with their entrees. Making sure their waters were filled and drinks kept coming. He was actually an excellent waiter. But she could feel his tension, and it fed her own.

She moved the chunks of lobster around on her plate, barely tasting anything. Cherry and Patti seemed to be enjoying their meal, but she caught her cousin's gaze on her once or twice and knew she wasn't fooling Patti at all.

When James suggested dessert, both Patti and Cherry

demurred, saying that they'd had more than enough last night. And they both somehow graciously made an exit, and Kate found herself alone with James.

"You aren't sparkling tonight, Kate," he said quietly. "Anything you'd like to talk about?"

"Nothing you could help me with," she said.

"I've been told I'm a good listener."

She had to smile at his attempt to help her. "I'm sure you are."

"Dessert or just coffee?"

"Just coffee—" But as she said the words, a frothy concoction passed by in a waiter's grasp, and she leaned forward. "What was *that?*"

He laughed. "One of our signature desserts. We've taken bananas foster from New Orleans and created our own version with Maui white pineapple."

"Oh my God."

"That settles that. You have to try it."

Kate sat back in her chair. James had been trying so hard to cheer her up, she felt horrible that her mood had dominated the entire dinner. So she resolved to be a better dinner companion for the dessert course.

"I will."

Jack didn't like the feelings that were flowing through him. He didn't like the stabs of jealousy that assaulted him every time he looked in the direction of Kate's table. He *especially* didn't like the fact that Cherry and Patti had left, and now his father was having dessert and coffee alone with Kate.

He couldn't believe that in less than forty-eight hours his entire life had been turned upside down.

Now she wanted the restaurant's signature pineapple dessert, and whatever the lady wanted, he'd deliver. But as Jack took the intricately crafted confection out of the kitchen, his gaze fell on another dessert, a chocolate mousse with tiny molded chocolates all around the side of the plate.

One caught his eye. A tiny, solid chocolate dollar sign.

Hurt, angry, frustrated, and not thinking clearly, Jack plucked the tiny molded chocolate off the plate and nestled it in the whipped cream of Kate's dessert.

Again, she could barely glance at Jack when he delivered the dessert to their table. He quietly set it in front of her, along with both their coffees, and left.

She picked up her spoon, and that's when she saw it. A tiny, molded chocolate dollar sign hidden among billows of freshly whipped cream.

And that was that.

Her eyes welled up, even as she pushed the tiny chocolate into the whipped cream on top of the dessert. She couldn't let James see this, or Jack would be fired for sure. Though why she should even care, she didn't know.

"Kate?"

She shook her head, her hand over her mouth. All of the tension of the dinner, seeing Jack, being so close to him and yet so far away . . . As her emotional control slipped, first one of the tears, then the other, spilled down her cheeks.

"Oh, Kate . . . I'm so sorry."

She shook her head again, holding up a hand as if to gesture him to wait. She wasn't a woman who usually broke down in public, and she hated having her private feelings exposed publicly.

"Take your time. We can just leave if you'd like."

She'd be damned if she'd ruin the entire evening.

"Give me a minute," she whispered.

*   *   *

Jack saw it all and hated himself all over again.

He caught a glimpse of her tears by candlelight, and the genuine concern in his father's expression as he leaned toward her. And Jack felt lower than an earth-worm, that he'd had to resort to such a petty little ex-pression of his feelings, that he'd had to hurt her so totally when he was the one who was jealous and upset.

He wished he could go back in time and not have given in to that truly petty impulse.

But he couldn't stop to analyze his feelings, not with five other tables to take care of. So, resolving never to hurt Kate again, *ever,* he immersed himself in his work.

If that meant he could never see her again, then that's what he would do. But nothing in this lifetime was worth hurting her.

Nothing.

"Kate. Let me help you." James hesitated, knowing he was treading in exquisitely delicate waters. "I know we haven't known each other long, but it always helps to share your problems. And I'd like you to consider me a friend."

"I do." She laughed self-consciously, then reached for her handbag and a tissue. She blew her nose, wiped her eyes, then tucked the tissue back inside her purse. "It's just—I think I've ruined everything."

"I take it it's a man you're talking about."

"He—" Fresh tears welled up. "He *hates* me, and I don't know why."

"Can I give you a little insight into the male psyche?"

"Please."

"We can sometimes be goddamn fools when we're overwhelmed by a woman."

"Oh, he's not overwhelmed with me."

James smiled across the table. "How can you be so sure?"

She hesitated.

"I met my wife on an elevator, and after I got one look at her, I not only got off on the wrong floor, I walked right into a wall."

She laughed at that, through her tears, and he found himself charmed by her vulnerability. And he wondered if his son knew what he was throwing away, what a treasure he had right under his nose.

"He keeps accusing me of—being after a millionaire husband."

"Are you?"

"No! I know he's just a bartender, and I don't even care. I mean, I guess he works several jobs around the resort—" She covered her mouth with her hands, suddenly horrified. "Oh! James, I just want you to know—you have to know that anything that happened between us, it was totally consensual. I mean, I wanted things to happen . . . Oh God, I don't even know what I'm saying. I just don't want you to fire anyone—but then I haven't told you his name." She hesitated. "Do I have your word you won't fire this man? I don't even know if he has any savings."

He smiled, touched beyond words. "You have my word. But how do you feel about him?"

She looked away, and he admired her classic profile, noticed the slight trembling of her full lips. "I really thought . . . I've never felt . . ." She turned toward him and those beautiful green eyes filled again. "Oh James, if I'd been on that elevator and met this man, I would have walked into a wall, too."

He felt his heart lift. *Wonderful.*

He sat back, took a sip of his coffee. "What happened?"

She considered this, then looked across the table at him and said, "I don't think I'm all that comfortable going into any detail."

"I understand."

"Let's just say that—maybe I made a fool of myself. I think that maybe we got a little too close a little too fast. He—when I first met him—it hit me pretty hard, you know?"

He nodded his head, indicating he was listening. Just as he'd suspected. That was why Jack had been so upset with him the other evening.

"Do you think that the two of you could possibly talk this out?"

"He doesn't seem to want to listen. All he wants to do is—*oh!*" Suddenly self-conscious, she looked down at her hands.

James took another sip of his coffee, considering

"Let me tell you a little about a young man I know." When she glanced up at him, her cheeks still slightly flushed with embarrassment, he said, "My son, of course. He's grown up with money, and one of the hardest things for him has been trying to find a woman who's not just after his considerable fortune."

"That has to be hard," Kate said quietly.

"It can make a man bitter. You can see the worst of human nature. And your young man, who works here, I'm sure he's seen a lot of it, too. Maui has more millionaires per capita than anywhere else in the world. So a lot of women come here looking for their rich man. 'Show me the money,' if you know what I mean."

She nodded.

"So sometimes a man can become extremely cynical."

Kate picked up her spoon and took a taste of her untouched dessert. "I can see how that would happen."

"But that doesn't mean that underneath that prickly exterior, he doesn't want to be loved."

She considered this, and James refrained from filling the silence. He wanted her to think about it.

"You're right," she finally said. "I've only been here three days. I have a week to get to him, to get him to see the real me."

"That's the spirit. Believe me, Kate, if anyone can bring this young man to his senses, I believe you can."

She studied him, and her expression softened. "You're the sweetest man. And a very good listener."

James leaned forward. "You're walking into walls over this young man, and I have a feeling he wouldn't be as angry at you if he weren't walking into those proverbial walls himself."

"Think so?" She looked so hopeful, so young and full of her future, his throat tightened. And he suddenly wanted things to work out for his son and this woman, more than he'd ever wanted anything for a long time.

"Kate," he said, reaching for her hand. "Fight for him. Get past his feelings, make him talk to you. You have far more power in this situation than you know."

"Thank you." She leaned across the table and kissed him gently on the cheek.

Jack, watching them from across the candlelit dining room, turned away and thought about all he'd lost.

Chapter Ten

❀ The following morning, Kate found herself out by
the pool for a sunrise yoga class. Both guests and
employees at the resort were encouraged to attend. Patti
and Cherry had talked her into it, even though the only
one of the three of them who had ever done any yoga
was Cherry.

"Yoga is *it*," Cherry had told them that morning as she
helped them drag their lazy, protesting bodies out of bed.
"Remember when Madonna told Oprah she doesn't even
use weights anymore? No weights, no treadmill or Stair-
Master, nothing but yoga. It's key. I've never had a
better body since I've started my practice."

And, Kate thought as she attempted to get into the
cobra pose, *with a body like Cherry's as evidence, you
couldn't really work up a serious argument against taking a yoga class.*

"You'll never have a double chin with this pose,"
Cherry whispered to her encouragingly.

"I may not live to enjoy that double chin," Kate whispered back. Why had she thought yoga would be easy, merely a simple series of stretches? This was hard work! Her body was sheened with sweat, but some of those poses, or *asanas,* as Cherry had called them, actually felt quite good.

"Now curl your toes on the mat and come up into Downward Dog," Matt, their instructor, said calmly. And Kate knew why her cousin had been enjoying her swimming class so much. Brad Pitt's hunky twin was alive and well on Maui. With an instructor like this one to look at, Patti would probably take up surfing next.

All three women watched their instructor, then imitated him and curled their toes under, then raised their bodies up.

"Elongate the spine," Matt said, his voice low and soothing. Mr. Zen.

"For him, I'd do anything," Patti muttered. Then she whispered, "Cherry! Cherry, that guy back there is looking at my butt!"

Not a hard thing to do, Kate thought, *considering that all three of us are pointing our butts up at the sky, stretching like, well, downward dogs.*

"Downward dogs," Cherry whispered. "They're all dirty dogs if you ask me—uh oh, Kate, red alert! Mr. Fling at eight P.M., right behind us."

Kate didn't look back until the pose called for it, and then she stretched her neck cautiously and snuck a peek. There Jack was, clad in only a pair of black athletic shorts, his feet bare. And he looked good, damn it. Too good. So that was how he maintained that gorgeous body.

They moved into the triangle poses, and when they reached the *asana* called Bound Warrior, Kate had to sneak another peek. To her dismay, Jack was no beginner. He'd easily moved into the advanced version of the pose, leaning down low and clasping his hands together in a seemingly impossible contortion.

And all she could think of was the various contortions they'd gotten themselves into during their one ill-fated night together.

"He *is* gorgeous," Cherry murmured. "I can't decide whether I think he or Mr. Legends of the Fall over here is sexier. I swear, this island is like a candy store for women."

"Take the Pitt look-alike; he's probably less trouble," Kate muttered, focusing on keeping her balance.

"Ah, but there's something about a dark-haired guy . . . my, my!"

And Kate gritted her teeth, knowing that Cherry had caught sight of Jack in the advanced version of the yoga pose. Well, she wasn't going to look at him again. He'd made his opinion of her very clear last night, with that chocolate dollar sign on her dessert.

One thing she was sure of, she was never going to give him the opportunity to hurt her again.

He couldn't keep his eyes off her and was so glad he'd snuck into yoga class and found a place almost directly behind her.

Kate looked so good in her peach-colored tank top and gray running shorts. Her dark hair was pulled off her face in a ponytail, and her feet were bare, the toenails painted a bright pink. She looked good enough to eat.

Jack shook his head to clear it, then concentrated on his friend Matt, realizing that he'd been staring at Kate and hadn't moved into the next position.

She wasn't bad. He didn't think she'd been doing

yoga that long, as she stayed with the beginner's versions of the poses, but she was extremely flexible.

His mind, traitor that it was, flashed back to that night in the cabana, and he remembered, in vivid detail, exactly how flexible she'd been. And Jack took a deep breath and hoped those erotic memories wouldn't cause him to totally embarrass himself in class.

He hadn't slept well last night. He'd been too ashamed. Before he'd fallen into a restless sleep, he'd decided that sometime today he was going to talk to Kate and at least apologize for what he'd done. Then if she never wanted to see him again—well, he'd work on convincing her that that was a really bad idea.

When class was finished and Kate was taking a swig out of her water bottle and wiping her face with a small white hand towel, she noticed Jack approaching her.

"Gotta run," she whispered to Cherry and Patti, who both seemed much more interested in mooning over the glorious Matt. "I'll meet you guys back at the villa, and we can go snorkeling."

"Sure thing," Cherry said, never taking her eyes off Matt. Patti didn't even register her comment.

Kate turned and fled.

Jack watched her go, disappointed. But he couldn't really blame her.

He wasn't going to make another scene. The resort wasn't that huge; it was like its own small world. He'd run into her again or make sure he did. He still had a little window of time.

Back at the villa, Kate took a quick shower to relax her aching muscles, then wrapped herself in a large, plush white towel.

"I'm going to miss you all when I go home," she said, giving the marble shower stall wall a pat. She moved over to the huge tub and caressed the gorgeous pink Italian marble. "And I want you to know that if I could figure out a way to take you all home with me, I would."

"Talking to yourself again, Kate?" she heard Cherry call as she came in the front door, and Kate had to laugh.

"I love this bathroom! This is what I want for Christmas!"

"Ain't that the truth," Cherry said, walking into the bathroom, going straight to the mirror and inspecting her face. "Do you think the lines around my eyes are getting worse?"

"No, it's just the harsh, unrelenting, and unforgiving glare of this tropical sun."

Cherry turned toward her and frowned. "Very funny. Listen, I think our Patti has the hots for Matt, and she's considering a fling."

Kate took another towel and began to dry her hair. "Considering my stellar track record, I'd say she's delusional."

"Have you taken a good look at that man's body?"

Kate sighed. "There has to be more to life than sex."

Cherry raised an eyebrow. "There is *nothing* more to life than sex for those of us who aren't getting any."

"Oh, please, like you've ever had any trouble in your life!"

"Actually," she said, turning toward the mirror and examining the very faint lines around her eyes, "I think I intimidate men. They rarely ask me out. Or at least the ones I want to ask me out rarely do."

Kate had never considered this. "That must be tough."

Cherry sighed. "I'm not quite sure what to do about it. Are you still up for snorkeling?"

"If you are. What about Patti? Do you think we should leave her with Matt?"

"I heard that," Patti said as she came in the front door. "Nope, I'm ready to go. All we have to do is stop by the concierge's desk and ask where the best beach is."

"Don't forget your sunscreen, Sugar. You look like you already have a bit of a burn."

Patti stuck out her tongue at Cherry. "I'm just a little flustered. You know, Matt."

Kate stopped drying her hair. It looked like Patti was really serious about having her fling.

"Doesn't he look just like Brad Pitt did in *Legends of the Fall*?" Patti said, standing in the bathroom doorway and holding on to the frame. "He's just so *yummy!*"

"He could be Pitt's evil twin," Cherry said. "In fact, I like that nickname. Pitt's Evil Twin and Mr. Fling. Hmm, I'm getting good at this naming stuff."

Kate didn't like the sound of this. Her cousin had just been dumped at the altar days ago; she wasn't ready for a sexual adventure.

"Patti . . ." she began.

"Don't say anything. I don't want to hear it!" her cousin retorted. "I endured four and a half years of boring, unexciting sex with Roger, including the humiliation of doing a striptease for him in front of the TV while the NASCAR races were on, so if I want to have a fling—"

"You stripped for that jerk?" Kate said.

"Only down to my bra and panties, but it didn't matter, he was into the race, and he told me to get out of the way."

"And that should have been your first gigantic clue,"

Cherry said. "Sugar, I'm *so* glad that wedding never came off. He did you a favor." She glanced at her watch. "Let's get going. We don't want to miss those fish."

One of the customers at Uncle Albert's restaurant had told Kate she had to get her snorkel and mask at Snorkel Bob's, so they went to the well-known rental place first thing. After renting their equipment and looking at some extremely funny postcards, all three women headed for the beach.

They spent all morning snorkeling. Cherry and Kate fell into fits of laughter when Patti finally got the hang of her snorkeling equipment, managed a good look underwater, and erupted up in a froth of waves to shriek, "Oh my God, there's a ton of fish down there!"

"We're not in Kansas anymore, Toto!" Cherry called out.

Even the people sunning themselves on the sand had laughed.

As Kate floated on the surface of the water and looked down at the various tropical fish beneath her, she began to relax. The yoga hadn't been all that relaxing once Jack had arrived on the scene, but now, floating in this glorious ocean, hearing the sound of her own breathing and looking at nature at its absolute finest, she could feel herself starting to unwind.

And she wondered, as she floated, if she ever really wanted to speak to Jack again.

Yes and no. There was a part of her that wanted to tell him off, to really go at him and ask him how he had the nerve to sit in judgement of her. There was another part of her that was so scared he'd do something to hurt her again that she didn't want to chance it.

Patti drifted by and grabbed her hand, and Kate surfaced, treading water and sliding her face mask up on top of her head.

"I just wanted to tell you, Kate, that I think I'm finally over Roger."

Kate frowned. *On day four of our vacation? That was quick.*

"No, I'm serious. I was floating along, and I was watching this little yellow fish, and I suddenly realized that I was happy. Really, really happy."

Quick tears stung Kate's eyes. This was the best news she'd had in a long time, and the whole point of their trip. "Then I'm happy for you, Patti."

"It's strange, you know? I was thinking to myself, would I have had as great a time with Roger if we'd gotten married and come here on our honeymoon? And I know the answer is no."

"Not if there were any sporting events being broadcast," Cherry said, swimming up. "That villa has a pretty nice TV. And ESPN."

Patti laughed.

"Don't even get me started on the liquor cabinet," Cherry said.

Patti glanced at both women, then said, "Let's hold hands."

"You are so summer camp," Cherry said, but she did as Patti requested.

The women held hands so they formed a circle of three, floating along in the turquoise tropical water.

"Good friends, good times," Patti said. "I just want you both to know how much you mean to me, because I love you both."

"Oh God, I can't stand the mushy stuff," Cherry said, but Kate could tell she was deeply touched.

"Hey!" Kate called out to an elderly woman with an outrageously colored swimming cap who was swimming nearby. "Would you take a picture of the three of us?" Earlier, at Snorkel Bob's, she'd bought a bright yellow waterproof disposable camera, and now Kate decided she wanted to capture Patti's happy moment.

"Of course, love," the woman said, with a strong Australian accent. She took the camera from Kate, swam back a bit, and called out, "Smile!"

And they did.

Jack had walked the resort's length and breadth, and still no sign of Kate.

She could be out sight-seeing. She could be shopping, or eating another dessert at a restaurant outside the resort. Maybe she'd driven up to Lahaina to see the sights.

Still, it frustrated him.

The longer the amount of time that elapsed between yesterday night's dinner and today, the guiltier Jack felt. He had to come up with a way to act in a reasonable manner where Kate was concerned.

Like that food fight. She'd dumped flour on him accidentally, and he'd actually thought it was kind of funny. Then she'd laughed, and he'd had this crazy urge to see her covered in powdered sugar—preferably naked, but a man couldn't have everything he wanted, at least not right away.

So he'd dumped half the bag on her, and she'd reached for the butter, and the next thing he knew, they'd been rolling around underneath one of the long kitchen tables.

He sighed, shading his eyes as he scanned the resort's beach. Where could she have gone? For as much as she frustrated him and made him crazy, and as much as his heart began beating faster and his stomach knotted when he caught sight of her, he realized one basic fact about the way he felt about Kate.

When she wasn't around, he missed her.

"I can't make up my mind," Kate said. "Maybe I'll get them all."

They'd snorkeled for hours, then had lunch at a little outdoor fish stand right by the beach. Kate had read about it in one of her guidebooks, and the concierge had assured her that it was definitely a place frequented by the locals.

Now they were having dessert—flavored shaved ice with a custard-like ice cream on the bottom of the paper cup.

"If you make a decision quickly, then you can eat it, and after we go shopping we can come back and have another one," Patti said. "There aren't too many calories in ice, are there?"

"It's the syrup, Sugar," Cherry said. "Literally. Hurry it up, Kate."

She gave the menu up on the wall one last look. "Guava shaved ice with fresh coconut ice cream. Large." She turned her attention to the two women. "You guys want to go shopping?"

"Yeah!" Patti said. "I want to get my mom some of those carvings and a pareo. And I think Dad would really like a print to hang in the restaurant."

"Good idea." Kate thought about this, then reached for her shaved ice, and the three women walked to one of the outdoor tables and sat down. "But I think I'll get a cab and head back to the resort."

"Kate, we can drop you off," said Patti. "What are you going to do?"

She'd given it a lot of thought. Part of what was making her crazy about Jack was that having been deprived of any sex life for some time, he'd awakened her body, and it was vigorously protesting this fact, as in *more, more, more*. So Kate had come up with a compromise.

"I'm going to have a massage."

"Wow! At the resort's spa?" Patti said.

"Yep."

"That actually sounds like a good idea," Cherry said, but at Patti's worried look, she said, "But Patti and I have a date with several stores."

He was getting desperate. Desperate enough to try a little white lie.

All right, a whopper.

"Hey, Lanie," Jack said, approaching the activities desk. "Could you help me out with something?"

"Sure, Jack. What do you need?" Lanie worked the front desk, and the slender redhead was one of his father's favorite employees. James McKenna thought of her as a daughter, as she'd worked for the resort since she was eighteen and was now in her late twenties. His father had a talent for making his employees family.

"I have to deliver some flowers, personally, to a Miss Kate Prescott. Right around two this afternoon. Any idea where she might be?"

"Let me check, and see if she's signed up for any activity," Lanie said, turning to her computer keyboard and typing in some information with her beautifully manicured fingertips. "Ah, here she is. She's getting a massage at that time in the spa. You might want to catch her as she comes out at three. The whole procedure should run about an hour, and she has Roberto. He's one of the best."

Roberto. Jack would have been jealous if he didn't know and like Roberto, and also know he had a live-in partner named Geoffrey.

Well, well, well . . .

"Thanks, Lanie. I think I'll do exactly that."

Entering the resort's spa had been like stepping into another world.

Again, she'd experienced the theme of opulence and marble, one of almost Roman decadence. Kate had been ushered into a private room and given a light terry robe. She'd undressed, donned the robe, and then been taken to meet her masseur, Roberto.

Now, just about finished with the massage, she lay facedown on the massage table, her buttocks covered with a towel, every muscle in her body totally relaxed.

Roberto had been an absolute dream. The man's hands had worked magic, and he'd had a great sense of humor as well. For the first time since she'd seen Jack, Kate could honestly say she felt totally relaxed.

Things were looking up, absolutely. Patti was happy, and that was all that really mattered. And her traitorous body had finally settled down. If it could talk, it would probably be saying, *I like, I like, I like, yeah, yeah, yeah . . .*

Kate turned her head and placed it in the cutout portion of the table. It had been formulated that way so she could lie with her head straight down, her neck straight. She could see through to the floor beneath her. But now, with her eyes closed and every muscle in her body totally relaxed, Kate just felt great.

She was in a fabulous mood. Nothing could disturb her now.

Jack hesitated just outside the spa's huge double doors. He was supposed to be a beach butler this afternoon, to a divorced woman, her three kids, and her boy toy boyfriend, but he'd asked Matt to take over for him.

Jack knew the risk he was taking. If he was caught bothering Kate while she was having a massage, no question about it, his dad would fire his ass faster than he could get on a plane and head back to Boston.

But he couldn't seem to stop himself. He had to see her.

Glancing to the right, then the left, he quietly opened the door and slipped inside.

She was in the third room on the left. He would have recognized the beautiful curve of that naked back anywhere. It had haunted his dreams.

He stared at that back, the way it sloped down to her cute little butt. Memories assailed him, all of them extremely erotic. What had he been thinking, that he could ever leave this woman alone?

"Roberto?" she murmured, and he knew she'd heard the door open. He had to act fast before she turned and saw him. Moving toward her, he put his hands on her shoulders and started to massage the muscles there.

"Mmmm . . ." She moved into his touch, practically purring, and it took all of his willpower not to just stretch out beside her on the table and start kissing her.

He was in big trouble. As good as fired. What the hell had he been thinking?

He cleared his throat. "Listen, Kate . . ."

Kate the cat who had been purring just seconds before reacted like he'd tossed scalding water on her. She shot up from the table, half-sitting, then madly reached for the small towel.

The view was glorious. Worth getting fired for.

"What the hell are you doing here?"

"Listen, I just had to come by and—"

"And what, destroy what little relaxation I've had this entire vacation?"

"Kate, listen, I've been looking for you all day—"

"I don't care. I don't want you anywhere near me! I know what you think of me. Damn it, Jack, get out, *now*, before I scream this place down!"

He was about to do exactly what she asked when he heard Roberto's voice outside the door. So he did what any sane man about to lose his job would've done. He dived beneath the draped table and hid.

Kate lay back down as Roberto came bustling in. He'd always reminded Jack of the actor, Nathan Lane; he had the same build and sweet face.

"How are we doing?" Roberto said.

We *being the operative word*, Jack thought.

Roberto didn't wait for Kate to answer as he touched her upper back.

"My, we're still quite tense. Honey, you should meditate or something."

"Or something," Kate agreed, and Jack almost jumped out of his skin as he looked up, craning his cramped neck. He realized there was a cutout in the massage table for a client's face, and Kate was looking right at him.

"All right, what's going on?" Roberto said as he worked his magic on Kate.

"There's this man," Kate began.

"There always is."

"Well," she said, staring right at him, "this one is particularly odious."

Jack couldn't believe what he was hearing. "Odious?" he mouthed, and she just grinned down at him. "Yep," she mouthed right back.

"I hear you," Roberto said calmly. "I'll just work on this tension, and you just breathe him right out."

"That sounds good," Kate said, then she stuck her tongue out at him, and Jack almost laughed out loud.

"Do you want me to press a little harder?" Roberto asked. "You really are tense."

"Do it harder?" she said, looking right at him, and Jack, looking up at her face, caught his breath at the suggestive tone of her voice. *What a little witch!*

"Yeah. I can do it as hard as you like."

"*Can* you?" Kate said, grinning down at him, and Jack realized that she was enjoying his predicament, seeing him trapped beneath the massage table, all six feet of his body painfully scrunched up.

"All right, Roberto," she said, and to Jack's ears her voice sounded almost unbearably sexy. "Do it as hard as you like."

"You go ahead and moan and groan if you need to, Kate. Just get it all out."

"Oh, I plan to."

And she moaned. And groaned. And all he could think of was that the exact same sounds had come out of that beautiful mouth that night they'd spent together. She'd been so incredibly wild and uninhibited that she'd taken his breath away.

And she knew it.

Jack knew she was enjoying his torture, because once, between moans, she'd had the nerve to wink at him! He kept looking at her, and it was almost as if the extended eye contact was making him even hotter for her.

"All set," Roberto finally said. "You're limp as a dishrag."

Too bad, Jack thought, *that the same couldn't be said for me.*

"Thank you, Roberto. Would you help me up?"

And Jack realized, at that moment, that Kate was leaving nothing to chance. She didn't want to be caught alone with him. A bad sign.

"Here you go," Roberto said, and Jack assumed the masseur was helping her into her robe. "The showers and steam room are just down the hall."

"Oh, I'm going back to my villa. I have a hot date with a marble tub full of bubble bath—a nice, long, sensual bath."

"And Mr. Odious is a bad memory?" Roberto said.

"Mr. Odious has about as much of a chance of sharing a bath with me as this island does of falling into the Pacific."

Jack stifled a sigh.

Message received and understood.

Kate made it back to her villa in record time. Hours would pass before Cherry and Patti returned from their shopping spree, so she had the place to herself.

She filled the tub with hot water and poured in a generous amount of plumeria-scented bubble bath. She got herself a glass of very good white wine from the villa's refrigerator and set it down on the edge of the tub. Then she pulled her hair up on top of her head with a band and spread a black charcoal and clay facial masque generously on her face, then tied on a gel eye mask.

Total and complete pampering, that's what she felt like. She might even give herself a pedicure afterwards. That massage had set the tone for her entire evening.

As she slid down into the scented water, Kate knew she should have felt elation at finally having been able to resist Jack. But somehow, she didn't feel too happy about the way she'd treated him.

She'd sunk to his level. And it disappointed her.

Oh well. She couldn't dwell on her one island mistake forever, her pathetic attempt at a fling. She was only on day four of probably the most glorious vacation she'd ever have the opportunity of taking in her entire life, so she was going to make the most of it.

Closing her eyes, she tilted her head back on the edge of the tub, against the luxurious bath pillow. Felt around for her glass of wine and took a generous sip.

And chilled.

Jack walked slowly back toward his employee apartment, taking the long way right past Kate's villa. Just more torture, but he had to.

There was no point in trying to see her. No point in trying to talk to her. She'd already judged him. How ironic that she'd done the exact same thing to him that he'd so expertly and thoroughly done to her. *Karma, all right. What you send out you get back, double time.*

He was walking past her doorway when he almost ran into Rosa, one of the maids. Eight months pregnant, she insisted on still working, and now was almost buried beneath a stack of thick, folded white towels.

"Rosa!" he said, delighted to see her. There were several of the employees who knew who he was, but had been warned by his father not to breathe a word to anyone for the duration of the ten-day experiment. But as long as they were both alone, who was to know?

"Jack!" she said, her pleasure evident in her shining brown eyes. "When did you get back on the island?"

"I've been here for a while. Let me take those towels for you."

"Thanks." She handed them over willingly. "Sometimes my back . . ." She rubbed her lower back, her face scrunched in discomfort.

"Why don't you go put your feet up somewhere, get a glass of juice or something?" he suggested.

"I just have to finish up here, then I can go home."

He knew without looking that the villa she was referring to was villa number six, and that his Miss Prescott was inside, relaxing in a tub of bubbles.

And Jack knew exactly what he was going to do—and that his job, and the deal he'd made with his dad, was as good as over if he was caught.

He didn't even care. Madness.

"All you have to do is deliver some towels?"

"Yes, and make the beds."

He formulated his plan quickly. "I'll do it for you. Go to the bar and get that fruit juice. Get off your feet until Bill comes to pick you up."

The relief in her eyes was all the encouragement he needed.

"You make beds?" she teased.

"You forget my infamous stint in military school."

"That's right." Rosa hesitated, then said, "It would be nice to get off my feet."

"Go," he said. "Just unlock the villa's door for me."

And with that, he sealed his fate.

Kate, after her glass of very good wine, had decided that the only thing the moment called for was a song.

Uncle Albert had karaoke night at the restaurant every Thursday, and she was usually the person who got up on stage first, set the mood and got everyone started. The family used to joke that while everyone else had an inner child, Kate had an inner ham.

So she had a repertoire of songs she especially liked.

Tonight's selection had to reflect her mood, so she was in the midst of a rousing rendition of "You Don't Own Me," when she heard the front door of the villa open.

"Hel-lo!" she called. "Cherry? Patti?"

"Housekeeping!" said a high-pitched, feminine voice.

Oh. Well. That was fine. They wouldn't care if she sang.

"O-kay," she called back. She leaned farther back in the enormous tub, bubbles frothing around her shoulders and neck, and continued to belt out the song. "Don't tell me what to do, don't tell me what to say—"

A brisk knock on the bathroom door interrupted her solo.

"Yes?" she said.

"Towels." Again, that same high-pitched voice. She sounded awfully young to be a maid, but who knew. Kate bet the hotel got employees of all ages. Everyone wanted to live in paradise.

"Come on in," she said. "I'm not shy."

She heard the bathroom door snick open, then the slight squeak of sneakers as the maid walked across the bathroom and began hanging clean towels on the racks.

She decided to start over.

"You don't mind if I sing, do you?" she said, from behind the face masque.

"Not at all. In fact, I think I'd rather enjoy it."

"Great." Totally uninhibited, feeling terrific after her massage, Kate began the song all over again.

"You don't own me, I'm not one of your little toys—"

She'd gotten to the big buildup and was belting out, "Don't tell me what to do" when a very distinctive and recognizable baritone joined in, their voices blending perfectly.

"Don't tell me what to say . . ."

"Aughhhhhh!" she said, ripping off her eye mask, shooting to her feet and staring in horror at the one man she'd never expected to see in her fantasy bathroom.

Jack!

"What the hell are you doing here?"

He only grinned.

"What have you got on your face?" he said.

Her eyes widened as she remembered the black clay facial masque and with a groan she slid into the tub and rubbed her face like mad, taking the entire masque off and probably some of her skin as well.

When she surfaced, sputtering, after staying underwater for as long as was humanly possible, he was still there. The nerve!

"If you were a gentleman, you would've left by now."

"I think we've already established I'm no gentleman, and you're no lady."

They stared at each other.

"What exactly is it that you want?" she said, keeping her eyes on him. To her absolute horror she could feel her nipples growing hard and that peculiar sexual softness permeating her body. That damn glass of wine, the massage, and bantering with Jack earlier—well, her body was primed for action, even though her rational mind was fighting to be heard, shouting something along the lines of, *This is a really, really bad idea . . .*

And she had the feeling he was reading her and knew exactly what kind of struggle was going on inside her.

"I thought," he said, slowly walking toward the tub, "that I wanted to apologize to you for last night. And I do." He moved a little closer, and she slid back in the tub, sloshing water over the side until her back was pressed as far away from him as she could get.

"But," he said, moving slowly closer, "seeing you in nothing but bubbles makes me start thinking about other things."

"What kinds of things?" she said, her throat suddenly tight and dry. She cleared her throat, but couldn't look away from him.

He moved closer, leaned in for a kiss.

"I'm drunk," she said when his lips were a breath away from hers, desperately trying one last time to salvage the situation.

He kissed her softly, and she was lost.

"Good wine," he whispered. "How much have you had?"

"One glass," she admitted.

"Cheap date," he whispered. "Is that all you need?"

He was searching for permission in her eyes. Leaving it up to her.

Damn it. She was absolutely insane, but this man had been haunting her dreams for as long as she'd known him.

Knowing she'd be sorry later but not caring, she grabbed a fistful of his polo shirt.

"Get in here," she whispered.

He laughed, then peeled the shirt over his head in record time.

Chapter Eleven

❀ She'd never had a better time in a bathtub. And the way Kate loved baths, that was saying something.

Jack locked both bathroom doors and rid himself of his clothing in record time, flinging shirt, shoes, and shorts madly around the bathroom. Within the minute he was naked and in the tub with her, then she was in his arms, then he was pressing her against the cool marble as he kissed her, and kissed her, then kissed her again. *Like we're both starving for each other,* she thought in a daze, then she stopped thinking as his hands slid over her body, up to her breasts, and reawakened every primal urge she'd ever possessed.

You are not in control of any of this, a desperate, quiet little voice in the back of her head insisted as she cried out and arched up against those hands. And Kate was a woman who needed control, who feared not being in control. It was something that had been set in her soul from the age of five, when she'd lost everything dear to her in one horrible moment in time.

Ah, shut up, came another voice, shockingly powerful, silencing the first. She recognized its wisdom and smiled against his mouth as she just let go and surrendered. Took that long fall into an ecstasy so strong, so irresistible, she couldn't fight it any longer.

There was no other word for what Jack did to her. It would be like trying to resist a tsunami; it came at you with such elemental, powerful force. As that tag line from one of the Star Trek movies had said, "Resistance is futile."

She was shocked by how ready she was for him, but her body had a sixth sense when it came to this man. Chemistry, electricity, who cared what it was called when it made you feel like this?

"What happened to just dating and getting to know a person?" she gasped against his mouth as he slid his muscular arms beneath her bent knees and pushed her legs apart.

"Fuck dating," he gasped back, and the rough, masculine force of his words sent a sharp thrill through her. The bathtub was slippery from all the bubble bath she'd used, and he couldn't seem to stop slipping. Neither could she.

That little rational voice wouldn't go away; it reared its ugly head one last time.

"Jack," she gasped out as he kissed his way relentlessly down her neck. "Will it really hurt you if I only use you for great sex?"

"It shouldn't, unless you like it really rough."

She laughed, they slipped, she grabbed his shoulders, and he swore, then lifted her out of the tub, both their bodies covered with bubbles.

"Shower," he said, and sounded so like a caveman,

communicating with one-word grunts, that she started to laugh.

"Yeah!" she managed to gasp out as he started toward the shower. Her body felt unbearably sensitive every place he touched her.

He carried her into the glorious marble stall, then turned on the water full force, hot and strong. It sluiced down over both of them, and he pulled her against him, right up against his chest, then lowered his head and kissed her as the water poured down over both of them.

She'd never felt more *alive*.

And she knew exactly where he was going and what he wanted as he maneuvered her up against the smooth marble side of the shower stall, because she wanted it, too. Couldn't think about anything else, didn't have room for it in her brain. Her arms came up around his neck, and she just held on as he lifted her hips, tilted them, pushed her legs apart and found her, sliding roughly inside her with one powerful thrust, right where she wanted him most.

She closed her eyes as her legs started to tremble, and he held them close against his waist. Then he lowered his forehead to hers, and she realized he was just as affected. And in the only corner of her mind that was still vaguely coherent, she realized Jack was as shaken up by this as she was.

Then he started to move, strong, powerful thrusts, and she just gave it up.

He thrust into her with such force, and it seemed as if every moment they'd been apart since that first night was behind that masculine strength. She kept kissing him, gripping his shoulders with a strength that had to hurt, but he barely seemed to notice.

She broke their kiss and moaned, feeling as if something had to happen to relieve the pressure, something had to come out of her. He grabbed her hair with one hand, held her still, kissed her again. He parted her lips and slowly slid his tongue deep inside her mouth, mimicking that other sexual rhythm, and she felt it all the way down in her belly.

Within minutes, they slid down the smooth marble wall, slowly, coming apart. Then he moved up over her, parted her legs with his body and slid inside her. And she felt that amazing shock that jolted her body all over again.

She was clawing his back and almost there when she heard voices coming from far away, then Jack's strangled curse. Feeling as if she were coming out of a fog, she looked up at him, then her entire body tensed as someone pounded on the bathroom door and called her name.

Cherry.

"Oh God," she whispered, "the door—"

"Locked it," he whispered against her mouth. He shifted, moved deeper inside her, and she moaned.

"Kate? Is that you? What are you doing in there?"

She almost started to laugh in nervous reaction. But thinking quickly, Kate cleared her throat and said, "You know me, it's just this *incredible* bathroom! I love it!"

"What?" Now Patti joined in.

"It's this shower! Just ecstasy!"

Jack chose this moment to tweak her nipple between his thumb and forefinger, and she yelped.

"Well, I *guess!*" came Cherry's voice through the door. "Kate, you're one sensual woman!"

"Oh yeah," Jack whispered, and Kate covered his mouth with her hand. He started to move, and as she was just at the brink, her head fell back, and she groaned softly.

"How long a shower are you going to take? Patti and

I want to show you all the cool stuff we bought. What, are you fooling around with the handheld shower attachment and thinking of Mr. Fling?"

Jack stopped pumping into her and Kate, her face totally aflame, just covered her eyes with one hand and wondered how things could get any worse. She felt his hand gently removing hers from her face, then she chanced a glance up at him as he cocked an amused eyebrow and mouthed the words, "Mr. *Fling?*"

Her humiliation was complete. And she hadn't even come.

"You're going to have to pay for that," he whispered, his warm breath tickling her ear. He leaned back, looking down at her, his lower body pinning hers to the shower stall floor. His expressive eyes were filled with repressed laughter.

Some little devil inside her that was never far from the surface with this man came to the fore. "Oh yeah? Make me!" She stretched her arms languidly above her head and watched the way he looked at her breasts. Then he lowered his head, kissed her, and got to work in earnest.

"Kate!" Patti pounded on the door. "When are you going to come out?"

"I'm coming!" she called.

"Almost," Jack whispered in her ear. He cupped her breast, and she moaned.

"Can I just come in and get some of that aloe lotion?" Patti said. "I think I got a little sunburn."

"No," Kate managed to gasp out, "I'm almost finished!"

"Not quite," Jack whispered. He pushed in really deep, keeping up an incredibly sensual rhythm, and she reared up and bit his shoulder to keep from screaming.

"Kate, let Patti come in and get that lotion, she's really burned!"

Kate couldn't answer. This was the kind of sex every woman fantasized about in her wildest dreams, the kind she'd always wanted. The kind that made your eyes roll back in your head and your mind go completely blank. At this point, she wouldn't have cared *who* walked into the bathroom, she *couldn't*—couldn't talk, couldn't think, she only knew she had to finish—

"Kate, you're really hogging the bathroom—"

"She's *just* about *done!*" Jack bit out, and just as he said the words she felt that inevitable tightening, that glorious point of no return, and she grabbed his shoulders so tightly she felt him wince, then whispered, "*Yes!*" as her whole body came apart.

And he followed her, finishing just a split second behind.

She didn't know how long they lay on that cool marble shower floor, she only knew that when she came to, Jack was breathing deeply, as if he'd been running for his life.

"Oh . . . my . . . God," she managed to squeak out.

"I think"—he took a breath—"that we should really think"—another breath—"about dating." He took another breath, then said, "You know, see each other."

"Dating? Are you kidding? We're *way* beyond dating."

He lay back on the marble floor, his forearm thrown over his eyes. He started to laugh, then she did, too.

She thought of something incredibly funny, rolled toward him, and whispered near his ear, "Do you think I'm easy?"

He came up on his elbow and looked down at her. "You're easy to be with. There's a difference."

"I am not! All we do is fight."

He traced a lazy finger over her collarbone, and she was amazed that her skin could spark to life with just that light a touch.

"We're not fighting now," he whispered.

"No, we're not." She felt a little flare of hope. There might be a chance for an actual relationship with this man, as opposed to just sex.

Not that she was complaining.

"But we can't do this all the time," she whispered.

"Why not?"

She thought about this for a moment, searching for a logical answer.

"I don't know." She snuggled closer. "I like you a lot better this way than arguing."

"Men get testy when they don't get—"

"Laid."

"What they want."

"Sex."

He kissed her. "Sex with you, Kate."

"That may be the sweetest thing you've ever said to me."

"Great. That was pathetic." He kissed her again, slowly and thoroughly, and she felt everything start up all over, it was that easy with this man.

"Can we just live here?" he said, when he broke the kiss.

"I think you need to leave," she said, but her voice was soft, sexually satiated, and lacked all conviction.

"Really?" He took her hand and moved it to points south where a certain part of his anatomy was already starting to stir.

"Oh my."

He smiled down at her, and she could tell he was disgustingly proud of himself.

"Hey, it's out of my control."

She started to laugh. "Oh, *please*—"

He moved over her, gently parting her legs as he slid inside, filling her completely. "Don't tell me what to do," he crooned in her ear, and she laughed again.

"This actually works with other women?"

"Baby, only with you."

He left shortly afterwards, rinsing off in the shower and then letting her dry his back as he grabbed a towel and attended to the rest of his body.

"No manhandling," he'd whispered, "or you'll get me going all over again and they'll find my exhausted, emaciated body at the bottom of that tub."

Before he'd left, he took her face in his hands and said, "I can't resist you, Kate. Date me." She liked the intensity she saw in those blue eyes.

"What do you think?" he whispered, and she knew he wasn't going to leave without an answer.

She hesitated.

Jack smiled down at her. "I'm sure that I'm up for this, Kate. I'm just not sure about you."

She loved it when he teased her, so she teased right back. Something about this man made the most outrageous statements come out of her mouth.

"Oh I'm *up* for this all right, I'm just not sure if *you* are. And that worries me."

The corners of his mouth twitched. "Baby, don't even waste time worrying. But I have to be honest. I'm wondering if you're going to be able to keep up . . ."

"Yes," she whispered back, putting a finger to his lips, and was so surprised to see the tiniest bit of relief in those blue eyes. He'd actually been worried she was going to say no. She sighed. "I'll date you. But what if we're really bad at it?"

"Not a chance." He hesitated. "I really am sorry,

Kate. About what I did last night, the thing with the dessert. It was stupid. I hated myself after I hurt you."

"I know." She kissed him. "No more of this millionaire stuff. I don't care what you do or how much money you make. You have to believe that."

He'd stared at her for a long moment, the strangest expression on his face, then said, "I really believe you mean that."

"I do."

Now, after seeing Jack to the villa's door, Kate glanced down the hallway in the direction of the bedroom that Patti and Cherry shared. Well, she had some apologizing to do as far as hogging the bathroom, so she might as well get it over with. She went into the bathroom and got Patti's bottle of aloe lotion, then started down the hall.

Both women were busily rearranging the contents of their suitcases, trying to fit in their various purchases, when she walked into the large bedroom.

"Hey guys!" she said brightly, handing Patti the lotion. Kate had showered with Jack, dried off, dressed in a pair of panties, and tied a gorgeous green pareo around her body that matched the color of her eyes. She felt as if she had energy flowing throughout her entire body and just couldn't stop smiling.

Cherry turned around and grinned at her. "Kate, you're glowing! I'm taking a shower as soon as possible! Any chance of renting Jack out for private parties?"

"Nope."

Patti was all smiles as well, and though Kate didn't want to talk about what had just happened, she was more than happy to look at their various purchases and hear about their day.

But they wanted to hear about hers.

Not mentioning the massage, she told them that Jack had come over and things had just sort of . . . happened.

"So now," she said, "we're going to try and date!"

"That's wonderful!" Patti said.

"Why ruin a good thing?" Cherry said.

"Oh, I don't know. Maybe these islands have softened my brains."

"Kate," Cherry said, folding one of the brilliantly colored pareos she'd bought and setting it inside her suitcase, "do you think you're the only woman on earth who's ever dreamed of having really hot sex with no repercussions? Puh-leeze! You, at least, had the courage to act on it! And you'll have some wonderful memories to take home with you when this vacation is over."

"Yeah, I will," she admitted, though the thought of leaving Jack and never seeing him again was doing funny things to her stomach.

"Well, I'm impressed," Patti said, spreading lotion on her shoulders and arms. "Remember our first night here at that little Italian deli, when you said you thought you'd barely be able to go out on a date? And look at you now!"

"She's just a quick study," Cherry said, and all three women laughed.

James was relaxing in the living room of his penthouse when Meredith called.

"Meredith?" he said into the phone as soon as he recognized her voice. "What's wrong?"

"Nothing, James. I think it's what's *right*. Hank and I had dinner at the deli tonight, and as we were taking a walk on the grounds, I saw Jack heading back toward the employee housing."

"And?"

"He looked extremely happy. He was whistling. I

even recognized the song. 'You Don't Own Me.' I just thought you'd want to know that he looked very happy."

"Thank you, Meredith." And as James hung up the phone, he smiled.

Jack lay in bed in his studio apartment and wondered at how he'd been lucky enough to find a woman like Kate. Beauty, chemistry, passion, caring, and all of it wrapped up inside the sweetest soul he'd ever met. She'd even forgiven him for all the stupid things he'd done to her since she'd arrived on the island, and a man couldn't get much luckier than that.

If he couldn't talk her into staying on the island, he'd fly back to wherever she was from—once he was no longer an employee here—and kidnap her.

He frowned. Caveman techniques wouldn't work with Kate. No, he'd have to take a more subtle approach, slightly more discreet. And he'd have to find a way to break it to her that he wasn't a bartender, that he was filthy rich, loved his work, wanted her with him for the rest of his life, loved—

Loved her.

I love her. The feeling came to him so easily, felt so right, that he didn't even try to fight it. He'd fought long and hard enough, determined to believe the worst of her when there was nothing bad to believe.

He'd fought so hard because he'd known he was taking that long fall.

He loved her. It had happened so quickly and hit him out of the blue. He hadn't planned for it to happen, but now that it was here, he was a happy man. Now that he'd just made love to her to the point of total exhaustion and knew he'd see her again tomorrow, he could finally relax.

He loved her. Kate Prescott, a woman he'd made

love to hours after they'd met. He'd bumped into her, and she'd rocked his world. He wasn't his businesslike, safe, and careful self around her; he was a crazy version of himself, risking his job and the entire resort for a glimpse of her, a word.

Now the only reason he wanted to take over the resort was to be able to lay it at her feet, give it all to her.

He smiled into the darkness. *Kate.* A woman who'd thrown a drink in his face and completely driven him to distraction for the last few days. A woman with a smart mouth, a sharp mind, a funny and unique take on life, and a body he couldn't seem to keep his hands off.

And she didn't give a damn if he had money or not. Though he wasn't quite sure how he was going to break that little truth to her. She'd probably be pissed at him, but what else was new?

He loved her. Well, okay.

He sighed, rolled over, and tried to sleep.

Kate lay in her bed and thought about Jack.

She was starting to fall for him, and that wasn't good. If this was just a fling, she couldn't afford to feel deeply. She couldn't bear the thought of starting to love him and then losing him. It would hurt too much.

But she couldn't seem to stay away from him or stop thinking about him.

A bartender. A general Jack-of-all-trades—literally—who, in his thirty-something years on this planet, still hadn't found himself or what he wanted to do. He seemed like such a terrific guy, she couldn't believe he hadn't advanced further in his work.

But she wasn't naïve enough to believe she could change him. If all he ever wanted to do was serve exotic mixed drinks to guests in bathing suits at the edge of the Pacific, then that was fine with her. If he wanted her to stay, if he gave her any indication that they could have a future together, maybe she could ask James to help her find an assistant chef's job on the island.

She only knew she wanted to be with him—and the intensity of her feelings terrified her.

Something had happened in that bathroom. The obvious was several incredibly spectacular orgasms. But on a deeper level, something else had happened. She'd felt herself starting to give over to him, to surrender to the powerful pull between the two of them. Kate knew she wasn't in control, and it scared her. What could possibly be just a vacation fling for him was turning into much more for her, and her emotions, her heart, everything she was and would ever be were at risk.

She wasn't the sort of woman who was cut out for a fling. Deep inside, she knew she wanted it all—the husband, the kids, even the goddamn white picket fence.

She wanted a family, because even though Patti had shared her own with Kate for so many years, she'd lost hers so long ago, and that wound had never fully healed. It probably never would until she had a family of her own. And the scariest thing was, she wasn't sure that Jack was a steady enough man to give that to her.

A bartender. A good-looking, happy-go-lucky bartender at perhaps the most fantastic resort in Hawaii. A man whose job put him among gorgeous women every day of his working life.

She sighed. No wonder he had no desire to advance to a more complex job. The one he had now was every guy's dream.

She frowned. But something didn't click. He didn't seem like the irresponsible type. There was more to Jack than he was letting on, and she didn't think that more included a wife and kids she didn't know about. There was just something that her intuition was screaming at her that didn't fit, but she couldn't quite figure out what it was.

More than anything, Kate wished she could confide in Patti, but she couldn't. Her cousin had just had her heart broken, and it would be painful to tell her that she was falling in love. Even though Patti had claimed she was healed, Kate knew how moody her cousin was, up one day and down the other. So to bring all her problems to Patti when she was struggling with so many of her own, she couldn't.

And Cherry . . . Cherry seemed like the sort of woman who understood all the rules in the battle of the sexes and really got what a true fling was all about. She also seemed like she could handle it, and accept the way life sometimes turned out. Kate wasn't sure Cherry would understand her feelings.

One step at a time . . . one little step. Go out with him, see what happens, take some time to observe him . . .

Oh God, in her worst nightmare, maybe she'd be the one sitting next to the airplane window and crying the entire way back to Chicago, drinking her Bloody Marys.

She didn't even want to go there.

Kate sighed, rolled over, and tried to sleep.

Kate had turned in early that night, leaving Cherry and Patti in the living room with some microwave popcorn and a great cable movie—*Legends of the Fall.*

"Why do you think he cut his hair?" Patti asked, watching Brad Pitt as the tortured hero.

"Oh Sugar, why do men do anything?" Cherry reached for a handful of buttered popcorn.

"Good point."

They watched the film in silence for a while, then

Cherry said, "You know, all things considered, I think Kate's having the best vacation of all of us."

Patti reached for another handful of popcorn. "Yep. I'd agree."

Cherry sighed. "Sure beats a luau."

Chapter Twelve

Kate woke to the sound of the phone shrilling softly by the side of the bed.

She reached for it after a few rings, realizing that Patti and Cherry had probably gone to the breakfast buffet and weren't in the villa to answer it.

"Hello?" she said, and her voice sounded uncharacteristically husky with sleep.

"Hey, sexy. Is that your usual morning voice?"

She smiled, sat up. Jack.

"Yeah."

"Hmmm."

Silence on his end of the line, but it wasn't uncomfortable.

"I've come up with a date," he said.

"You have? Something outside a bathroom, I hope."

"You're complaining?"

She had to laugh. *Men!* "Nope."

"Okay. Here's the deal. I'll pick you up at six. Dinner. You and me."

"Dinner?"

"Yeah, you know. You, me, food, conversation. Maybe dessert. Too risky for you?"

Kate leaned forward. *Yeah. Risky.*

"Kate?"

"I'd love to. Six tonight. Casual?"

A short silence, then he said, "No. Get dressed up. Put on the prettiest dress you brought with you. And heels."

She smiled. "I brought this little black dress—"

"I can just imagine." He laughed. "Sleep in, we might have a late night."

She already knew where this dinner would probably lead. Kate leaned back on her pillows and tried to relax. "What are you up to today?"

"I just finished working the breakfast buffet, so I'm going to go take a nap, then later I'm a beach butler for some family from Michigan."

The image of Jack stretched out on a bed taking a nap was unbearably sexy.

"No," he said, and she jumped at the realization that he knew exactly where her thoughts had strayed. "If I see you before six, we won't sleep."

"Yes, *sir!*"

He sighed. "Why do I just not believe you?"

She laughed, he said good-bye, then she hung up the phone and snuggled back down beneath the covers.

She was insane, that was all there was to it. All she knew was that if this was insanity, well, she'd never felt better in her life.

The front door of the villa opened, and she heard Patti's voice saying, "Ka-ate! Oh, Ka-ate! Pancakes!"

She could continue her snooze after breakfast.

* * *

As Jack walked away from the main lobby, a thought struck him.

Romance. Women loved all that stuff. And while he'd never set much store by it, he found that he wanted to make Kate happy. So he headed for the resort's main gift shop and walked in the door.

"Hey, Florence," he said, greeting the gently rounded, petite, white-haired woman dressed in a brilliantly colored muumuu behind the main register.

She glanced around the shop, making sure they were alone, then said, "Jack! Your father said you'd be working at the resort just like a regular employee, but I have to say that I didn't really believe him."

"Here I am, just off the breakfast shift."

Florence laughed, then came around the counter and scooped him into a warm hug. "I'm so glad to see you back here where you belong!" She stepped back, eyed him and said, "What do you need?"

"There's this woman."

Florence raised her eyebrows. "Excellent! Flowers, chocolates, perhaps a card?"

"That all sounds good. How about—" Suddenly he was struck by his limited budget. "How about three perfect red roses, and . . ." He walked over to the chocolate display and studied it, then said, "That box of six truffles."

"Excellent choices. Are they to be delivered?"

"Yeah. Villa number six. Kate Prescott."

"And a card?"

He frowned. "Something elegant. Nothing too fussy."

"It's as good as done. Do you want to charge that?"

"No, I'll pay cash." He pulled out his wallet, paid,

signed the small card, and gave Florence a kiss on the cheek good-bye.

As soon as Jack left the shop, Florence picked up the store phone and pressed one of the lines. "James? Jack just left. He ordered candy and flowers for that Miss Prescott in villa number six. What do you want me to do?"

She briskly wrote down what he told her.

"Three dozen long-stemmed red roses? And that's the thirty-six ounce assortment of Teuscher chocolates and truffles? Got it."

When she hung up the phone, she was grinning.

"Kate! Kate, you're not going to believe this!" Patti's voice was high-pitched and excited, and Kate opened the bathroom door, toweling off her hair.

"What?"

"My God, Sugar, he bought out the gift store." Cherry was carrying in a vase of a dozen of the most beautiful red roses Kate had ever seen in her life. Patti had another, and the deliveryman from the gift store had a third.

"What?" she said, standing there in a candy apple red pareo, holding the towel she'd been drying her hair with and staring at the flowers.

"And chocolates," the deliveryman said, handing her an enormous golden box, along with a small card. "You're Miss Prescott?"

"Yes," said Kate, thinking that this was what it felt like to be in a dream.

"Sign here, please."

Dazedly, she did so. But as he started to leave, she said, "No, wait! I can't accept these! He's just a bartender, this will bankrupt him."

"Kate, let him give to you . . ." Cherry began.

"Let him give to *me!*" said Patti, grabbing the generous box of chocolates and heading for the bedroom she shared with Cherry. "I'm a little depressed today, and I remember reading an article that said there's something in chocolate that's good for depression."

"There's something in chocolate that's good, period, and those look like they're from Switzerland," Cherry said, taking off after Patti.

Kate sat down in the living room and stared at the vases of roses.

What was Jack doing? This was insane, his spending this kind of money on his limited budget. It didn't show a whole lot of fiscal responsibility. And he was also taking her out to a really nice restaurant for dinner tonight? Her mind made up, she started toward her cousin's bedroom.

Patti and Cherry had each taken out a truffle and almost taken a bite when Kate yelled, *"Stop!"*

They both stared at her, incredulous.

"I really *like* this guy," Kate said, horrified to find her voice trembling. "And he can't afford this, so I'm sending it back!"

Cherry stared at her, then carefully set her chocolate truffle back in its exquisite little paper cup. Patti did the same.

"Kate," Cherry began. "I think Jack's the sort of man who gets a lot of pleasure out of giving. I think you'd hurt his feelings terribly if you sent all this back, and I'm not just saying this because I want to eat some of this chocolate, though I'm honest enough to admit that I do."

Patti just stared at her folded hands. Then she said quietly, "Kate, let him give to you. Don't be so controlling. I think it means a lot to Jack to be able to give all this to you. Be glad he's not stingy like Roger was. I mean, his idea of a honeymoon was a quick drive up to Wisconsin and a bratwurst dinner, not a beautiful place like this."

"Bratwurst?" Cherry raised a perfectly shaped eyebrow. "*Bratwurst?* That and that striptease and you were even *contemplating* marrying this beast?"

Patti shrugged her shoulders.

Cherry turned back to Kate. "You know, if a man's stingy with gifts, chances are he's stingy in bed. And both Patti and I know, from yesterday's adventure in the bathroom, that Jack is anything but stingy in that department. We heard you making all that noise, Sugar. So why are you so surprised that he'd go all out with a few presents?"

Kate sat down on the queen-sized bed across from her cousin, her friend, and the enormous box of expensive chocolates. And considered what Cherry and Patti had said.

Damn it, they were both right. She was scared and trying to control things.

Not a good idea.

Kate ran her hand through her damp hair. Looked up at the two other women. And grinned.

"He's nuts," she said finally. "Oh shit, I'm truly doomed. Pass me one of those truffles."

Patti and Cherry only smiled.

Afterwards, Kate asked Patti to take a walk with her on the beach.

They both put on their bathing suits and high SPF sunscreen, then walked to the far end of the resort's beachfront property where fewer people were sunbathing. Then Patti lay out a large beach towel on the sand, and they sat on it and stared at the waves as they frothed up the white sand, then slid back into the ocean.

They'd been quiet as they walked, but now that they were both sitting, Kate glanced at her cousin. As usual, Patti knew something was up and just waited for Kate to tell her what it was.

She pulled her knees protectively up to her chest and laid her chin on them.

"I don't know if I can do this," she whispered.

"With Jack," Patti said.

Kate nodded her head, then her eyes filled and she dropped her forehead to her raised knees, ashamed of her weakness.

"Oh, Kate." Patti put a hand on her shoulder, but didn't say anything.

Kate looked at her cousin, her eyes damp. "I've just screwed things up so badly. I thought I could be all sophisticated and go for this stupid fling, but now . . . things have happened so fast . . ."

"You love him," Patti said simply.

Kate lowered her head and started to cry. Patti moved closer, then put her arms around Kate and waited until she stopped crying.

"What am I going to do?" Kate whispered. "I can't do this. He wants me to go out to dinner with him tonight, and that only means we'll get closer, and probably make love again, and I don't know if when it's time to leave if I can even get on that plane home, and then if he doesn't want me . . ."

"He does," Patti whispered confidently.

Kate sniffed, wishing she'd thought to bring tissue. "You read too many of those romance novels."

"Don't you ever wish life could be a little like that?" Patti said, her tone wistful.

Kate hadn't thought of this. "What do you mean?"

Patti stopped hugging Kate and sat cross-legged, her hands in her lap in front of her. "You're not going to like what I'm going to say, because I'm coming from emotion, and you're trying to be logical and stay in control."

Kate had to smile. How well Patti knew her.

"Kate, I was really hurt by what Roger did to me, but seeing you and Jack together has helped me to heal."

"What?" This was the last thing she'd expected to hear from her cousin.

"Seeing the sparks fly when you two are together made me see what Roger and I *didn't* have. And I think that relationships are so hard, they can get so mixed up, that you have to have that spark, that really intense chemistry, to keep them going. When you threw that drink at Jack, that was the moment I knew that I didn't feel for Roger one-hundredth of the feeling that you already had for Jack."

Kate sat silently, considering this.

"And when you came out of the bathroom last night, I wish you could have seen yourself! You were lit up like a Christmas tree! You looked so beautiful."

"Really?" Kate said. She felt shocked, hearing Patti's words, and she knew they were true.

"Really. So beautiful. You looked like a woman who had been well-loved by the man she loves."

"Sex," Kate said. "Terrific sex, but sex."

"Nope. There's more to the two of you than that. I have never, ever seen two people more fascinated with each other. You guys are just . . . irresistible to each other!"

"So you don't think it's just me to him? You think he feels it, too?"

"Yep. You looked so beautiful last night, Kate, that was the exact moment I let Roger go, once and for all. Because I realized that I want what you and Jack have together, and if I never feel that, I don't want to settle for something safe and secure and boring. That's what I did with Roger, and it didn't even turn out to be that secure. He dumped me."

"Patti—" Kate began.

"No, don't sugarcoat it, Kate. When a man says he needs time to find himself or he has to have some of that space to work on his own issues or he doesn't want to get married right away, it simply means 'not you.' Not you. Roger was saying, not *me*. And I was devastated, because I'd put so much time and energy into the whole thing with Roger, and then I see you and Jack and I had this big epiphany."

Kate remained silent, waiting.

"I realized you shouldn't have to work so hard to get someone to love you. It's either there or it's not. And it's there with you and Jack, Kate. And I think you should embrace it, go for it, *treasure* it. So few people in life ever get what the two of you have, a huge love, the love of their life, a fine romance—even a passionate fling! So many people live their lives playing it safe and sitting in judgement of other people."

"I never thought of it that way."

"So maybe in a few days you'll get on that plane to Chicago because for some reason it doesn't work out with Jack. But you'll always have those memories. Those moments. You'll always be able to remember those feelings. Just keep telling yourself, *so few people have it, or ever have it.* Even if you only have it while we're here on the island, you're one of the very few that ever does."

Kate could feel herself gathering both courage and conviction from her cousin. She'd never thought of her fling with Jack this way, but it felt right.

"Kate, you have something with Jack that's worth moving toward, worth fighting for. And for the record, I think Jack is meant for you, and you're meant for him."

"You're the best," Kate said, linking arms with her cousin. "How did you get so smart?"

Patti looked out over the ocean. "Everyone thinks I'm so quiet. What I'm really doing is watching all of you." She glanced at Kate and smiled. "You learn a lot that way."

Cherry was leaning out on the metal railing surrounding the villa's balcony when she saw Kate and Patti walking slowly up the beach toward her.

She knew Kate had probably wanted some time alone with her cousin in order to talk with her about her feelings for Jack. And for a moment she'd wondered what it would be like to be that close to a woman, to be able to confide your deepest fears and heartbreaks, your vulnerabilities.

She'd never had that luxury, though she'd longed for a close woman friend all her life. She'd never known her mother, hadn't had a sister, and by the age of twelve she'd realized that the way she looked had been upsetting to other women. Cherry had realized early in life that most women were in some sort of subtle competition with each other, and—with no false modesty—she'd realized she had the sort of flamboyant and luxurious beauty that caused men's heads to snap around when she walked into a room.

Needless to say, she didn't have any female friends.

Until now.

Until Kate, fearless, smart, compassionate Kate. Kate was a fighter and loved as hard as she fought. And privately, Cherry thought she had a pretty good chance of nabbing Jack. He was crazy about her and, as he was just a bartender, lucky to get a woman like Kate.

And Patti. Patti, whose dreamy, ethereal blonde looks concealed a sharply intuitive mind and a heart so

large and loving that Cherry was surprised she hadn't
been hurt far worse than she had. But Patti also had a
spine and would go to the mat for those she loved. All
Cherry had to do was remember the way Patti had insisted she stay at the villa when she had nowhere else to
go, and her eyes would start to sting with tears she'd
quickly blink back. She'd learned long ago that emotions were a total luxury, and she certainly couldn't afford them.

"Hey, you two," she said. "While you were down at
the beach, I asked Matt to give me a lift to a local market. I bought some steaks and chicken and stuff to mar-
inate them in, along with some other things so we can
try out this grill and have a full-fledged barbecue for
lunch."

"What a great idea," Kate said. Cherry noticed that
her eyes were red and swollen, but wisely said nothing

"Can we make potato salad?" Patti said.

"You can make whatever you want," Kate said, heading toward the sliding glass doors that led inside to the
living room. "I'm going to try and take a nap."

"Kate," Cherry called after her.

Kate stopped, turned.

"I have some killer perfume if you want to borrow it
for your dinner date tonight."

"I'd like that," Kate said, then entered the villa.

She looks tired, Cherry thought. Patti had sat down at
the patio table and had kicked off her sandals. She was
staring out at the ocean, a few hundred feet away.

"We need to help her with this," Patti said. "Kate's
kind of fragile right now."

"I know," Cherry said, and she realized she was finally going to be part of a female relationship that
worked.

*   *   *

Kate couldn't sleep. She tossed and turned in her cool bedroom, finally gave up, went in the bathroom and splashed water on her face, pulled on shorts and a top, and let herself out the sliding door that faced the ocean.

She could hear Patti and Cherry in the kitchen, deciding what side dishes to make for lunch, but she decided to take a walk down to the beach, this time to the more crowded side.

She wanted to see Jack.

It didn't take her long to find him. He was playing cards with the family from Michigan, a boisterous game of poker that was clearly getting quite rowdy, with lots of laughter and joking. While the father and three of his older sons were in the game with Jack, the mother and her two daughters were sunbathing not that far away. Jack had supplied them with a cooler of drinks, but now he seemed to be providing the entertainment as well.

"How does this boy keep *winning*?" the patriarch of the family roared, throwing down his cards. "Sure you don't want a cigar, Jack?"

"Can't smoke on duty," was his reply as he eyed his cards. He glanced up and saw her. "I'm out," he said suddenly. "Just for the next few hands."

One of the sons looked up from his cards and saw Kate. "We can wait."

"Nah." Jack grinned. "You're right, I've already taken too much of your money. Deal me out of the next few hands. But I'll be back." He stood up, grabbed his soft drink, and headed toward her.

"Hey, what's up?" he called, and she felt a little burst of pleasure at the way he was so obviously glad to see her.

"I wanted to thank you," she said. "For the flowers and . . . and the chocolates. They were really lovely."

"Ah, it wasn't much," he said. "I wish I could've given you more."

She frowned, puzzled. *More?* He'd given her too much, considering what he probably earned in a month. But maybe she was wrong, maybe the tips were incredible, and he didn't have to worry financially as much as she thought he did.

"It was plenty, Jack," she said. "In fact, I was a little worried about . . . well, I mean, you're also taking me out to dinner tonight . . . and I thought . . ."

He was looking at her with a very strange expression on his face, and Kate realized she'd stumbled into an emotional minefield.

"I thought maybe . . . maybe we could go somewhere less expensive."

The minute the words were out of her mouth she regretted them.

He looked away from her, and she had a feeling he was trying to contain his annoyance. When he glanced back at her, she sensed a definite chill.

"Let me ask you something, Kate. If we were to go dancing later on tonight after dinner, would you want to lead?"

His question stunned her, and all of a sudden she saw herself through his eyes. Trying to make everything work according to a little master plan of her own.

Controlling because she was so scared.

"Forget it," she muttered, turning on her heel and walking off.

"No," he said, coming up beside her, then walking right into her path so she bumped into him before she could change direction. He grasped her upper arms, so gently. She couldn't look up at his face.

"Am I that horrible?" she said.

"Kate." He waited until she looked up at him. "Kate, do you trust me?"

You, I trust. My heart, I'm not so sure about.

She nodded her head.

"Do you trust me to make the decision as far as where we're going to go tonight?"

Miserable, she nodded her head. "Do you still want to go out with me?"

"Yes!" He pulled her into his arms and rested his chin on top of her head. "Yes. I just don't want you telling me what to do, even if you think it's for my own good."

She rubbed her cheek against the front of his polo shirt. They were silent for a moment, and he just held her.

"I think," Jack said, "that a lot of people depend on you to be strong and to do things for them. Am I right?"

Kate thought about that. She was her uncle's right-hand person at the restaurant; her aunt had always counted on her to be sensible and strong. And when it came to her relationship with Patti, it seemed that she'd always been the leader, Patti the follower.

"Yeah." She let out her breath slowly, softly, and relaxed against his chest.

"Well, you don't have to be strong with me," he whispered, his breath warm against her ear. "You get to relax, and let me do the work."

It sounded wonderful . . . and frightening, to relinquish that control.

"Can you let me?"

She nodded her head.

"Mad at me, Kate?"

She shook her head, her throat tight.

"Want to go dancing later?"

She punched his chest lightly, and he laughed.

* * *

Kate barely touched her lunch, she was so nervous. And it wasn't that the food was bad, because Cherry and Patti had outdone themselves.

"Kate may shine with desserts, but Patti, you really know how to make a mean potato salad," Cherry said. "I swear, between those desserts the other night, those truffles, and now this feast, I'm going to have gained about ten pounds once this vacation is over."

"We're almost halfway through it," Patti said wistfully. "Day five of ten."

"Oh, don't mention it," Cherry said. "I'd like nothing better than to stay in paradise forever. I think Jack has the right idea, living here."

Kate forked up another bite of potato salad, chewed and swallowed. Normally she loved Patti's potato salad, but today she barely tasted it.

Jack's dancing analogy had really gotten to her. Did she always have to lead? That had to be why she had so much difficulty with men, because if she were honest with herself, she didn't trust most of them. She'd seen her girlfriends go through so much trouble with their boyfriends, and then Patti's horrible breakup with Roger.

But they were all weak men. And Jack's not weak.

He might be only a bartender, but he was a strong man. She'd hurt him when she'd implied he couldn't afford their date, or that he might be overextending himself.

She was ashamed of herself for voicing such thoughts to him. And she realized that they'd actually had their very first fight since they'd officially started dating and emerged relatively unscathed.

Ah well, let it go. He has.

"Want me to do your makeup tonight, Kate?" Cherry said.

She glanced up. "Yeah, I'd like that a lot."

Cherry smiled, a very wicked little smile. "Do you want to go for the angel baby innocent look, the smart sophisticate, the party girl, or a little bit of the slut?"

"The slut," Patti said, her mouth still full, then she laughed.

"What do you think?" Kate said.

"Me, with a guy like Jack . . ." Cherry didn't even hesitate. "The slut. Men love it. You know, the black liner, the shiny mouth, wild, sexy hair—the basics. Men. They're so predictable. So easy."

"Then the slut it is," Kate said. "Pass me those chicken wings."

Later that afternoon, Patti had her second swimming lesson and decided she was going to seduce Matt.

She was toweling off afterwards when she said, "So, am I your last lesson for the day?"

"Yep."

She took a deep breath. "We had a barbecue today for lunch, and we fixed way too much food. Would you like to come over tonight around six-thirty and help us eat a bunch of it?" She knew men and she knew food, and they were almost always a perfect match.

"Wow, that'd be great."

Kate stared at herself in the bathroom mirror. Cherry had clearly outdone herself.

"Wow," she said. "*Wow.*"

"You're a stunner, Kate," Cherry said, starting to gather up her makeup. "And you should go beyond that natural look once in a while."

While most women had a little zippered bag that stored all their makeup, Cherry had a case that resembled a fishing tackle box, filled with pots and tubes and brushes.

She'd worked magic. Kate felt she'd never looked better, more sexy, more confident. And her hair! It framed her face in a wild, sexy mass.

She felt like a goddess.

"Give him hell," Cherry said as she packed up her makeup case.

Jack arrived promptly at six. She answered the door, and he just stared.

"Jesus," he whispered.

"Nope, just me," she said brightly as she stepped outside. She put her hand gently on his forearm and looked up at him, willing herself to say the words that were so hard for her to articulate.

"Okay Jack, I'm totally in your hands."

He couldn't seem to stop looking at her, and Kate silently blessed Cherry. Nothing made a woman as confident as knowing she'd really shaken up the man she adored.

"Baby, you're in big trouble."

Chapter Thirteen

❀ They didn't even leave the resort.

Kate resisted the urge to ask Jack where they were going as he led her toward a sleek bank of elevators off the main lobby. The doors slid shut, and he inserted a key card, then pressed one of the buttons.

For one wild moment she thought he was just taking her to bed, no dinner and no date, then the elevator doors slid open and she walked out into a fantasy.

A penthouse.

The double doors leading to the lavish living area were open, and she saw a small round table with two chairs, set with beautiful silver, exotic flowers and flickering candlelight. The culinary smells filling the air were incredible, and her chef's sense of smell totally appreciated them.

"Jack?" she said, stopping at the foyer, puzzled. This wasn't what she'd expected.

"Friends in high places," he said, smiling down at her.

"Oh."

"Come on, Kate. Dinner awaits."

So she stepped into the dream.

"Too innocent," Patti said, staring into the villa's bath-room mirror.

"Sugar, you *are* innocent," Cherry said, collecting her makeup.

"But I wanted something—I don't know, a look with a little more of an edge."

"You're the wrong type," Cherry said, packing up her makeup case. "If I put all that black liner on you, you'd look like a little girl who was playing with her mother's makeup. Think of it positively. Men love that whole innocent thing. Makes them feel like conquering heroes, your first lover, that sort of thing. I'd exploit it."

Patti sighed. "I don't even know if he likes me," she whispered.

"He's coming to dinner, isn't he?" Cherry patted her shoulder. "I'll lay low, stay in our bedroom, read. He won't even know I'm here. And if anything happens, the two of you can use that downstairs bedroom." The villa had three large bedrooms, two upstairs and one down-stairs. Patti and Cherry had one, Kate the other, but the one downstairs was free.

Patti sighed. She hoped to put it to good use. Her one dream since arriving on the island and seeing Jack and Kate strike sparks was to have some sort of fling her-self. If she was honest with herself, sex with Roger had been rather ho-hum for quite some time. She'd thought she'd be safe marrying him. Safe and protected.

She'd never thought about being dumped. Or bored. Matt wouldn't be boring.

"I'm going to just let things take their course," she

said, more to give herself encouragement than anything else.

"I'd use a little booze," said Cherry, tapping a finger against her chin. "Get things going. Mai Tais. You have to admit, you're in the place for it."

Patti looked in the large mirror, catching Cherry's eye. "Too obvious." She sighed again. "*You* could get away with that. Me? Nope."

"I know. I'll whip you two up a pitcher of Daiquiris. That's nice and subtle."

"You think so?"

"I *know* so. Just let me get down into the kitchen before Pitt's Evil Twin gets here."

Jack walked Kate to the table in the dining area overlooking the Pacific and pulled out her chair. Once she was settled, he took his seat, then looked at her across the small, intimate table.

Stunning. She'd somehow transformed herself again, and he found himself wishing they could just whip through the various courses and head straight to the bedroom.

But he couldn't do that to her. Romance, that was what he wanted to give her. An actual date. A night she wouldn't forget. And as his father was visiting close friends on the island of Oahu and wouldn't be back until late the following day, Jack felt safe in using his private floor of the extensive McKenna penthouse.

He found himself wanting to impress Kate.

"Wine?" he said, and she nodded.

He took the bottle of wine that was chilling by the side of the table and expertly opened it—one of the skills from all his years of actual bartending. He poured her a small amount, she tasted it, then he filled her glass and his own.

"Trying to seduce me?" she said, and the mischievous expression on her face made him smile.

"Why do you say that?"

"Oh, nothing." But she blushed slightly, and he had the feeling her mind was on the same track his was.

"I'll get our salads," he said. Pierre, a friend of his who was now one of the master chefs at the resort, had fixed an extraordinary meal for the two of them earlier in the day. Now all he had to do was head to his private kitchen and bring out the salad and bread, and, later, heat up the main entree. Dessert was simple as well.

And then . . .

Then was totally up to Kate.

"Hi," said Patti after she answered the door. Matt looked even more handsome; he'd taken a shower and was dressed in a pair of nice slacks and another polo shirt. He'd made the effort to dress up a bit, and she was glad.

"Hey. You look really cute."

Cute. That one word was the bane of her existence.

"Come on in," she said, her heart beating madly in her chest. "I thought we could eat out on the patio."

"Fine with me."

Cherry heard the villa's doorbell from her bedroom, and she briefly set down the Michael Crichton paperback she'd bought at the gift shop.

Matt had arrived.

She sighed. Kate and Cherry were women unlike any she'd ever met. They seemed so—*innocent,* for want of a better word, almost retro. Maybe it was that whole Midwest ambiance. Maybe it was because both of them had been protected and loved for most of their lives and had been part of what sounded like a really wonderful family.

Living in Las Vegas, she'd seen a lot, much of which she wished she hadn't. If Patti's and Kate's romantic escapades resembled something you'd find in a romance novel, her love life—her whole life—was straight out of a horror novel. She'd just about given up on men before she'd come up with her scheme to nab a millionaire.

And even that wasn't going as planned.

She hadn't expected this vacation from her life, ten days of not having to worry about anything. Ten days with two extraordinary women who'd made her believe that female friendship was actually possible. Ten days to relax and reevaluate her life and figure out what the hell she was going to do with the rest of it.

She picked up her novel, determined to read. She wasn't that worried about Patti. Matt seemed like a nice enough guy, and if he gave Patti a good time in bed, that would go a long way toward making her feel like a desirable woman again.

If only it were that easy . . .

She'd seen too much of the seamier side of life, and it had shaped her. She couldn't seem to let it go. Seeing Kate and Patti pursue what they wanted in both love and lust had brought a lot of bittersweet feelings to the surface. There had been nights in this villa she'd lain awake and thought about how her life might have been different . . .

Don't go there.

She picked up her novel and began to read.

"Daiquiris?" Patti said brightly.

"Cool."

She went into the kitchen and brought out the pitcher,

along with two large glasses. She poured Matt a drink, then one for herself, and sat back down.

"This is really nice of you," Matt said, then took a swig of his drink.

Nice. Cute. She couldn't stand it.

"Would you have sex with me?" she said.

Matt spewed his drink back out, then wiped his mouth with the back of his hand and stared at her, incredulous.

Kate sighed as she set down her fork. They'd progressed to dinner, and the shrimp and pineapple curry had been out of this world. She hadn't eaten as much of it as she'd wanted to, she was just too nervous around this man.

"Didn't like it?" Jack said, and she could tell he was concerned.

"No, it was fabulous. It's just . . . I'm a little . . ." She glanced down at the plate in front of her. "Nervous," she finished softly.

"Kate."

She glanced up at him.

"Nothing has to happen. Okay?"

She nodded her head.

"I didn't bring you up here with any ulterior motive."

She narrowed her eyes at him. *Please.*

"Okay, so I did. But I want you to know that you're in charge, and I'd have to be a total pig to make sex a conditional part of this date."

"So we're kind of starting over?"

"In a way."

She leaned back in her chair. "I find dating kind of complicated. I never know if I'm doing the right thing."

"Tell me about it."

"Oh, please. Bartending in paradise? The women must just fall at your feet."

"That hasn't always been my experience. And I haven't always been a bartender."

"Really? What else have you done?"

"I took some business classes once. And put a lot of thought into going into resort management."

"What do you want to do now?"

He took a sip of wine. "I think my life is going to change drastically in the next week, and that's all I'm going to say."

She leaned forward. "Now you've intrigued me."

He smiled. "Good."

"And that's all you're going to say."

"Yeah."

"Hmmm. Okay, then would you answer some questions I have about dating? It would relieve a lot of my nervousness."

"Sure. Fire away."

"How soon do you think is too soon for a woman to sleep with a guy?"

He shook his head, starting to laugh. "Don't go there, Kate."

"I guess I'm just a little self-conscious, thinking that you might find me too easy."

"Easy is not a word I'd *ever* use to describe you."

"Answer the question, please."

"I don't know. I mean, it's not like most guys aren't going to try and get what they can, but . . . Jesus, Kate, I feel like I'm walking in a minefield. Ask me another question."

"Okay. How many men in a woman's past are too many?"

"These are *not* easy questions. And most guys don't want to know."

"So if you ever asked me, I shouldn't tell you."

"I'll never ask. Dessert?"

"In a second. Do you think that sexual attraction is a firm foundation for a relationship?"

"It has to be there." He grinned. "Why? Not feeling those sparks anymore?"

"You know I am."

"Me, too."

She couldn't seem to stop looking at his eyes. *Uh oh . . .*

"Kate. Guys lie all the time. You know that old equation about previous sexual partners, that men will multiply by three while women divide by three—"

"You're kidding!"

"You never heard that?"

"Never."

"Well, you hear a lot tending bar."

"I guess so."

They were silent for a moment, then Kate said, "I can't stand this."

"Stand what?"

She stood up and backed a little away from the table, feeling his eyes on her the entire time. Dinner had been torture of the most primitive kind, having Jack across the table from her and yet not having him. She slid one of the straps of her black dress off her shoulder, sensing his attention on her every move.

"I think we should retire to another room for dessert," she whispered.

His eyes darkened, narrowed, and she felt that masculine attention totally honed in on her. *Such a heady feeling . . .*

"Oh, Miss Prescott," he said, leaning back in his chair and clasping his hands behind his head, "I like your style."

She realized he was waiting for her to make the next move, and it gave her an incredible feeling of feminine power. And she remembered Patti's words to her earlier on the beach, about making herself some wonderful memories.

Kate slipped first one strap off her shoulder, then the other, then she let the sexy little black dress slide down her body and pool at her feet. And as she was wearing nothing else but a pair of incredibly wicked black lace panties, thigh-high black stockings, and those high heels he'd requested, she knew she had his attention.

"Why don't you . . ." Then she started to laugh with pure pleasure as he caught her up into his arms and headed off in the direction of the bedroom.

"Have *sex* with you?" Matt said incredulously. "I thought we were having a barbecue."

And Patti burst into tears.

"Hey! *Hey,* I'm sorry. Patti, I just—I'm not sure what it is you want—"

"Am I that *horrible*? That *cute*? That *nice*? Am I *never* going to find a man who just wants to—" She hiccuped. "Just wants to—"

"Come here," he said, and dragged her into his lap. And she lay her head against his shoulder and cried into that strong, muscular swimmer's chest.

Half an hour later, she'd told him the entire story. Roger. Her lackluster love life. Being stood up at her wedding in front of five hundred family members and friends. Jetting out to the resort because of her father's generosity.

And feeling about as desirable as a can of dog food.

"That's so untrue," Matt said. "I think you're really cu—beautiful."

"You do?"

"Yeah."

"So, would you—do it?"

Matt hesitated. "Patti, you got stood up by your fiancé just a few days ago. I don't know if I'd feel all that good about having sex with you right now."

"But what if I was really, really sure that it would be okay? And we could use condoms, and if it's bad with you, then I'll *know* there's something wrong with me."

He laughed at that and kept her in his lap.

"Let me think about this."

They sat in silence for a moment, then Patti said, "Oh my God, I promised you a meal and then I only gave you a drink! You must think I'm a terrible hostess."

"Actually," Matt said, "this is the most interesting evening I've had in a long time."

"Chicken or steak?" she said as she slid off his lap.

"Steak."

She fed him, all the while telling him the pressure was off, what had she been thinking, please forgive her. Matt just laughed and ate and complimented her on her potato salad.

"It's better than my mom's, and that's saying a lot."

"Thank you." At least she could excel at something. Potato salad was pathetic, but it was something.

They drank a few more daiquiris, then retired to the downstairs bedroom.

Cherry closed her book with a sigh. Damn that Michael Crichton! She knew better than to start one of his books if she didn't have time to finish it. And now she just had, and it was three in the morning, and surely Matt would have done the dirty deed by now and left, so she could go down into the kitchen and get herself a glass of juice before turning in.

Dressed only in a silky little chemise, she tiptoed

down the villa's stairs and into the kitchen. Opening the refrigerator door, she got out a carton of guava juice, then a glass from the cupboard. Filling it with ice cubes, she poured herself a glass, put the carton in the fridge, and was about to go upstairs when she heard voices. Coming from the downstairs bedroom.

Well, well, well . . . So Pitt's Evil Twin did *spend the night . . . Good for Patti.*

She couldn't resist walking toward the closed bedroom door, tiptoeing carefully over the beautiful Oriental carpet, determined not to make a sound. Just to check up on Patti and make sure she was okay. She wouldn't really eavesdrop. After all, curiosity had gotten her in trouble more times than she wanted to admit . . .

Carefully, Cherry approached the door.

"Kate," Jack gasped as he slid off her, fell onto the king-sized mattress, and rolled to his side. *"Jesus . . ."*

She didn't even know how he could talk. Or why he would want to.

"You okay?" he whispered after a short silence.

She lay on her stomach, her face turned to the side against the cool Egyptian cotton sheets. She didn't think her legs worked anymore.

"Mmmm," she managed to get out, keeping her eyes closed. He started to laugh, then moved closer to her, put his arm around her, kissed her mouth.

"No," she whispered. "Wait. It'll take me a little time before I can do it again."

He frowned. "That's supposed to be my line."

She laughed, and he lifted her so she was on top of him, her legs straddling him, her breasts pressed to his chest, their faces inches apart.

"Kate," he said, tracing her lips with a fingertip.

"Fresh coconut ice cream with bittersweet chocolate sauce."

"You fight dirty."

"And some of those shortbread cookies."

She kissed him. "You're just making sure I have enough energy for the rest of the night."

He mock-frowned. "How easily you see through my master plan."

"I'll tell you what," she said. "Bring those babies in here, and I can think of a couple of really interesting things we can do with that chocolate sauce. Maybe the ice cream, too. Are there any sprinkles . . ."

But he was already out of bed and heading toward the kitchen.

Patti hadn't enjoyed herself so much in—she couldn't remember when.

She and Matt had decided on a game of strip poker and currently she was down to her lacy white bra and panties and he was down to pale blue boxer shorts.

And she could tell he was interested in her. Big time.

"We're going to take this slow," Matt had said out on the patio after their dinner. And he'd been as good as his word, kissing her between card games and making her feel like the most desirable woman in the world. They'd brought in another pitcher of daiquiris and a box of condoms—just in case—so the sky was the limit as far as she was concerned.

Roger, the marriage dodger, was fast fading into distant memory . . .

She'd even told Matt about how seeing Jack and Kate together had made her realize that Roger had done her a huge favor by not showing up on their wedding day.

"Yeah, Jack's crazy about her," Matt said, then hiccuped slightly.

Patti lowered her eyes. Her fantasies of sex with Matt were fading fast. Sex wasn't so good an idea with both of them having had this much to drink. He was pretty well wasted, as was she, and she knew she wouldn't have sex with him this way. She knew he wouldn't insist, he was just that kind of guy. But she'd had so much fun with him this evening, it had been such a long time since she'd just laughed and teased and had so much fun with a man. She couldn't remember the last time she'd felt this way, and it felt good.

Besides, she still had a few days at the resort, and now that she'd seen him almost naked, she knew she wanted to sleep with him.

"It's been difficult for him, you know?" Matt said, studying his cards with slightly unfocused eyes. He blinked, then squinted. "All that money, and all those women who were after him for it."

"What money?" Patti said. "He's a *bartender.*"

Matt started to laugh, then laughed so hard he had to put his cards down. "That's really funny! No, Patti, he's loaded! Filthy rich! His dad owns this resort and about seven others—"

Both of them were startled by the sharp crash, the sound of breaking glass they heard just outside the bedroom door.

"Damn!" Matt said, and got to his feet. "Stay back, Patti! Someone's broken in." He started toward the bedroom door.

She grabbed his arm, then called out, "Cherry?"

"Cherry?" Matt said.

"My roomie," Patti explained, and then she saw Cherry peek her head around the bedroom door. She looked shamefaced and stunning, her strawberry blonde hair set off by the emerald green silk of the sexy chemise.

"Whoa," Matt said when he caught sight of her entire body.

"I dropped a glass," Cherry explained. "I'll clean it up, and then it's off to bed for me."

"Get in here," Patti said.

Matt glanced from one woman to the other. "Wait a minute, this is beginning to feel like one of those *Penthouse* letters . . ."

"You should *get* so lucky," Cherry said. She turned to Patti. "I didn't hear a thing." Then she put her hand over her mouth, clearly realizing she'd blown it.

Patti stared at first one, then the other. "Both of you. *None* of what Matt just said leaves this room. Understood?"

"I don't even understand what he said," Cherry said. "I can't get my brain around this." She turned to Matt. "He's *rich?*"

Matt nodded. "But I wasn't supposed to say anything." He glanced at the second pitcher of Daiquiris, sitting on the bedside table, then lowered his head. "Shit, he's going to kill me."

"No, he won't," Patti said. "No one's going to kill anyone, unless it's me killing either of you for saying anything. I don't want Kate to be hurt." Patti touched her forehead, then glanced up at Matt. "I can't feel my forehead. How much did we drink?"

"A lot," Matt admitted. "You were nervous." He hesitated. "Me, too."

"This is utterly charming," Cherry interrupted, "but I want to get things straightened out before Kate gets home from her hot date with Mr. Fling—oh, excuse me, I meant Mr. *Millionaire.*" She turned toward Matt. "Are you telling me he makes her scream *and* he has money? He's a fucking *millionaire?*"

Matt bit his lip, glanced at Patti, then back at Cherry. Slowly, he nodded his head.

"Really rich?"

Matt nodded.

"Filthy rich?"

Matt nodded again.

"As in, he owns this entire resort?"

"His dad's handing it over to him in a few days."

"Then why," Cherry continued relentlessly, "is he making it look like he's a bartender? Is it something to do with fooling Kate?"

"No. No, I don't think so. His dad wanted him to work at the resort as an employee for about ten days so he could get a real sense for the people who would be working for him. But at the end of that time, James McKenna is retiring and giving everything over to Jack."

"So he's not a bartender," Patti said.

"Hell, no. He's got an MBA from Harvard. Up until a few months ago, he was managing the Boston property."

"Jesus," Cherry said as she sat down on the king-sized bed.

"Kate's going to kill him," Patti whispered as she sat down next to her. "That drink she threw in his face will be nothing compared to what happens when she finds out he's been lying to her."

"Hell, *I'm* going to kill him," Cherry said.

After a moment's hesitation, Matt sat down next to Patti. Cherry glanced over at him. They eyed each other uneasily. Finally, Matt stuck out a hand in front of Patti.

"Matt."

"Cherry." She reached across Patti and shook his hand.

"Nice to meet you."

"The pleasure's all mine."

"We have to take some kind of oath," Patti said, "hands on top of each other like that scene in *The Three Musketeers.*"

"Cool with me," Matt said. "My ass is on the line if any of this gets out."

"Kate's *heart* is on the line," Patti said. She put her hand down on her thigh, and Matt placed his hand on top of hers. They both looked at Cherry.

"You are *so* summer camp," Cherry said, but she put her hand on top of Matt's. Then Patti repeated the process with her other hand, and Matt and Cherry followed suit.

Their hands remained together as Patti whispered, "None of what Matt said tonight leaves this room, even after Jack tells Kate he's loaded, and they live happily ever after . . ."

"Oh, *now* who's telling a lie?" Cherry said. "After discovering this, I'm convinced he's just having fun with her."

"No," Patti said. "*No.*" She took a deep breath. "But if he is, the three of us have to get on that plane back home, and never let her know about this evening."

"What?" said Matt, confused, touching his forehead.

"Three as in *me, Patti,* and *Kate,*" Cherry said. "*You,* Mr. Pitt, are staying here."

"Who? Oh. Okay," Matt said. He rubbed his forehead. "Damn those Daiquiris. I can't think straight."

"Can you even keep a secret?" Cherry demanded.

"When my job is on the line? You bet. Not to mention my friendship with Jack. He's a great guy."

Cherry nodded her head. "Okay, I'm off to bed, and

I still have to get that broken glass cleaned up. Any other bizarre little rituals the three of us have to go through before I can drift off to dreamland?"

"Nope," Patti said.

After Cherry left, Patti turned toward Matt. Her blue eyes filled with tears.

"You know Jack better than I do. Do you think he's just playing with her?"

Matt shook his head. "No. I don't. I've never seen him happier."

Patti considered this. "That's what I think, too."

"I'm really sorry," Matt said. "I guess I really screwed up our evening."

Patti smiled up at him. "No, you didn't. I feel great."

Matt frowned. "I thought you couldn't feel your forehead."

"Yeah, but I've started to feel a few other things."

He gave her a considering look. "Really."

"I don't think you should go home this wasted. Why don't you spend the night?"

"Patti, I don't know—"

"Just sleep. I promise." She lay back down on the bed and patted the mattress. Matt hesitated for just a moment before he joined her.

"Where are you going?" Jack mumbled from the bed.

"I have to get back," Kate said, struggling into her little black dress. It was almost morning, and for some reason, she felt she wanted some distance from Jack. She had to get away from him in order to process everything that had happened between them on this first date. And thank God they'd thought to take a shower together after their little bout with the bittersweet chocolate syrup.

"Come back to bed," he said, and his voice sounded

so unbearably sensual, all raspy and morning sexy, that she almost gave up and fell back into bed.

"Nope. I'm going back to the villa."

"I'll walk you back."

He did, right to her door, then kissed her so sweetly she felt tears sting her eyes.

What are we doing? Where is this going?

But she didn't say a thing to him as she quietly let herself inside.

Chapter Fourteen

❀ Kate barely had a chance to relax between the sheets of her bed and close her eyes before the phone rang. Not wanting Cherry or Patti to wake up, she grabbed the receiver.

"Hello?"

"Kate. I have a plan."

"Jack? What plan?"

"For our second date."

"We barely finished the first."

"I know. But I just thought you'd want some advance warning about our second one."

She smiled. "Okay." She snuggled back against her pillows, pleased beyond all reason that he would want to call her so soon after they'd parted.

"Sleep in really late. Then meet me in the main lobby at three in the morning."

"Three? Where are we going?" Her imagination went wild. "Night diving?"

"Too risky."

Like what I'm doing right now isn't.

"Haleakala."

She sat up in bed. "The volcano?"

He laughed. "The *dormant* volcano. Let's not ask for trouble."

"I read about it in a guidebook. It's one of the places on Maui I really wanted to see."

"So we'll see it. Wear warm clothes, like a sweatshirt and socks. And a jacket."

She frowned. "I didn't pack any."

"Go to Costco and get some."

This was a man who was good at solving problems, and also had an unconscious air of authority. Why hadn't he moved any further up the job ladder? It was puzzling.

"That's a plan," she said. "What are you up to today?"

"Working the front, greeting guests, helping them get settled in, carrying luggage. I'll be one of those guys in the golf carts, loaded down with bags."

"Don't work too hard," she said.

"I won't. I'll see you at three."

"Okay." She hung up the phone, slid down into bed, and was asleep before she'd taken five deep breaths.

Cherry lay awake in her bed and thought about how the world worked.

Well, the universe was laughing in her face, because as up front as she'd been about wanting to find a rich man to take care of her, and as hard as she'd tried to manifest that reality, one of the richest had been right beneath her nose.

Jack. Mr. Fling. No, make that Mr. *Millionaire* Fling.

She'd been around wealthy men before. You couldn't have worked all the jobs she had in Vegas and not met up with some of them. But most had been old and liver spotted, flabby, overweight, and bald. Not sexy bald, like Bruce Willis in his prime, but Elmer Fudd bald, without one ounce of sexual energy. She'd wanted money and security, but hadn't been willing to go that far to get it.

And now Kate had found everything a woman could ever want in one big gorgeous package.

Cherry didn't begrudge Kate her good fortune, but now that she knew Jack was rich, she was worried as to how this entire affair was going to play out. Patti was a dreamer and wanted things to work out. Kate wasn't the sort of woman who would survive being toyed with all that well. That first night at the deli, she'd all but confessed she didn't feel that confident with men.

Actually, the hardest hearted and most realistic of the three of them was her, and she wasn't sure *she* could've had an affair with a man as attractive and compelling as Jack and been able to walk away unscathed.

Oh, who was she kidding; her heart would be shattered.

This promised to be a real mess.

Cherry sighed. She'd already decided that if Patti was okay with it, she'd change her ticket from Vegas to Chicago and help her get Kate home.

Hell, maybe she could find some kind of work in Chicago and stay in touch with Kate and Patti. They were the most genuine women she'd met in years, and she had the strangest feeling she was actually going to miss their company once this whole wild vacation was over. In fact, she knew she would. They were on day six of their ten-day vacation, and Cherry knew she would never, ever forget or be able to repay Patti and

Kate's generosity in allowing her to stay in this villa with them.

Missing people was something she'd learned not to do, as she'd changed homes and lives as easily as a cat walked through its nine lives.

She glanced over at the bedroom door as she heard it ease open. Patti stood there, in just her bra and panties, her face glowing.

"Looks like you had a good night," Cherry observed. Patti's whole demeanor was incandescent; she was lit up with feminine sexual energy and looked much like Kate had after *L'Affaire de Bathroom.*

Was she the only woman on this island who couldn't get laid?

"We didn't do it."

"You did something."

Patti sighed, then came over and sat on the side of Cherry's bed. "He's just the best kisser."

Cherry raised an eyebrow. "You expect me to believe that both of you were in your underwear, smashed on daiquiris, and all you did was kiss?"

Patti blushed. "Ah, we messed around a little. Boy, Roger didn't know a whole lot about a woman's body, let me tell you!"

Cherry started to laugh. "I'm happy for you."

"Me, too." Patti got up and walked toward the bathroom, then paused. She glanced back at Cherry. "You know, Matt said he likes the way I look."

"Well, why wouldn't he?"

"I don't know. I guess a lot of my life I've thought I just didn't quite—that I wasn't in the same league as a lot of other women. You know, not that pretty."

And suddenly Cherry knew why Patti had been willing to settle for one of the Rogers of the world.

"You're nuts," she said. "I think you're beautiful, and

when I worked as a showgirl in Vegas, I was around some of the most stunning women in the entire world."

"Really?" Patti said, and Cherry knew that she was in a position, this very moment, to give Patti an emotional gift.

"Sugar, a lot of beautiful women are empty inside. Dead. They don't have the capacity to really love and feel. You do. You feel more than anyone I've ever met in my entire life. You *care* more. *That's* what makes a woman beautiful. That's what makes anyone really beautiful, and don't you ever forget it."

She watched as Patti considered this and saw by the subtle changes in her friend's face that her words had gotten through.

"I believe you, Cherry," Patti said softly. "If anyone would know about being beautiful, you would."

She headed off toward the bathroom and shut the door. Within minutes, Cherry heard the shower running. And wondered at the irony of it all, that Patti should think she wasn't beautiful.

"Kate," Patti whispered into the dark bedroom. The shades were drawn, her cousin a mere lump beneath the covers. "Cherry and I are going to go sign up for some of the activities at that desk. Do you want to come along?"

No answer.

"Tough night," Cherry said. "Let's just go and sign her up with us. If Jack has other plans for her, we can always cancel her reservation."

"Okay."

They walked from the villa to the main lobby and found the activity desk where they met Lanie, the woman who was in charge. But the gorgeous young redhead seemed distracted. Her eyes looked red and swollen, as if she'd been crying.

"Is something wrong?" Patti finally asked, when a totally distracted Lanie had made her third error into the resort's computer.

"I'm sorry," the woman admitted. "It's my friend Angie. She sings in the lounge every night, and she just got word that her mother's had a serious heart attack. Angie's at the hospital with her, and I'm worried about both of them."

"How awful," Patti said. "Is there any way we can help?"

Lanie laughed. "Not unless you know a singer we can hire for a few days who's pretty good and can do all the standards."

Patti was thinking about this when Cherry said, "Maybe I can help you."

Lanie looked up.

"I used to sing in Vegas, at the Starlight Lounge on the strip. I had a whole show and came on right after the magic act."

Lanie hesitated.

"And I have an audition tape with me."

"Can you bring it to me?"

"Sure."

Lanie looked at Cherry as if she were sizing her up. "How fast could you be ready to sing?"

"All I'd need is about an hour and a half with the musicians. What kind of outfit did your friend wear?"

"A sexy, glittery kind of gown. Like Michelle Pfeiffer in that movie about the Baker Boys."

"Got it. And I've got a few dresses like that with me."

Lanie smiled at the two of them. "Get me that tape!"

* * *

They went back and found Cherry's tape, dropped it off with Lanie, and told her that the two of them would be by the pool, near the bar. And while they lay in the sun, both Cherry and Patti studied the various brochures they'd taken from the activity desk.

"The road to Hana sounds good," Patti said. "A friend of my mom's took that drive and said it was fabulous."

"It does sound good. How about a helicopter ride over Haleakala?"

"Hmmm." Patti studied her brochure. "I'd do it. Have you ever been in a helicopter before?"

"Sure."

"Not me." Patti sighed. "I wish I'd lived your life."

"Nah, you don't."

"Cherry?"

They both turned their heads as Lanie came running up, the cassette tape in her hand.

"I'd like to hire you for the week." She quoted a sum of money that made Cherry sit up straight, then said, "I phoned the musicians who usually play with Angie and told them there's been a change of plans. Can you meet them in the lounge at three?"

"Sure."

"And bring all the dresses you brought. James McKenna will make the final decision about which one you'll wear tonight."

"Fine."

As Lanie hurried away, Patti said, "You have the most exciting life! I can't believe you're going to be singing in a lounge tonight."

"I was just at the right place at the right time. I'm sure she could have got another singer if we hadn't been there."

"This is so great . . . wait, if she hires you for the week, you won't be able to come back with us."

"No. But you know what, Patti? When I'm done with this weeklong gig, I'm going to fly out to Chicago and see you guys. I want to meet your mom and dad and have a meal at that restaurant of yours."

"Really?"

"Really." Cherry pushed up from the chaise lounge. "Let's go back to the villa, I have some dresses to iron."

Kate staggered out of the bathroom, wrapped in a towel, another around her hair, as Patti and Cherry came bursting in. She listened as they talked about the activities desk, the singer whose mother was hospitalized, Cherry's audition tape, and the fact that she was making her Maui debut as a singer tonight in Neptune's Lounge at the Kalani Resort Hotel and Spa.

"All this happened while I was sleeping?" Kate said, sitting on one of the stools at the kitchen's breakfast bar, eating a piece of sweet white pineapple. "God, if I'd stayed in bed any longer, the two of you probably would have taken over the resort."

The phone rang and Kate picked it up. "Villa number six," she said, then, "What are you doing, calling again?" Out of the corner of her eye, she saw Cherry and Patti glance at each other.

"I'm on break," said Jack. "I just wanted to hear your voice."

"Oh," she said, slightly ashamed of the way she'd sounded. "I didn't mean that the way it sounded."

"Sure you did."

"Actually," she said, "I kind of like hearing your voice, too."

"Well, that's good. Actually, I also called to ask you

if you had any problems with getting to Haleakala on my bike."

"I hope you mean a motorcycle."

"Funny."

"I don't have a problem with it." And she remembered the first time she'd seen him on his motorcycle, when they'd driven to the resort in their rental car, their very first day on the island.

"Do you have a helmet I can use?" she said, remembering that he hadn't bothered to wear one the first time she'd seen him. He had a wild streak, and she knew she liked it. He brought out the wild streak in her.

"One for each of us."

"Good."

"Did you get those warm clothes?"

"I was just leaving for Costco as we speak."

"Get warm socks. Your feet will freeze."

There it was again, that easy air of authority. It was so obvious to her that he could be so much more than a bartender, but it wasn't her decision to make. And Kate resolved, at that moment, to stop thinking about this man's potential and to love Jack just the way he was.

There. She'd admitted it to herself. She'd finally taken that long fall.

Oh God, I'm in so much trouble.

"Kate? You still there?"

"Yeah. Warm socks. Okay Mom, I'll even bring an extra jacket." They both laughed, and she hung up, feeling a little shaky, then turned her head to find both Cherry and Patti staring at her.

"What?" she said.

Both women seemed to have lost the power of speech; they simply stared.

"Okay, don't say a word," Kate said, turning on her

stool so she faced both of them. "I don't even care that he's a bartender and doesn't seem to have as much ambition as I do. He's a hard worker and a great guy, and that's all that matters."

The two women glanced at each other, then back at her.

"What is it?" she demanded. "Why are the two of you acting so strangely? It's not like I can't take care of myself. I'm a big girl, and I'm just having this . . . fling."

Patti looked away.

"What?"

Cherry sat down on the bar stool next to her. "I guess Patti and I are a little concerned that you're going to get hurt."

Yeah, me too.

"Maybe I will be. Maybe I won't. But I went into this with my eyes open, and if I get hurt, it's no one's responsibility but my own."

Cherry glanced at Patti, who couldn't meet her eyes.

"Will the two of you tell me what the hell is going on!"

Patti cleared her throat. "Cherry and I are worried about how the whole thing with you and Jack is going to end, and we both feel a little guilty because we feel like maybe we egged you on, the way we talked at the deli that first night. You know, those goals we all set out to accomplish." Patti hesitated. "The fling."

"You are *so* not responsible for that. I'm totally responsible for my own decisions." Kate took a deep breath. "Listen to me, both of you. I'm scared, too. But I couldn't resist this whole thing with Jack, and I don't know a woman who could. There's just—" She hesitated. "There's something that happens when we get together, I can't explain it, it's just what it is. And if it means that in a couple of days I'm heading back to

Chicago with nothing but memories, then I'll deal with it. In the meantime, I have to go to Costco and pick up a few things."

"What things?" Patti said.

"Warm clothing. I guess it gets pretty cold up on Haleakala. You go through seven or eight climate changes as you go up the mountain, if I remember it right. It's a pretty high volcano."

"You don't need to go to the store for warm clothes, Kate. I can lend you some," Cherry said. "How does a sweatsuit, a warm jacket, and a thick pair of socks sound?"

"Why would you pack that kind of stuff for a trip to Hawaii?" Patti said.

"Sugar, when I left Vegas, I *left Vegas*. I packed up everything I own into those two huge suitcases."

Patti hesitated. "Then where are you going to go when this vacation is over?"

"First to Chicago to visit you two, then . . ." Cherry hesitated. "Then, as usual, it will be wherever the wind blows me."

"Wow," said Patti. "Man, I wish I could travel like that."

But Kate, studying the expression in Cherry's eyes, thought, *no, you don't.*

"Warm clothes, huh?" she said instead. "Let's take a look."

Cherry outfitted Kate with everything she would need, saving her a trip to the store.

"Cute outfit for a date, huh?" Kate said, laughing as she studied herself in the mirror in the forest green sweatshirt and matching sweatpants.

"You look adorable," Cherry said. "He'll love you in

it. Here, this is my warmest pair of socks. You have running shoes, don't you?"

"Yeah."

"Do you need gloves? A hat?"

"You *are* prepared!" Patti said, sitting on the bed and watching the two of them.

"I think I'll take both," Kate said. "The concierge told me it can get pretty cold up there, especially right before sunrise."

"That will be really romantic," Patti said, "watching the sunrise."

"It's supposed to be a very sacred place," Kate said, starting to take off the warm clothing. "What were you guys going to do today?"

"I'm free until around two, then I have to get ready to rehearse by three," Cherry said.

"You do know that Patti and I can't miss your opening night," Kate said.

"You guys don't have to come."

"Cherry!" Patti said.

"Okay, you can come."

Kate had to laugh. "I feel like lying out by the pool and maybe ordering lunch. A sandwich, some fries, or maybe those Maui onion rings."

"Now that sounds like a plan," Cherry said.

Jack knew he was getting very specific sexual signals from the woman whose luggage he'd just delivered, but he was choosing to ignore them. He'd guess she was in her early fifties. In incredibly good shape, she'd changed into an extremely skimpy bikini before he'd arrived and had kept deliberately moving into his personal space as he'd stacked the luggage by the king-sized bed in the master suite, making him uncomfortable.

"Have a drink with me," she said, touching his forearm. "Just a little one."

Her husband, a harassed-looking man in his sixties, had already left to play golf. It was pretty obvious they were a couple who chose not to spend a great deal of time together.

And Jack knew that, as annoying as this woman's advances toward him were, she was an individual who was in pain, and lonely, and probably thought she could assuage that feeling by having a sexual encounter with a younger man. She could feel desirable for a brief moment and hold those uneasy feelings at bay.

But not with him.

"Can't do it. Not while I'm working," he said with a bright smile. "But thanks for the offer." Not waiting for a tip, he skillfully maneuvered himself out the villa's door, then sighed with relief as the lock snicked shut.

His father had been right, and before the week was out, Jack knew he was going to tell him so. If he'd just slid right into an executive position, he wouldn't have had the countless experiences this ten-day period had offered him. There was absolutely no way he could have understood what the people under him went through on a day-to-day basis without working those same jobs himself. And how would a younger man, brand-new on the job, handle a situation like the one he'd just extricated himself from? Jack made a mental note to create a series of seminars to address the various problems employees faced.

Nothing like a little knowledge and preparation to avert a disaster.

And speaking of disasters, he had to find a way to tell Kate the truth. He couldn't wait until the last minute to tell her that he didn't want her to leave. And he couldn't figure out how he was going to break the news to her that he wasn't just a bartender.

Oh, by the way, the bartender thing?—a total smoke-screen. My father built this resort from the ground up, I've lived here every summer since I can remember, and he's retiring and handing it over to me to run in a couple of days. And besides making Cosmopolitans and Mai Tais, I also have an MBA, a Porsche, and a closet full of designer suits . . .

Jack sighed as he started up the little white golf cart and headed back over the winding path toward the main lobby. Maybe the wisest course of action would be to take Kate somewhere where they both had some privacy, where she couldn't run away, and just lay the whole thing out. Clear things up, once and for all.

He brightened, thinking of his favorite house. It was secluded and comfortable, a place he'd purchased primarily as a haven for when he needed to be by himself and think.

And it would be the perfect place to tell Kate.

Kate was walking back from the poolside bar with two orders of Maui onion rings, dipping sauce, and three large sodas when Cherry whispered to Patti, "You know, I lived in Vegas for eleven years and saw some weird shit. But nothing beats this whole mess."

"I know," Patti said. "It's like something out of a book."

"I hope Jack tells her the truth pretty soon," Cherry whispered, then she lay back on the chaise and closed her eyes as Kate approached.

"I can't stop thinking about what Matt said; it's like it's eating a hole inside my stomach," Patti whispered back, then turned her attention to her book.

* * *

Later that afternoon, while Cherry headed back to the villa to shower and get ready for her rehearsal, and Patti decided to stay out by the pool and continue reading, Kate found herself walking along the beach again. And thinking about Jack.

She didn't want to believe that he was the typical young man working a glamorous job in paradise and having affair after affair with the women who visited the island. She didn't want to see herself as one of that crowd. But there was a chance that she was seeing what she wanted to see in him and that the reality of his life was exactly what she feared most.

"Kate? Is that you?"

She glanced up to see James McKenna, dressed in a pair of khaki shorts and a green and white Hawaiian shirt. And she smiled.

"Hi."

"May I join you?" he said, and she was touched by his manners, his formal way of making sure he wasn't intruding.

"I'd like that."

They walked in silence for a while, then James said, "I trust you're enjoying your stay with us."

"Very much. Though I haven't had as much time to bake cookies as I thought I would."

"Don't worry about it."

"I'll send you some recipes once I get back to . . . Chicago." Her voice faltered at the thought of it. She couldn't bear the idea of being separated from Jack by thousands of miles. God, she was weak.

"Kate? Are you sure you're all right?"

"No, I'm not." She didn't even hesitate to tell James the truth. Kate didn't know why or how, but she'd grown enormously fond of this older man during the short time they'd gotten to know each other.

"Anything I can help you with?"

"Perhaps." She took a breath. "Can I ask you a question?"

"Certainly."

They continued their leisurely walk along the shoreline, letting the surf curl up over their bare feet.

"Hypothetically, of course," she said, grinning up at him.

"Of course."

"James, do you think it's possible to fall in love with a person in a matter of days?"

"You're asking the wrong man. I think it's possible to fall in love in a matter of minutes. In a heartbeat."

They continued their walk for a few paces, then Kate said, "That was the way it was with you and your wife, wasn't it? After you walked into that wall."

He laughed. "Yes, it was."

"She's been gone for a long time, yet you still wear your wedding ring."

"You don't forget a love like that any time soon, Kate."

They were silent for a time, then James said, "Do you think you're in love with your young man?"

"I don't think I am. I know I'm in love with him. I just . . . love him." They both stopped and looked out over the dancing waves, sparkling in the intense tropical sunshine. Kate's eyes stung, and she blinked back tears. It was one thing to admit to herself that she loved Jack, another to actually say it out loud to another person.

It made it real.

Patti had guessed, but Kate hadn't confirmed it. Actually saying the words to James made her feelings real.

And more terrifying. Now there was no turning back.

"Do you think he loves you?"

"I do when we're together. It's just—sometimes when we're apart, I wonder if I'm just one of many." She glanced up at him. "Promise not to fire him?"

"I give you my word."

"I wonder . . . he seems so sharp and has this kind of air of . . . authority. I wonder why he doesn't seem to have any *ambition*. And then I think that maybe tending bar is his way of being irresponsible and having all these affairs with the women he meets here. And then I think that maybe I'm just making up this big story in my head."

James sighed. "It happens, those affairs. I can't deny that. You see it all the time, people behaving in different ways because they're on vacation. But Kate, I think it's a very good sign that you only have these doubts when you're not with him. If you were seeing things about him when you were spending time together, that's when I'd advise you to be careful."

"Good point. And it's not that I want to change him, because I love him just the way he is. There are just these little inconsistencies, and my intuition keeps telling me that something's not adding up. There's more to Jack than he lets on." Realizing she'd slipped and revealed his name, she looked at James and said, "You can't fire him."

"No, of course not," James said. "But listen to your intuition. And I'm very glad to hear you love this young man for himself."

"Well, my aunt Connie always told Patti and me, 'Never fall in love with a man's potential. What you see is what you're going to get.'"

"A wise woman, your aunt Connie."

They started walking again, keeping to a leisurely pace.

"How's your son doing?" Kate said.

"I have a feeling his life is going to change profoundly in the next couple of days."

"For the better?"

"Definitely."

"That's good to hear."

"It's time. He's been too ambitious and used that drive to keep from having a significant relationship. But he's met this very special woman—"

"Wow. It must be catching."

James smiled. "I think he's going to ask her to marry him. I hope he does. And I can't wait. I'd like a couple of grandchildren to love and spoil."

Kate sighed. "That sounds so wonderful. I hope it all works out the way you want it to. That he loves her and wants to marry her."

"If he's smart," James said as he looked down at her, "he'll never let her go."

Patti was immersed in her novel when a shadow fell in front of the printed page. She looked up and saw Jack, in his usual uniform of khaki shorts and coral-colored polo shirt with the resort's logo on the upper left side.

"Hey Patti, have you seen Kate?"

"I think she went back to the villa."

Jack scanned the people around the pool, then his gaze took in the part of the resort's beachfront property he could see. "I was hoping to catch her here. I can't really go to the villa now."

"I'll tell her you were looking for her." Patti held out her large soda. "Want some?"

"Sure. Thanks."

As he took a sip, she said quietly, "Why is it, Jack, that I think there's a whole lot more to you than meets the eye?"

He set the soda down on the small table next to her lounge chair, then sat down on the chair across from her, his hands clasped between his knees as he leaned toward her.

"Why am I not surprised that nothing much gets past you?"

She grinned. "Because nothing much does."

"Well, you're right. But it's nothing I can talk about right now."

"But you're going to tell Kate," she said.

"Yeah," he admitted.

"That's all I was worried about. See, she doesn't have family to speak for her, except me. So I'm just saying what has to be said, you know what I mean?"

"Yeah, I do." How had he *ever* thought this woman was a silly little piece of blonde fluff? Or the consummate con artist, for that matter. Patti was simply all heart, and she loved her cousin, Kate. Probably as much as he did. And that love could make her a tough little broad.

Jack found that he really liked her.

"You mean she has no family here. Her family's back in Chicago, right?"

"No. Her mom and dad were killed when she was a little girl."

The look on his face told her that she'd shocked him, and then that he hurt for Kate. What hurt her hurt him. That was a good sign.

"What?"

"She was five years old. My dad went over to her house and got her. She was with a sitter. He brought her back to our house that night and she never left."

He was staring at her, an incredulous look on his face.

"How did they . . . die?"

"A drunk driver. They were coming back from their eighth anniversary dinner. My uncle and aunt were very happy, and they adored Kate."

He was silent, simply staring at her.

"She seems so strong, Jack; she's strong for everyone else, but underneath . . ."

He glanced away, and she sensed he was fighting strong emotion. The thought of Kate losing her parents at such a young age had affected him deeply. As if he knew how deep that pain could go, how completely it could scar you.

How it was never too far away from you, no matter how many years had passed.

"Underneath there's this terrible vulnerability. And I don't want to see her get hurt, so if she's just a vacation fling to you—and I want you to know that I don't think you feel that way—I want you to cut her loose. Stop it now. Give her a few days here to heal before she gets on that plane back to Chicago."

"No," he said quietly. "No, I'm not cutting her loose because she's not a vacation fling, and you and I both know it."

Her eyes filled, the book snapped shut, and Patti sat forward.

"That's all I need to know, you don't have to say anything else! Thank you, Jack! Thank you so much for trusting me!"

"Not a word to Kate, okay? Because if I have any say in the matter, she's not leaving this island."

"I swear! I think you guys are perfect for each other!"

He smiled at her, and she could swear that Jack, cocky, self-confident Jack, actually seemed a little shy with her!

"I have one question for you, though. How do you handle her temper?"

Patti laughed, remembering the drink that Kate had thrown in his face a few days ago. "She's a typical Taurus. Kate keeps it all inside, rarely lets it out, but when she blows—man, watch out! I just get out of the way until she gets it out of her system, and then she usually wants to talk."

"Hmmm." He considered this. "That's good to know."

"Do you think I'm goofy, you know, the astrology stuff?"

"Are you kidding? My mother was into all that stuff; she had an astrologer who would draw up a chart every time my father . . ." He hesitated. "Every time he opened a new business." He eyed her. "What are you?"

"Cancer. Can't you tell? Kate says I'm the moodiest person she knows. You?"

"Capricorn."

"That's a pretty ambitious sign for a bartender." She didn't dare say more, as he gave her a look that told her he had a pretty good idea he wasn't fooling her. Not one bit.

"Mr. Fling, huh?" he said, abruptly changing the subject. "Did you come up with that one?"

"Nope. Cherry did."

"Hmmm." He considered this.

"We christened you Mr. Fling the first night we were here, when we saw you buy coffee at the deli. It was the way you walked."

"You're kidding."

"That's no Capricorn walk. What else is going on?"

He got up, stretched. "I have to head back to work."

"You're evading the answer, Jack."

He started to walk away from her, then called back, "Scorpio Moon!"

She laughed, then mock-fanned her face with her hand. His laughter floated back to her, and she noticed that several women unobtrusively watched Jack as he left.

But it didn't matter how many women watched Jack, or wanted him, Patti thought, smiling contentedly as she settled herself back on her lounge chair, her novel all but forgotten. Because the important thing was that there was only one woman Jack wanted, and that woman was her cousin, Kate.

Chapter Fifteen

❀ Cherry opened the door to the small dressing room backstage at Neptune's Lounge, stepped inside, closed it securely, and took a deep breath.

The rehearsal couldn't have gone better. James had decided on one of her dresses, an emerald green, glittery confection that she adored. He'd asked her to wear her hair down, soft and wavy. He'd checked the song list and even picked out her shoes. And Cherry had suddenly understood that millionaires really paid attention to details and never missed a thing.

She walked over to the dressing table and sat down. Put her head in her hands and blew out a long, slow breath, trying to relax.

This job was a godsend. James had already told her that she could sing with the band as long as she wanted to. It looked like Lanie's friend, Angie, wouldn't be coming back for quite some time. Though Angie's mother was out of danger—barely—Lanie had told

Cherry that Angie had decided to take some time off and
take care of her mother until she was on her feet again.

So the position of lounge singer was open. And she
had it. She didn't have to go back to the States. She could
hide out here in paradise for a while until she thought of
what to do next.

Cherry glanced up, finally noticing the huge bouquets of flowers throughout the small dressing room.
Puzzled, she stood, then walked over to the first of
three, a dozen exquisite white roses. And plucked out
the small card, opening it.

*Thanks for saving us on such short notice. Break
a leg tonight. James McKenna*

Sweet. But according to what Kate had told her, this
particular millionaire was already taken, even though
his wife had been dead for years.

The second bouquet was a wild riot of tropical flowers, orchids, plumeria, and birds of paradise, an explo-
sion of color, fragrant and exotic. She opened the
envelope.

Wow! We know you can do it! Break both *your
legs! Love, Patti and Kate*

Cherry grinned. *Those two.*

The third was from Lanie, several stalks of delicate
white orchids in a pot, with a note expressing her sin-
cere thanks.

She sighed. One thing she wasn't used to was kindness, and she'd had nothing but kindness since she'd arrived at this magical island in the Pacific. Cherry sat
back down in front of her dressing table and looked at

herself in the large mirror, taking in the face and figure that had been the source of so much confusion and pain.

But then she thought of how her luck had changed, once again. Her life. And she would embrace it.

As Jack left his shift after hauling around more luggage than he ever wanted to remember, he decided that he'd tell Kate the truth after they came down from Haleakala. He wanted her to experience the sacred place without any other distractions, with nothing to take her attention away from it.

But as soon as they started down from the volcano, had breakfast, and then arrived at his house, he was going to come clean with her. He couldn't stand this double identity stuff, this false role. He felt like he was caught in a trap of his own making. Well, his father's, if he were really being picky. All he knew was that he *hated* lying to her, even by omission.

And he had a feeling that, when Kate found out the truth, she'd be pissed.

That temper. Those vivid green eyes would flash with fiery emotion. She might even throw something else at him. The downside was, he knew she was going to be angry with him. But the upside was that all those passionate emotions were let loose in the bedroom. Or in their case, the cabana and the penthouse.

He grinned. What a woman. Having Kate in his life was well worth a huge argument. He just had to find the right way to tell her. And he was confident he could.

Kate finished frosting the elaborate, three-layer white chocolate coconut cake, then stepped back. Frowning, she studied the dessert. Something was missing. After a moment, she picked up a handful of crushed Macadamia nuts and sprinkled them on the top.

Perfect.

She'd decided to bake Cherry a cake to celebrate her grand opening. Now finished, she'd take the cake back to the villa so that she and Patti would be totally prepared for the little celebration they had planned.

Glancing up, she saw Jack stride into the kitchen. And as always, her heart sped up, her breath quickened, and that strange feeling, like fluttery little butterflies, invaded her stomach.

He grinned as he caught sight of her, and she melted.

"Nice cake," he said as he reached her side.

"Thanks," she said, then didn't say anything else as he put his arms around her waist, pulled her close, and kissed her.

Unbelievable. There were kisses, and then there were kisses. And this man's kisses made her totally vulnerable and only able to think of one thing she wanted to do.

He broke the kiss and smiled down at her.

"Ready for tonight?"

She nodded. Sometimes she couldn't even trust herself to talk around Jack. He flustered her, when he looked at her that way with those blue eyes.

"Who did you bake it for?" he said, then glanced at the cake.

"Cherry. It's her favorite, and she's making her debut at Neptune's Lounge tonight."

"Oh. I heard about Angie's mom, but hadn't heard who was going to replace her. Cherry sings?"

"She had a whole act in Vegas."

"You going to see her?"

"Of course."

"I'll meet you there—"

They were interrupted by a shout, and as Kate glanced toward the sound, she saw that one of the prep chefs had cut himself badly. The young man was holding his hand and staring at the blood spilling from the cut as if that hand didn't belong to him.

Jack moved so quickly it was a moment before she realized he wasn't still at her side. She watched as he swiftly reached up into a cupboard for a first-aid kit. Then he led the shocked young man over to the sink, where he talked to him in a soothing voice as he washed and wrapped the wound, then arranged for another of the chefs to take him to the hospital for stitches.

Cool, calm, collected, and totally in control.

Kate frowned. *Something's wrong with this picture . . .*

But then again, maybe bartenders had ample opportunity to deal with accidents of all sorts. She was wondering about this as Jack approached her.

"Quick thinking," she said.

"Yeah, well . . ." He glanced down at his shirt and her gaze followed his. The coral-colored polo shirt was stained with blood.

"You'd better get that in some cold water before it sets," she said.

"Yeah." He raked his fingers through his dark hair, and she could sense his frustration. "Can I meet you at the lounge tonight?"

She studied his face for the fleetest of seconds. And detected the tiniest bit of doubt and uncertainty in those dark blue eyes. She liked the way Jack took nothing for granted, and was asking her if she still wanted his company.

"Yeah. I'd like that."

"Great. I've got to go." He gave her a quick kiss, then headed out the kitchen door. But as Kate watched him, those doubts assailed her again.

Something just wasn't right.

*   *   *

Neptune's Lounge was packed the night of Cherry's debut. As Kate and Patti walked into the luxurious club, James came up to them.

"As I knew you two would come, I arranged for you to have a table up front."

"Thank you," Kate said, letting him take her arm and guide her through the crowd to their table, right up by the band. Patti trailed behind them, taking everything in.

Jack caught sight of Kate the second she entered the club. In that little black dress, who could miss her? And saw his father escort her to the front table.

But he'd get the first dance.

To say that Cherry blew them all away would be the understatement of the year.

She looked absolutely gorgeous, Kate thought, as she watched Cherry slowly walk to the front of the stage, undulating and glittering in an emerald green dress that made her look like a movie screen siren from the forties. And Kate had the feeling that Cherry knew exactly the effect she was having on the men in the audience.

After a brief chat with the audience, Cherry signaled the musicians, picked up her mike, and began to sing, moving into the first of a series of classic and romantic songs.

Night and day, you are the one,
Only you, beneath the moon or under the sun . . .

"Dance with me, Kate."

She'd seen Jack approaching their table, dressed in a very nice suit. He looked absolutely incredible. And Kate stood, knowing there was no place in the entire world she'd rather be than in his arms.

She took his hand, and he led her out onto the small dance floor as Cherry continued to sing.

Night and day, why is it so,
That this longing for you follows wherever I
    go . . .

He eased her close, and Kate rested her head against his shoulder. They moved to the classic song as if they'd been dancing together all of their lives, and she realized it was going to be impossible to leave this man.

She might fly back to the mainland, but her heart would always be with Jack.

James watched the two of them dancing from the shadows of the club. The way they moved together, the way Jack looked down at Kate, the way she whispered something in his ear that made him laugh—it made his heart constrict, as he remembered Caroline. And he knew that his son was beginning the most joyous journey of his life.

And its torment won't be through,
'Til you let me spend my life making love to
    you . . .

His smile widened as he saw the way Jack held her. James had a feeling that he wasn't going to have to wait all that long for those grandchildren.

Patti was playing with the straw in her Mai Tai as she watched Jack and Kate. She glanced to the side as she saw James approaching her table.

"Would you like to dance?" he said when he reached her.

She nodded, then stood up. He took her hand and led her out onto the dance floor.

"Don't they look just great together?" she whispered into his ear as they started to dance.

He smiled down at her and nodded his head.

Cherry was having one of the great nights of her life. The first song had ended, and she smoothly started the next one, a smile in her voice as she thought of how appropriate it was to Jack and Kate.

Witchcraft.

Those fingers in my hair,
That sly, come hither stare,

She knew Jack wouldn't let Kate go, that he'd want more than one dance with her, and she watched them as she sang. And saw how James was looking at them.

He obviously approved.

A few hours later, Cherry had officially brought down the house. Two encores later, Kate and Patti knocked on the door of her dressing room, and she let them in.

"I didn't know you could sing like that!" Patti exclaimed.

Cherry simply laughed as James poured her a glass of champagne.

Kate stood to the side, enjoying her friend's success. Jack had left just moments before, telling her he'd meet her in the lobby at three. And she knew he might not have felt comfortable, coming back to the dressing room with her, what with his boss right there. Plus he'd been carrying heavy luggage all day and might have wanted a short nap.

One that she probably wouldn't get. She glanced at

the clock on the dressing room table. One thirty-five in the morning. And James had just popped open another bottle of the bubbly.

"Hey," she said brightly, "why don't we go back to the villa and continue this celebration?" She glanced at Patti, who grinned. They'd made a quick trip to a party store, and after Cherry had left, the main living room of villa number six had been totally transformed, what with all the banners, balloons, and streamers.

Not to mention a killer cake and other goodies.

Patti grabbed the bottle of champagne, then Cherry's arm. They started out the door, and Kate grinned at James, "Party at our place?"

He laughed. "I like the way you think."

Jack glanced around the lobby one more time. It wasn't yet three, but he was impatient to see Kate.

He hadn't felt comfortable going back to Cherry's dressing room, not with his father there. But after tonight, when he told Kate the truth, that would no longer be a problem.

He glanced up as he saw her enter the enormous lobby, then grinned at her outfit. The dark green sweats were sort of baggy, but on Kate they looked adorable. He had a feeling she might have borrowed them.

"All set?" he said, walking up to her. Then he frowned. That jacket didn't look too substantial. "Wait here a sec."

He approached the desk, then asked the man behind it if housekeeping could bring them a blanket.

"Jack! Is that really necessary?"

"Yep. You have no idea how cold it gets up there."

Once he had the blanket, he held out his hand, she took it, and they headed outside to the parking lot. He stowed the blanket in one of the motorcycle's storage compartments, handed her a helmet, put his on, then climbed on his bike.

Kate hesitated for just a fraction of a second, then got on the bike behind him. She hung on tightly as he started the engine, backed the bike out of its parking space, then headed them out of the parking lot and onto the deserted, dark road.

Their journey had begun.

It was strangely fun, riding on Jack's bike, holding on to him, in the middle of the night when it seemed like the entire island was fast asleep. She liked being able to touch him, even smell him. Now she knew she was losing it, when she even liked the way he *smelled.*

They passed small clusters of houses, towns where very few lights were on, then sugarcane fields, the silky stalks rippling in the night breezes. Then they finally reached the bottom of the volcano and began the climb.

Haleakala. *The house of the sun.* Jack had mentioned to her that the road they'd be taking to the top was the world's most rapidly ascending road. And because of the altitude at the very top, temperatures at dawn and dusk could drop to nearly freezing.

Jack maneuvered the sharply curving switchbacks expertly, and Kate had an intuitive feeling that if he'd been alone, he might have taken the road a little faster. She was grateful he didn't, as she might have gotten scared.

They climbed the side of the dormant volcano on Jack's bike, and Kate saw the vegetation change, from cactus plants and eucalyptus, past the tree line, to the strange, dry, brown desert littered with lava boulders.

And it was *cold.*

They parked the bike, and Jack reached into the compartment for the blanket. At that point, with a cold wind blowing in the darkness and Cherry's jacket totally inadequate, Kate was glad to let him swathe her in the thick blanket, covering everything but the very tip of her cold nose.

"Okay?" he whispered, and she nodded.

They walked, or rather, he seemed to know where he was going and she followed him, letting his bigger body act as a windbreak. As they approached the edge of the crater, Kate felt the ancient power of the place enfold her, almost capture her soul.

She'd never seen—or felt—anything like it.

The deep crater was swathed in a velvety layer of cloud. What she could see almost resembled a moonscape. Grey and pink cinder cones peeked above the foglike clouds, and she could make out swirls of red sand. The windworn lava formations had an eerie quality to them, and she could intuitively understand how the ancient Hawaiians had always considered this to be a very sacred place.

A powerful, natural presence could be felt here, a silence so profound it enfolded her. Enveloped her. Kate knew this view would be a part of her consciousness forever, and she actually felt she could feel the power of the gods and goddesses. Here, in their ancient and sacred home, the Hawaiian kahuna priests had performed so many sacred rites of initiation.

Jack had moved them up to the very front of a railing, to the edge of the crater where they had an excellent view. He stood behind her, his arms around her, helping to keep the blanket tightly around her. And now, Kate realized there were lots of other people around them in the darkness, coming to see this extraordinary place at sunrise.

Then it began.

Dawn slipped over the rim, lighting those extraordinary clouds. Though there were masses of people around them, utter silence reigned.

"Maui," Jack whispered in her ear, and Kate knew he was referring to the tale of the demigod Maui slowing the path of the sun and making the day longer by lassoing the sun with his rope. The creation chant she'd read had said that Maui had harnessed each ray of the sun. But when he finally released those rays, he left some of the ropes dangling, and the chant said you could see them at sunset when they slipped into the darkening sky.

The horizon fairly glimmered, slowly lighting with shades of pink, red, gold, and orange, each color and its various shadings blending into the next.

Bars of light shot color into the clouds, while the shaded areas turned a deep purple. Kate couldn't stop staring, then realized she was crying, tears running down her face from the sheer beauty in front of her.

She felt Jack's arms tighten around her reassuringly. He was standing behind her, his chin resting on her head, saying nothing. She wondered if he could tell she was crying, then found she didn't care.

He'd understand.

The memories flooding through him were so bittersweet.

The last time he'd been up here, his mother had been with him, wrapped in a blanket, so weak she'd been held in his father's arms. He'd been only eleven and had held her hand so tightly, as if by hanging on to her he could keep death away.

And now he was here with Kate.

He heard her sniff and knew she was crying. And he kissed the top of her head. He hadn't known why he'd thought of taking her here, he'd just trusted his instincts. Now he was glad he had. Something inside of him had shifted, settled, and he knew that all he'd ever want in this world was the woman in his arms.

Now all he had to do was convince her.

They watched the sunrise in silence, and even after most of the other people had moved away and gone inside the round, glass-paneled Visitor Center, they remained by the railing, staring out into the extraordinary crater.

Jack, Kate decided later at breakfast, was an incredibly friendly guy.

They'd started back down the hill, maneuvering past huge groups of helmeted bicycle riders coasting down the side of the dormant volcano to sea level. Now, still up in an area with lots of trees that looked nothing like what she'd always thought Hawaii should look like, he'd pulled over into a local eatery. The minute he'd walked in the door, almost everyone in the place had greeted him.

He'd introduced her to all these people, and they'd studied her, then him, then smiled. And Kate had wondered what they were thinking.

He'd ordered them each a huge breakfast, Portuguese sausage, eggs, and rice for himself, and banana macadamia pancakes for her. "The two best things here, and we can share," he'd whispered to her after he'd placed the order.

And Kate found herself simply nodding her head. She felt so open, so vulnerable, after their trip up to Haleakala, as if her heart had just opened up and there was nothing she could do to close it or guard it again.

Out of control . . .

They ate outside, on a huge lanai that overlooked a lush garden.

"Are you going to get fired for taking so much time

away from work?" she said, taking a sip of absolutely excellent coffee. Then she wondered why she should be worried for him.

"Nah. Matt's covering for me."

She loved looking at him. Listening to him. She loved kissing him. And she realized, between bites of those luscious pancakes, that she could wake up next to this man every single morning for the rest of her life and never get tired of that face, those eyes.

"Kate?"

She blinked. "Yes?"

"Do you have just a little more time before you need to get back?"

"Sure."

"Good. I have one more place I'd like us to go."

She nodded, too full of emotion to talk right then, and concentrated on her pancakes.

He took her to a house.

It had the feel of a little hideaway. Snuggled back among some trees, it looked like a little ranch house, and as Jack let her in the front door, he dropped the keys into a bowl on a table by the door.

"I'm house-sitting for a friend, I have to check on his pets," he said.

She nodded, taking in the house. It was bigger than it looked on the outside. Casual, furnished with a simple style and brilliant, pure colors. A tropical house.

She liked it.

The pets turned out to be three cats and two dogs, two Shepherd mixes with deep brown eyes. The dogs glanced at Kate, then at Jack.

"It's okay," he said, ruffling the hair on one's ruff.

Then they pranced over, wagging their tails and whining.

"They're beautiful," Kate breathed, squatting down and petting them. She laughed. "And they really like you."

"Yeah, well, I feed them."

Once he'd attended to the animals, he returned to the living room. She'd sat down on a comfortable couch, and he joined her, sitting close.

"Kate," he began, and she could tell he was uneasy. "There's something I have to tell you."

Everything in her went still. *This is it.* He was about to give her the good-bye speech, a little early, just because he was a nice guy and wouldn't play it out to the very end or not say anything at all.

"Okay," she said quietly. Cautiously. Her heart actually ached.

He seemed to be searching for the right words. Finally, after what seemed like an interminably long moment, he opened his mouth.

She put a finger over his lips and her eyes filled.

"I have a pretty good idea of what you're about to say," she began, her voice shaking, her stomach in knots.

"I don't think you do—"

"Jack," she said, interrupting him. "Could you—not do this right now? I'm feeling kind of fragile."

"Kate," he whispered, and his dark blue eyes had an almost agonized expression in them, "it has to be said."

"But not right now," she whispered back. "*Please.*" Not knowing what else to do, she leaned toward him and kissed him. "Please," she whispered against his mouth. "I just want this moment, right now. Nothing else."

He hesitated.

"Please, Jack." Their lips were almost touching, and she kissed the side of his mouth, then his lips, then touched that place on his neck between his jawline and his shoulder and felt those muscles jump, react to her. "Please."

She knew she'd won when she felt his arms come around her waist, when he pulled her into his lap and began to really kiss her. But a part of her knew she was only postponing the inevitable.

He lay in the big bed and watched her sleep. Afternoon light filtered through the blinds, so Jack got up quietly and closed them. Then he lay back down and closed his eyes as he listened to her slow, even breathing.

She was exhausted.

About forty minutes later, he watched as she slowly opened her eyes. She glanced around the shaded bedroom, and he knew she was remembering where they were, coming to the present moment from her dreams.

Then those beautiful green eyes were turned on him, and he felt that peculiar sensation in his stomach, as if he were on a roller coaster and they were poised on the top that split second before plunging back down.

He stroked her cheekbone with the back of his hand, touching her so gently.

"I knew you were trouble the minute I met you," he whispered.

"Well, I wasn't looking for you, either."

He smiled into the darkened bedroom. His Kate. His wonderful, complicated, prickly Kate.

"I was looking for you after that first time," he said. "After I bumped into you on the path." He lowered his head and kissed her, loving the way she softened beneath him. So wonderfully willing, every single time.

She broke the kiss, then lay back against the pillow, her dark brown hair fanned out behind her head, and she'd never looked more beautiful to him. Or more vulnerable. He moved up over her, settling his body between her thighs. And he sensed the exact moment she started to emotionally pull away.

He lowered his head, his lips against her ear. "Stay with me, Kate," he whispered, then kissed the side of her neck. "Stay here with me. Don't pull away." He raised his head slowly, looking down at her.

Her eyes filled, those lips trembled, she averted those green eyes.

Shit.

She took an unsteady breath. "I know this has to end—"

"No. Not true."

"Don't, Jack. I'm a big girl. I just—can we not talk about it today?"

He studied her for a long moment, then suddenly remembered how he'd felt the first time his mother had taken him to Haleakala.

Emotional. Overwhelmed. So open.

"Oh baby, I'm sorry." He slid his arms around her, rolled gently to the side, moved so she could put her head on his shoulder. "Whatever you want."

He stared at the ceiling, and within minutes could feel her tears on his shoulder.

He was hurting her. But if he told her the truth now, he'd hurt her even more. He had the feeling that Kate hadn't really risked her heart since that night so long ago when her uncle had come to her parents' house and taken her away.

He could understand that. He'd been just as scared after his mother died. What was the point of even attempting to love someone when it was so easy to lose them?

"Let's sleep a little more," he whispered, then turned

so they were spooned together, and he could hold her as she slept.

"Okay," she whispered, and he heard her tears in that one word. His stomach tightened, and he wished he could take all the hurt away, that nothing would ever hurt Kate again.

As he held her, as she finally fell asleep, he knew he'd never meant for any of it to turn out this way.

When she woke up, she was alone in the darkened bedroom. For just an instant, Kate pulled the covers over her head and hid.

Coward.

He'd been trying to tell her the truth, that both of them were going to go back to their respective worlds in a few more days, and she was such a huge baby that she couldn't deal with it.

Well. Maybe it would be easier if they never had that little talk. Maybe she should just get on that plane, grow up, and realize that this was what having a fling was all about.

There was just one tiny little catch—her heart refused to go along with it.

"Kate?"

She threw the covers back off her head and sat up, part of the sheet clutched protectively to her chest. Jack stood in the doorway, naked.

Now there was a view she could look at for the rest of her life, as well.

"Shower?" he said.

Kate made up her mind in an instant. If she only had a little time left with Jack, she wasn't going to waste it being mopey.

"Sounds great." She slid out of bed and started toward him.

* * *

The shower was outdoors, amid a glorious garden. And Kate laughed out loud when one of the dogs came galloping over and darted beneath the fall of warm water with them.

"Max!" Jack said, but the unrepentant dog merely darted out of reach and began to shake himself dry.

"I don't mind," Kate said. She reached for the shampoo.

"Let me," he said, and she almost started crying again at the way he shampooed her hair, his touch so gentle, so tender.

After they got dressed, he surprised her by firing up the barbecue and making what he told her was *huli-huli* chicken, seasoned with a soy sauce marinade. She fixed a salad from the produce she found in the large refrigerator.

They ate dinner out in the garden, overlooking masses of tropical plants and brilliant flowers. Max and Sheba begged shamelessly, and Kate kept laughing at the expressions on their doggy faces.

"Their owner's a real pushover," she said, giving Max a piece of chicken.

"That's true," Jack said. "Would you be able to whip these two into shape?"

"Nope," Kate said, then laughed. She stopped midlaugh, noticing the intent way he was looking at her. "What?"

"Spend the night with me, Kate."

As if she could refuse him anything.

He took her back to the resort early the following morning, and as Kate walked slowly down the path to the villa with Jack, holding hands, she knew she would never forget her first fling.

And her last.

"I'm working the bar today," Jack said. "Come by around noon and I'll have a surprise for you."

"Okay."

He kissed her good-bye and she watched him walk away. God, she was even in love with the way he walked! He turned around, their eyes met, then he grinned, turned, and continued on his way.

She let herself into the quiet villa, then walked down the hall to Patti and Cherry's bedroom. They were sitting up in bed, talking.

"Hey," Kate said, knocking softly. "I'm back."

"We weren't worried," Patti said. "We knew you were with Jack. Did you have a good time?"

"Wonderful. You guys should get up there, to the volcano." Kate yawned. "I'm going to take a little snooze."

"Sounds good," Patti said.

"Take one for me," Cherry called out as Kate left.

Once Patti and Cherry were alone, the two women glanced at each other, then at the door.

"She loves him," Patti whispered. Kate had never been able to hide anything from her.

"This," said Cherry, "is going to end badly."

Chapter Sixteen

❀ Cherry left late that morning for an early rehearsal, and Kate was fast asleep, so Patti decided to take a walk on the beach. She set off in the direction she and Kate had taken a few days before and found that the gentle sound of the waves and the feel of the trade winds on her skin soothed her agitated spirit.

Strange, how this whole trip had come about because Roger had left her at the altar. She and Kate wouldn't even be in Maui if it hadn't been for her father and a set of nonrefundable tickets for a honeymoon. So much had happened on this tropical island in the days since her wedding-that-wasn't that she felt as if she'd been transformed into another person.

Yes, she'd managed to get over the worst concerning Roger, chiefly because she'd realized and come to terms with the fact that they hadn't had that great a relationship to begin with. After seeing the way Jack looked at Kate, Patti knew she'd never settle for anything less.

But now, with Kate deeply in a relationship with Jack and with Cherry embarking on a brand-new career as a lounge singer, Patti felt as if she were drifting. Drifting through her life, as if she were being tossed along in the ocean, without anything solid to cling to, with nothing to ground her.

It wasn't envy, exactly. She was just wondering when something in her life would change for the better. As she stopped and stared out over the waves sparkling in the bright sunlight, she suddenly felt tired and so discouraged, as if every single choice she'd made up to this moment in time had been the wrong one.

"Patti?"

She looked up to see James McKenna striding across the sand toward her.

"How are you?" he called out, and she had a sudden intuitive flash that he really meant it, he wasn't just making conversation.

Still, she hesitated, then shaded her eyes and blurted out, "Not that good."

"Anything you'd care to talk about?" He'd reached her side, and now, as he smiled down at her, she thought that he had the kindest, most compassionate eyes of any man she'd ever met.

"Yeah. You're a good listener. And you don't have that many preconceptions about me."

"We could have lunch by the pool. My treat."

"That would be nice."

"So, all I thought I ever wanted was a home and babies and a husband who would come home every single night and want to be with me." Patti reached for another fry and dunked it into the ketchup on the side of her plate.

"Those are admirable goals. Good choices," James

said, reaching for his iced tea. He enjoyed talking with Patti. Right away, he'd recognized her as a gentle soul who spent most of her time helping others, but not necessarily asking for that help herself.

He found that he wanted to wipe that sad look off her expressive face. He'd seen her on the beach, staring out over the waves, and had known she was struggling with something. And problems were always more easily solved when shared.

"Not such good choices when you quit your job right before a wedding that doesn't come off."

"Can you get your job back when you go back home?"

"Nope." Patti reached for another fry. "The woman who worked under me moved right up, they promoted her. There's no place for me now."

"A clothing store," James said. "Did you enjoy working there?"

"I've always loved clothes." Patti leaned toward him, and he saw the flare of genuine passion in those clear blue eyes. "I was one of those little girls who really dressed her dolls. I've loved to sew and knit since I can remember."

"Kate made the mud pies," James guessed.

"Yep. And I made enough outfits for all our dolls and stuffed animals."

James laughed. "You two must have been quite a handful."

Patti grinned. "We kept my mom hopping."

"I have a proposition for you," James said, leaning back in his chair. "You know that a lot of people come to Maui to get married."

"That would be really romantic."

"I've watched other resorts get the bulk of that business because they have jewelry stores and wedding bou-

tiques right on the resort grounds. We have a gift shop
that also doubles as a florist, but other than a second gift
shop with more clothing, we don't really have anything
that can compete."

Patti leaned forward, and he knew he'd sparked her
interest.

"Like a pretty boutique that would carry dresses suit-
able for a bride? Like some really gorgeous pareos, or
long floaty things? And maybe some nice shirts for the
groom? And jewelry?"

"My thoughts, exactly."

"And darling shoes, and something blue, and maybe
even a few simple veils or headpieces for the women
who want to go that route—"

He almost laughed out loud. Those blue eyes were already full of dreams, and he knew he'd found the perfect person to give this project to.

"Have you ever done any designing?" he said.

"This is so funny! If you could see my bedroom, I
have a trunk full of drawings, I almost designed my own
wedding gown . . ." She hesitated. "Even though the
wedding was a bust, my dress was gorgeous."

"I'm sure it was. Is there any way your father could
fax me a few of your best designs?"

"Sure. I know exactly which ones!"

"Patti," James said, leaning forward, "I'd like to
offer you a job. It's kind of up in the air right now, un-
defined shall we say. But the area I have in mind for the
store is going to be vacated in just a few days. I'd like
you to stay and take a look at it, give me some ideas as
to how to decorate it so that it would appeal to a woman
coming here to get married. Especially the front windows. And then I'd like your help in stocking it with
items that would appeal to brides of all ages."

"Oh my God!" She sat back in her chair, and James

had to fight to conceal his grin. The enormity of what he was asking her to do had just started to sink in.

"The mainland is always just a plane flight away," he reminded her gently.

"I know, I know . . ." She covered her mouth with her hand, then looked at him, and he could see the bright sheen of tears in those incredible blue eyes. Her hands began to move expressively as she talked. "It's just—this would be so perfect! I wasn't really looking forward to going home and facing all the relatives, asking all those questions, and becoming 'poor Patti who was dumped at the altar, who couldn't keep her man.'"

"So we have a deal?" He held out his hand.

The hand she offered him actually trembled, but when he took those slender fingers in his and shook her hand, he found her grip to be strong and sure.

"Yes," she said quietly. "Yes, James, I'll stay here and work for you."

Kate bellied up to the bar and just enjoyed watching Jack for a minute.

He was happy, she could tell. He had a real winning way with the customers, laughing and talking with them, helping the children decide what ice cream concoction they wanted to try, gently flirting with the not-so-striking women and making them feel special.

He was just a good guy.

He caught her eye, walked over to where she sat, and asked, "And what can I get for you?"

"Nothing from the bar," she whispered back, and he laughed.

"Tonight," he said. "I'll pick you up at nine, when I'm off my double shift. Don't eat too much dinner; I have a surprise planned."

"Give me a hint."

"A picnic."

"I love it!"

"Good." The bar was absolutely packed, and he glanced quickly around at all the customers. "I've got to go."

"I understand. Nine. I'll be there."

He flashed her that smile as she left, and Kate felt her heart turn over in her chest. Oh, she had it bad.

As Cherry walked back toward villa number six after her rehearsal, she suddenly realized she no longer wanted to find a millionaire. The thought slipped into her mind so easily, she knew she'd been thinking about this particular question for some time. But now she was sure. It was no longer important.

Oh, she wouldn't turn one down if she tripped over him, and he asked her out to dinner, but it was no longer the driving force in her life. And no longer the reason she was here on Maui.

She'd found something far more special here in the tropics. True female friendship.

She'd sung in a lot of nightclubs, but the previous night had been a unique experience for her. No one had ever thrown her a party after an opening night, and no one had ever been as happy for her as both Kate and Patti had been. She'd actually almost cried when she'd walked into the villa after the show and seen the way those two had decorated the living room, with streamers and banners and balloons.

And Kate! That cake she'd baked! What had touched Cherry so deeply was that Kate had remembered which dessert she'd liked the most from their decadent night of desserts and had recreated a cake that had been really close to the one she'd adored.

Simple caring had been Cherry's undoing. She didn't

know how she would ever thank Kate and Patti, because between the two of them, they'd set her on the road to a brand-new life. And this one was so good, she wasn't sure she wanted to change it for quite some time.

She let herself into the villa with her key card, then started down the stairs for the kitchen and a glass of juice. Kate was there already, puttering around. Streamers still hung from the ceiling of the living room, along with a huge glittery banner that read, "CONGRATULATIONS, CHERRY!"

"Hey," Kate said, and Cherry thought she'd never seen her look better. That shiny, dark brown hair was pulled off her face in a high ponytail, and Kate's skin just glowed. Amazing what an incredible sex life could do for a woman's skin.

"Hey." Cherry reached into the fridge, grabbed a pitcher of pineapple juice, and poured herself a glass. "Jesus, between the flowers Jack sent you and the bouquets from my opening, this place is beginning to resemble a funeral home."

Kate laughed. "How did your rehearsal go?" she said.

It was strange, getting used to someone actually being interested in what she was doing. Actually caring. Most of her life, she'd come home to an empty apartment. She wondered if Kate and Patti realized how lucky they were that they'd grown up with that kind of caring. Did they take it for granted?

"Really good. We're rehearsing a few new songs, ones I haven't done before, so I might do some singing in the shower."

"That'll be fun to listen to."

Cherry had to comment on how Kate looked. "You're just *glowing,* Kate! God, I wish I'd had a fling while I was here."

The minute the words were out of her mouth she regretted them. She saw the slightly worried expression cloud Kate's expressive green eyes, and Cherry knew she'd said the wrong thing. But trust Kate, she'd cover up her emotions like an expert. Cherry was sure she wouldn't confide in her.

"Sex, sex, sex!" Kate teased. "Is that all you think about? It's not all there is to life."

Cherry sauntered over to one of the chairs by the round table in the dining area and sat down. "I look at it this way, Kate. Sex is like air. It's not that important unless you're not getting any." And she was pleased when Kate really laughed.

"How's Jack? Are you seeing him tonight?"

"Nine o'clock. A picnic."

"I'm sure it will be some picnic, with that man."

"Cherry . . ." Kate hesitated, and Cherry set her empty juice glass down, suddenly realizing that Kate might actually be asking her advice.

As if my life is anything at all to emulate.

"Cherry . . . could you . . . I mean . . . what I want to ask is . . ."

"How do you end a fling?"

"Yeah." Kate seemed relieved as she came around the kitchen counter and sat down in one of the dining room chairs. "I think Jack was trying to tell me something last night at this house he was sitting for a friend, and I couldn't . . . I asked him to stop because I thought he was going to tell me that . . . that we were over."

In a flash, Cherry realized Jack had been trying to tell Kate the truth about who he really was. And hadn't succeeded—yet.

"Kate, I think you should let him tell you what's on his mind. Maybe he was going to feel you out, see how serious you were about him, and whether the two of you could get something going when this vacation is over."

"You think so?"

"Sugar, I have *never* seen chemistry like the two of you have! He'd be a fool to throw it away. Let me ask you this, would you relocate to Hawaii to be with him?"

"In a heartbeat."

"That's the right answer. So tonight, if he wants to talk, let him talk. Find out what's going on with him."

Kate considered this. "So if he wants to talk, I should just let him?"

"Yeah. I would. Maybe he has something he wants to tell you, like he has a couple of million dollars stashed away somewhere."

Kate rolled her eyes. "Yeah, right."

"Hey, stranger things have happened."

The phone rang, and Kate lifted the receiver. "Villa number six." After a few seconds, she handed it to Cherry. "For you. James McKenna."

Cherry took the phone. "James. Hello."

"I have a personal favor to ask of you."

"Well, maybe I have a personal answer."

He laughed. "There's going to be a wedding at the re-sort tomorrow night, and I just remembered that Angie was supposed to sing. Would it be asking too much to have you take over for the evening? The same guys you sang with before, all the old wedding standards . . ."

"Don't even worry about it. I'll do it. It's before my set at Neptune's Lounge, right?"

"It shouldn't even overlap, there should be a couple of hours in between."

"It's as good as done." She hung up the phone and told Kate.

"Oh, we got a notice about that wedding. I guess it's

going to be held right on that large strip of grass above the beach, so it's just outside our patio. I'll get it."

Kate handed her the announcement, and Cherry read it. It was cunningly designed to look like a wedding invitation. It basically told guests that there would be a wedding outside their patios tomorrow evening at sunset and that they were welcome to come out onto their patios and watch the proceedings.

"How romantic," Kate said, and Cherry could tell where her thoughts were headed. But in romance, as in anything else, a wise woman proceeded one step at a time.

"Get him to talk to you, Kate. And make sure you tell him how you feel! I mean, what have you got to lose? I'd go all out for a man like Jack."

Kate reached across the table and grasped her hand. "Thanks so much, Cherry. I couldn't really ask Patti, she hasn't had as much experience with life. Hardly any. My aunt and uncle kind of sheltered her, you know?"

"Yeah." Sheltered. It sounded wonderful.

"I'm going to see what we can fix for dinner tonight. Anything you can't eat when you're singing?"

"Nothing too creamy. No dairy."

"Got it." And as Kate headed into the kitchen, Cherry sat back and realized she hadn't done so badly in the advice department after all.

Tell her, Jack, she thought. *Tell her tonight before everything blows up and out of your control.*

Patti blew into the villa about half an hour later, and Kate had never seen her cousin more excited.

"I'm *staying!*" Patti shrieked as she came into the villa, then ran down the stairs where Kate was preparing dinner and Cherry was lying on the sofa in the living room, reading a magazine.

"What?" Kate said, washing her hands and coming into the living room as she dried them on a dish towel.

"I'm *staying! Here!* In *Hawaii!"* Patti's smile was so bright it seemed to light up the entire room; she was incandescent with joy.

"How are you going to do that, Sugar?" Cherry said, coming up off the couch.

Briefly, Patti explained about the job that James had offered her in the soon-to-be-created bridal boutique. Kate felt as if her head were reeling, things were changing so very fast.

"So we can *all* stay!" Patti said, grabbing Cherry's hands and dancing her around the room. "You with your singing, me with the boutique, and Kate with . . ." She turned toward Kate, and to her horror, Kate felt her throat closing with intense emotion. As much as she was upset about what would probably happen with her and Jack, she simply couldn't diminish Patti's joy.

She ran to her cousin and hugged her tightly. "Oh, Patti, I'm *so* happy for you! Are you sure this is what you really want?"

"Are you kidding? Being able to design wedding dresses? My own boutique, that I can lay out exactly the way I want? Here? At this resort?" She laughed. "Pinch me quick; I have to be dreaming!"

"You're not dreaming, Sugar," Cherry said. "It's that James McKenna. He has a way of seeing that dreams come true."

Patti stepped back from Kate, and Kate's throat closed again, but this time from seeing the utter happiness in her cousin's face. Finally, something was going right for Patti.

"Finally, *finally* I'm going to do something really daring!" Patti said. "I don't want to be poor little Patti, shy little Patti, pathetic Patti who was duped and dumped by Roger . . ."

"You'll be Patti the successful businesswoman *in Hawaii!*" Cherry said. "I think this calls for a slice of that fabulous cake, Kate!"

As Kate dished up the cake and joined in the merriment, she wondered if she'd be heading back to Chicago all by herself.

Jack arrived promptly at nine in just swimming trunks, with a plastic cooler in one hand. Kate came to the door and let him inside the villa.

"You look tired," she said when she saw his face.

"I don't feel that bad," he said. "Not now. Ready to go?"

"Am I overdressed?" She'd dressed casually, in shorts and a T-shirt.

"Always." He smiled at her, that smile that got her going before he even touched her, and she knew that he didn't care about her clothes. Knowing Jack, she wouldn't be wearing them long. "You'll just need a bathing suit for where we're going."

"Should I put it on under my clothes, or just wear the suit?"

"Wear your suit and one of those pareos. We're not going far."

She went to change, and when she came back, Patti was telling Jack all about the boutique.

"I know he's wanted to do something like that for a long time," Jack said. "You, Patti, were in the right place at the right time. Congratulations, it'll be a lot of fun having you on the island."

"You guys have a good time," Patti said.

"I'm not going to take a purse or a key," Kate said. "Where we're going, I might lose it."

"Good idea," Patti said.

"Be back at a reasonable hour, children—*not!*" Cherry called from the living room. Jack just laughed.

They walked along the winding resort paths, between tropical foliage, and Kate noticed they were heading toward a particular pool area, with water slides and private grottos.

"I thought this area was all shut down after dark," she remarked.

"Only for those not in the know." And before she knew it, he'd slipped them both beneath the ropes that cordoned off the area.

"Jack!" she said, but he hustled her farther inside, where they couldn't be seen.

"I've done this a million times before . . ." he said, then stopped. "Not with a woman."

"I'm sure."

"Come on, Kate. I used to sneak in here all the time when I was a kid."

"You lived on the island as a child?"

She sensed his hesitation, as if he were choosing his words. And she suddenly realized she knew nothing about this man, his family, where he'd gone to school.

"Yeah, I did."

She wondered if his parents were still alive, and if they lived in a modest little house. Perhaps his mother was a maid, and his father drove for one of the tour lines.

She wouldn't pry.

"No other women, Kate, I swear."

She decided to stop being such a pain and just enjoy their date.

"Okay. Lead on."

He led her to the top of the elaborate pool area, to the beginning of the slide.

"It's kind of cool going down the slides in the dark. Matt and I used to do it all the time as kids."

"I would've thought they'd turn the water off at night."

He grinned at her. "That's where having friends in high places comes in."

"I'm just not going to ask anything else."

"Take your pareo off and leave it on that chair over there. We'll come back for it."

"Aye aye, sir. Or should I say, aye yay yay!"

He laughed, then took her hand, the cooler in the other.

And they jumped.

Water swirled all around them, and before she could really register what had happened, they were in one of the pools at the bottom of a slide. At night, the only reality she had was Jack's body, his arms around her.

"This is neat," she admitted. "It's nice being all alone."

"My plan all along," he whispered in her ear, and she laughed. "Up for a few more slides?"

She nodded, and he headed toward the edge of the pool, where she could hear a sound like that of a small waterfall.

"Lie down and let the water carry you," Jack whispered. She did as he requested, and found herself sliding down another long water slide, into another pool. She moved away from the bottom of the slide, and Jack joined her soon after, the small cooler still securely in his grasp.

"This is too much fun," she whispered as she swam up to him.

"No, you're too much fun, Kate. One more slide?"

She nodded.

The third slide deposited them in a huge pool, and Jack swam over to a large, rocky ledge. He set the cooler up there, then climbed up, reaching down and offering Kate his hand. He hauled her up easily, and they sat side by side.

"This is great," she whispered.

"Never let it be said that I don't take you to the nicest places," he said, and she had to laugh.

Then he started to unpack the cooler, and she was touched beyond words by what he'd brought. A small candle and a book of matches sealed in a plastic freezer bag. Jack lit the small white candle, and the light flickered brightly, illuminating the nooks and crannies of the grotto.

"And now," he said, producing a small bottle of wine and two plastic wineglasses. "A toast to the best time I've ever had in my life. You, Kate."

He poured her a little into the glass, and she pretended to taste it, much as she had at their penthouse dinner. "A fine wine, I think."

"Good." He filled her glass, then his own. "We'll start with our first course."

How he'd managed to pack so much food into such a compact cooler astounded her. They feasted on Vietnamese summer rolls filled with rice noodles, basil, Chinese parsley, mint, chives, lettuce, and shrimp, and moved on to crab cakes fixed from small blue Hawaiian crabs.

"I just brought three appetizers, so you could try more food," he admitted.

She was touched by the fact that he'd thought of what she loved to do as a chef. Try new food and think about how it had been prepared. It was her favorite thing to do.

Well, second favorite . . .

"And last but not least," Jack said, "we have vegetable tempura."

"This is wonderful," she said, reaching for a piece of sweet potato. She glanced at him, feeling like teasing. "But I hope you remembered dessert."

"You think I'd risk being caught out here alone with you without something sweet?" he said. "*Haupia* cake. White cake filled with creamy coconut pudding."

"Oh my God."

"I thought you'd like it."

Patti was feeling confident after her triumphant day and asked Cherry if they could go out to the bar by the main pool, which was still open and surrounded by flaming tiki torches. As Cherry only sang in Neptune's Lounge every other night, Patti knew she had the night off.

"Sure, Sugar, just let me throw on a pareo."

They wandered over and approached the crowded bar. And immediately Cherry found herself surrounded by guests who had enjoyed her singing the other night. Patti could tell it was a heady feeling for her friend, so she approached the bar and ordered drinks for both of them.

She didn't recognize the bartender, a blonde man with a mustache.

"Two Mai Tais," she said.

"For you, cutie, anything," he said.

Matt was tending bar that night, and he perked up as soon as he spotted Patti. Maybe tonight wouldn't be such a bad night after all.

He didn't care for the new guy he was working with. Just a feeling he had, but he'd learned not to ignore those feelings when they came to him. His name was

Greg, and he'd only worked at the resort for about a week, but his skill as a bartender told Matt that he'd been tending bar for a long time. Very smooth moves.

He watched as Greg handed Patti two Mai Tais.

"This cake," Kate whispered. "Unbelievable."

Jack, stretched out on his back, started to laugh. "You're so cute when you eat, Kate."

"Do you think I'm a pig?"

"What? No. Where do you get these ideas?"

"Just wondering."

"No, I like the way you eat. You know what they say, a woman who can really enjoy a meal is one sensual woman, and she can also enjoy other physical delights." He raised his head, looked at her, and wiggled his eyebrows.

"Spare me."

He frowned. "No?"

"Not even tempted. Not when I'm this full."

"My master plan has totally backfired."

Kate lay back and began to laugh. He was so open about what he wanted, you had to love him. "Maybe we should both jump in the water and swim, risk a cramp or something."

"Get over here."

"Ooh, I just love it when you order me around and act all macho."

She got on her hands and knees and crawled carefully over the cement ledge to where Jack lay on his back. He raised an arm and she lay down next to him, snuggling into his muscular shoulder.

"I like this," Jack said. "You, me, a cave. Fire and food. We could just live here, Kate."

"You are *such* a barbarian!"

"And you love it." He kissed her swiftly, then lay

back down. "Comfy?" he said, and she burst out laughing.

"We're lying on cement!"

"I know, I couldn't figure out how to get a blanket down here without getting it wet."

"I'm not complaining."

"Sure you are," he said, then she shrieked with laughter as he hauled her up on top of his chest, her breasts pressed against his muscled chest, her legs splayed out on either side of his legs.

"There. That's better," he whispered. "More comfortable?" He ran his hands up over her bare back, then down again. And her teeny black bikini offered scant coverage.

"Not by much. You're so hard—" She stopped as she felt his body stirring beneath hers, then glanced at him. Those dark blue eyes, filled with laughter only seconds ago, were looking at her with that peculiarly intent look that made her go weak in the knees.

"True," he said, then cupped the back of her head with his hand and eased her down so their lips met.

And Kate felt that fire start to shimmer in her belly. She was lost.

Patti sat at the bar, watching Cherry hold court. Her friend was the belle of this particular ball, no doubt about it.

"Here you go," said a male voice.

She glanced up as the blonde bartender put another drink in front of her.

"I didn't order this Mai Tai."

"It's on the house," he said, with a friendly smile. "What's your name?"

"Patti."

"Greg."

"Nice to meet you." She picked up her drink and took a sip.

"Who's going to be on the bottom?" Kate muttered against Jack's mouth as he slid her bikini bottom off and flung it aside.

"I'll volunteer," he said, raising his hand. "I don't want you to bruise your butt on the cement."

She laughed, then gasped as he slid into her, hard and hot and so ready to go. Her bikini top had long been discarded, and now she braced her hands against his strong shoulders as her head fell back.

It just got better and better with this man.

Then she couldn't think rationally anymore, she could only feel . . .

"I don't feel too good," Patti muttered, her head in her hands.

"You okay?" a voice said.

She glanced up and saw the blonde bartender.

"No. I think I'm going to head home." She started to slide off her bar stool and was shocked at how her legs didn't seem to want to obey her.

"Do you want me to help you home?" That same voice.

"I . . . oh . . . I don't know . . ." Patti tried to stand and realized she had to hold on to the side of the bar. What was wrong with her? How much had she had to drink?

"Let me help you back to your room," said Greg.

Something, some sixth sense, made Matt turn around just as Greg slipped his arm around Patti's shoulders.

Wrong. Wrong, wrong, wrong.

He didn't even question his judgement as he leapt

over the bar and raced to the couple. "Hey Patti," he said as he reached them. "You okay?"

She shook her head, then glanced up at him, her blue eyes clouded and unfocused. "Matt?"

"Yeah." He glanced over at Greg. "I'll take it from here."

"Hey, I was only going to help her get home—"

"Yeah, well, I'll take it from here." Something about this guy chilled him. He gathered Patti close to his side, but her legs kept splaying out and he realized that some of the guests were starting to give them a wide berth.

"Shit," he muttered, then slung her up over his shoulder.

"You," Kate said quietly after her third orgasm, "can do anything you want to me. You know that, don't you?"

Jack's quietly satisfied laugh told her all she needed to know.

"And this cement?" she whispered. "Like a featherbed."

"You are so full of it."

She leaned toward him and whispered in his ear, "I was."

He laughed.

"Patti, I need your key card to get us into the villa," Matt said patiently.

"Purse," she whispered. "Oh, my head . . ."

He balanced her on his shoulder as he rooted through her purse, finally finding the key card that would let them into the villa. He eased the door open, dropped her purse in the hallway, and steered Patti into the enormous marble bathroom.

"Matt," she said, and he was horrified to see she was crying. "My stomach . . ."

Then she threw up all over him.

Cherry glanced up as the handsome blonde bartender set the Mai Tai in front of her.

"I didn't order this drink," she said.

"It's on the house," he said.

She narrowed her eyes at him. If there was one thing she'd learned while trying to survive, it was that nothing in life was free. And she wasn't too bad at sizing up a man in a glance.

This one was trouble.

"Thanks." She knew she wouldn't touch it. "Did you see a pretty blonde woman here? About five eight, really cute. Big blue eyes?"

"She just left. She wasn't feeling too good."

Some inner warning system came to life. Patti sitting at this bar. The free drink. She knew his type, had met so many like this man during her years in Vegas.

"You're a little shit, you know that?" she whispered.

His head shot up, and for an instant she could see from the expression on his face that she'd nailed him.

She reached out and grabbed the front of his coral-colored polo shirt, bringing his face a mere inch from hers. When she spoke, her tone was very, very soft.

"You listen to me, and you listen good. If you've hurt my friend in *any* way, I'll track you down and make you wish you were never born."

She let him go abruptly, then got up and left the bar.

"Kate," Jack whispered.

"Hmmm."

"We should get going."

She kissed the side of his neck. "Where's your sense

of adventure? I thought we were going to sleep out in the wild. You know, like a slumber party."

"You're not cold?"

"Nope. It's nice, next to you. Like sleeping near an oven."

"I hope that's a compliment."

"A really nice Jenn-Air."

He laughed, snuggled closer. "Whatever you want." He closed his eyes, content to have her in his arms.

Chapter Seventeen

Matt managed to maneuver Patti beneath the shower, where he soaked them both and rinsed off their clothing at the same time.

"I feel awful," Patti moaned.

"You'll feel better once you puke some more," Matt promised her. Either that bastard of a bartender had put an enormous amount of booze into her drink, or he'd been testing out one of those date rape drugs. Either way, he wasn't leaving Patti until she was okay.

"I'm sorry," she whimpered, then he watched, hating her pain, as she clutched her stomach and doubled over.

Damn it, what had that bastard put in her drink?

"Patti," he whispered. "Can you stick your finger down your throat and force yourself to throw up?"

If she didn't get better pretty soon, he'd have to call 911.

*   *   *

Cherry raced to the villa, reaching the door and fumbling in her purse for her key card, then letting herself in. She stopped outside the bathroom, standing in the hallway as she heard the shower running.

Had she misinterpreted the situation? Had Patti just decided to come back to the villa early and take a shower before she went to bed?

No. Cherry trusted her instincts; they'd gotten her out of some pretty desperate situations more than once. That bartender had been just as bad as she'd thought he was.

She was about to pound on the bathroom door when she heard Matt's deep, masculine voice.

"Yeah, that's right Patti, just like that. That's it. No, you have to really stick it in deeper."

Cherry frowned. *Matt?* What was Patti doing with Matt in the bathroom?

"I can't get it down my throat, it makes me gag," Patti said. "Matt, this doesn't feel so good."

"You have to, Honey. I know you don't like it, but it's the only way . . ."

"Am I the *only* person on this *entire island* who can't get *laid?*" Cherry yelled. "What the *hell* is going on in there?"

A short silence ensued, then the bathroom door opened with a quiet *snick.* Matt stood on the other side, the door open only a few inches.

"She's drunk," he said quietly. "Something that bartender put in her drink. I'm trying to get her to puke."

"Oh." Now it all made sense. Cherry felt about two inches tall, but she pushed past her embarrassment, her only concern for Patti.

"Did he use that drug, the date rape . . ."

"I don't know. She seems to be getting better, she's puking a lot."

"I'll get some Seven-Up."

They worked on Patti for the rest of the evening, until she'd thrown up so much that Cherry didn't know how one human being could expel that much and still be standing.

Actually, by that time, Patti was in her bed, her stomach cramps had subsided, and she was sitting propped up with several pillows, a large glass of Seven-Up on the bedside table.

"Why would he do that?" she asked Cherry.

"Because there are some pretty bad people out in the world, Sugar." Cherry glanced at Matt, sitting on the foot of Patti's queen-sized bed. *What a guy.* A real champ. Nothing had fazed him, even when Patti had thrown up on him the second time.

Cherry glanced from Matt to Patti. Kate might not be the only one of them to find a man on this island.

"And," she said, "there are some pretty good people out there as well." She smiled at Matt. "Thanks for helping her."

"Hey, I just had a bad feeling and followed my instincts."

How well she knew that feeling.

Matt was dressed in one of the villa's soft white terry robes, and his clothing was being washed, along with Patti's, in the villa's washing machine downstairs off the kitchen. Cherry would make sure that before he left he ate something, had a hot shower, and had slipped into his freshly washed clothing.

"Your clothes should be done in about an hour," she said.

He glanced up at her, pushing back his long, damp blonde hair, and once again she was impressed by how much he looked like Brad Pitt in *Legends of the Fall.* But she found that she wasn't going to call him Pitt's

Evil Twin anymore. Maybe Pitt's Excellent Twin. She almost laughed out loud as she thought, *Are you a good twin or a bad twin?*

"I think I'll spend the night," Matt said. He glanced around the room. "If it's okay with both of you. If you can spare a pillow and a blanket, I can sleep on the floor by her bed."

His devotion to Patti touched Cherry, and she knew she was a notoriously tough nut to crack.

"You can sleep up here with me," Patti said softly, "unless you're scared I'm going to puke on you all over again."

Matt started to laugh as he looked down at Patti, and Cherry caught her breath at the expression in those eyes.

None of them could sleep much. Later that night, in the dark, Patti whispered, "It's going to be really bad when Kate finds out about Jack and his millions."

"You think so?" Matt said.

"No, it's going to end up all nice and pretty and wrapped up in a bow like in one of those romance novels," Cherry said. "Of course it's going to be a disaster, unless he's thought of a way to tell her tonight."

Patti started to cry, and Cherry felt horrible.

"Hey," Matt said. "Hey, it'll be okay. I promise you."

Cherry swallowed against the tightness in her throat. There were times when she hated her cynical side, but life had taught her too well.

"Oh shit, don't listen to me, Patti. Jack will tell her when the time is right." She crossed her fingers beneath the covers. "I bet it won't be that bad."

She was glad Matt was here to give Patti comfort, because she was certainly lousy at it.

*   *   *

Kate came awake with a start, as Jack nudged her shoulder sharply.

"Kate," he whispered. "We overslept. We've got to *move*."

She blinked, then came awake in a heartbeat. She and Jack, stretched out stark naked on a cement ledge, over a crystal-clear pool surrounded by tropical flowers in the resort's lush water slide area.

"Where's my bikini?" she whispered as she glanced quickly around.

"Shit. I don't know. I kind of threw it. Any idea where my trunks are?"

She started to laugh. "I think I threw them over there. Oh, *no!*"

She could hear children's excited laughter in the distance.

"I think," Jack said, "that unless we really move it, those kids are going to get a lesson in human sexuality their parents don't want them to have."

"What are we going to do?"

"Wait here," Jack said, then she watched in amazement as he began to scale the side of the slide, alongside the water, heading up to where they'd started their adventure the night before.

What was he up to? Kate couldn't even begin to fathom what he was doing, but she looked around the ledge and began to pack up their cooler, carefully gathering up any litter and cramming it into the plastic container.

Jack was back within minutes, triumphantly holding her pareo.

"You'll be covered," he promised her. "You grab the cooler, I'll keep hold of your pareo and make sure it doesn't get wet."

The children's voices and laughter sounded closer.

"*Now,*" Jack said. "*Go.* Down the first slide. I'll be right behind you."

There it was, that unconscious, completely natural air of authority. Not having a lot of time to think about it, Kate jumped off the ledge into the water and headed toward the slide.

Jack was as good as his word. Her pareo was dry as he handed it to her.

"We have to share it," she insisted.

"Kate, if someone sees us . . ."

"Oh, big deal! There are honeymooning couples all over this place, it practically screams sex! So we got a little carried away, we can just look like we're newlyweds and plain stupid. You know, crazy about each other."

"Hmmm." He smiled down at her. "Who has to act?"

She had to laugh as she shook out the pareo. "Stand next to me, you barbarian." She glanced down at his naked body. "Besides, I think that qualifies as a lethal weapon and should be kept under wraps."

"Damn it, I don't have a key," she whispered as they reached the door, unseen by anyone so far. They were standing as close to each other as possible, the pareo wrapped around both of them.

"This just gets better and better," Jack said, but she could hear the laughter in his voice.

She knocked on the door. After a moment, Matt opened it.

"Oh man," he said. "That must have been some date."

"Shut up and let us in," Jack practically growled, and

Kate tried to stifle a laugh as they sidled into the villa, moving carefully so the pareo wouldn't come undone.

"What's going on?" Cherry came down the hallway, then glanced at them. This time, both perfectly shaped eyebrows shot up. "I'm not even going to ask," she said, turning on her heel.

Matt was clearly enjoying this. "You want me to go get you some clothes?"

"Sounds like a plan," Jack said, so Matt left.

"Come into the bathroom with me, Jack," Kate said.

Then she heard Cherry say, "Wait, let me get my sun-tan lotion, I don't know how long you two are going to be."

"Oh, that's funny. I'm just going to get some clothes and let Jack have the pareo."

Within minutes, Kate had wrapped herself in another pareo, and Jack had folded the one they'd shared in half and knotted it around his waist. And Kate had to admit, he didn't look half bad.

"Where's Patti?" Kate said.

Briefly, Cherry filled both of them in on what had happened.

Kate was so upset she could barely restrain herself from running into the bedroom and checking on Patti.

"Let her sleep," said Cherry. "She had a hard night."

"Describe this guy," Jack said, and Kate turned, surprised at the sound of his voice. And she knew with absolute certainty that she never wanted that particular voice directed at her.

Cherry quickly filled them in, then Jack went right to their phone and punched in a number. Within minutes, it was clear to Kate that he was talking to James McKenna, telling him everything. When he hung up, Jack said, "That guy's as good as fired, but I suspect he's already gone."

"I have a feeling you're right," Cherry said.

"I have to thank Matt when he gets back," Kate said. "I don't even want to think about what might have happened if he hadn't been there."

As if on cue, Matt appeared with clean clothing for Jack, and Kate suggested that she cook everyone a big breakfast.

She walked Jack outside. He'd showered at the villa, changed clothes, and now looked confident and cocky once again.

Actually, he'd looked confident and cocky in that damn pareo.

"What are you up to today?" he said.

"Oh, I don't know. Maybe another massage after my night on that cement mattress."

"I thought you said it was like a featherbed."

She smiled, then kissed his cheek. "I had a wonderful time."

"Listen, Kate."

Everything stilled inside her. Waiting.

"I have to work this wedding tonight, but afterwards . . . we have to talk."

They had to talk. She knew this was true. Still, it didn't keep her from hurting. But she admired Jack, for being honest with her and wanting to settle everything before she left tomorrow for her life back in Chicago.

Suddenly, making desserts in her uncle's restaurant seemed like the last thing she wanted to be doing with the rest of her life. And she knew that if this was it for her and Jack, she would miss him for the rest of that life.

"Okay," she said quietly.

"Hey," he said, tilting her chin up with his hand, so gently, so she had to look at him. "Stop thinking the worst. Just promise you won't get too mad at me."

"I never get that mad."

He started to walk away, still facing her. "That's not what Patti's told me."

She waved her hand in a dismissive gesture. "Nah. That was when we were kids."

"Let's hope so," he called back to her.

Meredith walked into James's office with a sheaf of contracts. James was bent over a design, a gorgeously simple wedding dress. Curious, wanting to see more, Meredith walked to his side and peered over his shoulder.

"She's quite good, don't you think?" James said.

"She certainly has an eye."

They studied first one design, then another, before Meredith said, "You weren't really planning on opening a bridal boutique, were you, James?"

James McKenna smiled as he set the designs aside. "No. But what good is all my money if I can't help people make their dreams come true?"

"Speaking of dreams, we've got that wedding this evening." Meredith knew James had a policy that anyone on his staff who wanted to get married on the resort's grounds only had to ask. Then he gave them outrageous discounts on everything from flowers to exquisitely catered food. The man was a total romantic.

"I know. Jack will be working it. His last job before I hand the resort over to him," James said.

"He's done quite a good job, don't you think?"

James looked up at her. "Oh, I never doubted he could do the work. I just wanted him to find a nice girl and walk into a wall."

Meredith laughed. "I couldn't even seem to catch my

breath after I met Hank. I didn't sleep properly until he finally asked me out."

"Then you know what I'm talking about."

"I do, indeed And I like our Miss Prescott for Jack. I saw them dancing together at Neptune's Lounge. They fit."

"Yes, they do."

Kate hesitated outside the bedroom door and listened as Patti and Cherry packed their bags, all the while excitedly talking about the small apartment they were going to be sharing in the resort's employee housing.

She'd never seen her cousin this happy. And as for Cherry, Kate wasn't sure why she'd felt this, but she'd always had the strangest feeling that her friend didn't really want to go back to Las Vegas. There didn't seem to be anything for her there.

Hawaii promised to be wonderful, full of promise for both of them.

And as for her . . . well, she wouldn't be able to bear it here if Jack told her they were over. What was it he'd said last night?

You're too much fun, Kate.

A toast to the best time I've had in my life.

A good time. Fun. Those were fling words, but nothing Jack had said to her hinted at something more long range. Something committed.

We have to talk . . .

The dreaded relationship talk. It usually meant that things were not going well. Or were just about over.

Kate sighed. Squared her shoulders. Whatever happened, she had one more day in paradise. They were leaving—correction, *she* was leaving at around two in the afternoon tomorrow.

And it would be a long time before she'd be able to afford to come back.

Jack couldn't think of anything besides how he was going to tell Kate. And he bet this was a first—the first time a man was actually dreading telling the woman he loved that he was a millionaire.

Any other woman would be thrilled.

Any other woman wasn't Kate.

"Jack?"

He glanced up to see Meredith Wilkins coming toward him on the resort path, dressed in a peach-colored shirtwaist dress.

"Meredith. Good to see you." He mentally racked his brains, trying to figure out if he was in some kind of trouble. Meredith had been a sort of mother figure to him after his own had died, and they had an easy familiarity with each other.

He genuinely liked her. And she'd put up with a lot of his mischief over the years, the summers he'd spent here.

"Jack. One of the pool men found a pair of swimming trunks and a black bikini in the water slide area. You wouldn't know anything about this, would you?"

He cocked his head as if thinking, but his twitching lips gave him away. He looked away, trying not to laugh. "You got me."

"Do you think Miss Prescott will want her bikini back?"

"Yeah." He glanced at her. "Let me deliver it?"

She snorted, giving him a clear indication of what she thought of that idea.

"How on earth did the two of you leave the area?"

Grinning, he told her.

"Why Jack, I think you're actually blushing."

"Nah, it's just a little sunburn."

*   *   *

"Our last supper here, and I think we should go back to the deli where it all started," Patti announced. "Now that I feel well enough to eat."

"I'm glad Cherry is staying here to keep an eye on you," Kate teased. "Have you bothered to call Uncle Albert and Aunt Connie and let them know what you're up to?"

Patti sighed. "Kate. You don't think I'd let you fly home all by yourself, do you? James said I could go home for a few days if I wanted to, then he'd send me a ticket so I could come back."

Kate felt her eyes filling, and she glanced away. Patti came and sat next to her on the couch in the living room and put an arm around her.

"You're not going back, either. I know it. Jack feels the same way about you that you do about him."

"That's those romance novels talking."

"What's this with you and Cherry knocking what I read? No, it's because I see the glass as half-full and always will."

Kate took a deep breath. "I hope you're right." She glanced at her watch. "Let's get this early dinner over with. I want to watch the entire wedding."

They went back to the little Italian deli where they'd had their first meal on the island and ordered the same pizza with four cheeses. They also split a bottle of very good red wine. And Kate was absolutely determined that her uneasy, shaky mood was not going to affect this last vacation dinner.

"We've come a long way in nine days," Patti said. "I said I'd be over Roger and boy, am I!"

"That Roger," Cherry said, then took a sip of her wine. "Mister Bratwurst. He was like a character in a bad horror movie. Between that aborted striptease and his knowing absolutely nothing about a woman's body, marriage to him would have been *intolerable!* The two of you could have been an entire Oprah show, hell, a two-hour Oprah prime-time *special!* And just think what Dr. Phil could have done with your marriage!"

"It boggles the mind," Kate said.

Patti laughed and raised her wineglass. "Here's to *me!*"

They clinked glasses.

"Cherry?" Patti said.

Cherry sighed. "No, I didn't find my millionaire. But I don't want him anymore."

"You don't?" Kate said.

"Nope. I found something a lot more valuable."

"What?" Patti said.

"You guys," Cherry said, then she set her wineglass down. "Oh damn it, now I'm going to cry and I hate it when I cry."

Patti started to laugh. "Cherry! It feels good to cry."

Cherry reached for her purse and took out a tissue. She carefully wiped her eyes, then blew her nose. "I know you guys won't believe this, but I've never met two women like you . . ."

"Oh, I believe it," Kate said, and laughed.

"I'm used to women who don't like me, who judge me by the way I look . . ."

And Kate decided, at that moment, that she would never tell Cherry what she'd thought when she'd first seen her on the plane. She'd assumed that a woman who looked like Cherry would never have any trouble with men.

How wrong she'd been.

She put her hand over Cherry's. "I'm so glad we got

to know you, Cherry. You added so much to our time on the island."

"Yeah, banging my fist on the bathroom door and telling you to hurry up."

All three women laughed at the memory.

"No, I know what Kate means," Patti said. "I'm so glad you and Kate started talking on that plane while I was sleeping."

"Kate, you were the one who really brought us all together. I overheard you talking to that stewardess and couldn't help but jump in. If you hadn't been so open, I never would've met the two of you. I'm so glad it all happened the way it did."

"Me, too."

"Okay," Patti said. "Kate, your turn."

Kate tried to smile and raise her wineglass, but her smile was shaky and her vision blurred as she set down her glass.

"I'm sorry, guys, I can't do this . . ."

"Kate, it's going to be okay . . ."

"No Patti, it's not. He told me this morning that we have to talk. He wants to talk to me tonight after he's done working the wedding. And you know what that means."

"That he wants to talk to you?" Patti said, glancing at Cherry.

"No, that we have to have one of those damn relationship talks, and that usually means the whole thing is over. But he's being a good guy about it, he's treated me really well, and he's not giving me any false hope. So I guess I had my fling, and it was everything I thought it would be." She raised her glass, then drained it.

"Hey, easy on the wine, Kate," Cherry said.

"Maybe getting a little buzz is the answer. Maybe it's

the only way I'll get through this evening." Kate stopped talking as their pizza arrived.

"Are you sorry you had an affair with Jack?" Cherry said as their waiter walked away.

Kate hesitated. "I thought I could do it. The physical part of it; I can't describe what it is he does to me, what he makes me feel. I couldn't resist him. But this part, now that I'm finally leaving . . . it's too painful." Her eyes filled again as she looked at Cherry. "I didn't count on it hurting this much."

Cherry and Patti glanced at each other, then Patti said, "Maybe what he wants to tell you has nothing to do with your relationship. Maybe it's more to do with *him.*"

"Oh, sure. Like what?"

"Oh, I don't know." Patti fiddled with a bread stick. "Maybe something in his life that he's scared to tell you. Something from his past."

"Sounds like one of your books," Cherry said.

"Books can be a lot like life." Patti patted Kate's hand. "Think positive. I know he cares about you. I don't think he's going to let you leave. I mean it. Just . . . no matter what he tells you, don't go losing your temper and blowing up."

"Kate, blow up?" Cherry said. "I find that hard to believe. You're one cool little cucumber, walking around the resort with Jack in nothing but a pareo, having wild sex in a bathroom with him . . . need I go on?"

Kate had started to laugh.

Cherry leaned forward. "Listen, Kate, you can't know what Jack wants to tell you until the actual moment arrives. So don't go working yourself up. Let things unfold, believe that things are going to turn out for the best." She sighed. "I don't know if sleeping in the same room with Patti has softened my brains, but

I'm beginning to believe that you and Jack will end up together."

"Coming from you, Cherry, I find that remarkable," Kate said. "Come on, enough about me. Let's eat this pizza before it gets cold."

James finished dressing for the wedding. Though Hawaii was notorious for its informality, he always wore a suit to a wedding unless it was a clearly informal affair. But tonight's wedding was more formal, and he'd dressed for the occasion.

And he was nervous.

Kate was leaving tomorrow at two. He'd already checked with Patti. James also knew that if things with Jack and Kate didn't work out, she'd be flying home with her cousin.

James could only hope that his son would rise to the occasion.

Love was a scary business. Even if two people found each other, life didn't always guarantee a happy ending. But James had come to believe that the real happy ending was having the courage to love and be loved in the first place. To really know and love another human being. It just made you a better person. It strengthened your soul.

He sighed, then walked over to the wall where his safe was hidden behind a painting. He pressed a hidden button, the painting rose smoothly out of the way, and he used the combination to open the safe.

Once he'd opened it, he took out the small black velvet box that contained the engagement ring he'd given Caroline so many years ago.

"I hope it works, Caroline." He hesitated. "I wish you were with me tonight, but I have a feeling that if you were still here, Jack wouldn't have turned out the way he did." In many ways, James felt he'd failed as a single father, especially when he'd forced Jack to attend an extremely strict military school for a short time.

He snapped open the ring box and eyed the ring, then slowly took it out of the box. And he angled the piece of jewelry in the light, looking for the inscription he'd had engraved inside the gold band.

All the way. Trust Sinatra to put everything good he'd ever felt about his wife into one song.

All the way. There was no other way to love. And he wondered if, when Jack was finally put to the test, he would realize it.

Slipping the ring box into the pocket of his suit, James headed toward the door.

Chapter Eighteen

Kate stood out on the lanai of her villa, leaning on the iron railing and watching the wedding guests slowly starting to congregate. White plastic chairs had been set out on the lush green lawn, tiki torches lit. The plumeria tree right by villa number six filled the air with its distinctive scent. The sun was headed down toward the ocean and would soon dip into the horizon. The last of those infamous ropes that the demigod Maui had left dangling would slip into the darkening sky.

Sunset. The perfect, most romantic time for a wedding.

She thought about how ironic it was that their trip should start and end with a wedding. One that had been aborted, and this one that, hopefully, would go off without a hitch and be the perfect symbol of two people and their commitment to each other.

She saw James McKenna arrive, handsome in a suit. He caught sight of her and gave her a quick wave. She smiled and waved back, suddenly caught by the realization that she would miss him terribly. How was it possible that this island and its people had managed to wrap themselves around her heart in such a very short time?

Tomorrow she'd drive their rental car to the airport, board a plane, and fly back to Los Angeles, where she'd get on another plane and fly to Chicago. Her uncle and aunt would pick her up and probably take both her and Patti out to dinner, wanting to hear all about their trip. How she was going to put into words what had happened to her was beyond Kate.

Cherry came out onto the lanai and leaned on the railing beside her.

"You old cynic," Kate said, turning her head. "You're actually going to watch this?"

"Believe it or not," Cherry said, "I actually believe in the institution of marriage. And I think it's wonderful when two people love each other and have the guts to take the plunge. So yes, I'm going to watch the entire thing. And sing afterwards."

"Hmmm." Kate considered this.

"Are you okay?"

"I think so." Then she saw Jack, in that classic resort outfit, the khaki shorts and coral polo shirt. He was helping some other men set up long tables at the far end of the lawn, and Kate assumed they would hold all the food for the reception after the wedding.

"Maybe not so good," she muttered.

Cherry followed her gaze, then sighed.

"Cut him some slack, Kate. Don't be too hard on him."

"Yeah. I went into this with my eyes open; I can't really blame him."

Cherry laid a hand on her arm. "I want to see you guys make it. I'm not that much of a cynic."

Kate found herself oddly touched. "Thanks."

Patti came out onto the lanai and over to the railing on the other side of Kate. And as Kate glanced at her cousin, she was surprised to see tears standing out in her clear blue eyes.

"Hey," she said and put an arm around Patti's shoulders. Cherry came to Patti's other side and took one of her hands.

Patti sniffed, then wiped her eyes with the back of her hand. "It's just . . . I don't want Roger back or anything stupid like that . . ."

"Thank God," muttered Cherry.

"It's just that . . . I wish it could've worked. I wish I could've found someone worth marrying. I guess . . . I wish I was getting married. But to the right man, you know?"

"Yeah," Kate said. "I know."

"Yeah," Cherry said.

The ceremony was beautiful, the minister an eloquent speaker as he talked about love and the commitment necessary to ensure that love flourished and deepened over the years. The bride wore a gorgeous, simple, white gown and a stunning crown of flowers in her upswept blonde hair. The groom looked elegant in a suit. And Kate's throat tightened at the way the two of them looked at each other as the minister spoke those timeless words.

When they kissed, after they were pronounced husband and wife, she actually had tears in her eyes.

Jack found himself oddly moved by the ceremony in a way he'd never been before. And of course he thought of Kate, as each word of the ceremony was spoken, and as he watched the bride and groom.

That was it. He was asking her to marry him tonight. He glanced toward the lanai of villa number six, where he saw Kate, Patti, and Cherry all leaning on the railing.

As soon as he was done serving, he'd tell her everything.

The wedding was in full swing when James came by their villa.

"Please come join us," he told them. "There's so much food, at least have a drink. But feel free to eat."

Kate and Patti decided to take him at his word. Cherry had already descended the steps and joined the musicians she'd be singing with. She'd dressed in a gorgeous flowered sarong and had put a hibiscus flower in her strawberry blonde hair.

Kate hadn't eaten much pizza, and now found she was hungry. She'd have to face Jack in the buffet line, as he was carving prime rib, but maybe she'd skip the meat and just fill up on appetizers.

Not really knowing what she was doing, feeling totally insecure, Kate got in the buffet line, with Patti right behind her.

Jack saw Kate slowly heading toward him in the buffet lines and was grateful. He found that he didn't like being separated from her for a long period of time.

Oh, he had it bad. And he was sure. As sure as he'd ever been of anything in his life. And all of a sudden the enormity of what his father had gone through hit him with a whole new meaning. He thought of losing Kate after years of being together, after having a child with her, and found himself with a whole new level of respect and admiration for his father. And understanding.

He concentrated on carving perfect slices of prime rib and placing them on plates. The sooner this wedding was over, the sooner he could tell Kate he never wanted her to leave.

Kate was just a few people away from Jack when her world fell apart.

The man in front of her, heavyset and in his late forties, had obviously had a few too many Mai Tais.

"Jack, you rascal! What the hell are *you* doing serving food?" He roared with laughter, and as Kate turned toward him, she didn't see what was so funny. But Jack had glanced at her and then this man and had the strangest expression on his face.

"Hey, Roy, good to see you," he said. "Prime rib?"

"What, getting bored sitting in your office and counting all that money?" And again this Roy laughed; he seemed to be getting off on his own wit.

"Right," Jack said calmly. "Medium or rare?"

"How's your dad? He still planning on retiring?"

"Yeah," Jack said quickly. "Come on, Roy, I've got to keep this line moving."

"So he has you carving prime rib now, does he?" Roy laughed again, and jabbed his date in the ribs. She gave him a look that left Kate in no doubt how she felt about that little move. "Is that how he made his millions, starting at the bottom and working his way up?" He laughed again, and Kate was getting peeved. She didn't like the way this man was making fun of Jack.

"Move it along, Roy," she said. "And stop making fun of him."

Roy slowly turned and looked at her, clearly annoyed as hell.

"Kate—" Jack began.

"What bug is up your butt, lady?" Roy demanded.

Kate refused to back down to this insensitive buffoon. "You're holding up the line, and your little millionaire jokes aren't funny."

"What the hell are you talking about?" Roy demanded.

"Kate," Jack said. "Kate, listen to me—"

"He's a *bartender,*" Kate said. "He works here. I'm sure he'd *love* to have more money, but he doesn't need to hear *you* making jokes about him."

"Jokes?" Now Roy was truly pissed. He leaned toward her and Kate could smell the liquor on his breath. "Lady, you're a fucking *idiot,* because I don't joke about something as serious as money. What are you, stupid? This guy"—he indicated Jack with a wave of his hand—"is worth *millions.* So's his old man, James McKenna. He *owns* this place. So don't you go telling me not to make fun of someone when all I'm doing is telling the damn truth . . ."

Her plate slipped out of her hand and hit the lush green grass, the food spilling at her feet. Kate stared at it stupidly, then looked over at Jack. Everything seemed to be happening in slow motion as she took in what this Roy was saying and realized the guy was telling her the truth.

Rich.

Jack.

James McKenna was his *father.*

That was who James had reminded her of. Jack. *That* was why Jack had always seemed to possess that unconscious air of authority. He was no bartender. He was the son James had talked about, the workaholic, the . . .

He'd lied to her. The entire time they'd been together. He'd lied to her about who he was, about his entire life. Kate closed her eyes as she remembered the way Jack had made love to her. Had that been a lie as well? Had he been playing with her all along? Was this Jack's sick idea of a joke?

She started to shake as she opened her eyes.

Kate saw Jack start around the serving table toward her and at the same time knew she had to get away from him. She couldn't deal with this, not now, not in front of a couple of hundred wedding guests. And she couldn't do this to the bride and groom, ruin their wedding, the beginning of their life when her own was going up in flames.

He'd *lied* to her. *Why?* The second she asked herself the question, Kate realized it didn't matter.

She turned and started to run toward the villa.

Patti went straight to James and told him.

"Oh no," James said quietly as he watched Kate race across the lawn, darting between wedding guests, Jack in hot pursuit.

"I'm getting Cherry, and then I'm going to help Kate," Patti said.

"I'm coming with you," James said.

"Kate!" Jack called after her.

"Get away from me!" she shouted back, reaching the villa's gate, slamming it open, then racing inside and starting to unlock the sliding glass door.

He reached her before she opened it, putting his hands on her shoulders. She whirled on him, shaking his hands off.

"Is it true?" she said, looking straight at him. "Jack?"

He swore softly, then met her gaze without flinching. "Yeah. It is."

She stared up at him, knowing all the hurt and anger she felt had to be showing in her face.

"Why?"

"I tried to tell you after Haleakala . . ."

She couldn't seem to take this all in. *This* was what Jack had wanted to talk to her about? But why had he thought it necessary to deceive her, especially after they'd made love?

"How could you . . . after what we . . ." Her brain didn't seem to want to function. "That night, after that first night, and the next morning at the bar . . ." Her voice started to shake and she stopped. Now his accusations of her being after a millionaire made a horrible, sickening sort of sense.

But she couldn't seem to get past the betrayal.

"I need . . . I have to . . . get away . . ." She slid open the sliding glass doors and stepped inside. He followed, right behind her, and Kate walked toward the kitchen.

"Jack—" she began, backing away from him.

"Kate, we can work this out. Just don't get mad, give me time to explain the whole thing—"

At that exact moment, Patti burst into the living room, closely followed by Cherry, Matt, and James McKenna.

Jack turned, and Kate could feel his frustration.

"Could we *not* have an audience right now? I need some time alone with Kate . . ."

"Okay," Patti said. "Kate, don't yell at him, I know he would've told you sooner, but—"

"Wait," Kate said, feeling her emotions start to freeze. "*Wait!* You *knew* about this?"

Patti stopped talking in midsentence, then glanced at Cherry as if her friend would somehow know what to do.

Kate's gaze went from Patti to Cherry. "You, too?" This whole situation was spiraling out of control and she didn't know how to stop it.

"What the *hell?*" Jack said, glancing around.

"How about *this*?" Kate said, backing away from all of them with her hands in front of her, fingers spread, palms out. She was headed toward the villa stairs that led up to the front door. "Okay, everyone who *didn't* know Jack was a millionaire, please raise your hand." She hated the intense sarcasm that colored her voice, but it was the only way she could keep the pain at bay.

Obviously, James didn't raise his hand. Patti looked at her, stricken. Cherry kept her gaze on the Oriental carpet. Even Matt didn't raise his hand.

"Got it," Kate said softly. "O-kay."

"Kate," Patti began. "It had to come from Jack—"

"*Don't* you talk to me. Not now. *No*." Kate started to back up the stairs, then turned. She had to get out of here.

Then she yelped as she felt Jack's fingers close around her ankle.

"Let me go, damn it!" She kicked out at him impotently.

"No." He held her gaze. "No, I'm not letting you go." He turned around toward the others. "Out! *Now!*" But they didn't move; all four of them seemed rooted in their respective spots.

Jack turned back to her, lowered his voice. "Don't do this, Kate. Don't run away."

"Let me go," she said as she struggled in his grip. She was perfectly cold inside. It was the only way she'd ever get through this.

"I hate the hurt you've been through," Jack said, his voice tense as he kept a tight hold on her ankle. "I hate that guy who hurt you, because you can't see me—"

"Oh, I think I see you just fine—"

"No, Kate. No. You don't understand. You can't let me get close to you, Kate, because you're scared to death—"

"I'm not the one who *lied* . . ." She kicked impotently, but he just wouldn't let her go.

"Yeah, I lied to you. I lied to everyone, okay? But I need you to hear this, Kate! Listen to me, and *don't run away.*"

"*Fine.*" She'd started to cry, hating to cry in front of him, hating him seeing how much he'd hurt her. She had no pride left, no dignity, nothing.

"You know when I knew, Kate? That first night. I *knew.* This was different."

"Oh yeah, pull out all the stops now that I've caught you in a lie."

He stared at her. "Jesus, Kate, don't do this."

"You have no idea what I've been going through in the last forty-eight hours. Well let me tell you, Jack *McKenna,* that nothing is worth losing my peace of mind—"

"Kate—" Patti said warningly.

"—and I want you to listen to what I have to tell you." Kate took a deep breath, fighting the tightness in her chest as she continued to struggle in his grasp. "You were nothing but a fling. That first night meant nothing to me. Tomorrow I'm flying home to Chicago, and in a few days you're going to be *nothing* but a pleasant memory. Oh, except for this little scene. So let me go!"

"I don't believe you," he said quietly.

"Boy, you rich guys are used to getting what you want, aren't you?"

He let go of her ankle at that one. "Kate—"

"Good-bye, Jack. It was . . . *fun.*" She started up the stairs.

He swore, started after her.

She took off one shoe and threw it at him.

He caught it.

"Jack," Patti whispered. "Let her go."

He turned toward her, incredulous.

"Yeah, Patti," Kate called out from the hallway upstairs. "Why don't you give him a try; the two of you seem to be able to communicate better than we ever did!"

Then the front door slammed behind Kate and all was silent.

After a short silence, Cherry said, "She won't get far, with only one shoe."

Patti wiped at her eyes. "You don't know Kate."

She'd grabbed her purse on the way out. Numb, Kate took off her other shoe, then ran to the lobby and out into the parking lot, found their rental car, and drove away from the resort. And she realized she had no idea where she was going, she only knew she had to get away from everyone.

Within minutes, she was crying so hard she had to pull the car to the side of the road. How could she have thought that Jack breaking off their relationship, ending their fling, was the worst thing that could happen to her? Surprise, surprise, something worse had happened.

He'd lied to her, and worse, everyone except her had known the truth all along.

She blew her nose, furious with herself. Instead of remaining cool and collected, she'd blown up, cried, and finally left. Now she didn't know how she could possibly go back.

Her mind raced, trying to come up with a workable plan. She'd just go somewhere and stay the night. She'd come back to the resort right before her flight; she was practically already packed. She'd get her plane ticket out of the villa's safe, throw her bags in the rental car—Patti and Cherry could just stay on the island—and she'd drive herself to the airport, return the car, and fly home.

That was when she really burst into tears.

Ten minutes later, when the sobbing had subsided, she put the car in gear and started her search for another place to spend the night.

Jack remained at the foot of the stairs, his head bent. Silent.

No one said a thing. James watched his son, knowing that what happened tonight would determine his entire future.

After a moment, Jack turned toward his father.

"It's over."

James's heart sank. Was he going to give up on Kate this easily?

"I'm done," Jack said quietly. "With the whole charade. You can have the resort. I don't want it."

James stayed absolutely still as hope began to fill his chest. Just hours away from finalizing their original deal, Jack was giving it all away for something far greater.

"All right," he said carefully.

"I just want you to know I'm not finishing that wedding."

"You're going after her," James said.

"If I have to tie her up, throw her over my shoulder and imprison her in my house, she's not leaving this island."

"Wow," said Cherry.

"*Yes,*" breathed Patti.

"Cool," said Matt.

James couldn't contain the smile that had started deep inside of him. *Good for you, Jack. You got it.*

As his son started up the stairs, he called out, "Jack!"

Probably only his short stint in military school caused Jack to stop midflight.

"You might need this." James reached into his suit pocket and took out the small black velvet box. He tossed it to his son, and Jack caught it, stared at his father, then opened the box and looked at the ring.

James's throat tightened. He knew Jack would understand the significance of what he'd just done.

Jack met his father's gaze for a long moment. "Thanks, Dad."

"Jack," said Patti. "I'm sorry."

"What did the last guy do to her?"

Patti hesitated, then said, "He lied to her. He had a fiancée on the side the entire time he was dating Kate."

Jack swore softly, then said, "Where's her plane ticket?"

"You're taking her *plane* ticket?" Matt said.

"I'm playing to win," Jack replied. "Where's the ticket?"

"In the villa's safe," Cherry said.

"Get it."

Cherry ran up the stairs and within minutes came back with the tickets.

"Take all three—she might try to use one of ours." She gave the tickets to Jack. He turned toward his father.

"Dad, would you hold on to these?"

"Certainly."

Jack handed the tickets to Matt, who gave them to James.

"Jack," Patti said. "I feel so bad, but I think I have a way of making this up to you."

"Make it quick."

Briefly, Patti explained her plan.

Jack considered it.

"Okay," he finally said.

*   *   *

She'd tried several other hotels and found them full. Not the brightest thing to do, race out of a resort and try to find another room during the height of Maui's tourist season. And of course, a lot of people got married and took honeymoons right around Valentine's Day.

So Kate had driven until she'd spotted a Denny's. She'd pulled into the parking lot, gone inside, and now sat in a booth by one of the front windows, nursing what had to be about her fourth cup of not-too-bad coffee. She'd stay here until the morning, then head back to the Kalani Resort Hotel and Spa.

She felt so bad she'd even turned down the waitress's suggestion of a piece of fresh coconut cream pie. And when Kate couldn't eat, she was in trouble.

She started as her cell phone rang, then reached into her purse. It could only be one person, the one person on the island who had her cell number. Kate wasn't sure she wanted to talk to Patti yet.

But much of her temper had cooled during the drive, so she snapped the tiny phone open and answered.

"Yeah."

"Kate."

Patti.

Kate found she couldn't say anything. So she waited. Finally, Patti spoke.

"I'm really sorry."

Again, Kate was silent.

"I mean it. There were so many times when I wanted to tell you."

Kate merely listened.

"I couldn't do it to Jack. And he was going to tell you."

Kate sighed. "Kind of a laugh, isn't it? Cherry was the one looking for a millionaire."

"Kate. Remember when Roger dumped me and we were talking in my bedroom at home? Remember what you told me?"

"Something really brilliant, I'm sure. I mean, look at my love life."

"You said that whatever's really meant for you, you can't lose it. Nobody can take it away from you. Just like if something isn't meant for you, or meant to be, no matter how hard you fight for it, it'll never be yours."

"Jesus. You were listening."

"It helped me, Kate. And I want to help you."

Kate sighed, feeling something loosen in her chest. "Yeah. I know."

"Remember our fortune cookie?"

"You cannot lose what is your own," Kate said softly, then took a sip of her coffee.

"You're not going to lose Jack," Patti said. "Because the two of you are meant for each other."

"You think so?" Kate said, settling back in her booth. She signaled the waitress, mouthed the word *pie,* and gave her a thumbs-up sign.

Cherry had never met a man like Jack. As she ran with him to the lobby, she had to admire him.

Matt and Patti were back at the villa, Patti keeping Kate on the phone until Jack could get to the Denny's. He'd gone back to his studio apartment and changed and come back to the villa just as Patti had first phoned Kate.

After talking to her for a few minutes, Patti had asked Kate where she was, then written the name of the restaurant on a piece of paper and handed it to Jack. He'd given her the thumbs-up sign, letting her know he knew where the restaurant was located, and dashed out the villa's door.

Now, dressed in jeans, a black T-shirt, and a black leather jacket and boots, he looked less like a resort employee and more like the man on the bike they'd first seen as they'd driven to the resort. Something subtle had happened when he'd quit that deal with his dad. It was as if Jack didn't have to pretend anymore or be anyone he wasn't. And if it was possible, he was even more magnificent.

But then, she'd always liked really self-assured men. It came with the testosterone.

"If she gets away from me and comes back here, stall her until I can get here," he said.

"You bet."

She admired the way he'd delegated everything. And she saw James McKenna all over again in his son, in that same powerful mind, that same relentless pursuit of what he wanted.

And he wanted Kate.

She *really* admired the way he'd confiscated Kate's ticket. This guy played to win, and there was something incredibly sexy about that.

Cherry had a feeling Kate had finally met her match.

"Kate, don't throw this away. It's worth everything."

Kate had finished her pie and another cup of coffee. Now she listened to her cousin and that deeply instinctual part of her personality told her that Patti was right.

"I know," she whispered.

"It's what I wanted to have with Roger, but he couldn't give it to me. You've got it with Jack, and he can give it to you. Don't let your fears get in the way. You have to go for it!"

"But after what I said to him—"

"Like water off a duck's back. Not that I'd recommend saying things like that too often, but Jack's a strong man. He can take what you dish out."

"That doesn't sound too attractive. About me, I mean."

Patti sighed. "Kate, I love you, but sometimes you let your temper get the better of you . . ."

Kate glanced up then, by instinct, and saw him. Jack. Coming inside the restaurant, glancing around, honing in on . . . her.

"Damn it, Patti, you kept me on this phone just so Jack would have time to . . ."

"Yep. Don't throw anything at him," Patti said, then hung up.

Kate dug around in her purse and tossed some bills on the table, then slid out of the booth. She was going as he was coming, but that didn't stop him from grabbing her forearms.

"Kate, Whoa, wait, stop right there."

She had a feeling that wherever she ran, he'd find her. So she stopped, looked up at him.

His face was pale, making his blue eyes even darker, if that was possible. The skin seemed to be pulled tightly over his cheekbones, and as she studied his face, she saw a small muscle jump in the side of his jaw.

"Kate," he said again, this time so softly.

A part of her just wanted to give over, lean into him, let him take her in his arms and hold her close. Another part of her was so scared, couldn't let it happen, couldn't risk loving this man and taking a chance on being hurt.

Looking into his eyes, Kate had the feeling she was in for the emotional battle of her life.

Chapter Nineteen

It felt, to Kate, like everyone in the restaurant was watching them. With great interest.

"Can we take this outside?" Kate said.

"You make it sound like a fight."

She cocked an eyebrow at him, and he sighed, then let her go and walked with her outside. She headed toward her car and was about to put her key in the lock when he took her hand.

"I thought we were going to talk."

"I can't do this right now, Jack." She felt as if she were about to fall apart.

"When?" She could hear the impatience in his voice. "You're flying back tomorrow, so when are we going to talk about this?"

"I'm not up to this, Jack."

"I think you are." Before she could reply, she felt him place a hand on either side of her waist, then turn her so she faced him. He stepped closer, and she found herself pinned against the car, his legs spread slightly, his body enveloping hers, his pelvis pressed gently against her. It wasn't as much an aggressive move as a containing one.

He took her purse, stuffed her keys into it, and threw it on the roof of her car.

"That's a pretty vulnerable position to put yourself in," she said, glancing down where his legs were spread.

"I'm trusting you not to kick me," he said. "Though I know you think I deserve it."

She sighed, looked away, then gathered her composure and faced him. Which was hard, when he was standing so close to her.

"What did you expect me to do, Jack? I shared parts of my life with you, but you didn't tell me anything about yourself . . ."

"I didn't want to make up a story." He held up a hand. "Yeah, I know I lied by omission. The whole thing wasn't my idea. It was my dad's."

"What?"

Briefly, Jack explained their ten-day deal. His dream, the Kalani resort, his father's imminent retirement, and how they had both agreed the ownership and management of the resort would be passed on.

"He thought I needed to work the resort from the ground up in order to understand the people I'd be supervising."

Kate considered this. "Smart man." She hesitated. "So it wasn't a whole big joke you thought up to play around with women's heads?"

"No. Though I have to say I was totally sick of women coming on to me when they were more interested in my bank balance."

She nodded her head. "Okay."

"You, I didn't see coming."

"Jack, you don't have to say anything. I knew it was just a fling going into it . . ."

"Will you *stop* with this fling shit? I told you back at the villa I knew that first night that this was different. You and me. Different."

"How?" She had to be sure.

He cupped the side of her face with his hand, stroked her cheekbone.

"You blew through all my defenses. Every idea I had about what I thought I wanted. I thought I was happy, I thought I had the perfect life, no involvements, just work. And I love my work. But then I saw you on that path, bumped into you . . ."

He stopped, clearly gathering his thoughts. Kate waited. She was still pissed enough that she didn't want to make this easy for him. And she had to be sure.

He had to walk straight into that wall with her. James was right about that.

"I saw you, and I thought, oh no, oh *shit,* because I couldn't ignore you. You bothered me, Kate. You really bothered me. It was like I couldn't think straight after I met you."

She knew exactly what he meant. He'd hit that wall. The hardness, that little core of emotional pain around her heart, started to crack.

"You bothered me, too."

"Yeah. Well. You bothered me enough that I went for that first night with you. And then, the more I got to know you, the more we fought, the more *I* fought it, I knew it was right. I knew that you were it for me." He took a deep breath. "But I don't know what I have to do to convince you of that."

Totally amazed that he was willing to be so honest with her, to lay it all on the line, Kate knew she had to respond in kind. So she whispered the first honest thing that came to her mind.

"I'm so scared."

He gathered her close into his arms, and she rested her head on his shoulder.

"You think I'm not?" he said. "If you're not, it's not worth it. Baby, I'm scared to death to take this leap with you. Because even if you get it, you might lose it."

And that was when she realized he *knew*. He knew her, knew what she was feeling, what was inside her, all the pain and fear and hope and desire, all jumbled up inside. She started to cry, amazed that she still could after all the weeping she'd done.

"Hey." He stroked her hair, let her cry. When she'd let all of it out, he whispered, "I know about your parents. Patti told me."

She nodded her head against his black T-shirt and found that she never wanted to move from the spot she was in right now.

He just held her for a while as they stood in the parking lot, leaning against her rental car and ignoring the customers as they came and went.

Then he stepped slightly back from her. She could see his face.

"My mother died when I was eleven."

Her eyes filled. She knew how badly that hurt. "What happened?"

"Ovarian cancer. She fought it for so long, but toward the end, my dad and I, we just didn't want her to hurt anymore."

She nodded her head, knowing there weren't any words. Then she placed her hand over his heart.

"It always hurts," she said. "It's always there."

"Yeah." He took a breath, struggled for a breath through the pain of remembering.

And Kate, as she looked up at Jack and felt his heart beating steadily against her palm, knew that somehow this man mirrored her. He brought out all of the most painful things that had happened in her life, made her face them. Because she'd have to face them in order to be with him.

She'd read somewhere that relationships were always about soul growth and that sometimes powerful physical attraction kept you with someone so that you could work on those lessons and get it all done.

"Do you sometimes feel damaged?" she whispered.

She saw the instant recognition in his eyes. "All the time. Like, there's only so much I can give, because if I give it all up to someone and then lose them—"

"You'll die," she finished for him.

"Yeah. That's it." He lowered his head and kissed her, and she gave over to that physical feeling for just an instant. Then he broke the kiss, touched his forehead to hers.

"I want to give it all to you, Kate."

"I know." Her body had started to shake again. "Me, too."

"Come with me," he whispered. "Please. Don't ask any questions, don't think about it, just come with me."

She knew she was staring at the abyss, she was right at the edge of the cliff. She was standing on that cliff looking at the water below, and she had to jump, not knowing how deep or cold that water was or if she would even survive the fall. But she had to take that leap, with this man, at this moment.

This was it, and if she didn't, her life would be less.

"Come with me, Kate," he said, stepping away from her. Making the choice totally hers. He held out his hand, and she remembered the first night she'd spent with him, when he'd held out that hand, and she'd so willingly taken it.

She hesitated for just a heartbeat, terrified, then held out her hand. Grasped his, and he squeezed her fingers, hard.

"Yes," she whispered. "Yes, I'll come with you."

She knew where they were eventually going to go. He'd brought her a change of clothing, along with some shoes. When she saw Cherry's green sweats, she knew.

Haleakala. *The House of the Sun.*

She changed in the bathroom at Denny's, as getting on Jack's motorcycle in a dress would've been difficult. Then she tucked that dress into one of the bike's storage compartments, along with her purse, and got on behind Jack.

"Did you ever get any dinner?" he said.

"No." Though she was still nervous and didn't feel like eating. At this point she hadn't eaten pizza or the wedding buffet.

"Want to eat?"

She had to eat something; she was starting to get sick to her stomach on nothing but pie and coffee. Too much sugar and caffeine.

"Yeah."

"I know this place."

She was sure he did. And it was another hole in the wall, where he knew a lot of the people and the food was fabulous. Chinese, Korean, she couldn't even tell, and for the first time in a long time Kate found she wasn't interested in the food. Not tonight. She just concentrated on eating enough to get her through the evening.

Afterwards, they went to the little ranch house, and this time when the dogs came running up in the dark and saw Kate, they whined and wagged their tails. And in a strange kind of way, being here relaxed her. She didn't know why, but she responded to the physical place.

"It's yours," she said as they walked inside.

"Yeah."

"The dogs?"

"Guilty as charged."

"And you let them run all over you."

"Yeah, I do."

"The ruthless businessman can't train his dogs."

"Ah, I wouldn't call me ruthless. Just . . . competitive." He slanted her a quick glance. "Are you good at training dogs?"

"Ruthless. They'll quake in fear." At the look he gave her, she started to laugh. "Nah, but dogs always love me because I'm in the kitchen, cooking something good to eat."

"They're good dogs, Max and Sheba. I haven't been around as much as I should, but now that I'm home to stay, they might get better."

"Hmmm." She considered this as she walked inside. Now that she knew the house belonged to Jack, she saw him everywhere in the simple, clean lines, the bright colors. This was a house designed to be lived in, a fun house, a house a person could give parties in. A casual house.

But it wasn't a home. Not yet.

She continued walking through it, getting to know him through his house.

"Your mom?" she said, when she came to the picture in his den.

"Yeah." He stood in the doorway, watching her.

The picture was heartbreaking, an eight-by-ten color shot of Jack and his mother on the beach, both of them so happy, smiling into the camera. He was younger, probably five or six, and the way she held him told Kate all she needed to know about the kind of mother she'd been.

"She's beautiful," Kate said softly. "So full of life."

What an incredible loss.

"I remember," she said, "the first time I couldn't remember what my mother looked like."

"What happened?" Jack said, coming up to stand behind her, putting his hands on her shoulders.

"I panicked. I started to cry, and I ran to my aunt and she helped me pick out three photos from an album. She had them enlarged and framed, and I hung them in the room I shared with Patti. It helped. A little." She took a deep breath. "But I felt so guilty because I was starting to forget."

"I know," he said. "I don't have that many pictures around the house because there are times I still can't stand to remember."

He followed her as she explored the entire house, and they ended up in the kitchen, making coffee.

"Almost three," he said. "We need to get going." He walked over to the main closet off the living room and pulled out a warm jacket. "Here, this is better than one of the hotel blankets."

"I felt so safe that day, wrapped in that blanket."

"Would you rather have one?"

"No. This will be fine." She put it on and it smelled like him, that clean masculine scent she would always associate with Jack.

"You look cute in it. It's too big."

"It's fine." She went back into the kitchen, drank the rest of her coffee, then rinsed the mug out and set it in the sink.

"Neat," he commented.

"All those cooking classes."

Then they walked out the door, fired up the bike, and headed up the mountain.

This time, even though Kate knew what to expect, it was just as extraordinary. And she knew that each time would be different. The same because it was a sunrise, but different because the colors, the light, would always shift and change.

"My dad brought her up here, right before she died," Jack said, his voice low, close to her ear. "She wanted to see the sunrise one more time."

They were holding hands, his arms wrapped around her as he stood in back of her. She squeezed his fingers gently, interlaced with hers, knowing there was more.

"I can remember holding her hand so tightly, then watching her face as she looked at the sunrise. I didn't want to look at the sun. I wanted to look at her."

Kate didn't say anything, she simply wondered if it was any easier at eleven than it was at five. Of course not. The only comfort anyone could get from losing a parent was if they'd lived a long and happy life, and even then it was difficult.

"There was something in her face, as if she rallied, one more time, coming up here. For a moment, as she looked at the sunrise, in her eyes, she looked the way she used to. And then she was so tired, and she turned her head into my father's chest and I knew—I felt she was ready to go. And as much pain as she was in, I didn't want her to leave."

"You were eleven," Kate said.

Jack took a deep breath, she felt his chest expand. Then he let it out slowly.

"I was guilty about that for years. Couldn't even admit it to myself. But just saying it to someone, it helps."

"You can tell me anything."

Pale sunlight had come up over the rim, illuminating the clouds in various shades of pink, from the lightest shade, almost white, to the deeper, darker tones.

"Kate," he said, and something in Jack's voice made her turn toward him, away from the dawn. She could miss this one. She had a feeling she'd see many more sunrises with this man.

"Kate," he said again, then pressed his forehead against hers. He took a deep breath, then whispered, "Help me."

She moved away from him so she could look up at his face, but kept both his hands in hers. And as she looked at Jack, she realized she'd never loved any man more than this one. All of her life she'd yearned for a family of her own, and she had a feeling this man was going to help her create one.

"I'm leaving today," she said softly.

"No, you're not. I'm not letting you go."

"Okay."

Jack stared down at her. "Okay?"

"Yeah. Okay." Then, totally confident about what was coming next, she whispered, "I hope you're going to get to the good part."

"This," he said, looking down at her, "is as good as it gets."

He held her gaze for a long moment. She saw the exact instant he gave in to it, saw it in those incredible blue eyes. "Kate," he said with touching vulnerability. "I love you. I'll always love you. Will you marry me?"

She nodded her head, not trusting herself to speak.

They were roaring down the side of the dormant volcano when Jack said, "Damn it, I screwed up."

Kate had to laugh. "Now *that's* romantic!" she called

out over the noise of the bike's engine. She still couldn't quite believe that he'd given her his mother's ring. The stunning band, set with a small but beautifully cut diamond, flashed in the morning sunlight.

She was surprised when Jack slowed the bike, then pulled over onto the side of the road.

"Take the ring off," he said, still astride the bike but turning so he could see her.

"What?"

"What I mean is, take it off and look at what's engraved inside. I forgot to have you do it up there."

Incredibly curious, she slipped the ring off her finger and tilted it so she could see what had been engraved on the inside of the simple band.

All the way.

"My dad felt that way about my mom, and I feel that way about you."

She couldn't speak. Her throat closed with emotion.

"Like Sinatra," Jack said, looking at her. "The song. You do like Sinatra, don't you?"

She cleared her throat, then said, "Are you kidding, he's a god at the restaurant! Uncle Albert plays his CDs all the time."

"Okay, then." He started the bike up again and pulled out onto the road.

They went back to his house, and this time walked straight back into the bedroom, where Max and Sheba sheepishly got off the large bed. Jack let the dogs out, and then closed the blinds so the bedroom was soothingly dark and private.

And it was different, this time, when they made love. Quieter, but more intense. Kate realized that nothing made love sweeter than a commitment that came from that place deep inside your heart.

"Jack," she whispered into the darkened bedroom as they lay side by side, her head on his shoulder. "I really love you."

He kissed her.

She snuggled closer. "I knew that first night, too. That it was different."

She could sense he was waiting.

"And I'm sorry, what I said on the stairs, about . . . it being just a fling."

"You were scared. It's okay, Kate."

A few minutes passed, then she said, "Jack?"

This time he slid down so they could look at each other in the dim light, their heads close together on the pillows.

"I don't think I could've . . . I've never been that way . . . it's never happened that fast with a guy . . ."

"Shhh," he said, stroking her hair. "It's okay. I know. Me, too."

"Really?"

"Yeah," he said, and she shifted her body as he slid up over her, cradling his hips between her thighs. He kissed her once, twice. "It's overrated, that whole bartender thing."

"Really?"

"Oh, yeah. It's the millionaire businessmen who get all the girls."

She punched him in the arm, and he grabbed her fist and kissed it.

"Kate," he said, and she felt her stomach muscles dissolve at the way he said her name. "I don't need any more of that. Because I got the prettiest girl, the smartest girl."

"A girl with a bad, bad temper," she reminded him.

"Oh," he said softly between kisses, "I'm going to keep her so happy, I'll only see her sweet side."

*   *   *

They made love again, and she'd almost fallen asleep when she opened her eyes, looked at Jack, and said, "Wait a minute, I'm supposed to leave today, and Patti and Cherry still don't know . . ."

"Go to sleep," he said, pulling the light sheet up over her shoulders. "I'll call them and let them know."

"Thank you," she whispered, then closed her eyes.

Patti had been on edge all night and into the morning, waiting for Jack's call. And driving Cherry insane. Because if there was one thing Cherry was absolutely sure of, it was that Kate was in good hands. Jack's hands.

Now there was one capable man.

She and Patti were sitting out on the lanai, watching the waves.

"God, I'm going to miss this place," Cherry said. "Employee housing just won't be the same."

"Yeah. But we'll still be here in paradise, so who's complaining?"

God, how she loved Patti's eternal optimism. "That glass is always half full with you, isn't it, Sugar?"

"It sure is. Life can turn on a dime, that's what my dad always says."

The phone rang, and Patti picked up the portable phone she'd brought outside.

"Villa number six," she said, then, "Jack! How are you? Is Kate with you? What? Oh my God! She actually said *yes?*"

"Hallelujah," Cherry said, settling back on the cushions of her chaise lounge and slipping on her sunglasses. "At least one of us got it right."

"When? That soon? Well, I can . . . sure, I'll call my mom and dad. What? It's all set up? Boy, you're a great . . . what are you going to be, my cousin by marriage?"

Cherry smiled as she reached for her glass of pineapple juice.

"Okay. I'll do all that. You're just going to stay up there for a couple of days? Sounds good to me. Give my love to Kate, will you? And Cherry's, too. Oh, and did you tell her about what you did with her plane ticket? Good, I wouldn't do that. Okay, I'm going now. Get some sleep."

Patti hung up, then turned toward Cherry, her face glowing with happiness.

"He asked her to *marry* him and she said *yes!* So sometimes life *is* like one of those romances I read, after all!"

Cherry started to laugh. "I give up, Sugar. Get me a book. You're speaking to one of the converted."

"All *right!*" Patti said, and dashed inside the villa. "I know just the one!" she called back from inside.

"Ten days," Cherry murmured. "Ten days, and he knew it was right from the first night. Now that's what I call a fling."

"Wait, you don't know the half of it!" Patti said as she came back out the sliding glass doors and threw a fat paperback novel into Cherry's lap. She sat back down in her lounge chair so she was facing Cherry. "Don't bother finishing up your packing, we're here for another week!"

"What!" This got her attention.

"We're comped at this villa through the wedding, and Jack is arranging to put my mom and dad in the one next door as soon as he can get them to fly over here."

Cherry pulled her legs up to her chest and started to laugh. "God, I just *love* the filthy rich!"

"I have to call my dad right now, let him know that

none of us are going to be on that plane home!" Patti picked up the portable phone and punched in the familiar number, then raised the receiver to her ear.

"Dad? I'm looking out, right now, over the most beautiful ocean. And I can't thank you enough for what you've done for me."

Cherry leaned back in her chair and sighed with utter contentment. Life just kept getting better and better.

"Yeah, I'm fine," Patti said. "A hundred percent. But there's a little something that I have to tell you . . . no, now don't go getting all upset; Kate and I aren't in any trouble."

"Are you going to tell your dad *any* of this?" Cherry whispered, but she already knew her friend's answer before Patti shook her blonde head and mouthed, "He worries too much." Then she turned her attention back to her father.

"Well, we were for a while . . . in a little trouble, I mean, but it all worked out. Wait, put Mom on the other phone, and I'll tell both of you at the same time. And Dad? Do you think you can close down the restaurant for a week or two? Oh, I don't think you're going to want to miss this . . ."

Jack had barely hung up the phone when Kate said, "What was that about my plane ticket?"

The woman had ears, he had to give her that. He'd been lying close to her in bed as he'd talked to Patti, and she must have overheard what Patti had said.

"Nothing important."

"You can tell me now," Kate said as she stretched and yawned, then snuggled into his side. "I'm well fed and sexually satiated, so I shouldn't attack."

He still hesitated.

"I know you fight really dirty," she said. "And you play to win."

"Oh, you have no idea."

She waited patiently, just looking at him, a mischievous light in her green eyes.

Shit. He had to tell her the truth. He glanced away from her.

"Okay, just don't get mad. Kate, I . . . stole your plane ticket. Out of the safe."

She was silent for so long he began to worry, then when he felt the bed start to jiggle slightly with her silent laughter, he grinned, turned toward her.

"Jack." She slid her arms up around his neck. "You're *such* a barbarian!"

"And this is a good thing, right?"

"The *best*," she said and kissed him.

He felt them catch that sexual fire that was theirs alone, and slowly rolled her over onto her back, kissing her the entire time.

Chapter Twenty

❀ Albert Cannelli, short and plump with a perpetually worried expression on his face, got off the plane with his wife, Connie, and stared blankly at his daughter as she rushed up to greet them and flung herself into his arms.

"I still don't understand," he said, staring at Patti after she'd hugged and kissed him. "*You* were the one who was supposed to get married, that *jerk* didn't show up, so I send you and Kate to Hawaii for ten days and now *she's* getting married?"

"Albert, Albert," murmured his slender, serene wife as she fell into step beside him. "You've got to roll with the punches, go with the flow."

"And this is my friend Cherry!" Patti said. "Cherry, my dad and mom, Albert and Connie."

"Nice to meet you," Connie said, holding out her hand.

"I've heard so much about both of you," Cherry said, shaking her hand.

"Don't believe any of it," Connie said, pulling her into a hug.

"You look like a showgirl," Albert said as he held out his hand, frowning.

"Dad!" Patti said.

"That's okay, Sugar. I was." Cherry shook Albert's hand firmly, then tucked her hand into his arm and smiled down at him. "I hear you make a mean tiramisu." They started to walk ahead.

Connie fanned herself with a hand as she glanced at her daughter. "That one, she could give men coronaries."

"You're probably wondering why I asked you both to come see me today," James said as he ushered Jack and Kate into his office. And as he covertly studied his son, he realized Jack looked good. Relaxed and happy. Well, not right now, but since his son had proposed to Kate, he'd never looked better.

Kate either, for that matter. A pair of gorgeous emerald earrings flashed as she turned toward him. Jack had tried to buy her another engagement ring, a bigger diamond, but she'd adamantly refused his offer, claiming she loved the one he'd given her. James had heard all about that particular squabble. So Jack had bought her those incredible earrings, claiming the jewels matched her eyes.

Oh, his son had it bad.

James settled them both in chairs facing his desk, then sat down himself.

"I want to talk about our agreement, Jack."

"What's to talk about? I reneged on our deal."

"What do you mean?" Kate said.

"Didn't Jack tell you?" James said. "He walked out

on our ten-day agreement only a few hours before he would have completed it."

The look Kate gave Jack was priceless, and James bit the inside of his mouth to keep from laughing out loud.

The look Jack gave her back, which clearly said, *don't say a word,* was even funnier.

Jack faced his father. "I made my decision, so I'm sticking by it."

"I understand," James said. "And as you know, I've been interviewing candidates for the position. Running this particular property."

Jack nodded his head. James could read his son perfectly. This was killing him, but he had too much pride, especially in front of Kate, to let on.

"James, could I say a word?" Kate began.

"No," Jack said quietly.

She turned toward him. "Please?"

"I'd hear her out, Jack."

James watched as Jack glanced first at him, then at his fiancée.

"Please?" Kate said.

"All right." He hesitated, then lowered his voice. "But don't beg."

"I'm not going to beg, I'm just going to state my case." Kate turned toward James. "I feel terrible, knowing that my own bad behavior cost Jack the chance to run this property. And I'd like to know, James, if there's anything I can do to make you reconsider."

"Kate—" Jack said warningly.

"You already have," James said, and both of them turned toward him, surprised.

"What do you mean?" Jack said.

"That night, Jack, when you told me you were done with the whole charade, that you didn't want the resort?

Son, I was never prouder of you than I was at that moment."

Jack stared at his father, and James could tell that he still didn't quite get it.

"You've got the resort, Jack. I want you to have it. I'm passing the property over to you on the day you and Kate get married. You passed the test I set out for you with flying colors. It was never about work. It was always about love."

His son sat very still, just looking at him, awe and astonishment and so much love and respect in his expression.

"You were afraid he'd never fall in love," Kate said quietly.

James turned toward Kate and nodded his head, smiling. "Though I wasn't quite prepared for you."

"Who was?" Jack said.

They were outside in the hallway before Kate said, "You never told me you gave up this resort to come after me!"

"A minor detail," Jack replied. She could tell her husband-to-be was on top of the world. He'd gotten his father's approval, and she knew these moments were crucial for men. And James was such a special man, what he'd gambled on giving his son was truly priceless.

She wanted to tease Jack; she loved to see that sparkle in his blue eyes. "You were willing to give all this up? For me?"

"Ah, don't go getting all mushy on me."

"Mushy! I think you're crazy!"

"Crazy about you," he said, and she shrieked laughter as he swung her up into his arms and for their penthouse.

*   *   *

Their wedding, on the beach at sunset, was everything Kate had ever dreamed of.

And Jack found that he adored her even more when he discovered how little she cared about all the preparation—except for their wedding cake, of course.

"I don't even care about the dress," she told him one night at dinner, with Patti and Matt and Cherry. "I'd walk down the aisle naked to marry you."

"Whoa, that would be a wedding I'd like to see," Matt said.

"Watch it," Jack said.

"What I meant," Kate said, tossing a bread stick at Matt, "was that it's the man, not the dress, and it's the marriage, not the wedding. Does that make sense?"

"Perfect sense, Sugar," said Cherry.

During their wedding ceremony, right at sunset on that stretch of beach where he'd pulled her out of the waves, Jack found that he couldn't look away from Kate. She'd told him she might cry, but all she did was smile, her happiness apparent for everyone to see.

And when he'd pulled her into his arms and kissed her after they'd both said their vows, all had felt right in his world.

He hadn't known how lonely he'd been until he realized he no longer was.

Earlier, he'd asked Cherry for a very personal favor. After everyone had finished feasting and giving the most outrageous toasts, she'd walked up to the mike on the bandstand and said, "And now, Jack and Kate will have their very first dance together as husband and

led Kate out onto the dance floor that had been outside on the lush lawn beneath the tropical

stars. And the musicians played the first few bars of
"You Don't Own Me."

Kate really laughed as he pulled her into his arms.

"Hey, I'll always think of it as our song," he whispered into her ear.

And they danced.

"Perfect," Patti said as she watched Kate and Jack
standing close together, talking with their guests. As
both Jack and his father were so well loved on Maui and
had so many friends, there had been quite a guest list,
not to mention all of the friends and family that had
been flown to the island from Chicago.

Cherry came up behind her and put an arm around
her waist. The band was taking a break, and so was she.

"You're not sorry you didn't get your millionaire?"
Patti said.

"Nope." Cherry took a sip of her drink. "I want *that*,"
she said quietly, and Patti followed her gaze in time to
see Jack give Kate a quick, but very tender kiss.

"Yeah," she sighed. "Don't we all."

That night, in their luxurious private villa, Albert Cannelli lay in his dark bedroom on an extremely comfortable mattress and sighed.

"What?" said his wife, Connie.

"Ten days," he finally said. "It makes no sense."

"It's not supposed to," she replied.

Patti and Cherry lay in their darkened bedroom, neit*
of them asleep in their queen-sized beds. The soun*
the waves outside were soothing, but Patti c*
seem to relax.

Finally, she spoke up. "Cherry?"

"Hmmm?"

"Tell me that someday I'll find what Kate has with Jack."

"Count on it, Sugar. You know why? There's something magical about this place."

James McKenna took a midnight stroll around his resort, and finally said good-bye. He wasn't leaving it, simply shifting into the next stage of his life. Actually, he was looking forward to living here for many more years, spending time with Jack, getting to know Kate, and playing with his future grandchildren.

As he headed back toward his penthouse, he looked up at the clear tropical sky and centered his attention on one particularly bright star. Right after Caroline had died, he'd picked it out for her. He liked to imagine she was up in the night sky she'd loved so much, looking down at him and their son.

"We did it," he said quietly. "Now he's on his own journey, that's his alone to take. And I have to say, darling, I envy both of them the trip."

Kate and Jack had both stayed at their wedding to the very end, until the last guest left, enjoying it immensely. Then they'd retreated to their penthouse, where he'd suddenly suggested they change out of their wedding finery, put on their bathing suits, and take one last walk on the beach.

"Hey, it's not every day you get married," he said.

"Yeah. And now we have a nice, calm, peaceful mar-
~e to look forward to."

"ou think so?" he said, and she laughed.

~ sat on the lush grass just above the sand, watch-
~moonlight make a sparkling path across the
the waves crash against the shore. Feeling the

"Jack. But you can call me Mr. Fling." He stood, then held out his hand.

"Okay, baby. Let's go."

"Lead the way."

She grasped his hand, and he pulled her to her feet, his grip strong and sure.

And they ran along the moonlit beach, holding hands and laughing.

soft tropical air against their bodies. Counting the stars, talking and laughing.

"I remember when you pulled me out of the ocean," she said. "I was so glad you did."

"I'd been watching you before that, playing in the waves," he confessed. "And I was just about getting ready to leave; I didn't want you to think I was spying on you. But I knew you were the same woman I'd bumped into." He grinned at her. "The one who disturbed me."

"Really?" That thought pleased her immensely.

"Really."

They were silent for a time, holding hands, just enjoying the night and each other.

"Hey," he said softly.

"What?"

He brushed his hand over her upper arm. "You've got sand all over you."

"I do not—" She stopped. Realization dawned, and she smiled. What a sexy, adventurous, imaginative man she'd married. How incredibly lucky she was, and how loving he was. Because the one thing she was absolutely sure of was that life with Jack McKenna would never be dull.

"Where is it?" she said, her voice softening. "I can't quite seem to reach it."

"Here and here and . . . oh yeah, right over here."

"I'd just hate to go back to my villa and track sand all over everything."

"You don't know about our outdoor showers?"

"Why, no, I don't believe I do. I just arrived here this morning."

"Would you like me to show them to you, Miss—"

"Miss Fling. But you can call me Kate. And your name is—"